# MATADORA

# ELIZABETH RUTH
# MATADORA

*Cormorant Books*

The publisher gratefully acknowledges the support of the Canada Council for the Arts and the Ontario Arts Council for its publishing program. We acknowledge the financial support of the Government of Canada through the Canada Book Fund (CBF) for our publishing activities, and the Government of Ontario through the Ontario Media Development Corporation, an agency of the Ontario Ministry of Culture, and the Ontario Book Publishing Tax Credit Program.

LIBRARY AND ARCHIVES CANADA CATALOGUING IN PUBLICATION

Ruth, Elizabeth
Matadora / Elizabeth Ruth.

Issued also in electronic formats.
ISBN 978-1-77086-208-1

1. Title.

PS8585.U847M38 2013      C813'.6      C2012-903500-9

Cover design: Angel Guerra/Archetype
Interior text design: Tannice Goddard, Soul Oasis Networking
Printer: Friesens

Printed and bound in Canada.

The interior of this book is printed on 100% post-consumer waste recycled paper.

CORMORANT BOOKS INC.
10 ST. MARY STREET, SUITE 615, TORONTO, ONTARIO, M4Y 1P9
www.cormorantbooks.com

*For my daughter Violet.*
*To life!*

*The afternoon says: "I'm thirsty for shadow!"*

FEDERICO GARCÍA LORCA
*SELECTED VERSE*

My bull-lover makes a matador out of me. She circles me and in her rough-made ring I am complete. I like the dressing up, the little jackets, the silk tights, I like her shiny hide, the deep tanned leather of her. It is she who has given me the power of the sword ...

JEANETTE WINTERSON
*THE POETICS OF SEX*

# Act 1

## Andalucía
### 1932-1933

SUNRISE IN LATE AUGUST, wind sweeps through the valley of the Sierra de Grazalema and the morning air shimmers with red dust. Twelve-year-old Luna balances on the edge of the white stone wall that circles the ranch house. She is captivated by the silhouette of a lone Sangre Caste bull on top of the hill, a valiant statue cut from the dawning light. She can't look away. Already she knows: love is a dark and dangerous animal. For love, you must be prepared to die.

The wind picks up, flattening the skirt of her work dress against her bare legs. She leans into it and its sad lament. Mama, it whispers, washing over her with the inevitability of loss. She scans the dry, yellow hill where the bull swings his head from side to side. She's wandered the silent cork forest in her rope-soled sandals looking for some evidence of peace but has yet to find the unmarked grave. She's searched the property each season, dug with bare hands under a common cypress tree. Recently, she searched her own image in Doña García's ivory hand mirror, hoping to find consolation there. But death offers no consolation to the living; she wants something more.

*Matadora*

Teetering, she spreads her arms out like wings. Today she'll lift her feet from the stony equator, soar with the birds chained so magically to the sky. Today will be the day she doesn't return to the house. She closes her eyes, face tilted into the rising sun, and prepares to give herself up to flight. With a silver coin squeezed in her palm, she jumps, and for an instant she's more than the orphaned bastard she was branded at birth, more than a servant; she is one of God's creatures. She can fly.

MANUEL WAS LEANING AGAINST the white stone wall when she jumped, with his notebook open in his lap, a pencil tucked behind one ear, and a pair of black binoculars hanging around his neck. At twenty-one, he was the eldest of Carlos García's two sons, a bronze prince with an intelligence for questioning assumptions, and a heart made to be broken. As he watched the girl sail into the air, inspired by the simple defiance of her act, an intrepid thought formed in his mind: perhaps, with enough faith, anything was possible. The thought didn't last long though, because gravity could not suspend its nature any more than the girl could, and she fell, landing beside him on her hands and knees. In a gesture of mutual defeat, or solidarity, he closed his notebook.

"What are you doing, Luna?"

"Nothing," she said, trying not to appear startled. She had no reason to fear Manuel. Not once had he scolded her for shirking duties, or demanded subservience.

Manuel pointed to the coin in her hand. "Is that my business, or are you reaching into Father Serratosa's pockets when he visits?"

Luna closed her hand around the coin protectively and sat cross-legged opposite him. "It's for my mother; it isn't stealing if I don't want it for myself."

He couldn't help grinning. Her rebellious nature impressed him, for he'd had to cultivate such boldness, if only to challenge his family's expectation that he become a bullfighter. "People have taken more for less noble reasons," he said.

Unfortunately for his parents, Manuel's real destiny involved the likes of Lorca and Whitman, not Manolete or Belmonte or Fransuello. He'd endured dreaded years of practising in the bullring to please his father, but he hated the sight of blood. To his father's great displeasure he'd been a poet from his first full sentence, which family legend claimed he spoke at the age of two, pointing to the sloping, graceful hill to the east of their house, and declaring that the sandy pyramid was breathing.

He watched Luna toss the silver coin from one hand to the other. Once again he doubted his own talent; he'd yet to publish a single poem, or prove himself in any measurable way. It was possible, he thought, that he'd made a mistake in following his passion, and that poetry would not bring him success, or worse, that he'd not succeed at creating a thing of beauty. The idea made him as uncomfortable as the hard stone wall pressing against his back.

As if looking to unravel a clue to her own happiness tangled in Manuel's serious expression, Luna turned the conversation to her current preoccupation. "Was my mother beautiful?" she asked. "Was she brave?

Manuel craned his neck to find the hill, but the bull was gone. "She loved watching the bulls as much as you do," he said. "That's all I remember."

It was a lie. He'd not forgotten the bold sensuality her mother had exuded; as a boy he'd noted an earthiness about the woman that had seemed organic. When she came in from her shack in the field to visit with Paqui, she'd been warm, unlike his mother. Accessible. He felt good in her presence. As a man, he understood that Luna's mother had possessed something rare for a woman of any class; she'd possessed herself, entirely. She'd been the kind of woman men desired without ever knowing why.

Luna leaned in closer, wringing her hands, hoping for new information to hold on to, but Manuel offered none. Her neck pulsed; the beat of her heart betrayed the vulnerability she tried gallantly to hide. "Sometimes I think it would be better if I'd died too," she said.

"What?" Manuel sat up straight, as though a sword had been slipped in place of his spine. "Don't ever say that to me."

"I wouldn't commit such a sin," she said. "But I was a mistake in the first place. Maybe I'm not supposed to be here."

With those words, a child's simple logic, Manuel was rendered helpless in the face of her pain. He didn't see her as she saw herself, a mistake; for he too possessed the irrepressible feeling of not belonging to the life he'd been assigned. They shared a temperament shaped by loneliness, the unfed craving to express themselves and be loved for it. They also shared a physical resemblance: both were long and reedy, naturally thin, with brown hair and almond skin, though hers was fairer. There was plumpness to their pouty lips, but there was ferocity behind her eyes — a wild mix of rage and ambition — that could not be found in his. "I need you to do something for me," he said, gently.

"Anything," she weighed the coin in her left palm. "Do you want me to practise my cursive writing every night instead of every third as we agreed? Do you want me to try reading from Cervantes again?" Her voice lifted in anticipation. "Or from another of your old bullfight magazines?"

He tore a piece of paper from his notebook. "My artists' circle is meeting tonight," he said. "I want you to slip this into Eugenia's portfolio without her noticing."

Eugenia Vidal was a young Córdoban painter who frequented his group with her twin brother, Jorge. She had deep-set, intelligent eyes and an oval face; her interest in challenging tradition was irresistible to Manuel. Luna thought Eugenia spoke about her work in a manner that made it more important than his.

"Give it to her yourself," Luna said, pushing his hand away.

"I've tried," he mumbled, embarrassed that, at his age, shyness was still matched by a predictable romantic nature, made more debilitating by the prospect of a woman's rejection.

"Oh, all right, let me have it." As Luna was folding the paper into the pocket of her work dress, Doña García's sharp voice pierced the air.

"Luna. There you are!"

Manuel ducked out of sight of his mother, barely peering over the wall, but Luna stood fast, dusting off the front of her dress; she would meet the challenge on her feet.

"Didn't you hear me calling?"

"Just now," Luna said, with an expression of practised blankness, the gaze of a worker who knew better than to appear either vulnerable or resentful. She would give away nothing of her true thoughts or feelings.

Doña García advanced. "Did I see you talking to someone?"

"Only God." She hopped over the wall and accidentally dropped the coin in the sand.

Doña García glimpsed her son, parted her lips as if she were going to speak and decided against it. Instead, she pointed at the ground where the sun had caught the metal of Luna's coin. "What's that?"

Luna shrugged, noted the unmistakable whiff of Manzanilla sherry sweating off Doña García's skin. A part of her wanted to admit that she'd rooted through Don Carlos's pants again while gathering the wash, to see the shock on his wife's face. Whose business was it if she'd claimed this section of the wall for her own mother's tombstone? A peasant deserved a proper grave. She intended to stash the coin behind a loose slab of stone along with the gold brooch, snatched from one of Manuel's city cousins the previous Easter, and the straight razor she'd found while cleaning the calves' enclosure, two pearl buttons snipped from Doña García's wedding gown, and the pair of scissors that helped get the job done — but she'd have to wait and find another. Each of these small victories, these tiny acts of resistance helped her to continue, day after day, in a home where she felt like an uninvited guest, unable to leave.

"I asked you a question, child."

"And I answered, Señora."

Doña García's neck and cheeks flushed, but she too was practised in the art of self-control; alcohol might loosen her tongue, yet nothing would provoke her. "If I find that you've been stealing," she said, "not even Manuel, over there, will stop me sending you to the nuns."

Luna clenched her jaw to hold her temper, but it was too late. Whenever she was reminded of her dubious station, loneliness slid under her tongue and pooled there like spoiled milk until she spat it out.

"I'm not paid in silver," she said, storming past. "How could it be mine?"


IN THE BRIGHT WHITE light of the ranch house kitchen, Paqui stood at the stove, stirring flour into a pot of boiling water for a migas. The radio was on, and La Niña de los Peines sang a throaty cante jondo. Paqui's lips moved silently, caught up in a private conversation with the music. She nodded and laughed out loud. Was it to the flamenco singer that she was speaking, or the blessed Virgin or to the family she'd left behind high in the arid Iberian mountains? She turned and found Luna standing in the doorway hesitating on an entrance.

"Where have you been?"

"I went for a walk," Luna said, advancing.

"One of these days you're going to get yourself into real trouble."

"I don't care."

"You should, mi hija." Paqui lowered her voice, almost to a

whisper. "It's not wise to forget your place." She gestured with her chin. "Over there, grind that pork."

"They don't own me," Luna said, meaning the family.

Paqui cocked an eyebrow as if to say, *you're wrong about that.* "Become useful," she said. "If you're needed, you'll be provided for."

"I can take care of myself."

"Is that so?" Paqui heated a pan of olive oil at the stove; some of it splattered onto her smock. "What have I been doing all these years?"

"I didn't mean it that way," Luna said, screwing the meat grinder to the corner of the table. "But why do I have to spend all my time in this house? Manuel doesn't clean and cook, and neither does Pedro." Her voice was barbed with the injustice. "I want to be like them."

"We're all servants," Paqui said, crossing herself and kissing her fingers. "Or, do you also think you don't belong to God?"

"I pray every night, Paquita."

"Good, then you are already rich."

But Luna was full of doubts: Why should she bother with prayer? What had Paqui's loyalty — to the García family or to the Father, Son and Holy Ghost — spared her? Not subservience, or isolation from her people, not having teeth pulled because she couldn't afford the gold to fill the holes in them. She certainly felt watched over, but by a different sort of trinity: Doña García, the unwinnable matriarch of the ranch, with her penchant for expensive liquor and drawer full of silk fans; Paqui, the old housemaid, the one who loved her without blood ties but could offer no future; and the soul in the sky who gave her life only to haunt it. She packed the meat into the grinder with a clenched fist.

"Do you think my father will come for me one day?" she asked. "I bet he's handsome and courageous; why else would my mother have loved him?"

"I've told you a thousand times," Paqui said. "He was a bullfighter."

Luna turned the crank on the grinder with one hand and caught the meat in a bowl out the bottom. "But you're not sure?"

"I never met him. That's what I heard."

Luna sighed. Her parents were destined to remain vague figures carved from snippets of information she'd gleaned, shadow people who emerged and receded from view. Other than herself, the proof that they'd existed was her mother's gold crucifix, which she wore around her neck. And, if what Paqui had heard about her father was true, he was likely dead. "What do you suppose it's like up in heaven?" she asked.

"How would I know that?" Paqui laughed. "Ronda is the farthest I've travelled." She turned up the volume on the radio to a Portuguese fado. Sometimes it was the tango transporting them to Argentina, or King Benny Nawahi's guitar taking them to Hawaii. There was American jazz, and Mexican folksongs, and Paqui's favourites, the saetas from Seville's Good Friday processions.

Luna raised her voice to be heard over the music. "Manuel says there might not be an afterlife. That we make our own heaven and hell right here on earth."

Paqui sucked her teeth and shot Luna a disapproving glare. "Manuel is filling your mind with stories," she said. "He can afford to consider such nonsense. You and I know better. Maybe Doña García is right that you spend too much time together. Stay here for the rest of the day with me."

"But imagine what it would be like to travel," Luna pressed. "To carry a name that people respect, to inherit this place."

"You can be so naive. If Don Carlos himself was your father you wouldn't inherit. You are a girl." Paqui poured the warm olive oil into the migas and stirred the dough with a wooden spoon. "How are you doing with that pork?"

"Almost done," Luna said, sounding a note deflated. She examined her hands. The one holding the bowl was covered in a raw mash and the other bore a knotted scar at the base of her thumb. She stared at it as though she had no idea how it got there. They were small hands, smaller than Paqui's, but they were just as strong and callused. *There must be a way to climb from one life to another, she thought, like stepping up a ladder towards the sky.* But there were two ways for the landless to rise out of poverty in Spain: revolution or bullfighting. "One day I'll have my own maid," she said, feeling one of her dizzy spells coming on. "I'll order her around and be waited on."

Paqui laughed again. "And how will you feed her?"

"Maybe I'll sell fortunes, like a Gypsy. Or write a book."

"Where do you get such ideas?" Paqui saw the hope clouding Luna's eyes and decided it best to spare her future disappointment by crushing it. "You think you're too good for this," she added, waving the wooden spoon in the air. "You think that when I was young I didn't dream of a different life. I'm an ignorant woman, but I know what I know: you have three options and the sooner you accept that the better off you'll be: you can marry and serve your husband, you can serve a good family as I have done, or you can starve."

Luna felt the room tilt from side to side and begin to spin. She gripped the tabletop for balance, parted her lips, poised to speak, but stopped short of confessing to another bout of vertigo. Paqui would immediately send her to bed with some bitter tasting herbs to drink and the shutters closing out the light.

"Mi hija, what's wrong? Is it happening again?"

"No," she lied. "It's nothing." She stared out the kitchen window across the field looking for the one thing she knew would slow the spinning, looking for the most solid, unmoveable thing she could imagine — an immense black bull. To her great relief the tilting ceased, the spinning slowed, and the room fell back to stillness. "I'm telling you," she said. "One day I will get out of here."

"Your mother used to say the same thing," Paqui snapped.

Paqui's tone was uncharacteristically severe and Luna's face tightened into a near grimace, as though she'd been struck by a blow she hadn't expected. Because of Paqui she'd grown up sleeping on a straw mattress in the maids' quarters attached to the house, while other children slept with their families on dirt floors in shacks out in the fields. Because of Paqui, she occasionally bathed in a tub of rainwater, not a muddy river. She rarely went to bed hungry. Although more of a grandmother than a mother to her because of her age, Paqui was the closest thing to maternal love Luna had known. Without her there was no solid, sure place to land at the end of a day.

"Don't be angry with me, Paquita."

"Never for long," Paqui said. She smiled and her missing teeth looked like tiny black squares.

LUNA AND MANUEL WALKED to the Venta by the highway. The sky glowed violet, but it was too early to see any stars. Jorge Vidal's elegant Vivastella was parked sideways in front of the small stone fountain that sat in the centre of the outdoor patio. Eugenia's dog was drinking from the third tier of the fountain. As they approached, he moved to rest at his mistress's feet. Eugenia and Jorge sat in white wicker chairs around one of the small tables with a dirty white tablecloth on it. Eugenia's short dark hair was severely parted on one side and set in marcel waves. A jasmine flower was pinned behind one ear, and she wore a turquoise shawl.

"Hola, qué tal?"

"Hola."

Manuel bent to kiss her on both cheeks, and took a seat next to Jorge, leaving the chair beside Eugenia free for Luna. She too sat. In the flicker and shadow of the overhanging string lights, Eugenia's charcoal painted eyes and bright red lips appeared huge and hungry — as surreal as the images she created on her canvasses. Her beauty was bold and inspired, and it sent a shock of desire through Manuel's body. Eugenia turned her attention first to Luna. "You're more grown each time I see you. So tall, and that hint of a widow's peak. It makes you look unexpectedly serious, like a García. You don't mind me calling you that, do you?" Eugenia leaned in and made a closer inspection. "Good cheekbones, thick eyebrows. You have the most beautiful dark eyes Luna. I'd like to paint you some day. Would you let me do that?"

Luna thought of the framed oil painting Manuel had found by the side of the road the year before. It had fallen off the back of a truck and the gilt frame was cracked, but when he gave it to her she didn't mind. The painting, he'd explained, was a poor imitation of the work of the great Velásquez, with its dark, majestic subjects, and their realistic finery. It showed a young woman dancing in the arms of a much older man in a formal suit and wide-brimmed Córdoban hat. His face was obscured, though the girl's tender, ambivalent expression was unavoidable. Her eyes were the darkest of browns. Almost black. Beneath the two figures the artist had painted the words, *Carbón quema, pero la luna alivia.* Coal burns, but the moon soothes. Luna had felt that she was Manuel's favourite little moon. Watching him light up in Eugenia's presence, she worried that she had been displaced. "Don't waste paint on me," she said, folding her hands in her lap.

Eugenia laughed. "False modesty is no virtue, child."

Luna ignored the comment. She saw that instead of her portfolio Eugenia had brought an ugly cloth bag, something a donkey would carry. It hung off the back of her chair.

"Do you like it?" Eugenia asked. "There's a flea market at the plaza de la corredera on Sundays. A mute sells them. I could bring you one."

"No, thank you."

Their waiter set a bowl of olives and a basket of bread in the centre of the table. He winked at Luna, as if to say, *You and I, we're not like them.* Luna immediately broke his gaze. She wasn't his ally. She was one of them — the artists and the privileged — if only for a couple of hours. In the company of Manuel's friends she was able to glimpse their lives, their possibilities, and imagine some for her own. She sniffed at the waiter dismissively.

"Para beber?" he asked, impatiently.

Manuel handed her a menu so she could decide for herself. "Luna, have whatever you like," he said. He was proud that he'd taught her to read, and saw nothing wrong with her showing off in front of his friends.

Luna took her time deciphering the words. Twice she named items out loud, and glanced up at the waiter to make sure he knew she could do something he probably couldn't. But when Eugenia said, "She's lucky you've taken an interest, Manuel," as though he was her trainer and she a wild animal that had been domesticated, Luna felt ashamed. She lost her confidence. Not wanting to order the wrong thing and embarrass herself or Manuel, she ordered a glass of water with ice.

"And the rest of you?" asked the waiter.

"Three beers and an assortment of tapas," Manuel added, decisively.

"Brandy for me," said Eugenia.

As the waiter left, Jorge scratched his ample belly with both hands. "I'm ready to be entertained," he said. "Where are the others?"

Eugenia lit a Caldo de Gallina cigarette. "You know novelists. They take so damned long to do anything; it's as if time has lost all meaning for them."

Jorge and Manuel laughed. Luna didn't. She noticed that Eugenia's hands were stained yellow, the colour bullfighters fear because it brings bad luck in the bullring. She didn't appreciate Eugenia's clever way of filling conversation with veiled insults. Eugenia and Jorge aren't very much alike, she thought.

Jorge was squat and prematurely balding, and he claimed there wasn't a creative vein threading under his skin, though Luna doubted it. Unlike his twin sister, Jorge was humble and generous; without him to drive the long distance between Córdoba and Sangre

Mío to meetings, Eugenia, who suffered fits of epilepsy and couldn't drive herself, would've continued painting in isolation, and Manuel would not have found his first love.

"How long did that last painting take you to finish?" Manuel asked.

"The one I just showed in Madrid? Six weeks. But it's terrible. I fooled the critics. I can't seem to get the canvas to match what's in my mind."

"If you could do that maybe you'd lose your motivation to paint," Manuel said. "I wish I wasn't so slow. My most recent poem has taken five months and is still unfinished."

"Is this what our circle is coming to?" Jorge teased. "A group of dissatisfied time-keepers. I thought only dictators and businessmen like me kept their eyes on the clock."

"You're right," Manuel laughed. "But, please, no talk of dictators. The Republic is in power now. I'm hopeful about the new constitution."

Jorge loosened his bow tie. "A union friend tells me some estates lock out workers rather than increase their wages. Or refuse to plant crops. How does your father feel about the reforms?"

"He resents being told what to do," said Manuel. "Especially by government. But for all his complaining he won't ignore the decrees."

"It's an exciting time," said Eugenia. "To think I can vote! I hope the government carries out its promises. What will the Church do now that schools are secular and divorce legal?" The waiter set their drinks down on the table. "Jacinto says there's a chance Federico will join us," Eugenia added, "to give a reading when he returns from Cuba."

"Imagine," said Jorge. "The most famous faggot in all of Spain, in our little group."

Manuel reached into the centre of the table, tossed two olives into his mouth. "I saw his troupe perform in the Grazalema village square last summer and I invited him, but I've heard nothing. Was he reading at La Pombo when you and Jacinto were there?"

"No, no," said Eugenia. "Not when I was there. I would've spoken to him."

Manuel spat the olive pits into his hand and flung them into a shrub. "What would you have said?"

"Something about his imagery," she said. "The earth. Nature. I would've asked him why it's violent and mournful. He seems to be saying we are prisoners of nature, but it's not what I would say about us." Eugenia reached around her chair and lifted the material of her bag. "I embroidered these words here to remind me of Wallada," she said. "Luna, you should remember them too."

Luna looked more closely at the thread that looped and swung into letters.

*I will give my cheek to my lover and my kisses to anyone I choose.*

"What does it mean?" she asked.

"That we shouldn't be slaves to tradition," Manuel said, and then he felt foolish and insensitive. Since the election he'd been swept up in the Leftist spirit of change and optimism, but the lives of peasants in the south remained unchanged. For Luna there was no choice but to trudge on, day after day, within the walls of tradition.

"Wallada was a Moorish Princess," explained Eugenia. "So proud of her beauty that she refused to wear the veil when she went into the streets of Córdoba. The local men accused her of being a harlot. She had those words embroidered onto her gown for the world to read." Eugenia turned in her chair to gain Manuel's full attention. "I prefer her vision of love to Federico's," she said. "I find elements of Dalí in his poems, and I appreciate the plays, but there's something too definitively tragic." Her turquoise shawl slipped, revealing one bare shoulder. Manuel couldn't stop himself from staring. "Objectively, love doesn't exist," Eugenia said. "It's merely how another makes us feel about ourselves. Wouldn't you agree? It's immaterial. Like air or, or ..."

Luna kicked Manuel under the table.

"Like faith," he said.

"Yes. Precisely. Not religion, but faith." Eugenia reclined in her chair. "It's no more real than that."

Luna felt for the page concealed within the front pocket of her tunic. "How do you know love doesn't exist?" she asked.

"I know because I've tried to paint it and failed."

"Maybe you need more practice."

"Luna!"

Eugenia laughed. "Leave her alone," she said. "She's probably right." Eugenia's words sparked with an erotic charge and she flashed Manuel a coy smile. "Perhaps I do need more practice."

Manuel tugged at the frayed edge of the tablecloth. For a moment he felt much too intense. He took a swig of beer and quickly recovered. "Does a tree not love the forest it grows in?" he asked. "Does a bird not love the sky that holds him up?"

"Of course not," said Eugenia. "Instinct makes him fly. Love is a choice."

"Is it?" asked Jorge. "Too often I've found love chooses me."

"Federico is writing of our natures," Manuel insisted. "We are the sky and the forest and the mountain. For him there's no separation."

Eugenia took a long, calculated drag on her cigarette and blew smoke towards the clouds. Either she could think of no retort or she was deciding whether or not she would fall in love with Manuel. She tossed the butt of her cigarette on the ground where it continued to burn. "Did you bring something to share tonight? Besides your little helper, I mean."

"I'm not little!" Luna said. "I'm almost thirteen."

"Next time," Manuel said.

He hadn't had the courage to share his work with the group since he'd fallen in love with Eugenia. In fact, with the exception of a few brief love poems, he'd been distracted and stalled in his writing.

"Why does your dog not have a name?" Luna asked. "He should have a proper name."

Eugenia fixed a dramatic gaze on Luna. "Because that's exactly what you expect." She reached down to pet him. "Good dog," she said, and Manuel was aware that he and the dog both regarded Eugenia with the same hopeful expression. "For a time I wanted to call him Dalí," Eugenia added. "I thought it might incense the elite."

"But you didn't," laughed Jorge. "Who else will pay for your canvasses and brushes?"

"I dislike the status quo," she said. "Not the wealthy individual." She reached out and cupped his cheek in her yellow-stained hand. "I adore you, brother."

"All I want is one great poem," Manuel said. "One faultless poem."

"You don't care about publication?"

"Yes, I care. And I envy your trips to Madrid. I would read on stage at La Pombo if I was asked, but I concentrate on the work. It's all we have."

"You have me," Luna said, not yet understanding the depth of loneliness that lives inside an aspiring artist, and which he rarely admits is there.

"She's so sweet," said Eugenia.

"No, I'm not," Luna blurted. Sweet was a condescending description better left for one of Paqui's sugary desserts, she thought. A fast way to put her in her place. Her shoulders curled and her frame assumed the nearly apologetic posture of someone who was meant to slip in and out of rooms invisibly.

"You've insulted her," said Jorge.

"Have I?" said Eugenia. "I didn't mean to." She turned in her chair and observed Luna frivolously. "How would you describe yourself?" she asked. "Tell us. Who are you, and what would you want if you could have anything?"

Luna hesitated, knowing better than to give an honest answer. Paqui would pinch her arm hard for expecting equality where none could be, and yet Manuel was waiting patiently across the table, as though he was genuinely interested in hearing what she had to say.

Who was she?

The question struck her as funny; no one had ever asked it before. She was a housemaid, of course. An orphan, prone to dizzy spells, as Paqui called them. Someone who loved animals, especially the bulls. But that wasn't all. Like Eugenia and Manuel, she was ambitious. She wanted to be recognized as an artist, hear her name whispered enviably on the lips of men everywhere. Fame. She wanted fame, but not for its own sake. What she craved was the legitimacy that came with public acceptance and, given the chance, she knew exactly how she'd get it, though she wasn't foolish enough to tell anyone.

"I would be Manuel's sister," she said, offering another wish instead.

"How delightful," said Eugenia.

"You flatter me," said Manuel, shifting in his chair. Being born into a land-owning family had innumerable advantages for which he was grateful, but such a confession left him feeling complicit in the inequitable social order. He'd tried, despite it having been seditious, to share his privilege with Luna by teaching her how to ride a horse, how to discern a griffon vulture from the rarer black vulture; he'd taught her to read and write. Was it cruel of him to offer her a taste of a sweeter existence? He smiled guiltily and turned to face Eugenia: "My skill improves the more I write," he said. "But no amount of practice can teach me how to capture my soul and translate it to the page. Either I am capable of that kind of passion or I'm not."

"And are you?" Eugenia stood without waiting for his answer. She wrapped her shawl tightly around her body. "My sketchbook is in the car," she said.

Manuel looked at Luna, as if to say, *This is it. I'll distract Jorge so you can slip her my poem.* It was a poem. What else would it have been? Luna had read it.

Luna lifted the fold of paper from her pocket, and when Jorge looked the other way she dropped it into Eugenia's bag.

They continued to talk until it became clear that the others weren't going to make it. Luna grew impatient, flipping through Eugenia's sketchbook and listening to her defend her mysterious choice of colour and subject: seven blue faces with red lips for eyebrows, a gigantic green mountain goat with donkey's ears, an upside-down vulture with Spanish flags for feathers. Eugenia refused to tell them what any of the images represented or how they were connected. When Jorge said he wanted to return to Córdoba before it was too late, Manuel paid the waiter and waved them off, Eugenia blowing kisses through the open window of the car as they pulled away.

"I hope you're invited to read at La Pombo one day, Manuel."

"Thank you," he said, but his mouth and throat were painfully dry. If he did manage to write enough poems to form a collection, who would publish them? He was, after all, the first-born son of one of Spain's most respected bull breeders. His poetry was meant to be written in the bullring. No one would risk embarrassing his father by proving otherwise. So he stood beside Luna in the grey striped pants that all the men wore, with his white shirt billowing in the wind, watching Eugenia disappear into blackness, wondering if the things he loved most would ever be his.

THAT NIGHT, THE WIND gained momentum, crossing the Mediterranean from Africa, blowing north up the coast, over the plateau, and catching and turning in the rolling hills around Sangre Mio. Manuel lay in bed fretting. Eugenia must've found the poem. What was she thinking? He should've handed it to her himself, but he lacked the courage. Feeling foolish and exposed, he threw off the cotton sheet, climbed out of bed and grabbed his notebook and pencil. Pulling on a sweater, he snuck outside. He walked behind the house, where Luna and Paqui shared a small room next to the black pigs in their enclosure and, once he was far enough from the house that his footsteps wouldn't be heard, he ran. Soon, he found a rhythm with his feet and began to loosen, sink into himself and the natural world surrounding him.

The smell of manure and cow's urine was familiar, if not comforting. The full moon was charged, illuminating his path and the olive trees that lined it. He made his way out to the far field, beyond the small training ring, with the frail skeletons of crumbling sunflower stems crunching underfoot. He avoided stepping on a scorpion and, a few paces on, an adder slithering across his toes.

He stopped at the high wooden fence, where he'd occasionally seen a little Scops owl, and when he ran one hand along the top rung he noticed something rough and knotty in the wood. He looked closely. Someone had carved a word there: Toro. He teased his fingers across the indentations of each letter, sounding the word out phonetically as he'd taught Luna to do when reading. Toro. It sounded awkward spilling from his lips, too tight, confining, like his old traje de corto.

He knelt and found a shallow trench running under the bottom rung of the fence. His father wouldn't have dug it. Why was it there? Confused, he glanced around. Off, in the dead of night, he spotted something else. As he approached, he saw that it was Luna's thin figure standing in a silver moonbeam. Her feet were together, arms high, and she held a dishrag in her left hand. Her chin was tucked in close to her body, playing at bullfighting as he and his brother, Pedro, had done when they were young. He raised his arm to announce himself, but she didn't appear to notice. A gust of the night's cold wind made him shiver. He took a few more steps. All at once the fine hair on the back of his neck stiffened. There was a bull out there! His black coat almost disappeared into the darkness, but his cuernos looked exceptionally sharp, their white tips glowing by moonlight. Manuel waved his notebook with one hand and pointed frantically with the other. "Luna, get out of there!"

As if she hadn't heard him, Luna spread her legs, dropped her shoulders, and pressed her heels into the grass.

"Have you lost your mind?!" Manuel shouted. "Run!"

She lifted her gaze for a second and once more rested it firmly on her enemy. She moved her wrist violently to taunt him with the rag.

"Hijo de Puta!" Manuel dropped his notebook and ran along the fence line, making as much noise as he could to distract the bull. "Run!"

Again Luna ignored him, stood her ground. She waved her imaginary muleta to entice the bull. Alone in the dark she could admit it: bullfighting was the perfect penance; by risking her life could she satisfy the need she had to prove its worth. Out of irritation, the bull rumbled and pounded the dirt and, to Manuel's horror, he charged.

Luna dropped the rag, turned and sprinted in Manuel's direction. She zigzagged as the bull gained on her, and with a pulse of breath between them, she dove to safety under the fence. The bull stopped, barely winded. Moonlight caught like blue flame in his eyes.

"What in hell do you think you're doing?!"

Panting, Luna pushed up onto both legs. She was unnerved by having been discovered, but wouldn't apologize. "Practising," she said.

"You could've been killed!"

"I know what I'm doing," she said, defensively.

"No you don't! He almost gored you."

"He's half blind."

Incredulous, Manuel asked, "Have you done this before?"

"A few times," she said. "But don't tell."

"Santo Dios!" Manuel rubbed his temples, tried to quell the pounding in his chest. "What's wrong with you? He could've ripped you apart." He paced, resisting the urge to shake her. "And you do know you ruined a potential fighter?"

She narrowed her eyes at him — angry and confused.

"The cloth," he said. "They have long memories. That bull won't charge in any ring now. See how much you know about bullfighting? Wait until my father learns what a crazy, stupid thing you've been doing!"

Luna tensed. Don Carlos's tempter was unpredictable, and

although it hadn't been directed at her, she'd seen him fly into a rage when Manuel wasn't working fast enough, or when he was caught writing poetry. Lately, Don Carlos was on edge because some of his workers had organized to demand a shorter workday and a cap on their rents. Luna didn't want to find herself on the receiving end of his anger. "Please don't tell," she said. Shame enveloped her as she scrambled to find the words to placate him. "I'm sorry, Manuel."

He softened in the face of her pain, slightly. His voice remained hard.

"Promise you'll never try it again and maybe I won't."

She flinched at his angry tone. He was the one person in his family she could trust. In Manuel's presence she was an equal, legitimate. He answered questions without judgment or ridicule. He kept her secrets as though she had a right to them, and she kept his.

"Promise it!" He repeated.

She looked as though she was considering lying but didn't.

"I can't," she said.

"Why not?"

She pointed to his notebook splayed on the ground. "Could you promise to stop writing?"

"That's different," he said. "Poetry is my future."

"Then train me," she said, with a tremor in her voice. "I know I'm a girl, but you talk with your friends about going against tradition. Train me and I'll make you proud."

There was the unmistakable ring of ambition in her voice, and an edge of confrontation that reminded Manuel of the times he'd tried, in vain, to explain a love of poetry to his father. His heart squeezed a little, knowing she too had nights when sleep eluded her, but instead of searching for love in the arrangement of syllables and stanzas, she was compelled into the field as if love was waiting for her there.

"I taught you to read so you'd have a chance to better yourself," he said, more gently. "Maybe one day you'll be lucky and marry an educated man."

"I don't want to be married off to some old goat or sent to work as a maid for a lawyer in Ronda." Her eyes flickered with rage and sorrow. "I want to be a bullfighter!"

"What?!" At first Manuel was shocked to hear her, but a sense of inevitability pressed in around them, as if each beat of her life had brought her to this place of asking. There, under cloak of night, he was forced to admit that she was more ambitious than he'd assumed, she had the fire and the fury that drives so many disadvantaged boys and men into the ring. She, not he, was made for it. A flash of daring hope behind her eyes confirmed the point, and yet what she was asking him to do was impossible. "Be reasonable," he said. "I can't train you."

"Fine," she spat. "I'll keep practising on my own. I'm very brave!"

"Yes. I've seen that for myself. Brave and foolish. Is this why you watch my father and El Mayoral in the training ring?"

"Of course," she said impatiently.

He could feel her desperate gaze upon his skin and it made him squirm. She thought he didn't need her, why would he? And yet she was wrong to think that. He was a shy, tender heart, sometimes a little too fragile, but he'd long suspected she was the better side of him, and he needed that. Exasperated, he took one of her hands in his. "If I could, why would I teach you something I didn't want to learn myself?"

"Because I'm asking," she said.

"Girls don't fight bulls, Luna!"

She pulled her hand away, beginning to feel light-headed. "I thought we were friends," she said, as everything began to spin. "I thought you were different."

LUNA HAD THE PERSISTENT delusion, as some children do, that she was all-powerful, and as proof of her power, she would occasionally face a bull in the field at night. Or, during the day, stand very still on top of the white stone wall, close her eyes, and call the wind to rise up. Not a moment later she would feel its warm caress upon her face or legs. She could often halt the dizzy spells through willpower, or with one of Paqui's herbal teas. There was no question that she held magic within her heart, tricks of pure light. She was lucky, touched by the angels. Or was it her mother sending blessings from above? Of course, her feelings of grandeur, her ability to bend nature, rested upon the exact opposite belief: that she was utterly powerless, stained, cursed and forsaken by God himself. Why else would she be so alone?

She longed for a friend her own age, a girl with whom she could share secrets, laugh, experience the buoyancy of living. But the other children at Sangre Mio resented her house privileges, and although she understood their envy, she felt no sympathy for them. They didn't roam the property alone at night as she did, or lay beneath the sunflowers at dawn, praying up at them as though their faces were those of the saints. They didn't know the beauty of a newborn calf, how its smell was of old blood and new metal, how it would sniff each mother in the field, accepting the first who offered milk. She alone knew those things.

Her closest companions, aside from Manuel, were the animals on the property. The sorrel mare, Batata, a three-legged stable cat, Fermín, who'd claimed her one Easter morning. The hunting dogs, and all the birds who'd manage to survive Pedro's sling shot. She was one of them, with a life as wordless and surreptitious as theirs. Animals act on impulse, she knew, but they love in a predictable manner — whoever feeds them, when the season for mating comes around — or not at all. They move inside the laws nature wrote for them.

She'd tried hard to win friends when she was younger, and it had almost worked. When she'd turned seven, Paqui had persuaded Doña García to pay Father Seratossa to come to the ranch and confirm her, and the other girls whose parents worked for the family.

There were nine of them, each in a white dress, each with a pair of thin gloves. Luna also wore a cream-coloured veil that Paqui had made for her from strips of discarded lace. With Doña García presiding, she and the other girls were lined up on the terrace, like untouched dolls, and one, by one, initiated into the Church.

Luna stood beside the grubby daughter of a field hand, the one with the overbite, who was beaming with pride at her salvation. The girl's jubilation was a curiosity to Luna who didn't feel much of anything except itchy and hot in the confining dress. After the confirmations, Paqui led them all to a table for a treat of quince jelly and cheese.

"Have mine too," Luna said, pushing her portion across the table in a blunt bid to win the girl's friendship. She hadn't yet learned that successful friendships between girls were delicate matters that, ironically, required a touch of cruelty and a thick skin. Rather than appearing needy and vulnerable, she should've tried to appear indifferent.

"Thank you," the girl said, happy to have the extra treat. She gobbled it up and in so doing, established, not so much a friendship with Luna, as a pattern of relating which, from then on, would require that Luna anticipate the girl's demands before she made them, defer to her wishes, and bolster her power.

After the day of the confirmations, whenever the girl with the overbite walked in from the field to collect water in clay jugs or to speak with Paqui about scraps of food for her family, Luna would follow her. Eventually, Luna was allowed to jump rope with the girl and her younger sister, though she was rarely permitted to take leave of her turning station at the end of the rope. They also played hiding games with a wider group of girls, and on more than one occasion Luna had given herself up after a long wait to discover that the others had all stopped playing and gone home. By her tenth birthday, she and the girl with the overbite sometimes played alone, and Luna looked forward to those times most of all.

One afternoon, in her eleventh year, she'd climbed the wall ladder over the calf enclosure and waited in the hay loft for her friend to arrive.

"Let's play master and servant again," the girl said, when she entered the enclosure. Luna lay back awaiting further instruction, and the girl climbed on top of her. "Wriggle about," said the girl, and Luna did. "Kiss me," the girl said, and Luna did that too. Not a peck, but a real kiss with their lips pressed together for a good long time, the kind of kiss Pedro gave many girls in the barn. Luna wondered if other friends played such games and why it had to be a secret, but the weight of the girl's body pressing down on her was a wonderful anchor, pinning her to the moment. She hadn't had a dizzy spell in months since they'd started this game. "This is good practice for when we have husbands," said the girl with the overbite.

With hay scratching under her work dress Luna opened one eye. The other girl's eyes were open too and both girls quickly separated. Not wanting to lose the connection, and assuming this was a new twist to the game, Luna craned up for another kiss.

"Don't!" the girl said, but it was too late, Luna had broken the rules: her tongue swam around in the other girl's mouth like a skittish fish. "Stop it!" the girl said, pushing off roughly.

Luna struggled to sit up. "I'm sorry," she said.

The girl sat up too, wiped her mouth with the back of her hand. "That was disgusting!"

Luna's neck and ears flashed red and the walls of the small loft began to spin faster and faster, rendering her arms and legs, her feet and brain, useless, turning her, not so much weightless, as matterless. Within seconds she could no longer find her bearings or focus on the girl's face. Hard surfaces disappeared; she couldn't tell where walls and floor began or ended. "We can play a different game," she said, desperate to re-establish some equilibrium.

The girl with the overbite placed one foot on the ladder, and started to climb down. "We're not friends anymore," she said.

LUNA WATCHED MANUEL KNEEL in the corral and draw a circle, the size of her serving tray, in the dirt with his finger. "I'm still not talking to you," she said.

"Pretend this is the bullring," he said, ignoring her comment. He took a pencil from his back pocket, broke it in half and placed both halves in the centre of the circle. "This one is the horse," he said of the shorter half. "And this one is the bull."

"It looks like a clock," she said, glancing over her shoulder to make certain that his mother wasn't outside. She should've been scrubbing the tile floor in the entranceway to the house, but when Manuel had called her outside, she'd made a quick pass with a wet rag and hidden her bucket and dry brush in an armoire.

Manuel pressed his thumb into the dirt, making small indentations, creating two paths away from each animal then crossing them back again. "A suerte should happen like this," he said. He repeated the paths, this time using both hands simultaneously. "Now you do it."

Luna bent down and easily copied what he'd drawn. She'd spied on so many bullfights in Don Carlos's training ring, though in all but one the toreros had fought on foot.

"Bueno," Manuel said. "Then it ends with the placement of the rejones, right here." He pounded his fist on the ground decisively and struck the longer half of the pencil to show how a torero on horseback pierces the bull's withers and tires him. "It's the job of the rejoneador to know which path the bull will take," he said.

"Rejoneador," she repeated, as though it were something regal.

Two horses exercised nearby, Batata, named by Luna for her round belly, like a sweet potato, and her new foal, not yet named. Batata sniffed the air and stayed close. Luna had ridden her bareback many times, when the family had gone to mass and she'd been left to fry pigeon in cinnamon or set out the pigs' feet.

They stood. Manuel dusted off the knees of his trousers. "If one hand of the clock does not move properly, Luna, time doesn't advance and the suerte fails. If either hand accelerates the suerte also fails. Me entiendes?"

"Yes, yes, so what? Your mother and Paqui are waiting in the house. Why did you call me out here?"

He chewed his thumbnail, nervously. "I'll do it," he said.

"Do what?" A rush of adrenalin flooded her body, her face reddened and she fought the urge to jump up and down. "Train me?!"

He peered directly into her eyes. "On one condition: No more sneaking around. It's too dangerous."

"Agreed," she said, bursting with joy. "Oh thank you, thank you Manuel!"

"We'll practise after dark as you've been doing," he said. "We won't interrupt your chores, and I'll find other animals. We can't use my father's."

Luna nodded. Don Carlos's ranch was a small business compared with the sprawling properties of other, more established, breeders. About eight hundred head of cattle at any one time, so each bull was valued. Each was branded with an 'S' for *Sangre* (after the ganadería, not after its owner, as was the custom) and with a number. This blood caste was as highly prized for its stamina and aggression as the great Andalucian Miuras, or the giant Serranos of Perú. Being among the fiercest, the Sangre caste bulls brought some of the highest prices at auction.

"We could still be punished," she said.

"Yes. But you were right," said Manuel. "I do talk about challenging tradition. I talk about taking risks. All I do is talk. If you're still willing to try it, so am I." He bit at the cuticle of one finger until he tasted blood. He'd spent his life avoiding the ring, but, ironically, through her he might step out of his father's world.

Luna blushed, flattered by the thought that she'd been persuasive, and the feeling of being little more than a dirty shadow most of the time was gone. She'd hardly dared to hope for more than scrubbing, shovelling, and mending, but she had wished that God might reveal a purpose to her life. Until Manuel had found her with the bull in the field, that purpose was a private indulgence. "I knew you'd help me," she said, wrapping her arms around him.

He hesitated before returning the embrace. Any Spanish torero worth the weight of his sword had passed through the ranch to test the bulls for his father. People said that was how Luna's parents had met. But his father's dream of siring the next Pedro Romero had been destroyed by Manuel. If it were discovered that Luna was fighting Don Carlos's strong bulls his father's reputation would be ruined. He would be furious. How forgiving of this plan would he be? Manuel thought of El Mayoral, the ranch foreman, negotiating with his father on behalf of the other men, for better working conditions. His father was angry about that, but ultimately he respected workers with ambition, as much as he loved bullfighting. Both gave him the opportunity to cheer for the underdog. "For now we say nothing," Manuel said. "If you're truly talented, I will tell my father."

"Yes. Of course. Anything you ask."

Manuel searched Luna's eyes and there was a quality in them, a degree of ambition that hadn't been so apparent before; ruthlessness folded over desperation. He knew she would stop at nothing to become a bullfighter. "You understand," he said. "I'm not offering to train you on foot and make you into a Matador de toros. You wouldn't be the highest category of bullfighter. But perhaps a rejoneadora is good enough?"

Luna looked over at Batata and her new foal and back to Manuel. "I do ride well," she said, and just like that, ambition took flight.

FROM BENEATH THE SHADE of a single holm oak, Manuel was peering through his binoculars at a dazzling hoopoe probing for grubs on the ground, when his brother startled him by jumping down out of the tree. "You and that girl had a lot to talk about," said Pedro.

"We were passing the time."

"Is that all?"

Manuel lifted the cord of the binoculars over his head, tried to weave around his brother, but Pedro stepped in front of him, blocked his path. Physically Pedro was their father, short in the legs and thick around the middle, not physically suited to fighting the bulls. But he was fearless and vain, and he liked blood. He liked killing. Although he didn't have the graceful physique to pull off artful passes, Pedro had the instinct of a murderer, and that, along with his Nationalism, were what distinguished him from his older brother.

"I once heard this crazy story," Pedro said, pulling a cigarette from his pocket, and holding it between his stubby fingers. "Maybe you know it too. About a girl in the colonies fighting on horseback. What a novelty. That kind of thing can be very profitable."

Manuel froze. The ground at his feet was crowded with the shadow of the overhanging tree. How much, he wondered, had his brother overheard?

"Don't look so concerned," Pedro smirked. "It's unlikely another girl could do the same thing. Not here. It would take a miracle. But, if someone trained her, you, for instance, and she turned out to be any good, bueno, with a dedicated promoter you could earn more in one performance than a schoolteacher earns in an entire year. More than our father or a great General earns in two months." He lifted the cigarette to his lips and grinned the grin of an entrepreneur.

"Is money all you think about?"

Pedro sniffed violently. "I'd give anything to have what you waste. God granted you the perfect physique for toreo and instead you play with children and rearrange the alphabet!"

"Luna's not a head of cattle to be traded at auction for your benefit."

"No, she's a housemaid, but for some reason you pretend otherwise."

Manuel clenched his jaw. He hated class arrogance from anyone, and especially from his own family. And yet, he didn't fully understand his affinity with Luna. Was it about his guilt? Was she another way to defy his parents? No. In a private part of himself, tucked away where temperament and passion collided — in his mutinous soul — Luna felt more like family than his own brother. He looked at Pedro, with his bulbous nose, small, deep-set eyes, and the indulgent grin that suggested an opportunist's nature. There was nothing on his brother's face that he recognized in his own. Four years separated them, but for all their differences it might as well have been four centuries.

"What do you want?" he asked.

Pedro exhaled a small cloud of cigarette smoke. "Half of your cut."

A wave of angry resignation rolled across Manuel's body. His brother's greed was boundless. Pedro hadn't shown the slightest interest in Luna until that moment, but excluding him from the plan would send him running to their father to try and win favour. "You've got some nerve," said Manuel.

MINUTES AFTER MIDNIGHT, LUNA found the testing ring open to the starry sky, a near-exact replica of a real plaza de toros — though smaller and less adorned. It sat in a pasture surrounded, in the distance, by the moonlit silhouette of sloping mountaintops. Manuel was in the arena, holding the becerro with a rope around its neck, and Pedro was over by the fence, ready with a garrocha — the rejoneador's long pole.

"You're late," Manuel said.

"Paqui couldn't sleep." Luna pointed at Pedro. "What's he doing here?"

"He knows about our plan."

"Oh no!"

Manuel stepped closer, lowered his voice. "It'll be all right. Let him think he has a role and he'll keep his mouth shut." He waved her to stand beside the calf. "Examine him," he said, in a louder voice. "First with your eyes, and then with your hands."

"Why?" She was still watching Pedro. "I already know what he looks like."

"Do you want lessons or not?"

She did as instructed, as though she'd not seen a calf up close before. Measuring from the top of his withers, he came up to her chest — she could see over his back, to where Pedro was leaning against the fence with a self-satisfied expression on his face, as though he was already counting the money he'd make from this affront to tradition. The calf was light and insecure on wobbly legs, young to be separated from his mother. His round, sorrowful eyes darted about, searching for an ally. Luna approached him slowly, held her hand out for him to nuzzle. Maybe he'd think she offered grass. She waited, and slowly he inched forward craning his neck. His dark eyes were wet and seemed the deepest in all of the world, deeper than Pedro's greed. The calf sniffed her fingers and blinked long, pretty eyelashes. "He's handsome," she said.

"Yes," Pedro called out. "But not for long."

Luna knew what he meant; the calves grew into cows or fighting bulls, and if they weren't brave or noble enough for the corrida they were sold and moved on to slaughter. Still, she resented the comment. Like his mother, Pedro was often dismissive of her, and delivered his statements of superiority so matter-of-factly they sounded inevitable.

She ran her small palm along the length of the calf's body, felt his ribs. He was beginning to lose his downy black undercoat. Most of his narrow neck and torso was already covered in a coarser, light grey standard coat. Still, he was already big enough to hurt her.

"He has some nasty bites under his coat," she said. "Maybe from flies."

"Look at his ears," said Manuel. "Inspect his hooves and his teeth."

"His teeth!"

"Yes, as with the horses, you know how to do it. You should know each part of him. Watch." Manuel spread his hand, and inserted his thumb and middle finger between the calf's wet lips, pushing around the outsides of his teeth, to the very back of his mouth, near his throat, where he was all gum and couldn't bite. Manuel squeezed and the calf opened his mouth. His breath was of sour milk and newly cut grass. His teeth lined up in two fine, white rows, and though they couldn't see it clearly under the moonlight, his tongue was pink and shiny. "Now the hooves," said Manuel.

Luna passed her hand along the calf's thick neck, across his soft chest, and down his left, rear leg, as she would've with a horse, warning him where she was going so he wouldn't be spooked. She curled the calf's pata up behind, tugged until he relaxed into her hand, and ran her thumb across the bottom. "Soft," she said. "No splintering. How old is he?"

"Two years."

She dropped the pata and returned to the calf's head, stroking one of his ears. "We should call him Gamuza. He's soft as suede."

"So, how is he different from you?"

She giggled, but saw that Manuel was deadly serious.

"I don't know."

"Think. Feel. What are his strengths and defects? Is he more or less afraid than you are? Is he stubborn? Is he passive?"

"I'm not passive!"

"Then tell us. How is he different from you?"

As Pedro approached, Luna considered the question. There was the obvious; the calf would soon have a full, tough coat where she had delicate human skin. He had four legs and she had two, though she sensed that wasn't what Manuel wanted to hear. She walked around the animal once more and he jumped. He was skittish, lighter on his feet than she was, though that too would surely change as he grew muscle. He was young, also like her, and though he didn't know it, his life was fated in a direction he could not alter. Luna tickled his upper lip as she would a horse's. To her surprise his thick lips quivered and he laughed.

"He has a good sense of humour," she said.

Pedro pinched her cheek a little too hard. "Definitely not like you."

She recoiled at his touch. Pedro was someone she'd grown accustomed to living around, but they usually ignored one another. He had a forceful personality, if entitlement can be described as a personality trait. Physical contact brought him into sharp focus, and she was reminded of how much she disliked him. She leaned forward, and rubbing her sore face, peered directly into Gamuza's eyes. She might as well have been peering into Pedro's as she said, "I'm smarter than him."

"No." Manuel was fast to correct her. "Don't make the mistake of arrogance, Luna. The moment you assume to know more than a bull you'll be in trouble."

"He's not a bull. He's only a calf."

"His temperament is already fixed. Each creature has its own intelligence and his is for the kill." Manuel almost laughed at himself, sounding like his father, but he too respected the animals, considered them works of art. "The most fiercely bred creature cannot become immortal without help," he said.

"Immortal? But —"

"Not you, though one day someone will have the honour of killing him, if he's lucky. If it happens in a grand arena, surrounded by the roar of applause, he'll die a king among beasts, a most dignified end. Better than the slaughterhouse. But you will have to injure him and see blood." Manuel patted the calf's developing withers. "Do you still think you can place the rejones on his back?"

"Yes," she said. She was certain she could, though it felt presumptive to say so, when Manuel, a grown man, hadn't found it within himself to draw a lance or sword. Luna wondered whether he would change his mind about training her. Did his distaste for the violence of bullfighting ever leave him feeling like a failed Spaniard? She looked up, saw impotence on his face, and thought she'd better do something to seem less threatening. "What if I love him and he loves me?" she asked, feigning apprehension.

"All the more reason," said Pedro.

"Manuel," she whined. "I cannot hurt Gamuza. I can't."

"Aiy!" Pedro was angered by her girlish weakness; he didn't know it was a facade. It didn't disturb her to watch Paqui snap the hens' necks, and she didn't gag, as Manuel did, at the smell of cows' hide being branded. "This will never work," Pedro said. "She's no torera."

Manuel released the rope and it dangled like a snake beneath the calf's neck. "Yes, she is," he said, more to her than to Pedro. "Luna was born struggling. She'll find the honour in it."

With that, Luna closed her eyes and tilted her head towards the sleepy face of God, asking Him to grant her that single wish. "Make me brave, like my father," she prayed out loud. "Make me the bravest bullfighter who ever lived." Since her confirmation she'd been praying at night, but those prayers were sent up for others, her mother, her father. Tonight she imagined being in the ring, wearing a colourful suit of lights, pink and turquoise, her favourite colours, with gold sequins that shimmered under the sun. She saw herself succeeding, escaping her low station. The bulls were powerful, but they were ultimately living a life of servitude. Who better to fight them? Moonlight washed over her face with a veil of cool blue, a flash of silver. She opened her eyes once more, and stared up at the velvet sky, pin-dotted with stars. The moon glowed as if made of white gold.

"I can learn," she said.

"Let's see about that." Pedro jabbed the calf in the rump with the spike of the garrocha, causing the animal to make a pained sound that was half surprise and half betrayal. He darted away, stopped beside the toril, watching them and swayed his head from side to side. He was hurt physically, yes, though not much. Mainly, he was humiliated.

"Why did you do that?" Luna asked, angrily. "After all my work to become his friend." But the instant she showed the calf her back, he charged her.

"Look out!" Manuel hollered.

Luna bolted, found a foothold on the small white shelf inside the wooden barrera, and threw herself over the wall, landing outside the ring.

Pedro fell to the ground laughing and holding his stomach, while the calf swerved around him. "Some torera you'll make," he said. "This one doesn't weigh fifteen arrobas."

It was Luna's turn to be humiliated, but she quickly turned it outward. "He's mad at you," she said, standing on her tiptoes, with her arms dangling overtop of the barrera, catching her breath. "You deserve it."

"You must learn to understand their nature and movements," Manuel said. "So you'll be able to predict them. All this pequeño had in him was a gesture of defiance."

"No true bravura," said Pedro, spitting on the ground. "Looks like he's destined for the factory not the bullring."

"I am destined for greatness," Luna said, balancing on the wall and stretching her arms up over her head, and instinctively, Manuel knew she was, the way we know the sound of our parents' voices before we ever learn their given names.

"Our little torera-to-be?"

"Torero," she countered. She was one of them now. An honorary brother.

"She ran on instinct," said Pedro. "What does that tell you?"

"What it tells me," said Manuel, "is that she's no different than you. I remember you running like that last year."

"Never."

"When we came upon that wild boar you were hurrying home for supper?" Manuel winked at Luna, and her heart made an extra beat for him. He wouldn't give up on her. He wouldn't turn his back on the things that he believed in. That's why she loved him. His kind of passion was unfaltering, loyal, a defence of those more vulnerable. And what was passion, if not the relentless expectation of something better?

Pedro turned and chased the calf to the other side of the testing ring.

"Again?" Luna asked, tentatively.

There was a long silence while Manuel searched her eyes. "Art is about love, Luna. It's dangerous, and there are no guarantees. Are you absolutely certain this is what you want?"

Excitement funnelled up through her body and gathered between her shoulder blades, turning them into sharp little wings. "Claro que sí," she said.

ONE WEEK LATER, MANUEL drove to Córdoba to see Eugenia, dreaming her reactions to his declaration of love. He parked the car on the waterfront, and found her waiting on the footbridge that jutted out over the Guadalquivir. As she approached him, sunlight shone through the purple cotton skirt of her sundress revealing her long bare legs.

They toured the Mesquite, strolling arm-in-arm beneath the striped arches, discussing the beauty of the architecture. They shared a meal of paella and a bottle of local wine, and discussed anticlericalism.

"Nuns and priests should be banned from teaching," said Manuel. "They use schools to spread Church propaganda and legitimize reactionaries."

"Yes, but ordinary Catholics feel attacked," said Eugenia. "They want their rituals and we are seen to be forbidding them. Are we against Church privileges or against its followers?"

They avoided the subject of his poetry. After supper, they made love in the recessed doorway of a narrow street not far from the Mesquite, and when Eugenia shuddered in his arms Manuel heard pigeons above them cooing. They walked to her apartment sharing a cigarette. She said, "We shouldn't see each other again, outside of the group."

"What? Why not?" Manuel was confused.

"You're very attractive," she explained. "I could fall into the habit of this. But I can't love you."

Manuel felt the wall of muscle in his chest squeeze too tightly. "You just did," he said, and feeling foolish for being sentimental he added. "What was that back there?"

Eugenia sent a smoky tendril into the night air. "I find your poetry to be small," she said. "It lacks intensity. This is the quality I value most in life. I'm sorry, Manuel," she said. "You might as well know it."

"Do you fuck all the men you disrespect?" He made a show of looking behind himself. "Am I at the front of a line?"

Eugenia tossed the cigarette on the ground angrily. "Grow up," she said. "You know better than to think I will be caged."

MIDDAY SUN SCREAMED OFF the white wall that surrounded the property. Luna shielded her eyes with one hand. As she rounded the chicken coop, she found the girl with the overbite and her sister, waiting to taunt her.

"Look who it is," said her former friend.

"I don't see anybody," said the other, staring directly at her.

Luna faced the girls with stony resentment. "Paqui has no eggs to spare," she said. "Get out of my way."

"People say your mother was cursed," the younger one said.

"She was a whore," said the other. "We all know it. Don Carlos's mistress!"

For a moment Luna was speechless. The stories that circulated among the workers were often fabulist, a form of entertainment for them. But didn't most stories begin from a germ of truth? Almost without thinking, she lunged, shoving the girl with the overbite, and sending her reeling backwards into the corner of the stone pileta. "My father is a brave bullfighter," she said, proudly. "And don't you ever speak about my mother again!"

The girl burst out laughing. "A bullfighter? Ha! Who told you that?"

Don Carlos stepped around the corner, into view. "It's vile to spread rumours!" he snapped.

The sisters' mouths dropped open. The one with the overbite lowered her eyes in deference. "Forgive us," she said.

Luna threw her hands to her hips with smug satisfaction. She had the more powerful ally. "Why don't you tell him the other rumour you spread?" she dared.

The sisters looked at one another, but neither girl spoke.

"No?" Luna pressed. "Why not?"

Don Carlos already knew the story: that a wild black bull, driven by passion, had overtaken Luna's mother one night in the field and fathered her. This terrible thought gave him a chill. "Get to work!" he barked. "All of you."

DON CARLOS REACHED THE far field where a dam was standing on the dry grass in between Pedro and Manuel, her abdomen stretching and contorting rhythmically as though it might rupture. She moaned but didn't look over her haunches in the direction of new life, rather she kept her head forward, focussed on her pain. The calf's rear end was sticking out of her body.

"How long has she been like this?" Don Carlos asked.

"Almost an hour," said Pedro. "I tried to turn it manually but it wouldn't budge."

"She won't be able to hold herself up much longer."

The dam was shaded from the sun by the shadow of the hill, and a half dozen other cows who sniffed the air but kept a respectful distance. A few bulls watched from behind a fence.

"What if we lay her on her side?" asked Manuel.

Don Carlos fiddled with the end of his salt and pepper moustache. "Another ten minutes and I'll have to pull it out."

Pedro lifted one hand to shade his eyes from the sun and saw

Luna coming upon them. "What is she doing here?" he asked.

"I can help too," Luna said, arriving at Manuel's side. She admired the animal's chocolate-coloured face, recognized it as belonging to Gertrudis, the cow who grazed closest to the house, near the south-east fence. She'd named her for a brown-skinned mountain woman who traded wild boar for Paqui's tapestries.

"This is no place for you," Don Carlos said. "A dam requires privacy," though what he believed was that a girl who witnessed the pain of birth would be dissuaded from having children of her own. A mothering cow has a nine-month gestation period.

"Por favor, Don Carlos. I won't get in the way."

Don Carlos hesitated, searching inside of himself for the will to enforce his own rule, but the burden of death, he suspected, was with her, as it was with him, pressing up against his consciousness, an exposed nerve. Little in the pain and guts of death was as hard to bear. "Suit yourself," he said. "She may not live."

Luna nodded. She'd seen guinea pigs birth dead pups, and, once, she'd watched a mad hog trample her own piglets. She'd spied on more than one foal's birth, and countless other calves, and how many times had she helped Manuel feed injured and abandoned birds? She was immune to such indignities. Life involved pain and loss and a labouring dam was merely a labouring dam.

For Carlos, any birth was a potential disaster. Luna's own birth had been that. He still remembered the bloody details: Though there was no official record, it was 1919, and the final day of the September Feria, the premier bullfight event of the year. He and Father Serratosa had returned from Ronda where they'd been celebrating with the toreros. Wet and drunk, the two of them stumbled through Paqui's kitchen door looking for something to eat, and found themselves to be uncomfortable spectators, as Luna's mother writhed in pain on the long wooden table.

Carlos froze. His heart thundered in his chest. He hadn't seen Elisenda in months, had been trying to forget her for her own sake, and for his. The last time they'd spoken, was when he'd ended the relationship at his wife's insistence. His head began to throb. Elisenda was having a baby in his house! Was this his baby?! The unusually hard rain outside pummelled the earth, violently uprooting the red, red sugar beets. A rusty stream flowed, painting everything the colour of pain.

Seeing him, Elisenda reached out with a limp arm. "Carlos?"

He didn't move, averted her gaze, but another wave of agony rolled across her body and she let out a chilling scream that turned his stomach and brought tears to his eyes. She was the only woman he'd loved. It was unbearable to hear her suffer. He stepped towards the table, but the priest's firm grip pulled him back. The warning was clear: Go to her and you are publicly admitting your sins. Go to her and I cannot help you.

He'd had other lovers but this one was different. Elisenda had been his for almost two years. She made him feel alive. Again Elisenda reached out for him, pleading with her eyes, and this time Carlos shook loose of the priest. He took her hand in his. "Mi amor," he whispered, kissing the fevered skin of her open palm.

Elisenda smiled weakly, until a more powerful contraction took hold and she screamed, gripping his hand hard, almost crushing it. He had no idea what to say, or how to comfort her. He looked to Paqui for guidance and she crossed herself, whispering prayers. "Dios mío. Por favor, save the baby." Paqui massaged Elisenda's swollen feet, fed her an ointment of thyme and hollyhock, which did little to dull her pain. After an impossibly violent series of contractions, Elisenda's hand went limp. She was losing consciousness. Panicking, Carlos shook her. "Elisenda, open your eyes. Elisenda the baby!" She did open her eyes, but they were dim and glassy.

As Paqui began to sob, the priest placed one hand on Elisenda's fevered, sweaty forehead and said, "She is in God's hands now."

Elisenda was not so resigned. She drew on the last of her strength and gave a final push, tearing her body and freeing Luna, who ripped into this world bloody and blue. Paqui caught her, and immediately saw that the cord of life was unusually short, and wound tightly around her neck. "Quick," Paqui said. "She can't breathe!"

Carlos dashed to the sink and fished out a bucket, and a dirty rag and the heavy blade of a carving knife. With it, he made the necessary cut. Colour flooded Luna's tiny face and neck and, at last, she took her first breath. When Paqui wrapped her in an apron and set her at her mother's breast, Carlos dropped the knife on the floor with obvious relief. "Qué buena suerte," he cried. "What good luck to be born on such an important day." But, minutes later, he was reminded that one person's good fortune often comes at another's expense. His lover's blood pooled on the floor.

Gertrudis moaned deeply, and strained against the next contraction. Her calf, still encased in its amniotic sac, tore a little farther out.

"Get ready to catch," Don Carlos said, moving into position. Gertrudis's legs began to buckle. "Mierda!" He pushed against her haunches with all of his strength. "The two of you, over here, put your shoulders into it! Luna, stroke her face."

Barely standing, Gertrudis pushed one final time and the calf's torso, front legs and head slipped out of her body. Don Carlos guided it to the grass like a pile of dirty clothes. Gertrudis had delivered a healthy calf, and her bones settled into a more peaceful arrangement, but she had no energy left for licking her calf to help it breathe. She didn't move around to sniff it, or mark it with her scent, so Don Carlos ripped off his shirt and handed it to Manuel. "Help it along," he said. Manuel knelt and hesitantly touched the calf; it was fragile, dark and skinny, more like a wet dog. "Vigorously," Don Carlos said. "I shouldn't have to tell you!"

Manuel tensed. What does it feel like to know your own father thinks you're a disappointment? At times it felt as though it had always been that way between them, distant and yet on the edge of eruption; other times the serrated tone of his father's voice cut him like a bullwhip. He used to wonder if he should give up on poetry to make his father happy, contort into the image his father had of him, rather than fail in his eyes. Indeed that thought was what had kept him training for as long as he had. In moments like that, when Carlos couldn't hide his antipathy, Manuel believed his father hated him. "You do it!" he snapped, tossing the shirt at his father's feet and storming off.

Don Carlos spat on the ground. The reservoir of anger he felt inside could easily spill over into violence and he didn't want that. "Keep going!" he shouted, in a tone of disgust.

Luna watched the interaction with an odd transparency; as if by instinct she understood that Don Carlos's anger and disappointment were with himself and not with Manuel. When he met her eyes, she knew that he understood it too, and the shared intimacy made her uncomfortable. Although she didn't want to leave Gertrudis in such a fragile state, she tore off after Manuel.

Pedro warmed the calf's chest as his brother had been asked to do, but felt cold and bitter in his own heart. His father couldn't hide that he favoured Manuel. It was evident to Pedro through his father's anger. It was for Manuel that Don Carlos had high expectations, placing his greatest dreams upon Manuel's shoulders. It was with Manuel he fought. Pedro felt that he hadn't been enough of a concern to warrant expectations. "Mira, Papi! Look, I'm done," he said, ever hopeful of impressing.

Don Carlos turned around. "Did you say something?"

PEDRO HAD BEEN THIRTEEN years old the first time it occurred to him that his father rarely noticed him. That was also the year Pedro had paid for his first sexual encounter, and the two experiences were connected, although he wouldn't think about how.

He'd been working in the barn alongside El Mayoral branding cattle all morning, proud to be the one to sear the ranch's initials into the hides of his father's newest acquisitions. After they were done, he waited for his father to come by and inspect his effort, which Carlos did. The brands were uniformly placed, Carlos said.

Pedro had held the poker down for the right amount of time and with the proper amount of pressure. Pedro beamed. He felt impressive and loved, and was thrilled to have his father's recognition, especially in front of the lead ranch hand. Then, as Carlos was leaving the barn, he casually called over his shoulder to his son.

"Good job, Manuel!"

Pedro clamped his jaw tightly, turned bright red. The pride of accomplishment he'd been feeling instantly melted away and he was embarrassed that El Mayoral had heard the mistake. He sauntered out of the barn, waving casually at El Mayoral as though nothing significant had happened, and yet he was full of rage; he could've been anyone to his father. Clenching his teeth against the feeling of invisibility, Pedro headed around the side of the house where he threw himself into an old wicker chair on the terrace and sulked.

He noticed a girl eating her lunch nearby. She was his age, a field worker from a farm near Sangre Mio. She'd come with her five sisters and their mother to help whitewash his house. He watched her eating a fig, and the deliberate way she'd peeled it and placed it on her tongue was unbearably suggestive. When she smiled at him, he'd stood and walked over to ask her name. Later, in the afternoon, unable to think of anything but her mouth, he'd hidden around the corner and motioned for the girl to excuse herself. She did. He dropped two coins in her hand. Next came a furtive kiss behind the barn, some awkward unbuttoning, and she was on her knees. They didn't see each other again, but the feeling of love being anonymous and conditional was familiar to him, and instantly became his model of the perfect sexual encounter. He would continue to seek it out.

"WHAT IS THAT?" LUNA asked, squinting in the dark to see.

Manuel was holding a ridiculous-looking contraption in his arms. "Working so soon with a live animal is maybe not the best way," he said. "For now, I'll be the bull."

"It's a chair," she said. "A chair with cuernos."

"No," said Pedro, impatiently. "It's a brave bull. Here, take this and run over there." He handed her the rejón, a hard solid spear, and pointed to the far side of the training ring. "When I say, Manuel will charge and you'll pretend that he's a bull and place the rejón, exactly as he showed you. Go on."

She darted across the sand and waited under the moon with the rejón in her hand as though this was one of the games she'd played with the field girls when she was younger and Paqui had let her slip away from her chores — like Civiles y Ladrones, where she was the policeman and they were the clever thieves; Tienta, where she was always "'it,"' and Mico, which the girl with the overbite had invented. She hated Mico most of all because she couldn't win. The sisters would toss a ball high above her head, and she'd try in vain to jump and intercept it. For years she'd watched enviously, while Manuel trained in his father's small ring, and Pedro played torero with their cousins, comparing imaginary cornadas, trading matchboxes and wine labels with pictures of famous Matadors on them. Now it was her turn. She dug her heels into the dirt of the ring. "Es fácil," she said. "I'm ready for you."

Manuel lifted the chair by two of its legs and held it out, the large white, curled cuernos mounted on the back. They'd been polished and they shone like ivory in the moonlight. He snorted and dug at the ground with one boot, then charged. Luna knew it was him, but the sharp tips were coming straight for her, so she stepped out of the way. Manuel swerved and chased her around the ring until she was running with her back to him, squealing and flapping her arms about in the air, out of breath.

Pedro waved them to stop. "Quiet! We don't want to attract the Guardia Civil. Return to your positions," he ordered. He moved to stand behind her, placed one of his arms beneath her right one, and the other beneath her left, where she held the rejón. "Feel what I do," he said, and she stiffened, finding his touch to be abrasive. Pedro nodded in Manuel's direction. "Try it again, this time not so fast!"

Manuel advanced slowly, making a low, menacing groan to sound authentic. When he was close enough, a few feet away, Pedro raised Luna's left arm in a firm, fluid motion, and brought the rejón down behind the cuernos of the chair. Manuel stopped and they all held their positions. "This is where you need to aim and hit," said Pedro. "Precisely this area of the bull's withers. It's the size of a coin. Do you see?"

She leaned in. The rejón was between the chair's legs.

"Easy," she said. "Let's play again."

Pedro released her arms. "This time on your own."

Manuel charged her again, from a different angle, and, feeling confident in what was expected, she placed the rejones behind his cuernos. "Done!"

Over and over they practised and she soon got the feel for the correct position of her arms, how her left needed to rise and fall as though it were a giant feathered wing, and how her right should remain slack, holding onto the imaginary reins of her horse. She repeated the motion so many times that she no longer had to think of timing, or of the distance between the "head" of the animal and his "withers." She simply knew. Each night she did as the brothers instructed and each morning she looked a little more confident, exhausted. She began to worry that her work in the house was getting sloppier and that Paqui would soon wonder why. Still, the threat of discovery wouldn't keep her from training. She'd found new kinship with the moonlight rolling over the hills, with the grey-blue film peeking through the morning clouds. She'd tasted the beginnings of belonging, what it was like to be someone else, better born, because faith had been placed in her, and when she stood praying at the centre of her own sweet universe, no García could better her.

Luna's discipline and focus offered up artistic permission for Manuel, too, and some of his best material came in the sleepy days after they'd snuck out to the field. Within a few months he'd begun a collection of poems called, "Birdsong. Canto de los Pájaros."

Danger for a torero is found in the twisted horns of a fighting bull, in the narrow reflection of a sword, but Manuel found it at the edge of night, under the pearly moon, knowing that for the first time in his life he had fully committed himself to his writing.

"Remember, your gestures are in pursuit of grace," he told Luna.

"What is that?" she asked.

"A state of charm that transcends beauty."

"But how will I find it?"

"Not find, become."


WHEN LUNA WAS A small child she'd spun around in tight little circles, faster and faster, until she made herself sick to her stomach or until she fell down. Despite her attempts, she couldn't replicate the particular kind of dizziness she experienced seemingly out of the blue. Spinning in circles was merely a challenge to the laws of gravity, her body in motion. The other, the vertigo that snuck up on her when she least expected it, was brought on by stasis, lack of movement, feeling she was trapped outside of love.

The very first time she remembered it happening was when she was four years old and in the kitchen grilling Paqui with questions about her mother.

"Why did she die, Paquita? Where is she now?

"God took her to heaven during childbirth," Paqui said, in as practical a manner as she could muster.

Luna still remembered the unmistakable click in her brain, the sound she felt rather than heard, as though in her child's mind a window she hadn't known existed had been unlocked, letting in the terrible truth. Her stomach turned and the room began to spin, slowly at first, then faster until she was unable to stand without falling and Paqui had to carry her to bed.

At first, Paqui had accused her of feigning illness to be excused from chores, but it happened more and more and Paqui decided that it was a side effect of Luna's traumatic birth, a frail constitution that needed additional support. She'd instructed Luna to eat a slice of ginger root each day and not mention the condition to anyone. Luna had complied. A weakness like that was a dangerous thing for a poor girl to share.

The bulls were Luna's real medicine, more powerful than any longing for friends and family. More powerful than the vertigo itself. They were representatives of death, and death, she'd come to believe, was about love. Christ's. Her mother's. Sometimes when she was alone and feeling introspective, she'd wonder whether she too was destined to sacrifice herself on the altar of love. She hoped so and, as quickly, she hoped not.

ONE NIGHT MANUEL DECIDED to take away the chair with the asti-blanco cuernos, and in its place he stood a calf Luna hadn't seen before. Her favourite horse, Batata, was tied nearby.

"What's the point of perfect technique," Manuel said. "If you waste it on a chair?"

"But that one is so cute," she said. "You see how, with his big ears and the ring around his eye, he looks like a silly clown? Let's call him Payasín."

Pedro rolled his eyes. "Stop naming them. How are you going to view them as enemies?"

"Enemies have names too," she countered.

"Pedro has gone to much trouble to find a calf for practice," Manuel said, to appease his brother. "Our neighbour doesn't know we've ... borrowed Payasín. He's here to help, Luna. What makes you think you have the right to refuse Payasín that honour?"

The calf turned, searching for the herd in the field, on the other side of the wall, and Luna glanced from one brother to the other. They both looked impatient, standing with their hands crammed into the front pockets of their pants: Either she placed the rejón and carried on with training, or Payasín returned to his herd unharmed and she returned to the house. She peered across the field where the satin moon set the whitewashed house aglow. She'd already made her decision.

According to Paqui, her father had been a fearless torero, with an unparalleled desire to experience the world. He'd promised her mother travel, said they would cross the ocean and dance in fine leather heels, but it didn't happen. One night he snuck off to follow his own freedom, and left her mother with nothing to look forward to, except an illegitimate pregnancy and the crushing boredom of drudgery. It saddened Luna to imagine it: abandonment that convinces you you're fated to deprivation, but she knew she was like him. She would leave this place to follow her ambition the first chance she got. Her mother had been forced to serve out the rest of her days at Sangre Mio for less than a pocket of coins, and because she'd disgraced herself, and the family she served, she sank deeper and deeper into an unmarked grave, but Luna was destined for something else.

She felt for the tough calluses on her own palms. *Why should her heart meet the same, hardened fate as her mother's?* She tightened the cinch on Batata's saddle, lifted her left leg into a stirrup, and hoisted herself up. Pedro handed over her rejón and it felt heavier in her palm than it had before. She forced herself to look Payasín in the eye, and he seemed to be asking for mercy, as though he could see through her skin, all the way down into her heart, to where pain originated.

"No puedo," she said, drudging up some apprehension.

"You know you can," said Manuel. "Focus. Emoción y técnica."

"You're not going to kill him," said Pedro. "Place the rejón. And stop looking at him as if he's one of us!"

Luna bit her bottom lip. After so much time spent together in training, Pedro had learned nothing about the inner machinations of her ambition. It was precisely because she believed the animals were her equals that she could fight them. She met Payasín's eyes once more and hoped he could understand: this was their only honourable way out of an impossible situation.

On horseback, Luna held the rejón across the horse's neck with her left hand while keeping the reins in her right. It was tricky wrist work and required good balance, much like el relojito, the jump-rope game she used to play with the field girls in the waning heat of the afternoon. All at once she couldn't get the song out of her head: *Al pasar la barca, me dijo el barquero, las niñas bonitas, no pagan dinero.* She tugged on the reins, turning Batata, and moving them into position under the stars. In truth, her instinct to fight was stronger than any latent instinct she might've had to protect the calf — or herself — and all she was seeing from her mount was a target. Her hands opened and closed, as if craving the hardness of the reins and the rejón. Her lips were moist and she swallowed decisively. Kicking Batata, she charged her little friend, lifting her arm and, with all of her strength, bringing it down again, stabbing Payasín's withers with the angled blade precisely where she should. Smooth resistance, cutting into his flesh was as easy as cutting into a tub of lard.

A kinaesthetic charge rippled through her body, as if she had electric veins that sparked with light. Something awakened and rose up from the deepest pit of her where a dark, primal urge to follow her instincts was born, and she knew that passion for the fiesta brava had indeed been bred into her while she'd slept within the protective circle of her mother's womb. Her skin was flushed; alive with a prickly energy, when she made the pinchazo, and she immediately wanted to go again, go again, as though marking Payasín from on horseback was an exciting new ride at the Feria de Abril. The calf moaned and twisted in no particular direction, in an attempt to get away from her, but it was already done. The rejón was placed. Payasín was injured, though not close to fatally. Luna had merely pierced his withers about three inches and caused a spray of blood to colour his coat.

She dismounted quickly, and leapt into Manuel's arms.

"I did it! I did it!"

"Estupendo!" he said, spinning her around.

"Not bad," said Pedro.

Manuel set Luna down and turned to examine the placement of the rejón. It was perfect, and he was relieved, and proud of her. Some of us spend too long concealing our natures, hoping and waiting and praying to be loved, while others risk everything to reveal themselves. She knew who she was.

LUNA WAS IN THE kitchen suffocating under the heady scent of partridge and stewed chestnuts, when Manuel entered the room cupping a bird in his hands.

"A blue rock thrush," he said.

Paqui pointed with a thick finger to the red dirt he was tracking across her clean tile floor. "Wipe your shoes," she said.

He held his hands out for Luna to see. The bird was covered in cobalt feathers and had a long black beak and round elegant head. One wing was folded neatly into its chest but the other struggled clumsily to fly.

"Pedro's slingshot?" she asked.

"One of his traps."

The bird again tried to flap its wing, but couldn't. Its small black eyes watched helplessly, defiantly. A bird that cannot fly is no longer a bird.

"What are you going to do with it?" Luna asked.

Manuel moved over to the butcher's block in the corner to fashion a miniature splint from string and matchsticks. "Save it," he said.

THE FOLLOWING SPRING, THE Confederación Española de Derechas Autónomas, CEDA, was busy persuading Catholics to unite against the Republican coalition government and defend Christian civilization. Manuel arranged to take Luna to Ronda to see her first professional bullfight at the Real Maestranza bullring. This was to be the next stage in her training: to witness the ringcraft of a master on foot. He waited to tell his mother until late the night before, when he knew she would be reading a magazine in the living room and half-way through a bottle of sherry.

"There's a meeting of my artist's circle in Ronda tomorrow," he lied.

"Hmm."

"I'm taking Luna with me."

Doña García lifted her bloodshot eyes as if to say, *You can't socialize with her in public, Manuel. What will people say?* But when she fixed on him, with his defensive posture, ready to argue the point, there wasn't enough fight inside of her for anything other than raising the soothing bottle to her lips.

At three o'clock Manuel parked one of his father's old trucks in front of the Ayuntamiento. Luna was quick to run down the street and search out the plaza de toros.

The crowd gathered six men deep at the sandstone entrance, and before the kiosk closed Pedro purchased their tickets. Facing them, beside the ticket window, was a large black and orange cartel advertising the event. *The greatest torero of all time*, it said, in thick lettering. *Juan Belmonte!* Luna clapped her hands together; after years in retirement, and a few fulfilling contracts in the colonies, Belmonte had returned to Spanish soil. They were catching one of his first performances.

Vendors outside the plaza sold pistachios, wineskins, toy banderillas and muletas for small children. A group of girls Luna's age disappeared around the side of the plaza to wait for the toreros' last minute arrival and possibly autographs. Luna checked her ticket to learn which tier and row and seat she'd been assigned. She clutched it to her breast as latecomers tightened in around them like a belt and squeezed them through the arched doorway.

Inside, Pedro rented three leather cushions from a young boy and pressed forward to find their section. "Over there," he pointed.

They hurried along the corridor to the third door where they climbed the stairs and emerged, facing the open bullring. A carnival of colour washed over them like holy water. Sun bathed one side of the ring in pure amber light. The other fell into shadow. The sand was a flat gold circle, smooth as velvet, and above them, a cloudless blue sky. The stands were packed all the way around, pale stone pillars and arches framing a flurry of motion as women in each section fanned themselves, handbills flew, and men argued and placed bets while their children ran the length of the stone bleachers. On more than one occasion Manuel had heard his father say that the Real Maestranza was a holy place, the most glorious bullring in Spain, some claimed in all of the world. Today, Luna knew it to be true. Her face betrayed the force of her passion. She looked part of something ancient there, as though no other world existed outside of toreo, and that art was religion.

Pedro found their seats and passed them each a cushion. They squeezed onto the bleacher between an old man in a silk scarf, with a girl of about five bouncing on his lap. A pregnant woman fanning herself sat in front of them. It was hot in the shade. The air was a fog of cigarette and cigar smoke. Luna's throat scratched. The floor, the cushions, the air, stank of sweat and beer. A moment later, trumpets sounded and they heard the beat of a drum.

"Look," Luna said, extending a sinewy arm. "At the far end!"

Two Alguacillas in red-plumed hats rode into the ring, leading the procession in order of seniority: First came the three Matadors, with Belmonte in the middle, parading before them in his blue suit — a glittering figure. The three cuadrillas trailed their respective toreros, each wearing a parade cape draped over his left shoulder. The banderilleros were next, with their rejones, and the puntillero identified by his black-on-black silk embroidered costume. Mercifully, he would use his short puntilla to sever the bull's spinal cord once the Matador was finished with him. Next came the picadors on horseback, each crossing himself as he entered the ring, followed by the monosabios in their red shirts, dark trousers and caps, and last, the muleteros, dressed the same as the monosabios but with mules to drag the dead bulls out of the arena. It was similar to what happens in a corrida on horseback, and Luna was entranced by the notion of facing a bull on foot.

When Belmonte was close to them he turned and peered up into the stands, and Luna saw that the epaulets on his suit of lights were finely embroidered. Tassels had been sewn along both arms in magenta, orange, and gold. She took in the beauty of his costume, as though it was one of the wall tapestries Paqui weaved: a bright, pulsing star on a hot summer night.

Pedro pulled the peak of his cap down over his eyes. "Look at his ssssuit," he stammered, imitating Belmonte's known weakness. "Who dresses him, his mmmadre?"

"What's so wrong with it?" Luna asked.

Manuel leaned in. "My brother can't stand to be upstaged by a better man."

"Mejor?" Pedro laughed. "That gordito has eaten too much Spanish sausage. And look? He has a long pointy nose and big ears and he's old now. Probably, he can no longer fuck."

"What do you know of it?" said Manuel. "A bullfighter is the world's greatest seducer. Belmonte will slay the bull with brutal precision and watch; the women in the stands will hear whispers of love."

The procession dispersed, though Belmonte remained in the ring sweeping his crimson capote back and forth across the sand to test the wind. His name was sewn on the gold underside in black thread. A stack of folded muletas balanced on the barrera next to him. "He must've drawn the first bull," Luna said, knowing there would be six, two for each Matador.

"Watch closely," said Manuel, as Belmonte moved into position. "You won't see this technique again."

All at once, a black Serrano with the number 38 branded into his hide beat across the ring. He slipped on his hindquarters but found his legs quickly, stopped and waited. He had huge black testicles and white horns with black tips. His face was soft, loving as it raged, and yet it was clear that he was confused with nothing obvious to charge.

Belmonte stepped forward and the bull swung his head.

"He's too big," Luna said.

"It's the braver the bull, not the bigger," said Manuel.

With four passes Belmonte moved the bull farther into the centre of the ring. He was impressive and restrained with his gestures, and hardly mocked the bull or played to the crowd for favour. He simply stood close to the animal, so close that an uninitiated spectator would've thought this was his final performance. When he was ready, he signalled for his picador, who entered the ring sitting atop his horse with dull armour and flat expression, looking like a passionless cousin of Don Quixote. His garrocha was eight feet long, and had a serrated steel point at the bottom, like the ones Luna had been using during her training sessions. His rusty spurs clinked as he moved his horse into position opposite the bull. "This is a small part of the corrida," Manuel warned her. "But an important one."

The picador's horse was blindfolded, and wearing no peto for protection. The mare waited obediently for the charge, mutely, because her vocal chords had been cut. The lone part of her body that protested, and it quivered violently, was her bottom lip.

"Why doesn't she run?" Luna asked.

"Sshsh," said Pedro.

But it was a good question and an ironic one, coming from her. Until she'd trained as Rejoneadora, Luna had found no place in this life other than the one she'd been assigned, and perhaps that's how the horse felt. She looked to Manuel for his answer, but all at once, the bull slammed into the horse like a clap of thunder and the pretty brown mare was being lifted off her feet. Luna shuddered, though her eyes were riveted on the spike of the garrocha, planted inside the bull's neck. Red blood ran down his ribcage. When the bull pulled back, she saw that the horse had been ripped open from chest to stomach. She wanted to beg God for answers as to why some must die so that others live on, but didn't. She looked to Manuel once more, to gage his reaction. He was trembling and his face had turned the colour of blanched almonds. He closed his eyes as the picador dismounted and his horse collapsed onto the ground.

"A necessary sacrifice," Pedro said.

"But why?" Luna asked. "He could tire the bull some other way."

Next, a blond banderillero pranced onto the sand in his slippers. He sighted the Serrano, found a good angle from which to approach, and lifted the pink and white banderillas dramatically, one in each hand. The bull looked tired, almost innocent, his belly heaving and his white tongue hanging stupidly out of his mouth, though his tail told a different story. The banderillero ran directly for him, blond hair flattened by the wind, and it appeared that he'd meet the same fate as the picador's nag, but he was a graceful dancer, lifting himself into the air at exactly the right instant. The banderillas went in silently, and anyone could see that he wasn't made from solid mass, but from shadow. The bull bucked and dug at the ground, and the colourful sticks bounced on his withers. "Bravo!" called out the pregnant woman in front of them.

For the third and final act Belmonte stepped into the ring and faced the angry bull alone. So small was he opposite the massive front of the defiant animal that Luna was no longer sure it was possible for any man to kill a bull, let alone such a short, slight man. But each gesture Belmonte made with the flick of his wrist and the swivel of his narrow hips caused the beast to come further under his submission, and the frenzied crowd reacted with jubilation.

"Mátalo! Kill him!"

Belmonte made a few more passes with his capote, impressively fanning it high over his head. He exchanged it for the muleta and a sword with a curved end. The music stopped, and in absolute silence he sited the bull along the length of that steel.

"Kill him well!" The crowd shouted. They wanted more and more of what appeared to be abject cruelty. Luna tensed on the bench with barely contained anticipation. The crowd excited and frightened her. It was the more ferocious beast. But she wanted their attention too: to be in their loving embrace. She waved her ticket and cheered for the magnificent animal trapped inside his own aggression, and for the man who was impossibly, elegantly, drawn to set him free. She'd long understood that pain and passion ran together, her mother's death was evidence of that, though with her eyes open to the bloody spectacle, she'd digested the brutality of life, and she accepted it.

Belmonte shook the muleta and taunted the bull until he charged, and when he made his famous arch, bending one arm to slay the bull instantly, young women in the crowd indeed swooned, though Luna was not one of them. She knew she didn't want to become one of Belmonte's lovers, at her unlikely age, or at any other. She wanted to become Belmonte.

"Coraje," she whispered. "He's so brave." She leaned over to Manuel and more quietly, into his ear: "When do I get my turn?"

DON CARLOS PUSHED HIS empty water glass across the patio table, and puffed on a cigar. "Not in this lifetime," he laughed.

"What if we train her," said Pedro. He was balancing his chair backwards on two legs. "She has good instincts."

Doña García scoffed, but held her tongue. This idea was so ridiculous that even her husband, with his soft centre, wouldn't indulge it.

"She's a girl," Don Carlos said, beginning to sound annoyed. "Her instincts are meant for other things."

Luna moved silently around the table with a clay pitcher, filling water glasses while they spoke about her as though she wasn't there.

"She's no smaller than some of the novilleros," Manuel tried.

"We could select the bulls for her," added Pedro. "Blunt their horns; no one would know. Her horse would protect her."

Don Carlos shook his head, disapprovingly. He didn't like a fight unless it was fair. Blunting the horns made a bull feel disoriented. "To afeitar is to make a scandal," he said. "It gives the bullfighter the advantage."

Luna set the pitcher of water down on the table in front of him. "It's permitted if there's a festival," she corrected.

Don Carlos tapped the lit end of his cigar on the edge of the table and ash fell on the ceramic tile. He looked up at her. "How would you know that?"

She couldn't meet his eyes for fear of confessing and enraging him, or further locking him into his stubbornness. Instead, she looked at Manuel, and so did his father.

"What is this?!"

The moment had come for Manuel to take responsibility for

training her, as he'd promised he would, but he fell mute. With his father staring, already disapproving, all parts of speech were caught in his throat, vowels and consonants, one piling on top of the other, reasons and excuses, choking him silent. He watched Paqui through the terrace doors, as she cleared plates from the dining room table, fiddled with the wild roses climbing the wall beside him, inhaling their sweet perfume. When it was obvious he couldn't find the courage to make the confession, loyalty to the man who'd fed and clothed her prevailed. "They've already trained me," said Luna.

"Cómo?!" Doña García was incredulous.

"Since last year. We practise after dark."

"Maletillas!" Don Carlos leapt up from his seat and lunged at Manuel. "How stupid can you be? Unregulated training!" He cuffed Manuel across the top of his head with an open hand. "You and your brother have been dragging your ugly bones around here for months, and the neighbours talk about thieves in the fields at night, but I don't have a problem. Now, I find that it's you stealing their animals so this girl can play dress up." He wagged his lit cigar in Manuel's face. "To make her into the torero you should've been!"

Manuel grabbed his father by the wrist, held the cigar at a safe distance. "I respect you, Papi. Will you not respect me?"

Doña García turned in her chair, tired of the tension between them. "Paqui!" she snapped. "Bring a bottle of sherry and some ice and lemon!" They were too alike, she thought. Stubborn. Turning around again she said, "Rest calm! Both of you."

It'd been several hours since Doña García's last drink and she needed one. Luna was driving her to it. The mere sound of the girl's name burned her ears. Paqui called it out of windows all the time, down hallways. She herself was forced to use it almost daily. The taste of it on her tongue had grown bitter through the years. It was bad enough she had to put up with seeing her face, a face that looked too much like Manuel's, and was a constant reminder of her husband's enduring love for another woman. The thought of Elisenda's bastard joining the family business was unbearable.

Don Carlos took a deep drag on his cigar. "I want the number of any animal she touched," he said. "You'll work to buy replacements." He looked at Luna and tapped the ash of his cigar onto the ground. "What you've done is dangerous and costly. You have spoiled fighters."

"I don't use a muleta," she mumbled, shame colouring her face.

Paqui slammed the bottle of Manzanilla down on the table. "Basta!" she said, braving her voice. "Enough!" "This time you've gone too far." She was loyal to the family, to her country, and to the Church, and she wouldn't have Luna insulting all three institutions at once. She waved a finger, directing Luna to kneel and use the skirt of her apron to clean up the fallen cigar ash.

"She's talented, Papi," Manuel said, pulling Luna up off her knees to stand next to him.

"Bad learners don't make for good bullfighters!"

"She's brave."

Don Carlos poured himself a swig of sherry, played with his cigar, twirling it in and around the fingers of one hand. He searched Luna's face for a glimmer of Elisenda, but didn't find any. "The law forbids a girl in the ring."

"Only if she were to fight on foot," said Pedro. "We've trained her in the Portuguese style. Already we have interest for a rejoneadora in some country ferias up north. She wouldn't compete with the real toreros. There's no harm in it."

Doña García was beginning to lose her composure. She sounded indignant. "Since when do you two get along? What kind of crazy proposition is this? No man would allow his housemaid into the ring. You know better! Find another, if this must be your plan, a Gypsy maybe. Luna belongs in the house with Paqui."

"Exactamente," said Paqui. She'd lost her husband and her baby to the influenza thirteen years ago. She wasn't about to lose Luna. She wished Luna could grow up to become more like the privileged women she'd served, those comfortably married to ganaderos or civil servants and powerful monarchists — those with the luxury of fine dresses and of feeling immortal, but that wasn't possible, and it hadn't occurred to her that immortality might require a suit of lights. She met Doña García's eyes with a clear and knowing expression of her own, and brief though it was, managed to communicate its threat: she'd kept her part of the bargain, not telling Luna who her father was, but unless Doña García used her influence to help keep the girl safe, she could no longer guarantee what revelations might slip from her lips.

Doña García reached for the bottle and topped up her glass with the pale, dry liquid. "Boys, you will harm your father's good reputation," she tried. "Have either of you thought of that?"

"I had the same reservation in the beginning," said Pedro. "But I thought of the money we could make." He brought his chair forward and set his elbows on the tabletop, with his hands clasped together and his chin resting pensively on them. He looked like a salesman, though he was seventeen years old. "Give us one temporada, Papi, one season, to try her out. If it doesn't work we won't mention it again."

Don Carlos twisted the hairs of his moustache and regarded Luna with a kind of objective appraisal she'd often experienced from his wife, as though she'd shocked him by having a will of her own. "I can't believe you did this, Luna. Tsk tsk tsk," he made a sound with his tongue while tapping his fingers on the table. "I cannot believe what I'm hearing."

"I meant no disrespect," she said.

"Don't blame her," Manuel said. "I convinced her to do it," he lied. "Think how it'll look if she succeeds. Think of the publicity for the ranch and what attention could do for the Sangre caste. Carlos García's talented daughter? It could be good for us all."

"Daughter?" Don Carlos sounded defensive. "What do you mean?"

"Qué ridículo!" said his wife. "I've never heard anything so absurd!"

Humiliated, Luna turned away from them. Her eyes began to water and she stared at the olive oil lamp hanging from a hook on the wall. She wouldn't give Doña García the satisfaction of seeing her cry. As the vertigo began to churn inside of her, she licked her pointer finger and passed it through the flame of the lamp. She conjured a fiery red bull — a giant beast with speckled horns that jutted sideways from his head — and imagined herself facing him, lifting a crimson cape, and commanding him to fall under her control. This time it didn't work. The table began to spin and then so were their faces.

"We'll gain access if ring promoters think she's a García," Manuel said. "It wouldn't be hard for her to act the part. She's lived here all her life."

"No one would have to know," agreed Pedro.

Luna leaned against the wall for balance, wrung her hands. She'd spent a year gaining the skill and technique any novice rejoneador needed. The world of possibilities had opened, like a great iron door, and if she were forbidden to continue, if Don Carlos slammed that door shut, she would remain a servant. "I started life with nothing," she said, daring to offend. "With less than nothing. But I don't intend to end up that way."

"Aiy!" Doña García sucked her teeth. "No me des mala sangre! Don't give me a hard time. Who are you to demand anything here?"

Luna looked at Paqui who was gesturing for her to be quiet and keep to her place. Paqui was nobody's fool. She could size up a scoundrel in ten seconds or less, make soup from wilted and decaying vegetables and make it last a week, scale a fish faster than Luna could blink. From the very first notes of their falsettos, Paqui knew whether it was Montoya or Caracol playing guitar on the radio, but she couldn't know the reckless abandon that coursed through Luna's veins: coming from a long line of servants, she possessed a practical resourcefulness that Luna admired, but her bones were filled with marrow — not with ambition. Not with what Luna's parents had passed on to her.

"I am a rejoneadora," Luna insisted, pressing her hands into fists. "You don't believe me? I'm not afraid of anything and I'll prove it." She took a deep breath, and held the air in her lungs, as if to endanger her life.

Doña García laughed. "Don't make idle threats, child. You're too young to know who you are."

"I'm not one of you," Luna said, blowing all the air out, "But I'm good in the ring." She looked into Paqui's angry face. "Paquita, you should see."

"And if you leave, who will be here to help me?"

Luna bit her lip, lowered her eyes. Without her, Paqui would have longer days managing double the work.

"Am I supposed to fund this adventure?" said Don Carlos. "Is that what you all think? I can't hire foreign labour now and I can't raise rents."

"She's asked you for nothing," Manuel said, without knowing he was playing to his father's weakness.

Don Carlos sighed at this. He shifted uncomfortably in his seat. His old dream of becoming father to a bullfighter had returned to mock him. He chewed the tip of his cigar pensively. Luna had the proper build to be a bullfighter. She had the spit and spark. Maybe she was the one. He balanced his cigar on the edge of the table and looked at his wife helplessly.

"Carlos, no!"

"I don't approve of how this happened," he said, pointing at Manuel with his free hand. "I hold you responsible, but next month when I test the young bulls and heifers I'll see her instincts for myself." He met Luna's eyes. "You will attend the tienta and if you're as good as they claim I won't prevent what's been set into motion. But you aren't stepping into another ring unless you succeed in mine first."

Luna nodded and caged the smile that wanted so badly to press out of her. *It's God*, she thought, *who's already decided this.*

Doña García pushed her chair away from the table. "How dare

you!" she said, leaning over and slapping her husband hard across his face. If it was a moneymaking scheme to her sons, it was more than that to Carlos and they both knew it. She stormed past Luna into the house.

Paqui crossed herself and ran after Helena sobbing. Through the terrace doors the two women exchanged a flurry of words and Paqui, who had sworn not to interfere with family matters, pounded her fists on the table and shouted, "No!"

ON THE NIGHT OF Luna's birth Paqui had pried the screaming infant from Elisenda's breast and held her out to Don Carlos. "Take her," she'd said. "She's yours." The accusation was searing: Elisenda had died as a result of his selfish desire.

Carlos shook his head, refused. He'd wanted to hold Luna, feel the sloping weight of new life in his arms, the warmth of her tiny body against his; he'd rarely held his sons at that age. Holding Luna would've been another act of betrayal, and if he held her he might not want to let her go. "I can't," he whispered.

Paqui's eyes narrowed. "Coward!" she hissed.

He was shocked by her open display of disrespect. It was more than insolent to speak to him in such a manner! But what could he do about it? She'd seen his weakness, she held the power. He was the servant now. "What should I do?" he asked.

As if she knew what fury awaited him in this life, and in the next, Paqui thought carefully before responding. His wife was upstairs, drunk. Father Seratossa was outside on the terrace expecting to leave with the newborn. There was one person who knew what had happened and who could love this child. "Give her to me," she said, holding Luna close to her heart. "I won't tell."

FROM THEIR SUNNY PERCH on the platform at one end of the training ring Luna and Manuel could see the flat tops of olive trees, and a few gall oaks bending and twisting like arthritic old men. They found El Mayoral in the stands, ready with his paper and pen. He'd take notes on each stage and assign a grade to each of the cows, though it was Luna who was going to be most harshly graded.

El Mayoral had already been out to the fields and selected three cows who showed bravery — they wouldn't test more at a time or the animals become excitable and guess that something unusual was on its way. The chief philosophy and technique of raising cows and bulls is tranquilidad, for them to be calm at all times.

Don Carlos sounded stern when he climbed up onto the platform. He moved swiftly. It was clear he'd treat Luna no differently than he would any other torero in that situation. Normally, he invited a retired matador to carry out the formal testing, or a novillero hoping to make connections and practise new manoeuvres, but today he'd invited Luna. "The purpose of the examination?" he began.

Luna couldn't help but giggle nervously.

"Do you find this amusing?"

"No," she said, soberly.

"I can bring in someone else."

"No, don't do that." She hid her unsteady hands behind her back. All the times she'd wanted to escape the kitchen to freedom, were insignificant compared with this felt moment. This was about love — his, theirs, and the unworthiness sitting at the bottom of her ambition. Behind them there was a green bush with tiny buds on it, and when the wind blew they clacked together softly like a curtain of beads.

"The purpose of the examination?" Don Carlos repeated.

Luna glimpsed Doña García leaning against the barrera, fanning herself. "A brave and noble bull for a father is not enough to guarantee the instinct to fight," she said. "Without a strong mother the result will be doomed."

"Entonces qué?"

"We're here to look at the gallop, humility and charge. To discover which cows will be selected for reproduction."

"And the others?

"La carne molida," Luna said, pretending to slit her throat. "Ground beef."

Don Carlos motioned for Pedro to pull aside the heavy steel gate and the cow thundered in and ran about, confused to find that freedom had walls. After a minute she stopped, the white patch on her chest heaving. She surveyed the enclosure. A lock of stringy hair hung over her forehead. She appeared controlled and solid. Black muscled coat, sculpted shape, but was she brave and noble? She ambled to the opposite side of the ring, and a trio of small brown birds trailed, feeding on her manure. El Mayoral recorded the cow's activity in his book.

"A good sign," Luna said. "She's confident."

Luna fanned her muleta in the wind, turning and loosening her wrist. The heavy red felt twisted and tangled, then untangled. She gripped the small wooden ceremonial sword sewn into its lining. Her shirt billowed; the wind messed her hair and cut through a tall aloe, making a faint whistle. Manuel had given her a pair of his old zajones to protect her legs from the cows' horns; the leather was making her warm. She wiped her sweaty brow with the back of her hand.

Don Carlos waved for the picador to enter the training ring. His nag was blindfolded but wearing peto because losing horses for the tienta was an unnecessary expense. The picador placed himself contraquerencia, and jangled his leg armour to provoke the cow to charge his horse. The cow was unimpressed. The picador shouted. At this, the cow quickly trotted away from him and waited by the toril. "A false start," Don Carlos said. He waved for a second provocation, but again, the cow was slow to react. He shook his head. "Let's hope the next one's better."

The cow was led from the arena. Luna looked at Manuel desperately, as though her future was slipping away. If none of them passed to the final stages of the examination, she wouldn't get to do her part.

At the first hint of noise from the picador the second cow bolted. "Better," she whispered, under her breath.

Knowing that a cow could begin strong and progressively worsen, Manuel made no judgment when the picador placed himself contraquerencia, ready to throw his first lance. The pole he used was long, the same as those used during the corrida, and during Luna's training, though the tip had been replaced with a much smaller one.

"Will it hurt her?" Don Carlos asked to test Luna's stomach.

She repeated what she'd heard Pedro say a thousand times before: "To a bravura it will feel like a mosquito bite."

The picador taunted the second cow and, as her cuernos slammed into the horse's ribcage, he stabbed her with his garrocha. There was a small amount of blood on the cow, though she didn't acknowledge her injury. The horse stood her ground, despite the impact. But the cow was manso, it turned out, clever, which is the opposite of brave, and when the picador next attempted to make her charge, she'd have nothing of it.

"Está en las nubes," Luna said, trying to stay hopeful. "She's daydreaming."

"You need the animal to return to the capote, and the sword," said Don Carlos. "Intelligence is not a desirable trait."

The cow had learned from the first lance that she didn't wish to repeat her injury. A *sensible decision*, Luna thought, though one that she certainly didn't appreciate. "Try again!" she shouted, as another moment to prove herself slipped away. A tiny green gecko scurried across the floorboards between her sandals, and El Mayoral drew a dramatic line across his page marking that cow for the slaughterhouse.

Manuel chewed his fingernail. As a boy, training with his father, he'd not been able to accept the rotten logic that intelligence in the animals was of so little value. Such a dismissal was an insult to him and his dreams, though later he accepted it; the smartest of fighting bulls, like clever poets, get in their own way by second-guessing. Art is better when it's driven by instinct.

The final animal of the day, the one with the white tail, charged beautifully, and with her head down. She was given a good note on her gallop, her charge and humility, so all at once Don Carlos shoved Luna to the edge of the platform.

"Climb down," he said.

She stepped into the ring and the cow watched closely, with eyes that seemed to see all, but the cow was, of course, colour-blind and couldn't see the red of the muleta. Placing herself in line with her rival Luna used the posture she'd been taught, slowly passing her muleta alongside her body, and behind it, mindful of her thighs and stomach as the cow passed. She made a *natural* on her right side three times, and each time the cow followed at the exact angle she'd asked for, with her head low. The cow was so close to her body that she could see the first anillo near the base of the horn. She knew the others were noting her gestures, but she concentrated on regulating her breathing. She repeated the naturals on her left side and the cow again impressed them.

"That's easy!" Don Carlos called down. "Anyone with a dishrag could bring the same result. Paqui could do it!"

Luna balled her fists, ready for an argument. There's nothing easy about standing in face of an angry animal, including a three-year-old cow.

"Pstst!" Manuel drew her attention. "Luna, tranquilízate. Don't listen. He's seeing if you can be distracted."

"It only looks easy!" she called out with renewed conviction. "I use observation and my intuition to judge her."

"It takes experience."

"Then I'll be even better next year!"

Don Carlos laughed. "You are arrogant enough to be a bull-fighter," he said. "Try something difficult now."

Luna gathered the soft red material of her muleta in one hand and again spied the cow. Each animal, she knew, had its natural and preferred distance from which it would comfortably charge, and each preferred one side to the other. This cow was cautious though ready to follow her commands. She held the muleta at waist height, and when the cow charged she swung it leftward and down and turned away from the cow until she was in a position to repeat the pass.

"Is that all you have?"

Doña García waved with her fan. "Stop it, Carlos!"

"Watch this," Luna said, spurred on by the attention.

She tucked her chin in close to her chest and beckoned the cow as though she had a sword ready and would finish her with it. As the cow began to charge she dropped to her knees for a Farol de rodillas. She held the cape high this time, blocking her own ability to see, and asked the cow to cross in front of her body, which she did. Holding her position with her knees digging into the sand, the white-tailed cow turned in a cloud of dust and Luna tasted dirt.

She felt sweat pooling under her arms. There was silence except for the cow's laboured breathing and her own. She stood, dusting off her zajones, spat on the ground and walked away from the scene slowly, on tiptoes, and next on the flats of her feet, to show her control and mastery.

She looked up at the platform and called out confidently. "Don Carlos, this one prefers about fifteen feet. On her right. Do you want me to test her at a closer range?"

"No," he said, looking stunned. "No, we don't want her to birth a bull that'll sit in the stands with the aficionados do we?"

Luna smiled and relaxed; he could see she had a talent for it.

"What's your recommendation, Luna?"

"Mark her for reproduction."

Don Carlos climbed down from the platform. "When does that take place?"

"Between January and June," she answered without hesitation.

"One more thing," he said, landing on the ground next to her with a heavy thud. "How old are the bulls when they're tested?"

Luna looked up at Manuel, knowingly, and over to Pedro who was practically jumping up and down beside the toril door. "Two years," she said, holding up the same number of fingers.

Don Carlos opened the door and removed the cow. "Looks like you'll get the chance to earn some of what you owe," he said. He embraced her for the first time, and an uncommon peace fell all around him. As Luna sank into him, and his approval, he felt more than a pang of regret. He felt her mother in his arms. Elisenda would've been proud. He kissed Luna roughly on the forehead with whiskers that scratched like wool. "She's saved herself!" he called out to the others and they all laughed, including his wife, for they understood that he could've been talking about the cow.

LUNA COULD HARDLY CONTAIN her excitement as their train rattled northward along the track like steel castanets. "Tell me again. The name of the place?"

"Burgos," Manuel said. "It'll be long to the north. You should rest." He tapped the toe of his shoe on the worn carpet and returned to the copy of *El Debate* he'd found on his seat. One editorial quoted the leader of the Confederación Española de Derechas Autónomas, CEDA, saying that fascism might be a sensible cure for the evils of Spanish Republicanism. Another article suggested that the Republic and its reforms were part of a Jewish-Masonic-Bolshevik conspiracy. The mood in the country was shifting to the right, Manuel thought. He glanced toward the exit for a second time.

"Where did Pedro go?" Luna asked.

"To speak with some men."

Pedro could've been off talking to strangers, but he could've as easily been with some girl. They all knew what he paid for in darkened fields or in the back room of the venta near the ranch house. In any case, he might be gone a while.

"Have you written anything for Eugenia lately?" Luna asked.

Manuel spoke without lifting his eyes from the newspaper. "She isn't the one," he said, as though there could only be one for each of us.

"But you love her. You said so in your poem."

He slapped down the paper. "You weren't supposed to read that."

Luna fidgeted with her hands, sat up on the edge of her seat, closer to him. "I'm sorry. But what did she do? You're angry with her. I see it on your face."

Manuel felt the muscles in his face stiffen. His throat constricted as he remembered his last conversation with Eugenia. Why did she have to be so detached and cruel? She could've rejected him without also maligning his work.

"She doesn't like my writing," he confessed. "She finds it to be vapid and sentimental." His shoulders sank a little. "I suppose it is too rooted in regionalism and tradition to be universal."

"Absurd!" said Luna. "She needs to feel special."

Manuel laughed. Luna's way of cutting through an experience so bluntly was endearing, and she was right: Eugenia did work hard at being subversive. "Let's not mention her again," he said.

Half an hour later Pedro plopped down in the empty seat across from them. "One horse," he said. "A large bay. She's got at least six years left in her."

"They're a jumpy breed," said Manuel.

"It'll cost more to find a mount when we get there, and there won't be much time. This way we don't worry about quartering."

"Why couldn't we have brought Batata?" Luna asked.

Pedro kicked off his shoes, and stretched his stinky toes. "They're fine with the other matter. As long as they get half."

"Half! For a horse and a few frilly shirts!"

Luna pushed herself up in her seat, arranged her skirt around her legs. "You found me a costume?" She'd been wearing the same work dress whenever she trained. It was beginning to thin and fray from washing.

"The jacket will fit you," said Pedro. "And the shirt. But there are no zajones. It doesn't matter. You'll be wearing a skirt. You will pin up your hair though, so it's not loose."

She pulled a long strand behind one ear, self-consciously. "What about a hat?"

"No hat. It rests with its previous owner. A young novillero, badly gored outside of Sevilla."

"He died?"

"He was careless," Manuel said, kicking Pedro. "He wasn't well trained."

The truth was that the novillero had simply met with bad luck. It had rained hard the afternoon of his performance, and yet the local official in charge refused to cancel his fight. The bull had charged straight for him and wouldn't be diverted by other members of his cuadrilla, and when the novillero ran for the shelter, he slipped in the mud. His had also been a country fight, unregulated. (Most novilleros took turns at the country festivals where they faced additional dangers.) There had been no enfermería on site, not a médico or a veterinarian, and with an unpredictable, second-grade bull, the novillero had exposed himself to significant risk.

"I'm well trained," Luna said, confidently.

It was no insult to her that they'd agreed, in advance, to give away half of her fee to a rival cuadrilla in exchange for an experienced mount and a barely used traje corto. Or, that because she was a girl her name wouldn't appear on the bill for the event. Her train ticket was paid for and she would be staying in a hotel for the first time, not sharing a room with anyone. She had one of Don Carlos's bulls to fight — Sangre #114 — and she was about to perform in her first real bullring as a member of the García family. What else was there?

THE FOLLOWING AFTERNOON THEY entered the makeshift plaza to find sawdust on the ground, and the ring promoter driving a heavy truck to help level and compact the earth. Loose sawdust in the ring makes it hard to breathe and to see. *I'll be mounted*, Luna thought. *It's much worse for those on foot.* The barrera was a patchwork of rickety old wood, barely standing, and the pens were small, agitating the bulls confined within them. The crowd was large and loud and this was new; her audience at the ganadería had been limited to the sidelong glances of olive trees, the expansive night sky, and occasionally, a nosy hunting dog.

Soldiers and priests appeared with other aficionados, shouting at one another, some waving the capes they'd brought with them. When the cuadrilla from the train sent one of their peons to deliver the new horse, she was a silver Andaluz with wide set eyes and a mane of silk, and she was a full hand taller than they'd led Pedro to believe, and two hands taller than Batata.

"What do you want to do?" Manuel asked.

"It's too late to exchange her for another," Luna said.

She mounted, knowing that the space between the end of her reach and the bull would be greater than she was accustomed to during practice. She'd need to compensate by lifting herself farther out of the saddle. Without having had time to practise riding, she was already taking an unusual risk. Pedro appeared waving his arms about. "There's a problem with blunting the bulls' horns," he said. "They won't allow it. We can use cotton caps, but we didn't bring any."

Blood churned in Manuel's chest, his fingertips went numb. "That's it; we're out. Tell them we aren't ready."

How stifled Manuel felt in his starched collared shirt and pants. How the cool northern air in Burgos chilled his lungs. Luna didn't know how inexperienced she actually was — like any torero she had no plan for failure, they'd not practised that, so the possibility of injury or death indeed felt remote. "Are you sure?" he asked with a voice that betrayed anxiety.

"God will protect me," she said, as the clarions called. She made the sign of the Father, Son, and Holy Ghost, kissed her mother's gold crucifix, and tucked its chain safely under her new shirt collar. She had faith and skill, and she was lucky.

THE SUN WAS LOW when she prepared to enter the arena on horseback in her scarlet and black traje corto. The embroidery was finely detailed, and she looked regal. The alguacil was mounted in his black velvet robe and red plumed hat, ready to lead them all into the ring and open the ceremony. He barely glanced in her direction. "What's your torero's name?" he asked. Pedro and Manuel lit up like twin lanterns at the assumption that Luna was a boy. They huddled to discuss a name.

"Buena Suerte?" Manuel whispered. "Good luck?"

"No, we can't tempt fate."

"What is he known for?" The alguacil persisted, impatiently.

Manuel turned around. "Heart," he blurted. "Pure heart."

And so she became El Corazón — not La Corazoncito, but the masculine form, undeniable.

The arena was large and the ground uneven; the chalk line made an imperfect circle and the smell of fresh manure and blood was pervasive. Luna had seen Sangre #114 before, visited him the previous day and again that afternoon, in the chiqueros, both times sneaking a peek without allowing him to see her in case he should remember her later and refuse her call to charge. She knew his tail was so long that it almost reached his ankles, but when he entered through the toril it was his square nose, and his cuernos veletos, she saw first. Right away he charged the shelter where the toreros stood, and when he pulled his head from the barrera, the cotton fastened to his cuernos tore and hung in threads.

Seeing this, Manuel's throat flashed dry. His stomach clenched and twisted. But the bull was slow, and after that first outburst, lumbering. Manuel squeezed through the burladero and distracted him with a capa de brega while Luna moved into proper position. Her horse responded to a loose rein and could be trusted. "The

tail!" Manuel shouted from behind the barrera. "Approach from
the tail!" His heart was a drum reminding him to breathe. *Pretend
he's the chair, Luna. He's nothing more than a chair.*

She turned her horse and positioned her rejones. "Toro!" she
called. "Eh, Toro!"

The bull was easily agitated by her voice and by being trapped
within the enclosure. He was ready for her. He charged.

Luna felt confident. The circle that was her clock of sand spun
out around, creating a larger and larger space, sending the crowd
into her peripheral vision, muffling their noise, hurling the ring
promoter and announcer, and Manuel, into insignificance. All that
mattered was her, on her horse, and the bull, and when she lifted
her left arm time itself was slain.

She placed the first rejón with precision and grace, exactly where
she was meant to, and her horse veered with a quickstep, clearing
them of the bull. It was much easier for her in the daytime, with
the stands full of cheering spectators, than it had ever been with
Pedro and Manuel under the moon. An uncomfortable heat spread
throughout her body. The crowd loved her and she felt it. But they
didn't know who she was.

She made another lap around the ring and again moved her horse
into proper position. Number 114 understood what was coming;
he wouldn't be so easily approached a second time. She patted her
horse's strong neck without taking her eyes from her enemy, and
he watched her too, as if marking her weakness with his beady
black eyes. Knowing she could afford him no time to strategize,
she gave a swift kick. The bull answered with a charge, and at the
last instant turned from her. That was when she brought down
the second rejón. "Done!" she shouted, speeding past him. The
crowd roared. Stomped their boots. Rattled and shook the rickety
stands. Most did not yet realize that she was a girl.

Was she still a girl? Had a taste for power and blood made
her less of one? Throughout history there had been a handful of
girls and women who fought on horseback; Manuel had researched

them and made her study their stories. Fewer had tried to fight on foot, and they were forced to work abroad, generally rejected by reviewers and aficionados. Would she face rejection later, when her real identity was circulated?

Having the one horse, she didn't change mounts for the placement of the colourful banderillas or for the final rejón, though if she took much more time her horse would tire. When the moment arrived she asked her horse to make a spectacular capriole, which the horse did, jumping and suspending them in mid-air with all four legs tucked up under her body, and when they landed again she galloped straight for the bull and placed the eight-inch-long steel blade in his shoulders. It broke from its wooden staff leaving a small flag that showed she'd conquered her territory. The bull bucked and twisted and staggered across the ring. He collapsed on the sand and rolled onto one side, gasping for air.

Luna watched the puntillero approach and assess the situation; once satisfied that the bull could not rally, he leaned over and slit the bull's neck. She turned and rode past Pedro, who was basking in the attention of reporters and photographers along the fence. Respected banderilleros and picadors slapped him on the back and reached out to shake his hand. She rode under the archway and out of the arena inhaling the tangy and wretched smell of fresh blood, heard the violence of the butchers' knives in the carnicería preparing the dead bulls' carcasses for sale as beef. Stopping in front of Manuel, she dismounted. "Did you see us jump? Did you see?" Adrenalin was still coursing through her body.

"I was jealous," he said, embracing her. Success was an intangible pleasure. Success was all hers.

As soon as they returned to their hotel suite Pedro showed Luna a copy of a review, published immediately after the fight. The ink was so fresh that it smudged off on her fingers. The headline of the local paper read: *VALENTISIMA Y HERMOSA* — valiant and beautiful. Pedro read the full review out loud.

"This afternoon, to my amazement, Miss Luna García Caballero distinguished herself in handling a novillo. She is young and attractive and it remains a mystery to me why any girl would bother to fight at all, but this little lady showed courage and skill in protecting her large mount. The placement of her rejones was as stylish and colourful as the tail feathers of a peacock. With dedication, this girl could become a respectable rejoneadora. First place: Esteban Calderon. Second Place: El Corazón. Third Place: Joaquín Reyes."

The telephone rang and Manuel crossed the room to answer it. "Hola? Con mucho gusto, Señor. Si … Si? I'll let her know. Mañana a las siete." He replaced the receiver in its cradle. "That was Chucho López," he said, loosening his shirt collar.

"The banderillero from the train?"

"His cuadrilla was impressed with Luna's performance today. They have a proposition they wish to discuss with us."

"Oh, no," she said. "They'll want their horse. I was going to name her Fortuna."

Pedro and Manuel looked at her, and at each other, and pealed into laughter. They ran at her and tackled her to the ground.

What the cuadrilla wanted, of course, was her. Since their novillero had been fatally gored, they were a gang without a leader, a business with no income. Either they disbanded or they found a new lead torero. When they saw Luna in the ring at Burgos they recognized the same potential for curiosity and profit that Pedro had recognized. She wasn't a matador, but she would do.

"WE'VE WORKED TOGETHER FOR three years," said Chucho, over breakfast the next morning. He was a tank of a man with hands so large they belonged on a giant, and one of them, his left, was missing its index finger so that he gripped his coffee mug with what looked like a vulture's claw. His hair was thick and black and matched the stubble on his face. He spoke with a full mouth of omelette, bread, and Manchego cheese.

"I've been peon de confianza from the start," he said. "Chief banderillero. With a rejoneadora I won't need to throw the banderillas, but I will remain in charge of the others." He looked at Pedro and Manuel to guess their reactions, and when he was satisfied they were in agreement he continued. "The Picadors are cousins. We have an experienced sword handler and we have the right horses. Naturally, we'd want regulation pay, plus lodging and travel expenses."

"What's in it for us?" asked Pedro.

"We have signed contracts in Mexico for next season."

Manuel set his coffee down on the table. "What about the fact that she's a girl?"

Chucho glanced at Luna. "She could be a three-legged dog for all I care," he said. "As long as she sells tickets."

CHUCHO AND THE CUADRILLA returned to Sevilla to prepare for the long journey to Mexico, and Luna, Manuel and Pedro returned to Sangre Mío to do the same. The mood among workers in the fields, in the training ring, indeed throughout the region, had shifted from cautious optimism to mounting fear about the future. The radio crackled a continuous commentary about CEDA's claims of reconquering Spain, purifying the county-side and restoring traditional values. Newspapers warned that if CEDA defeated the government in the November elections, it could trigger regional strikes and violent clashes between workers' committees and the army.

Inspired by reports of Luna's performance in the north, Don Carlos no longer expected her to work at anything but toreo. He offered to cover her initial expenses in Mexico, knowing his sons would repay him; what she earned there in one season would more than double his annual profit from the ranch.

Pedro worked to gain passports, and the many special permits they needed for fights abroad, while Manuel found a carpenter in Ronda to fashion wooden crates for their belongings and a special

one to transport Fortuna. One Friday, he and Luna drove into the city
on the narrow winding road, with steep drops down into the valley.
Luna had not made a car trip before. She laughed riotously the
faster Manuel drove, spurring him on to take sharper corners
and not to slow down when passing on the outer edge of the cliff.
Far below them lay a vast expanse of gold and brown and green
farmland that stretched out for miles. She clutched her seat with
both hands, flying, as the wind stole her breath and Manuel thought,
how much more of a risk-taker she was than him, right down to the
bone. She accelerated towards danger, like a true torero, rather than
withdrawing from it.

In the city they visited the shoemaker and the boot maker and
an expert tailor where Luna's body was outlined in chalk and chaps
were cut. Because his father's old truck had dim headlights, Manuel
didn't want to drive in the dark and so he'd arranged for them to
stay overnight at an inn across the street from the Real Maestranza
bullring. The woman at the front desk showed them the two
remaining rooms and Manuel inspected Luna's for security. "We're
close to the street," he said, stepping out onto the small balcony.
"Close your shutters tonight."

The sun slipped below the horizon and the sky above the plaza
de toros bled in pink and orange hues. "How beautiful," Luna said,
as if the bullring beckoned her like a round, white church. "Let's go
out and see it."

They stood at the sandstone entrance, pressed their ears to the
large wooden doors. Only the wind inside. They walked all the way
around. Luna ran her hand along the wall, still warm from the sun.
At the ticket booth they read the cartel announcing upcoming fights
and wound through narrow streets looking in the windows of white
washed houses, with their wrought iron grills. They sauntered past
the Arab baths and a few tapas bars. The smell of fresh tuna and
anchovies on tomato made Manuel's stomach rumble. They hov-
ered in the entranceway of a café where Niño de Marchena sang
Flamenco in his trademark riding clothes. They lingered on the

stone ledge of the Puente Nuevo looking out at the Serranía de
Ronda as the wind kissed their legs, and the air was perfumed with
the candied scent of oleander.

"Some of the world's greatest poets have written here," Manuel
said: "Rilke, Juan Ramón Jiménez. Alongside the greatest bullfighters." From the inspiration in his eyes Luna could see that
Ronda was a place for dreamers and so a place for dreams as lofty
as theirs. She scaled the immense wall of the rock face with her eyes
and pointed out the water far below.

"So green," she said.

"As if the sun has melted a pool of emeralds."

She looked up at him, caught a note of longing in his voice. He'd
chosen poetry over bullfighting, but perhaps he resented the ease of
her talent.

"You were good in the ring," she said. "Do you ever miss it?"

"Not enough," he said, truthfully. "There are moments, like
tonight. I remember the feeling of the hot sand underfoot, and how
immense the sky looks from the centre of a bullring. But, those are
a poet's observations." He shrugged. "Writing is my art."

She tried to stifle a yawn. "I'm so tired."

"Take care where you step," he teased. "You know how that
chasm down there was created, don't you? God had grown weary
of reminding the young girls of Grazalema to behave."

"Girls like me?"

"Especially girls like you," he winked. "God was so weary that
he could hardly keep himself awake. He yawned carelessly as you
did now, and one of those yawns was so big and so strong that he
couldn't cover his mouth to contain it. The yawn reverberated all
the way down to earth, where it formed that deep gorge."

"You're making that up," she laughed. "You don't believe in
God."

"Are you sure?"

Luna peered over the bridge for a second time. Manuel enjoyed
writing his imagination over top of hers: Was the praying mantis

on a window ledge simply cleaning his hands or was he preparing to dine on her while she slept? Was the sloping hill across from the ranch house a pile of dirt and minerals or was she a naked señorita, reclining? Palomas and black birds with sharp red beaks flew through the gorge and Manuel opened his notebook and began to write in it. They didn't speak again for a long while until Luna asked him to read her something.

"I can't show my poems," he said.

She studied his face intensely, noting the shadow darkening his chin and upper lip, and his unconvincing eyes. "Eugenia was wrong," she said. "If your writing is half as beautiful as you are, Manuel, your poems must be good."

He smiled, gratefully, and cast his pained gaze across the gorge. He kept his poems private for the same reason that Luna had been secretive about the stolen objects she hid for her mother in the stone wall: because sharing them would've been equivalent to sharing a dream he wasn't yet ready to let go of. He stepped away from the gorge. "When you fall in love one day," he said. "I hope it's with someone who respects you."

ONE MONTH LATER, CHUCHO and his sister, Marisol López, arrived from Seville. Luna was helping Paqui change bed linen for them on the second floor of the house with the bedroom door ajar.

"Why must she come to Mexico with us?" Luna asked.

"Sshsh!" Paqui said. "She's right in the next room." Paqui lowered her voice to a whisper. "She lost her Mama to cancer of the stomach, that's why! No one knows where their father is. You of all people should understand. Here, take this pillowcase."

"Still," said Luna. "I don't see why."

"People say her father is a Gypsy, Luna; that his mules carry contraband shipped from Gibraltar. In Sevilla they're known as The Immortal Eleven. Somehow, whether his gang is shot at by the Guardia Civil or by rival bandits, there are eleven of them."

"De verdad?"

"Sí. I hear she doesn't know how to ride. Maybe you could teach her?"

Luna wrinkled her nose. Paqui worried about her being without friends, but she had Manuel and she had the bulls. That was enough.

"It's a good thing Marisol is joining you abroad," Paqui said. "Not one of you can cook to save your life."

"I cook. You taught me."

"Yes, but you'll be too busy."

For days Paqui had reluctantly washed, ironed and packed Luna's new frilled shirts. She'd wrapped two months supply of dried camomile leaves and ginger root in cheesecloth, and blocked Luna's Córdoban hat to keep its shape. "Line the brim with paper," she'd said, "when it no longer fits properly." She'd tried to accept that there was nothing she could do to stop Luna from leaving, but it was impossible to feel good about being so far away from her. She could tell Luna the truth about Don Carlos and that might keep her at Sangre Mio, Paqui thought, but it might as likely send Luna running away for good.

"What about the dizzy spells?" Paqui asked.

Luna lifted a feather pillow from the bed, fluffed it, and set it down again. "I haven't had one for a long time," she said. "I think they've stopped."

Paqui looked doubtful. "What if it happens in the bullring?"

"I told you, I'm cured."

The floorboards creaked on the landing and the two of them turned to find a young woman cradling a small sewing machine in her arms as though it were an infant. "I was tightening some buttons on a shirt," Marisol said.

If Chucho resembled a rare black vulture, his sister was the Spanish imperial eagle with white shoulders and a deceptively gentle countenance. She was a few years older than Luna, and exceedingly pretty, with much paler skin than a Sevillana should have, paler than Chucho, light green eyes, and a kind of translucence that suggested vulnerability. Right away Luna disliked her. Pretty girls were worse than plain girls as far as she was concerned — they expected too much attention and gave too little. She'd seen how the field girls behaved, feigning interest in the bulls while they tried not to get their clothes dirty. They could haul water for miles but when there were men around they waited for doors to be opened and chairs to be pulled out for them, and they distracted the men by giggling whenever they made one of their stupid jokes. All of these things, Marisol looked as though she could do, and quite naturally.

"I'm embarrassed," Paqui said. "You've caught us gossiping."

"Don't be," Marisol said, brushing past them and rushing down the hall. "It's all true."

LATER, LUNA WAS OUTSIDE watering two horses at one of the stone troughs, the mysterious piletas that had been on the property for centuries, though no one knew how they got there or where they came from. When Manuel appeared, Batata immediately swung her head around to greet him. The larger horse dug at the ground with one of his front hooves.

"Qué hay?" Manuel asked.

"Marisol wants to ride," Luna said. She gave Batata's coat a quick brushing, lifted a saddle onto her broad back and, though the horse wasn't technically hers, she imagined that she was. Batata was part Andalucian and part Arabian, so was hardy and liked to be ridden, to carry Luna up to the top of the hill, where she'd look down at the Venta by the highway and the pet ostrich the owner kept there.

"I met her when they drove in," said Manuel. "She's very beautiful."

Luna rolled her eyes. She saddled up the second horse while the electric sound of cicadas buzzed in her ears, and led both animals out behind the barn, where Marisol was waiting. The light was clear and bright, as though the day demanded honesty.

"Which one's for me?" Marisol asked, nervously.

"The tall one," Luna said. She stepped into one of Batata's stirrups and threw herself up, on top of the horse. "Yours is named Churros," she said. "He's hard-looking but his nature is as soft as fried bread. He'll do as you ask."

Gingerly, Marisol lifted a foot to her stirrup and struggled to pull herself up, but Churros began to walk before she'd found her seat. "Help me!" she said, in a bit of a panic.

Reaching over, Luna pulled on Marisol's reins and stopped Churros. "He can sense that you're afraid," she said, trotting off ahead.

Marisol stiffened. Her face flashed red; she was older and should've been able to do everything better.

"Here," Manuel said, swinging himself up behind her. "We'll ride together." He took hold of the reins and they broke into a fast trot.

Manuel felt Marisol's smaller frame slide back against his body. She was warm and solid. Her hair was tied up and her neck exposed; it was tempting to lean forward and press his lips to the fine little hairs. He felt, for a moment, that he could pursue her, but something made him think that she'd want a rougher type. Maybe Eugenia had destroyed his confidence as a lover. Perhaps he wasn't ready for another woman.

A moment later they caught up to Luna.

"What'll you wear to the farewell party?" Marisol asked.

"Ni idea. I have no idea."

"I have one special dress. I wore it to my mother's funeral. It's white with tiny pink flowers on the skirt. I think I'll put my hair up in a high comb."

Luna shrugged, slipped her feet out of her stirrups. She wanted to appear indifferent, to show scorn for girls like Marisol whose costuming and performances were limited to attracting the love of a husband. When they hit the open field she slackened the reins over Batata's withers and galloped freely. Churros worked to keep up.

"You don't like me, do you, Luna?" Marisol called out.

"I feel sorry for you," Luna lied.

Offended, Marisol accidentally yanked on the reins, making Churros whinny and rear, nearly sending Manuel off his back. Marisol brushed the thick, dark hair from her eyes with obvious disdain. "I'm the one who feels sorry for you," she said. "You're not a real girl. Look at you. You're flat-chested. You have no hips. Your face and clothes are smudged with dirt. Your hands are dry and scaly. No one will ever want you. In the end, you'll be all alone."

Luna gripped Batata with her calves, straightened herself on the horse. "I don't care what you think," she said. "I'm going to be famous one day."

"So what?" said Marisol. "I'm going to marry Pedro, and have his babies." Emboldened by anger, she kicked Churros. The next thing Manuel knew, they were off, galloping. Luna and Batata were left to suck on their dust.

THAT NIGHT, PAQUI SET a Serrano ham out on the dining room table along with tortilla de patatas, partridge and stewed chestnuts, sardines on skewers, paella with red shrimp from Almería, and Luna's favourite, pescaito frito. There were sugary cakes, soaked in wine and syrup, and vanilla flan. The guests who'd come to bid farewell milled about — neighbours and friends from the region; Father Serratosa, Eugenia and Jorge Vidal, and others, whom Luna had not met — serving themselves and making toasts when, in a rare free moment, Paqui took her firmly by the hand and pulled her outside to the eastern edge of the stone wall, where they stopped on the sandy terrace. Luna beside a giant palm. Laughter carried outside, and a noisy black dog barked in the distance.

"What is it, Paquita?"

"Vamos a ver," she said. "Let's see." Paqui raised her eyes to the dark veil overhead. "On the night you were born I swaddled you in an old sheet, and paced, deciding what name would suit you best. When the storm cleared, I crept outside to search for inspiration. The moon was bright but the sky was black like this one," she said. "I knew; you were like that moon, rare and determined. I stood right here under it, and under all of them." She pointed to the stars above. "They pulsed then as they pulse now." Squeezing Luna's arm she added, "You're leaving me, mi hija."

"Only for a short time."

"No, you're leaving. It happens that every girl should one day leave home, but I hoped it wouldn't be this soon and for such a reason!"

"Don't cry," Luna said, reaching over and wiping Paqui's tears with her hand. If Paqui couldn't be strong and certain about this plan, how could she?

"I've taught you what little I could," said Paqui. "God willing, you won't starve."

"Bullfighters live high. Don't worry."

"If you were mine," Paqui said, but she stopped herself from spilling the rest of what was on her tongue. She swatted at the mosquitoes that pinched and fed at her ankles. "There are three more things you must know, Luna. First, God is watching. Do you understand me?" Luna nodded. "Second, when you need me go outside, wherever you are. Look up as I do now, look hard into the night." She pointed to the brightest star in the sky. "Find that one," she said. "See how steady it is? It's the most valuable of all the stars because you'll know I'm looking at it too. Come here, let me wrap my arms around you. No future husband of yours will be able to afford diamonds like those," she said. "See how they shimmer?"

"The third thing?"

Paqui swept the hair from Luna's eyes, cupped her cheek. "There will be suitors," she said. "But make them wait. You will know when it's the right one, as surely as I know you are meant for more than I can offer."

"How will I know that?"

"When you find yourself sharing this sky again," she said. "With someone other than me."

Luna laughed and disentangled from Paqui's arms. Her future was going to be filled with high Spanish saddles and toros bravos, not star-struck husbands-to-be. Her future was now or not at all. "I promise," she said, humouring Paqui.

"Good. Now let me get back to work."

When Paqui was gone Luna climbed up on the wall and walked around it until she came to her secret hiding spot. She dislodged the stone and carefully examined each of her stolen items and replaced them and the stone. She didn't know much about being part of a family except what Paqui had taught her and the rest was tucked away safely right there. She touched the crucifix hanging around her neck, and scanned the moonlit hill and the fields that had belonged, for generations, to the García family. "I must pretend to be one of them now, Mama," she whispered to the wind. She jumped down and headed towards the flicker of oil lamps coming from the house.

PAQUI WAS IN THE kitchen serving up a dish of pork, chickpea and vegetable stew when Helena found her. "Aiy, Señora," Paqui said, clasping her hand to her heart. "You startled me." She took a deep breath. "What is it? Why aren't you at the party?"

Helena's hands were shaking. Her face was moist with perspiration. She surveyed the kitchen, the heart of any home she'd once believed. She scanned shelves storing the best olive oil from Almeria and a fat little bottle of cooking wine from Jerez that made her mouth water. She looked at the windowsill brimming with potted geraniums, at the stove, bubbling with pots of water, and, for a second, at the large wooden table. She lifted her eyes. "Are you going to tell her?"

Paqui held Helena's gaze. She pitied the woman. With alcohol as her sole companion, drinking had gone from being a frequent enjoyment to a necessary crutch. Luna would hate her colluding with the family, Paqui thought, and yet she couldn't risk losing her position in the house. "No," she answered. "That's your husband's confession to make, not mine."

LUNA STEPPED INTO THE inner patio as Chucho was loading up his plate and approaching Don Carlos with a half-full pitcher of sangria. "Señor García," Luna heard him say. "I hope it's all right that I join you." Chucho sat without waiting for an answer. "I want you to know that the cuadrilla has great respect for you and your family," he said. "It's our privilege to work with your sons. And we will protect Luna on tour."

Luna scanned the room for Manuel and, instead, found Marisol, in the corner of the garden with her hair back in a high ivory comb and her wide face gazing up at Pedro. She'd pinched her cheeks and lips to rouge them the way Doña García used to do before her husband came home from long trips. Marisol looked much older than seventeen standing there while Pedro fingered the thin gold chain around her neck. What could she possibly be saying to keep him so entranced? Since when, Luna wondered, did Pedro stand still for that long? She saw Manuel and moved to stand beside him.

"There you are," said Manuel, slipping his arm through hers. Chucho got out his guitar and began strumming with his claw hand. "Why don't you join him on bandurria, Papi?" Manuel asked.

"It's been too long," Carlos said, feigning modesty.

"Nonsense." Manuel reached up beside them, to the wall where the instrument hung. He lifted it from its hook and passed it to his father.

Father Serratosa raised his drink. "Don Carlos is a master."

"Please, Father," said Manuel. "No titles. We're all equal under God."

Carlos swatted Manuel. "Show some respect," he said. He placed the bandurria in his lap and played to encouraging yelps and clapping. Soon enough he had his arm around Chucho. Both were slightly drunk, swaying and speaking too loudly. "Viva los toros bravos!" bellowed Chucho, and Don Carlos raised his bandurria as if it was the Spanish flag. It was clear to Manuel that Chucho had a gift with men: He'd won over the most stubborn, and his father hadn't noticed it happening.

"Ven aquí niña!" Don Carlos called out to Luna without breaking rhythm. He patted a cushion on the chair next to him. Luna sat. A few minutes later he slipped her the name of his Spanish contact in Mexico, the man who would host them — Don Ramón Santiago, with whom he'd gone to school in Ronda when he was a boy. "I haven't seen him in years," he said. "Not since he dabbled in breeding. He's a wealthy aficionado. You will stay at his riding school. He knows many impresarios who could offer you contracts."

"Thank you," Luna said, almost breathlessly.

"One thing," Don Carlos added. "There will always be a place for you at Sangre Mío, but if you fight under my name, make sure you are the best."

Luna nodded. Many times she'd hoped that her father was like Don Carlos — strong and generous, and successful with the bulls. "I won't let you down," she said.

Manuel watched Luna basking in his father's attention and longed to be recognized in such a public way. *It doesn't matter how old we get, he thought, or how certain of our mother's love, we don't stop craving the approval of our fathers, especially when they withhold it.* Nostalgia began to ache in his bones like cold water. Leaving home was what he wanted, but it meant stretching the thin thread that connected him to his family. Would it hold? He walked over to the food tables, plucked an apricot from a silver tray, and popped it in his mouth.

A moment later he heard a familiar voice that made his heart leap. He turned slowly to find Eugenia standing by the garden wall commanding the attention of a few men from their writing circle. With a glass of red wine in one hand and a cigarette in the other, she flirted openly — laughing too loudly, pouting her red, red lips, and occasionally brushing up against one man in particular. Manuel hadn't invited her, but neither had he specified to Jorge that she not come. Tentatively, Manuel lifted his hand to acknowledge her, and Jorge, seeing him first, returned the gesture. Eugenia smiled and leaned into her new lover.

Manuel blushed. Fresh despondency rose within him. How many times, he wondered, would he make a fool of himself for that woman? Eugenia showed no concern for his feelings or any fear of judgment. He should be grateful to have gotten away from her before he'd fallen any harder, but her brazen callousness was also brave, and made him want her all the more.

He took a deep breath and looked up at the full-sharp moon. Soon he would be looking at it from a different vantage point and that's what he needed — to get away from home, find new inspiration, to find his voice as a writer. Mexico would be that new beginning. He glanced at Eugenia and at his father, and wanted to believe it.

# Act 2

## México
### 1933-1936

ON A BRIGHT NOVEMBER morning, days after CEDA had been elected to power in Spain, Luna sailed into the Bay of Mexico, and descended the steam ship at the port of Veracruz. "I am reborn!" she shouted, bounding down the platform ahead of the others without a backward glance. By contrast, Manuel felt sluggish and hesitant; after more than two sickening months swaying on the sea, his body had, by necessity, fooled itself into believing it was rooted to that ship. The first thing he noticed as he stepped onto solid land was the weak wind and the language, which was like his, but sounded less serious, each letter and syllable indistinct from the next. He waited with the others while their trunks were off-loaded and Fortuna was led up from the hull of the ship.

Pedro paid a man to drive Fortuna to Don Ramón's school and another man to pull their belongings on a cart to the hotel where they would stay overnight. The following morning, they all piled into the second-hand school bus that Chucho had arranged for, and drove two hundred miles west, into Tlaxcala, the smallest of

Mexico's states, where the school was nestled in the hills of the central highlands.

Don Ramón's property was vast, bought with money he'd made from breeding and from investments in Spain and abroad. The most talented young novilleros in Mexico trained with him and the fee was high. As a favour to the García family, he would charge the cuadrilla nothing for the use of his stable and training ring and a steady supply of bulls to practise on.

"Welcome!" he called out when they parked in the long driveway lined with manicured lawns. He was loud and rotund with a crown of silver hair and a ruddy, pockmarked face. He wore an expensive suit, a gold watch and cufflinks, and a leather holster in which he carried a large revolver. Despite these extravagances, or perhaps because of them, he was unable to hide his boorishness — and yet Luna was already charmed.

"Look at his clothes," she whispered, under her breath.

On the front lawn, Don Ramón embraced Manuel first. "Your father is an old friend," he said. "And a great Spaniard. Ask for anything you need." He took Pedro's hand and then appraised Luna. "So this must be the lady bullfighter?"

"Con mucho gusto," Luna said. "It's an honour to meet you."

"I was surprized to learn that Carlos had a daughter with talent," he said, admiring her face and body. "Of course you're welcome here too. As long as you agree to train on foot, that is."

Manuel and Pedro exchanged nervous glances. "But she's accomplished on horseback," Manuel said. "That's her talent." In a more conciliatory tone he added, "As we've already discussed."

"Bueno, what she does in her spare time is of no concern to me. But my school is only for the bravest toreros." Don Ramón surveyed the details of Luna's face. "I don't see Carlos in you," he said. "Perhaps in your temperament?"

Luna's eyes swept ambitiously over his property, drinking in the million round suns of the orange grove. "I would like to think as much," she said. She shifted her weight from one foot to the other, knowing that in the family of bullfighters there was no higher position than a matador. "I'm most grateful to you for any opportunity," she added.

Don Ramón blew his nose into a red silk handkerchief and stuffed it into his shirt pocket. "No need for gratitude," he said. He looked at her once again, in her new white cotton dress and black heels, as though she was as rare and mythological as a unicorn. "I must tell you though," he said. "I've never seen a girl fight on foot. I'm not convinced you will succeed."

"I understand doubts," she said, before Manuel could intervene. "There are many things I too have not seen. God, for one. And still I find it in my heart to believe."

Don Ramón, accustomed to the ways of bravura, burst out laughing. "You have quick reflexes," he said, guiding her by the arm across his terrace. "That's a start."

While the cuadrilla unloaded their belongings from the bus, and Marisol and Pedro were directed into the guesthouse by a maid, Don Ramón led Luna and Manuel into a covered arena where a dozen boys and men stood practising their cape and muleta manoeuvres. "Over there," he said, gesturing to the young bullfighter in the centre of the ring with a magenta and gold capote. "Behind the others, you see? That is the orphan Armando Mendoza. He's the most determined young torero I've ever known. If you haven't heard of him already you soon will. Armando is five years older than you, Luna, and has performed all over the country on foot. His discipline and timing are impeccable. One day he will be a great matador."

Armando was dressed in a modest pair of knee-length pants and a loose shirt. His figure was lean and muscular. Luna clenched her jaw as if in competition. *Not so tall*, she thought. *Maybe too skinny*. Armando moved with grace; that couldn't be denied, but he rarely held his feet still and his expressions, both those on his face and those brought on by the movement of his capote, were not solemn or aloof, but dramatic and sandunga. She immediately recognized his style as being copied from some of the most influential matadors in history. Armando stopped what he was doing and joined her.

"May I present Luna García," said Don Ramón. "The rejoneadora I told you about. She'll observe for today. Tomorrow she begins with the muleta and sword."

"As you wish, Patrón." Armando made a stiff bow in her presence. "Bienvenidos," he said. "It is my pleasure to welcome you to the school of Taurine."

Luna smiled warmly. Up close he was less of a threat, almost pretty. His hair was thick and wavy, his grey eyes fanned by long lashes. "I see you follow the Sevillian tradition," she said.

"And you?"

Neither Manuel nor Pedro had spoken to her of a formal style on foot, though she knew Pedro Romero was a hero to their father. His was one of the founding bullfight families of Ronda, so she said, "Rondeña."

Armando forced a nod and the corners of his mouth pressed into an insolent grin. He was humouring her, or perhaps judging her. "In that case, Señorita, I hope I may be of assistance. Rondeña and Sevillana are as different as love is from passion."

"What would she know about that?" snapped Manuel. "She's fourteen!"

Don Ramón shot Armando a warning look. "Our friends are here to see your technique, boy. Not to hear your opinions."

"Of course," Armando said, deferentially. "I meant no disrespect."

Luna looked him in the eye. "If I pray soberly in the dark of a chapel and you pray out in the open field, under the sun, drinking wine and laughing, we are both talking to God."

Armando blushed, and Don Ramón jostled him. He turned to his guests. "We'll observe now."

For the next hour they sat on the sidelines while Armando pranced around the ring, an exaggerated flamingo, showing off and intimidating the other students, trying hard to impress, with much decoration and gaiety, and little subtlety or restraint. But he demonstrated capote skills, presented clean, precise footwork. Occasionally he glanced in Luna's direction, almost as though he couldn't believe he would be forced to share a training ring with her. It was obvious to her that Armando thought as highly of himself as she did of his adornos, the bloated actions some matadors make during the faena to express their mastery over the bulls. Once, he knelt with his back to an imaginary rival and another time reached out as if to grab onto a cuerno and lean on the bull's head with his elbow. Though he lacked a certain reserve and enjoyed these showy acts of vulgarity, Luna saw he did have the fine technique of any master-in-training and, without forethought, she jumped down onto the sand, kicked off her heels, hiked up the skirt of her dress, and tied it in a knot between her legs. She mimicked his gestures as though she too held a capote. From a distance, they looked like a man and his shadow.

"Luna!" said Manuel. "Get up here! Ven aquí!"

"Leave her," said Don Ramón.

Almost as soon, the other students gathered to point and laugh.

"Look at those legs!" one boy shouted.

"Yeah, jeered another. "What else is she hiding under that skirt?" He rubbed his crotch and blew her a kiss.

Manuel was on his feet, ready to cross the sand but Don Ramón gripped his arm tightly and held him back. "A pack of scrawny boys should be no match for a real bullfighter."

Manuel hesitated. If Luna were seen to be in need of his protection, the likelihood of her being taken seriously as a competitor would be undermined. He forced himself to take a seat again. To his relief, Luna turned to the boys and advanced fearlessly.

"Taking a break so soon?!" She hollered. "I was just getting started!"

"Started on what?" said, one boy. "Entertaining us or cleaning our ring with your skirt?"

Luna gasped. She blushed and hated herself for it. She hadn't worked so hard and come this distance to be treated like a servant! She looked over at Manuel who offered no support and at Armando who seemed to be enjoying the spectacle. She wanted to throw a shoe at him or turn and storm off, but those impulses were quickly replaced by a stronger one: In an effort to win, she untied the knot of her skirt and scandalously let it fall to the ground. "You haven't seen a girl before, is that it?" she shouted. "Acabemos con esto. Let's get it over with."

None of them moved. Not one boy made a sound, though Armando stared in disbelief. He looked her up and down, resting his eyes on her white skirt, laced with sand from the ring. "Maybe we should get to work," he muttered to the others. After that, the boys resumed training and Luna continued studying them, satisfied she'd indeed won the first battle.

Sometime near the end of the day, Armando called out to her, "With more flourish, Señorita García! Louder, Louder. Or, see how I don't bend my elbow. Do it as I do!" When he was finished he reluctantly walked her through the grounds without introducing her to anyone. He showed her the field where the bulls roamed, the stall where Fortuna and her other horses would be kept, and the location of the novilleros' toilet. "There is only one," he said, unbinding his shirt collar. His neck and face glistened with sweat and grime. His palms were callused, from months of manoeuvring the heavy capote.

"I require no special treatment," she said.

"Good," he said, running one strong hand through his damp hair. "You won't find any here."


"HE'S AN ARROGANT BOY," Luna announced when she sat at the table between Manuel and Pedro in the guesthouse kitchen. "I won't work with him."

"Stop being melodramatic," said Marisol. "It's tiresome." She stood awkwardly at the stove with one hand on her hip, serving from a pot of rice and beans. A set of red maracas hung on the wall beside her. She was baffled by the way the men indulged Luna. Luna was an actress, as far as she was concerned, with an over-developed need for attention that should be ignored. Marisol hadn't asked to come along on this adventure and she resented it already. In fact, she hadn't once, not in her entire life, wanted to leave home, including during the interminable years when she'd been held captive by her mother's lengthy illness.

"There is no one better than Armando," said Manuel. "He has a wrist."

"He has no self-control," said Luna. "He barely talked to me after practice and he didn't stop the others from mocking me. Neither did you," she said, sounding hurt.

Pedro was cleaning his fingernails with a pocketknife. He looked up. "From what I heard you didn't need any help."

"Find me another to learn from," she said.

Manuel sealed an envelope addressed to Jorge Vidal. "Luna, you knew this wasn't going to be easy," he said. "Armando is not unusual; naturally he doesn't want you here. There will be much resistance — from ring promoters, perhaps the crowd. Respect is earned, not given. You must learn to deal with him."

"But how?"

Marisol plopped a spoonful of warm rice and beans onto Luna's plate. "Have you forgotten already?" she said, impatiently. "We all do things we don't want to do."

THE FOLLOWING SUNDAY, CHUCHO drove the old school bus to nearby Tlaxcala city and parked outside the hotel. They checked in, dropped their bags, and headed straight for the "El Ranchero" bullring to fulfill their first contract. The brightly coloured cartel in front announced, *Rondeña Rejoneador*! and showed an illustration of Luna atop her horse. *See for yourselves*, it dared. *Is she as valorous as she is beautiful?*

"Manuel," she said. "Am I beautiful?"

"All the more so because you don't know it."

"Be honest," she said. "What do you see?"

He laughed. How could someone keenly intelligent in one arena be so completely unaware in another? "Bueno," he said, "let me have a good look ... To start, you're as skinny as a shovel. You should eat more. And you need a new suit ... But your posture is correct, and there's determination in the way you carry yourself. More like a man," he added. "Oh, and those big eyes are intoxicating. They don't hide your ambition."

"I like that," she said, pleased.

Twenty minutes before the event was scheduled to begin, the cuadrilla entered together through the puerta de caballos at the side of the plaza. Pedro was already pacing. "This fight will make or break us," he said, "Your performance must be flawless." He spoke severely, threateningly, as if he'd guessed that the best way to motivate her was to dare her to fail. But she was no longer at Sangre Mio, taking orders from superiors, and no one placed more pressure on her to succeed than she placed on herself.

"You don't have to remind me."

As instructed, Luna sought out the senior matador who was enjoying a cigarette in the shade. He stood elegantly in his red and gold suit of lights. "I'm humbled to share the bill with you," she said. "My cuadrilla speaks highly of your talent."

The matador scrutinized her body from head to toe and blew smoke in her face. "What harm can there be in a warm-up act?" he said, smirking. "The crowd enjoys the corrida buffa."

Luna coughed and choked. "Maestro," she said, steeling herself against another attack. "We're no company of clowns."

He turned away from her with the cigarette hanging between his lips. "Nice skirt, little tortillera," he said, under his breath. He snapped his fingers for someone to bring his horse.

Luna felt her face burn, swallowed her anger. She didn't know how to respond to such inhospitable behaviour from an adult, so she ignored it. She watched Chucho lead Fortuna in from the small open enclosure where the horses were being exercised. Fortuna was impressive at eighteen hands high, and dressed magnificently. Her white, pearly coat gleamed and her long silver mane was braided tightly with decorations. One red flower was tied to her forehead, and her tail had been carefully combed out and covered in a red and silver sequined strap. Her ankles were wrapped in white bandages, and her bridle and crosspiece adorned with red and white florets.

"You look better than I do," Luna told her, and she was ashamed of her outfit; the long skirt and second-hand traje corto, and all they represented. She hated that the senior matador had made her feel inferior, but who was she to think she could do this? She was a fake, a nobody. She mounted slowly and, leaning forward, slapped Fortuna's thick, arched neck. The horse snorted, transferring her weight from one hind leg to the other. *She's ready*, Luna thought. *Am I?*

She crossed herself as they passed the small chapel and took her place between the other bullfighters on their horses. A pasodoble played loudly, something that didn't happen in a Spanish bullring, and it added to her sense of displacement, but when she heard the universal excitement of spectators coming from the stands, she set aside the feeling that she was an imposter. A minute later, the trumpets sounded and two alguacillas rode her, and the other two bullfighters, out into the sun. Side by side the three of them crossed the arena and tipped their hats at the president's palco.

Manuel rushed through the wall of toreros and businessmen to the other side of the arena, with anxiety leaping under his skin. More than when he'd been in the ring himself, seeing Luna there was agonizing. All he could do was watch helplessly, and hope he'd done his job. The authorities and their elegantly dressed wives stood to acknowledge the bullfighters and the main judge tossed down the key to the toril door. One of the alguacillas caught it in his hat. The three bullfighters made the procession with their cuadrillas behind them on foot, each member carrying a capote draped over his left shoulder. Following were the mules and mule drivers. Once having made the round, Luna dismounted and handed Manuel Fortuna's reins. "You can do it," he said. Pedro held out a capote and Luna took it. She moved to stand beside the barrera, testing the wind, sweeping and waving the silk across the sand. Thankfully, the wind was low.

When the trumpets blew for a second time, she mounted again, and Chucho handed over a small ceremonial cup, which she drank from in one gulp. She screwed up her face as the alcohol burned her throat and passed the cup down to Chucho. Seeing Pedro and Manuel hide behind the burladero, she positioned herself opposite the toril, as was customary in the Portuguese style, and didn't take her eyes from the door. Seconds later, she held her breath, the chute flew open and out charged the bull they called Apolo.

Fortuna was off, galloping around the ring, and with a long pole Luna drew a line in the sand between herself and the bull. She and Fortuna circled twice before the bull stopped in the sun, at centre ring, confused. One of the peons ran out to retrieve the long pole and offered a shorter one, with a red flag on its end.

From twenty feet away, Luna taunted the bull, asking Fortuna to dance, side to side, having her bow and show confidence. Caballos Andaluz are trained to perform such intricate moves; they prance with high knees and a slow gait that would impress anyone, and the Mexican aficionados were particularly amused.

The bull was also impressed. He charged.

They were off again, and Luna prayed Fortuna would not slip or fall on the sand. The space between the horse's body and the bull's cuernos was less than an inch, though Fortuna was faster and more agile. Naturally, with the hot breath of an angry bull on her hide, Fortuna wanted to speed up, but Luna held her back; she needed a clear view and close range. They made one more circle of the ring, with the bull chasing, frothing at the mouth, until he slowed. Luna was a short distance away. She stood Fortuna in front of him, and made her dance. "Apolo!" she called, spinning her horse in a tight circle, three full rotations. "Apolo, look over here!" She galloped straight for him, leaning flat back, with her shoulders practically bouncing off Fortuna's rump. She reached over her head, stretching all the way out of her saddle, and placed the rejón on the bull's back. "Toma!" she shouted. "Take that!"

The crowd cheered, and expected Apolo to slow once more, but he didn't. Heaving, he continued to charge, and because a torero mustn't show fear or run from a bull, Luna didn't turn Fortuna away from him, but instead sat up in her saddle and asked Fortuna to dance them to safety sideways, and backwards, until they were practically into the barrera. She noted Don Ramón and Armando watching from their seats, sombre bajo. Luckily, the bull began to feel his internal injury and exhaustion, and slowed to a stand still, blood painting his hide, with his tongue hanging out of his mouth to taste the air.

She placed the second and third rejones, dizzying him with Fortuna's spins, charging him directly, although she held one rejón in each hand, and rode without the reins, demonstrating her horsemanship, to the crowd's delight. She placed one, swiftly, leaning sideways, and the second immediately after, from an upright position. The second missed and fell onto the sand and she almost followed, slipping out of her saddle, though she managed to hang onto Fortuna's back with her thighs and was able to right herself.

"Do you think I'm at the beach?!" she yelled at the cuadrilla. "Why does no one bring the cape or pick up what I've dropped!"

Two peons dashed out onto the sand, one using his capote to distract Apolo while the other passed Luna the stick she'd dropped.

She turned Fortuna, wasting no time. "Vente, Mira!" she called. "Come on Apolo! Look what I've got here!" It would've been an act of cowardice and more, of cruelty, to place sticks when he refused to charge, so she waited him out, though she needed the crowd's energy to finish the job. "What do you think?" she called out for support.

"Finish it!" Manuel called, inciting the spectators in the stands.

"Finish it!" the crowd repeated.

The bull's front legs had weakened and he was no longer able to chase her any great distance, so she rode by the burladero and demanded a sword. She didn't fear blood or death; not the way other people did. She had nothing to lose and that was her advantage. When Manuel handed her a sword she hoped the senior matador was watching. "Look at me!" she wanted to shout. "All of you look at me!" She made a turn around the ring and taunted the bull, this time with the crowd's assistance. He charged with all the life he had left, and when she was so close that closer would've meant disaster for Fortuna, she swung the sword and plunged. But

Apolo was stronger than she'd anticipated, able to hold his head high, and her sword had gone in part way.

"El a partillo!" Someone called from the stands. "El a partillo!" It was Armando's voice and this enraged her. Don Ramón was holding his head in his hands as though he couldn't bear to watch such disgrace, and Apolo, on his knees, was halfway between this world and the next. Blood flooded from his mouth and nose, and poured onto the sand like an open faucet. Spectators in the seats nearest to him moaned.

Luna dismounted fast and ran to Apolo, leaving Fortuna to find her way to the boards. She leaned over Apolo cautiously, in case he rallied, and removed the sword with both hands. His eyes rolled back in his head; he was close to the end. She knelt before him with one hand on her hip and flamboyantly made a bow, as Armando would've done. Apolo couldn't rise, he wanted to rise and pin her to the sand though he could barely hold his head. Next, she demonstrated her mastery by standing with her hand out over his cuernos. When she lifted her sword, in her other hand, and prepared to place it one last time, there was relief on his face. She put it in fast and he dropped like stone.

The crowd was on their feet.

"The ear! The ear!"

In truth, there were also whistles, because she'd taken too long to kill, and missed on the first try, but the majority were pleased and wanted to see ears awarded. They wanted to be a part of something great, and so would make her great. This was her first lesson in the authority of the people, which may not be formal, as with the judgment of the president in his box, but is more powerful and persuasive. As the mules were led in, tin bells clanging against their yoke, the president signalled to the alguacil to offer an award. Luna lifted her arms to recognize the highest seats in the plaza, and she pranced, much as Fortuna had pranced, almost skipping in slow motion into the centre of the ring. There, the alguacil hacked off Apolo's left ear and awarded it to her, embracing her for the honour.

Chucho jogged over to embrace her as well, and Apolo was hitched and dragged out of the arena. Luna lifted the ear up for the crowd to see, and girls tossed red carnations at her feet.

Covered in speckles of blood, she made the rounds with her cuadrilla, and for a moment Luna knew what it was like to be an artist, to be loved. Spectators threw fans and scarves and she picked each up off the sand, and tossed it back up to them. The bull's ear was a scratchy wet weight in her right hand and blood covered her fingers. She saw Don Ramón grinning and slapping Armando on the back, though Armando showed surprisingly little reaction, and looked stunned. As if she knew he'd expected her to fail, Luna tossed him the bull's ear and watched him clutch it to his chest. Bending over, as she'd seen Belmonte do that afternoon in Ronda, she grabbed a fist full of Mexican sand, held it high in honour of her gracious hosts and let it stream through her fingers and all down her suit.

"WHAT DOES IT MEAN, tortillera?"

"Cómo?" Manuel was standing in the doorway of the bedroom she and Marisol shared, holding his leather-bound journal.

"Tortillera, what the senior matador called me. I don't know what it means."

Manuel cringed. "Bueno, it means a girl who … Aiy, tortillera is … it's derogatory for …"

Marisol sucked her teeth, impatiently. "It's a dirty word for a dirty woman, Luna. Someone not even God could want. Don't use it again." Marisol held up a blue ankle-length skirt and a pale green dress. "We've gone through the whole closet," she said. "Which of these will you wear tomorrow?"

"Neither of them," Luna said. "I'll wear trousers, like Armando does."

"Qué absurdo!" Marisol tossed the clothes onto the bed.

"Luna, you know better," said Manuel. "Stop it. Marisol wants to sleep."

Luna flopped onto her bed, pulling the thick mosquito netting over it. She wondered if he wished she could be more like Marisol; competent in the art of domesticity, more companion than competitor. But how to be both female and a bullfighter? Outside the ring, she was expected to show modesty and virtue, and her class demanded subservience, and yet when she performed she was expected to be a showman.

"Must this be about my sex?" she asked.

"From the moment you lifted a sword."

Luna threw aside the mosquito netting. "I want people to take me seriously, Manuel. Remember the Moorish poet, Wallada? She refused to cover her face in public or keep to her place. I will be defiant too," she said. "But I will conform to tradition — bullfight tradition." She swung her legs over the edge of the bed. "I already restrict my food to fit my short jacket. If I have to dress the part of a bullfighter every hour of every day to be accepted as one, I will." She looked at him. "I will risk your approval."

Manuel flinched. She'd not before spoken so indifferently about his importance in her life and it hurt, though not in the sharp way physical pain does. He felt an unbearable and gradual tightening in his chest, as if all of the air was being squeezed from his lungs, and he was being crushed with the weight of a life much larger than his own. *At five in the afternoon*, he found himself thinking of Federico's famous bullfight poem: *At five in the afternoon, the wounds were burning like suns.* Of course he understood her need for acceptance; they were alike physically and in their desire to express themselves, but also in matters that concerned the heart. Acceptance in the ring meant everything to her, and offered her a place in a kind of family. Who was he to interfere with that? "Do as you please on Sundays," he said.

"You can dress yourself," said Marisol. "I have better things to do." At home she'd been responsible for administering her mother's medicine, exactly as the doctor had advised, preparing meals, cleaning the house. She'd held her mother's frightened hand without resentment, and lied about her own fears. She'd moistened the woman's lips with a damp cloth when she could no longer swallow to drink. Illness and hard work didn't offend her, but Luna's spoiled attitude did. She stormed about the hotel bedroom, gesturing with her arms while she muttered to herself.

"I didn't ask you to fuss over me," Luna said. "You're not my mother."

"You're lucky I'm not!"

Pedro pushed into the room and found Marisol with her hands on her hips. "Why is there shouting?" he asked.

As soon as Marisol set her eyes on him she burst into tears. "Take me to my brother," she said. "I want to go home."

It was the first anyone had mentioned Andalucía since they'd left, and it occurred to Manuel that the ache he'd felt most evenings was not because of the rain, which fell for too long throughout the region, nor was it because he was still in love with Eugenia, but because their small group of bullfight aficionados was too insulated, offering him little access to other people or fresh ideas. He missed his artist's circle. Without it he was lacking an intellectual life.

"I hate it here," cried Marisol.

"You don't mean that," said Pedro. "You're tired."

Marisol's eyes were glistening with sadness, but no fool, especially not the common kind like Pedro, could cross her line of vision without being seen clean through. She'd been run over by circumstance but she'd certainly not given up her sense of self or her sharp tongue. "Do not tell me how I feel!" she said.

In a clumsy attempt at tenderness, Pedro moved to put his arms around her and whispered in her ear. He promised to marry her one-day though Marisol suspected he might be trying to win another kiss. Still, she nodded, sniffled and wiped her face with her hands. When they separated again she said, "Fine, but we need a pair of pants for tomorrow. Maybe ask one of the picadors for his old ones, because Luna, the great matador of Mexico, will no longer wear a skirt."

"But if she draws more attention in pants," Pedro said.

"Her technique is what should be drawing attention," said Manuel. "Besides, what cuadrilla will work with a girl who dresses better than they do?"

"I'll talk to them," Pedro said. "They'll appreciate her commitment."

"No." Manuel raised one hand, the one holding his journal. "You talk and don't listen. I'm thinking of her future."

"Sí, you have bigger concerns, like your stupid scribbling!"

"Aiy, don't fight," Luna said.

Marisol lit the red candle hanging beside the small Virgin Mary wall shrine and both men fell silent. Pedro kissed his fingers then, a second later, lunged for Manuel's journal. Manuel shoved him against the wall and the journal fell to the floor, with its binding spread like wings.

Pedro scrambled to retrieve the writings and read the first stanza out loud:

*Does love still look for me in the land of dust and blood*
*under the Doorway of Sorrows on a street called Lineros,*
*or does she hope to find a king not a man?*
*Will she crave some starry wilderness, or the world I offer*
*and move swiftly like the Guadalquivir, in the curve of my hand?*

Pedro laughed. "Don't tell me you're still pining for that cock tease?"

Manuel ripped the journal from his brother's hands, clutched it to his chest. "Go to hell!"

"This is bullshit!" said Pedro. He smoothed his hair into place. "I came in to give Luna her cut." He pulled a wad of ten peseta notes from out of his pocket, peeled one off the top. "Here," he said, tossing the money into the air before turning on his heels.

Luna leapt off the bed, snatched the thin paper rectangle as it sailed towards the floor. She stood, admiring it in her hand, sniffed it to know what such a large amount of money smelled like.

Manuel watched her with a mixture of frustration and envy. Bullfighting was an earthy passion. Rough and roiling with violence. She was fully engaging with it while he floundered with his poems. He hadn't been writing nearly enough or every day, and the few poems he had finished were weak. Too often he expressed his theme of love, in distant celestial terms, and his imagery was platonic, pure and bright as fairy dust. A poet must be bold, he thought, as daring as a bullfighter, and yet he still hadn't learned to let go. He turned to Luna. "No pants outside the ring," he said, trying to regain some composure.

Luna folded her arms across her chest, stubbornly. "A torero doesn't wear a skirt."

Frustrated, Manuel threw his arms into the air. Luna beamed with satisfaction. She turned to Marisol. "You see?" she said, "I must dress as a matador if I'm going to be a matador."

"Have your way," said Marisol, climbing into bed as the crickets outside began to click and sing. "You always do."


LUNA SAT CROSS-LEGGED on her bed, composing a letter to Paqui by candlelight. She tried to be neat and impressive; Paqui wouldn't be able to read the letter, but Manuel had assured her that he would post it with his own letters for home, and have his mother to read it out loud to Paqui. *This money is for you,* Luna began. *It is the first I've earned. Buy something beautiful for yourself.* She folded the bill inside the notepaper, proudly, and wished Paqui could've seen her first performance, how the crowd had loved her. *I sleep on clean linen each night,* she wrote. *I don't have to wash it. Someone else does.* She drew a stick figure of herself atop Fortuna, and signed the letter, *Prospero Año, Luna*

LUNA WALKED INTO THE stable to brush Fortuna, and found her groomed, her mane already braided, and Armando leaning against a stall door, cleaning and polishing her tack. She was surprised to find him engaged in such a mundane chore.

"We're not all granted free tuition," he said, without realizing that, like his own, Luna's privileges at the school were conditional upon success. When she reached for the cloth and bridle he was holding he jerked them away. "I don't need your help."

"No, of course not," she said. "It's I who needs yours, right?"

Armando said nothing, but softening, handed her a cloth and Fortuna's bridle. "Don't tell Don Ramón. He'll think I'm lazy."

The heat of Armando's fingers was still pressed into the old leather. He pulled up a stool and sat with her brandy coloured saddle resting on his knees, and a crosspiece for the halter at his feet. After oiling the saddle he looked up at her in her shirt and pants. "You're good in the ring," he said. "Do you know that?"

"Yes, I know," she said. "But I will be great."

Armando's plump mouth pressed into a curve, almost against his will, and he laughed. Hearing herself through his ears, she laughed too. Pretty soon they were both wiping their faces.

"I will be great," she repeated, mocking herself.

"I will be the greatest," he said, imitating her voice and tossing his hair, as she'd done. He set the saddle on the floor, slid off the stool, and moved to lie in the hay alongside Fortuna. "It's funny," he said, "how we all sound the same." His black hair was spread out around his head — a dark halo — and the first strong sun of the day filtered through the metal bars of the stall door trapping his grey eyes within a prison of shadow. "What are you looking at?" he asked defensively.

"Nada." Luna plopped down beside him, leaned back onto her elbows to appear casual. She was staring though, riveted by the single, sudden thought that they shared the hunger. The red raw growl of ambition. They were making something of themselves and suffering the anxiety of not yet fully succeeding. They were both orphans — alone in the midst of a community of brothers, though ultimately belonging only to the ring.

"I've heard you have no familia," she said, rather callously.

"Forty mothers," he answered, without emotion. The nuns of Santa Mónica convent in Oaxaca. She pictured a stern flock of habits, the nuns' implacable natures pecking him towards perfection. "It isn't so bad," he said, laughing at her expression of concern. "Sister Margarita was the first to introduce me to the bulls. Her cousin was the great Raphaelito. Wherever I perform there are a dozen mothers watching over me." He spoke directly, as though the impact of his words left no residue on his heart, but she saw the pain clouding his eyes. She saw his attempt to hide longing and loneliness, because she'd been hiding it herself.

Sitting close to him with her trusted horse beside them, and the smells of worn leather, polish and hay all around, it was as if God were holding up a mirror so she might at last see her own potential. Armando was beautiful and talented and heartbroken, and there could've been no greater temptation: love itself was the corrida, and so Armando its first messenger. All at once, Luna wanted to distract him from his intense and faithful passion for the ring and redirect that passion onto her. She wanted him to want her as badly as he wanted to perform, crave her as he craved applause, touch her as she suspected Marisol allowed Pedro to do. Armando was five years older than she was, though he was an eternity away in accomplishment and knowledge. She was as full of fire as he was for it, but what did she know compared to him?

"Teach me," she said, without planning to.

"Qué?"

She meant all he knew of the capote, the grand flourish of his Faroles and Verónicas, the theatrical precision of his right arm crossing over his left arm and leg as he moved in to make the descabello. That and more.

He struggled up onto his elbows to face her, leaned in, and put his lips to hers.

A kiss is never just a kiss, and with Armando it was a breathless consolation she hadn't known she needed. It reminded her of the game she'd played with the field hand's daughter, although Armando hadn't demanded she be subservient. She permitted him to slip his tongue inside her mouth and press her onto the pile of hay, where they lay, body to body, for what felt like a very long time. *Desire is an art*, she thought, *like any other*, and she ran her hands through his hair, rested one on the back of his neck. She matched him, made no resistance when he slipped his hand beneath her shirt and moved it higher on her bare skin. He stopped himself.

"We shouldn't," he said, panting.

"Why not?" She placed her hand over top of his, on her chest. "I'm almost fifteen," she reminded him.

"We're bullfighters," he said, as though bullfighters risk greater danger than other people feeling passion outside the arena.

She squeezed his hand and pressed her chest out so he felt her. "Since when do you show such restraint?"

Armando blinked his long lashes. "You're brave and beautiful, Luna García."

"Prove it," she said, offering him her neck to kiss.


THE NEXT EVENING, IN Tlaxcala, they stood inconspicuously close to one another holding lighted candles as the beating of the drums announced the beginning of the posada — the first of nine processions leading up to Christmas Day. They walked at the front of the procession, behind Marisol and Manuel, who were dressed as Mary and Joseph. Marisol wore a poinsettia in her hair. Children and their families followed her, slowly moving through the village, going door-to-door singing hymns and praying for shelter from King Herod.

Manuel had reluctantly agreed to the honour of playing Joseph, and regretted the decision. He felt awkward at the front of the procession — fraudulent and baffled as to how others could so unquestioningly believe. Wasn't all this tradition a way to keep people from challenging the authority of the Church? Shouldn't they instead be searching for a way to improve the condition of people's lives? As Marisol walked beside him with her hands on her abdomen and a devoted expression upon her face, he could see that she had no such reservations. Marisol derived comfort from her faith, a boundless feeling of being loved. By candlelight she appeared gentle, serene, and yet Manuel suspected she could become fiercely protective, if need be. Still, he was struck by her pious beauty. Pedro has found a good woman, he thought, and he felt a tweak of desire for her, and was ashamed. He glanced over his shoulder and saw his brother walking at the rear with the Three Wise Men — prominent village leaders.

Armando was at Luna's side when they passed across from The Parish Church of San José on their way to the Plaza de La Constitución, and he leaned over and whispered in her ear, "I want to be alone with you." Luna pressed her tongue to the roof of her mouth, but said nothing. Marisol had turned to peer in through the ornate entrance of the church, and was watching.

The villagers gathered in the plaza by moonlight to say the rosary, and the children, excited, ran off to break the piñata leaving their parents to mingle with neighbours and friends. Gifts of food and drink were passed around — tamales, sugar cane, hot fruit punch, and the Rosca De Reyes — the wreath-shaped bread with candied fruit. Luna nibbled her piece while Armando laughed and joked with the others from the school. She felt nervous excitement jump under her skin and wanted to pull him aside. Instead, she scanned the plaza and found Don Ramón and Pedro with the priest, and Chucho, sharing a cigarette with a brawny looking man. Manuel was sitting alone on a wrought-iron bench in his white robe and desert sandals, staring at the Government Palace to the north. She went to him.

"What are you thinking?" she asked.

"Too many things," he said, wearily. "I'm surrounded by home and it makes me question why I left. Did you know this was one of the first places founded by Cortés?" He pointed across the street to the wall of colonial buildings fronting the plaza. "There's a bandstand over there that was a gift from King Philip III."

Luna sat down next to him. "So what?"

Manuel watched the priest move around the plaza, greeting his parishioners. "I write of love, but I'm not living the experience," he said. "Maybe I would be more productive if I fell in love again."

Luna laughed, and stifled it. Sometimes he could sound so absurd. Love wasn't a romantic thing that would better his art, it was a bullfighter facing immortality, a poet facing the same, it was ecstatic and painful, a double-edged desire to be both craved and feared. It had nothing to do with his lack of confidence. "You don't need anyone else," she said. "You are the artist."

"I suppose so."

She leaned into him, put her head on his shoulder as if the moon had granted her its mercurial power to sway tides and heal hearts.

"That's your problem," she said. "You're unsure of yourself." A moment later she stood and pulled him up off the bench. "Art is not a democracy, Manuel. It's a dictatorship, and you're the one in charge. You taught me that when we trained. Maybe if you believed it you'd write more."

LUNA AND ARMANDO BEGAN to meet early in the mornings before the other students arrived. They didn't fully undress, and Armando retained his self-control, despite Luna's best efforts to help him lose it. They played at being secret, tortured lovers, as they played at being matadors de toros. One act inseparable from the other. Armando's skin, his golden god-like skin, was the feel of her muleta, and the muscled length of his sinewy arm, was the muscle of her own arm as she learned better how to move the heavy capote. The smile he offered so rarely encouraged her to work harder. She absorbed him, inhaled him. His fresh energy was with her throughout the day and yet in sleep she dreamt not of circles or suertes, but of the painting of the young girl and her suitor hanging over her old bed at Sangre Mío, and she heard the low, dark murmur of love — a more dangerous proposition — waiting around soft slumbering corners.

One morning, far behind the orange groves where no one walked and no one could see them, Armando rolled on top of her, and she didn't stop him. She felt the cool earth at her back, tasted eucalyptus in the air. As the pastel sun lifted, Armando released himself inside her. *Power,* she thought. She'd studied it as a slave studied his master, yearned for it, and now it was mixing into her.

Armando rolled onto his back, and struggled to pull up his pants from around his ankles. A pile of silver coins spilled out of one pocket and their clinking music was hopeful, inspiring. Luna reached across the grassy dirt and traced the outline of one coin with her pointer finger.

"Pedro manages my money," she said. "Who takes care of yours?"

Armando sat up. "No one. I count each peseta myself."

"You do?"

"And I carry enough for an emergency. What if I need food, or a room for the night, or a fast escape? A man with empty pockets doesn't belong to himself; he's at the mercy of others."

"Yes," she said, slipping the coin into her pocket without him seeing. "You're right." Why had she not already thought of it herself? Money was freedom, and what was the use in having it locked up in a bank somewhere, or jangling around in Pedro's pockets. She should be able to get at it whenever she wanted. Snuggling in closer to Armando, she rested her head in his lap.

"Did I hurt you, Luna?" he asked, stroking her hair.

She felt a burning sensation between her legs, imagined a tear and traces of blood. "A little," she said.

All at once, Marisol was towering over them, blocking the sun. "I knew it!" she snapped.

"We're talking," Luna said, scrambling to cover herself.

Marisol tugged her up onto her feet, digging long fingernails into her arm. "I see what you're doing!"

"Let me explain," said Armando, standing.

Marisol looked at him sharply. "If you know what's good for you, you will disappear before I call for one of her brothers. "Váyase! Go!"

"Please don't tell," begged Luna.

Marisol turned around with the same fierce judgment in her eyes.

"You will take a hot bath immediately! What in God's name were you thinking? He's a man; don't you know he'll do whatever he can get away with."

"It wasn't like that," Luna said. "He's not Pedro."

"Foolish girl! You'd better pray I'm not forced to tell what I've discovered."

"What do you mean?"

"A pregnancy, of course. You could end up like your mother."

Luna shivered, touched her hand to the flat of her stomach. *Would God plant something inside of her and expect it to grow?*

FOR THE NEXT THREE days, Luna rode bareback each morning, galloping as fast and hard as she could to dislodge the pregnancy that might've been taking root inside her. She knew nothing of the science of conception, although she'd once heard from Paqui that girls who found themselves in trouble tried to knock the thing out. In the evenings she squeezed the juice of a lemon onto a kerchief, twisted it into a rope and shoved it up between her legs where it stung. Before falling asleep she prayed: *Dear God in heaven, forgive me. I cannot bear a child. It will end my career and I don't want to die, like my mother.*

IN FEBRUARY THEY WERE on the road again, this time headed for a weeklong bullfight festival in Mexico City, in the Valley of Anahuac, surrounded by imposing mountains and the high volcano called Iztaccihuatl to the east. As Chucho drove, Luna couldn't stop thinking about her body, each sensation, real or imagined, was magnified — evidence her life might indeed be imperilled. What would Armando and the others do if she were pregnant? How would she continue to perform? As the bus bumped along a dirt road, she meandered to the rear, past Marisol who was asleep with her head bobbing unsupported, past Pedro and the cuadrilla who were playing cards, to where Manuel was busily composing in his notebook. She plopped down next to him, tucked her knees up against the seatback in front of her. Manuel didn't respond so she poked him in the ribs. "What is it," he said, sounding annoyed. "I'm working."

She looked at his tense face, hiding important thoughts. He'd stopped shaving and was shrouded behind a full black beard and moustache.

"What is love?" she asked.

He tapped his pen on the cover of his notebook. "I'm in the middle of something, Luna. I don't want to lose momentum."

She sighed. She'd begun to miss those late nights of training at Sangre Mio, having his full attention. She missed how easy it once was to make him laugh. Lately, he was distracted and irritable, as if the incandescent solitude he needed for his writing cut a sombre, impatient edge across his personality. She stared out the window at the hilly green landscape and tried not to panic about the baby that might or might not be turning inside her. She suspected that, if she were pregnant, Armando would be forced to marry her. The real problem, she knew, was she didn't want to be a wife or mother.

Her opening performance was exceptional, and one of her most exhausting; she'd drawn last, so had had to wait until the other two toreros fought. Her second bull, though small in stature, bucked and charged and slammed his horns into the boards like a firecracker on four legs. He chased her fearlessly, and she and Fortuna had to outride him many times. In the end, she'd tired him enough to place sticks and kill. When it was over, and the spectators cheered, she knew she'd broken through another layer of resistance from aficionados and colleagues; they no longer expected that she'd fail. As she exited the ring Don Ramón presented her with two-dozen long stemmed red roses, and embraced her ardently in front of photographers and bullfight reporters.

AT THE HOTEL, SHE peeled out of her chaqetilla and the rest of her outfit eager to soak her sore muscles in the tub. She carried the roses into the bathroom in a vase and set them on a commode where she could smell them while she soaked.

The bath water was too hot when she slipped under and released the last of her performance. She set loose her hair from its pins so Marisol could wash it. "Lean forward," Marisol said, lifting water in a wide ceramic bowl and pouring it down over Luna's head. Rivers spread across her scalp, spilling into her eyes. She closed them, and for the first time in years remembered Paqui bathing her in an old tin washtub when she was small. "Mugriento," Marisol said, clucking her tongue as she performed the baptism. "Your hair is filthy."

"I should cut it."

"No. A man likes a woman with long hair."

Luna blushed at the memory of being discovered behind the orange grove. "I thought you disapproved."

"That's not what I meant," said Marisol.

Luna pressed her bony knees up close to her chest, flesh to flesh. The lamp sitting on a small table across the room shined blue through its silk shade, turning her body to a bruise. "Do men also like women who kill bulls?" she asked.

"No. All the more reason for you to keep it long."

"Aiy! My eyes." She rubbed soap from them.

Marisol handed her a cloth. "Use this," she said.

There was still such formality between them, despite their physical intimacy. Marisol's hands massaged Luna's head and neck, the balm of warm water washing away her sins, but neither one braved any real tenderness towards the other until Luna took the risk. She reached over her shoulder for Marisol's hand. "Gracias," she said. "For all that you do."

Marisol slipped her hand away and resumed her work. "We each have a job," she said.

"Is that all I am?"

"Now you want to be my friend," Marisol said coldly.

Luna tensed. It was true she had made no effort, but surely Marisol could've made it easier? She didn't understand Marisol, and was offended by her lack of ambition. But Marisol wasn't without goals; she'd set her sights on Pedro and she appeared to be winning him. "Perhaps I've been unfair," Luna said. "We don't know each other."

"What do you want to know?"

There were many questions to ask — of Marisol's Gypsy father and his disappearance, of her mother's death from cancer, and how she carried on undefeated. Leaning into the strength of Marisol's hands Luna said, "It's not my place, but how did you know you wanted to marry Pedro when you met him? You were practically strangers."

Marisol worked the shampoo into lather. "Manuel's heart belonged to his writing," she said in a voice so practical it made Luna shiver. "And to you," she added. "Pedro's belonged to no one."

"Does he love you as much as you love him?"

Marisol stopped what she was doing. They could hear the brothers arguing over the details of a new contract in the next room, as the bathtub faucet dripped time. "You don't measure love," she said. "It's like water." She ran the bowl through the water and filled it once more. "With some, love is warm summer rain, with others ice, but we need it."

"I need it," Luna said, the words pressing from breath and shaping on her tongue before she could kill them.

"Armando," Marisol nodded. "Yes, that was plain."

Again, Luna felt her face burn. "I don't want to have his baby," she whispered.

Marisol lowered her voice. "You haven't bled yet?"

Luna arched her neck. "What do you mean?" There was a look of panicked fear in her eyes and Marisol felt sorry for her.

"Didn't Paqui tell you about la menstruación? Down there," Marisol pointed. "Between your legs?"

"No."

Marisol gathered Luna's hair at the base of her neck in both hands, squeezed the water from it. "Women bleed every month," she said. "You should've started by now. Maybe because you're so thin ... You're lucky, Luna, you cannot be pregnant if you haven't started."

"You're certain?"

"Yes."

Luna took a deep breath, exhaled and felt each muscle in her body relax.

"You still have a chance with Don Ramón," said Marisol.

"Don Ramón!" Luna faced forward once more. "But he's old! I wouldn't want to —"

"Always it's something with you. You're too good for him, is that it? Be careful, Luna."

"Careful of what?"

"Of reaching for too much and ending up with nothing." Marisol wound Luna's hair on top of her head. "I see the way Ramón looks at you. He wants more than a celebrated pupil. You'd better start thinking like a woman, since you can't act like one. Bullfighting is for the young. What will you do after? There is more than the ring and your bulls. There are husbands and children, the needs of the flesh."

Luna shuddered. Don Ramón was her great champion in Mexico, but the thought of being intimate with him repulsed her, and yet if what Marisol had said were true, she'd be answerable to the tradition of the sexes too. How would she navigate Don Ramón's feelings and not ruin their chances? She slipped backwards against the smooth enamel of the washtub, rested her head on the edge conjuring Armando's breathless kisses instead. It was comforting to believe they were all she needed, but they weren't. She needed the bulls. Her lower back ached and some new pain wrung through her. "There is nothing more," she said. "Not for me. There can't be. Not if I want to succeed."

Marisol rinsed her hands in the bathwater and patted them dry on a towel, which she spread around Luna's shoulders. "Don't stay in too long," she said. "You could catch a chill." The door clicked shut. Luna thought, *Marisol is strong after all. A strong angel. She'd make the ideal wife for Pedro and a good mother to his children.* Indeed, Marisol was the kind of woman Luna would've wanted to marry if she'd been a man. A tangy, metallic odour hit her. It was ferrous, earthy, the smell of ripening. She looked down into the bathwater and gasped. Blood was flowing from between her legs. Crimson paint of life, or death. But unmistakeably proof of flesh.

IN THE CAPITAL, MANUEL strolled wordlessly through Chapultepec Park. He admired locals out for a boat ride on the lake and families beside it, picnicking. He was amazed to see a red-tailed falcon flying not far overhead, and from beneath the Ahuehuete trees, imagined what it must've been like to be a wandering Aztec from the thirteenth century coming upon such an oasis. He followed the loud squawk of wild parrots to an empty stretch of parkland where he encountered no one else for fifteen minutes. This is the place, he thought, impressed that such natural beauty had been protected from the bustling urgency of the city surrounding it.

He crossed out of the park and headed towards the Condesa delegación, where he met the clean lines and easy curves of the Art Deco architecture. There, the gritty streets and crowded scenes, the lighted faces, were as inspiring as the park had been. Artists and Leftists made their homes in la Condesa, he knew, and there, among the bohemians, he felt his own creativity resurfacing. The first stanza of a new poem came to him whole, and he stopped by the side of the road and quickly jotted it down in his journal.

Thirsty and ready for a break from the sun, he stumbled into a café.

"Take any table," the waiter said, gesturing to the empty space.

Manuel sat at the nearest one, strewn with newspapers. He ordered hot chocolate and sweet bread and settled into reading. It had been twenty-four years, one editorial reported, since the Mexican constitution was passed. Another piece warned of dangerous divisions within the Left. Manuel decided to try to write a poem about that. He stretched his legs, and while he wrote he sipped his drink, tasting the sweet bite of cinnamon. Being away from the others, being in the company of his own mind, opened up a space inside of him; he could feel it already, the space wherein he might form meaningful words. He promised himself to take time alone more often.

After an hour of scribbling in his notebook, he stood and walked around the café, studying the artwork on the wall. There were posters — one red with a golden hammer and sickle on it, promoting the Mexican Communist Party, and the other, blue, advertising a music festival that had already taken place. Along the rear wall he found a display of black and white photographs by a local artist, depicting the neighbourhood. Each image presented a peculiar juxtaposition of subjects — a stony church and a prostitute leaning against it wearing nothing but a priest's black and white collar, a beautiful young mother, smiling, with a dead dog in her arms. The images were obviously staged, and the photographer, a surrealist; for a moment Manuel thought of Eugenia again, her way of looking at the world, and the poems of his she'd rejected. He wondered what she'd think of his "Birdsong" collection. He'd been pushing himself to take risks with non sequitur. It made sense, he thought, in the thematic contexts of love and flight that strange objects and distractions might appear out of nowhere.

At the end of the display there stood a high wooden barstool with a small book for viewer's comments, and a copy of *El Machete*, the Mexican Communist Party Newsletter. Flipping through it, Manuel learned that the café was a regular meeting place for party members who were affiliated with an artist's union. He flagged the waiter over. "When do the artists meet?" he asked.

"Monday nights."

"That's tonight," said Manuel, excitedly.

The waiter pointed to the bar. "There's a sheet of paper over there. If you want time on stage put your name down."

At the counter, Manuel stared at the paper contemplating the prospect of an audience. Could he read out loud to a room full of strangers? Perhaps if he wandered the neighbourhood for a few more hours, had a proper meal and returned. Still, his hand wouldn't lift the pencil. Reading in public could interrupt his recent progress. Then again, no one here would know him. He reached for the pencil and added his initials to the sheet. That way, he thought, he could change his mind at the last minute without being identified.

AT NIGHT, THE CAFÉ was bustling. Men and women sat at small square tables, drinking and singing and filling the place with the hollow noise of empty glasses. Most people obviously knew each other and Manuel felt out of place. He was reconsidering his reading when a woman he'd not seen before, with thick black braids wound up on top of her head, waved him to join her table. "Over here, Comrad!" she called through the crowd. At first, he wasn't sure she was speaking to him and he turned around to see if there was someone else behind. "No, you," she said, raising her voice and pointing sharply. "You mustn't sit alone." She motioned him to an empty chair next to her. "We can see you're new," she said, when he arrived at her side.

Manuel scanned the half-dozen faces looking up at him from around the table. "That's very kind of you," he said. Two tables had been pushed together to make a longer one, and he sat between the woman and a young man with a thin moustache. "Manuel García Caballero," he said, extending his hand.

"A Spaniard," chirped the man with the moustache.

Manuel nodded. "I manage a bullfighter who's been performing here," he said.

"Really?" said the woman. She assumed his profession marked him for a Nationalist. "I don't think we've ever had one of your kind in here."

"I'm not very good at it," Manuel laughed. "If that makes you feel any better."

"It does, a little," the woman admitted.

"My name is Jaime Sanchez," said the man with the moustache. "I'm a lithographer. She is Concepcion Pena Gutierrez. The photographer."

"Those are yours?" Manuel asked, pointing to the rear wall.

"Only if you like them," she teased.

Up close, Manuel could see the woman was older than him, in her early forties, he'd guess, and very attractive. Charming dimples appeared on her cheeks whenever she smiled. "I'm an aspiring poet," he said. "Lately, I find myself thinking a great deal about how an artist's life might inform his work."

"I would rather tell you how I became a Communist," she said. "Communism is my life."

"Are you party members?" Manuel asked, looking around.

"We're members of L.E.A.R," she said.

"The League of Revolutionary Writers and Artists," explained the man with the moustache. "Here, have a look." He tossed Manuel a publication entitled, *Frente a Frente*. "If you want to contribute, let us know."

Manuel flipped through the small magazine, reading titles of articles on communism and socialism, and before he could ask more questions, another man, this one with a head of tumultuous black hair, crossed the room and set down a wooden crate that was to be the small stage.

"Welcome Comrades," he said. "I will start tonight. I want to tell you about my woodcutting. With this art form I align myself with the campesinos, who continue to live in the tradition of good taste. Some of you know I admire the American cinema, but I've decided I will no longer be oppressed by its bourgeois, capitalist aesthetic."

The café burst into applause, and Manuel found himself clapping along with the others at his table, although he questioned the speaker's assumptions. Good taste was a political matter. He agreed. But the suggestion that folk art was a purer form of expression because it was connected with the peasant class made Manuel uneasy. Ironically, it reminded him of the Rightists' call at home for a return to purity and tradition.

The next man to take to the stage recited a story from memory about an injured construction worker who had no rights to compensation, and who, while bedridden and recovering, had been left by his wife and children. The worker survived his injuries, the storyteller said, but to what end?

Manuel enjoyed listening although the tale seemed to be more of a polemic than it was a well-crafted piece of art, and that bothered him. He hoped, with his poetry collection, to leave room for readers to form their own opinions. After the storyteller, a pretty, young essayist with hair the colour of wet sand hopped up onto the crate to deliver some scathing words about the editor of a right-wing magazine. At last, it was Manuel's turn.

He stood on the crate with his heart drumming inside his chest and the backs of his knees sweating. He was thinking his poems wouldn't be political enough for this crowd when he opened his notebook. The chorus of voices in the café faded to a whisper. People stared. "I'm a little drunk," he said, clearing his throat. "But not enough to forget that I am nervous." He took a deep breath and began to recite from "Birdsong."

*Love is an alphabet*
*an apple, in the beginning*
*bountiful temptation, I regret*

*still, I would marry on that cross*
*die a thousand deaths or more*
*to elevate my heart, such lofty measures*
*to fly above this besotted earthly floor*
*an albatross*
*an angel, forgotten*
*I would fly, and let my winged body cry.*

At first his delivery was stiff, airless — there wasn't enough breath behind his words to deliver them with conviction, but he quickly began to connect with his writing, follow it, rather than try and wrestle it into a performance, and that helped him to relax into the moment. Before he knew it, the trill of his rrrs came more easily, and the lushness of Andalucian poetry pressed out between his teeth. When he forced himself to look up from his pages, the audience appeared to be captivated. A feeling of elation overtook him, and he carried on with confidence. There was applause between the first and second poems and again when he was done, and he heard the woman with the braids shouting, "Bravo!" He closed his notebook and felt a little disappointed that his time on stage had gone by so quickly.

He spent the rest of the night, and early into the morning, discussing art and politics with his new friends. Having a community of intellectuals around him once again was inspiring, and he couldn't pull himself away. Before sunrise, he reluctantly said goodbye and promised to read their publication and return as soon as he was able.

Outside, the streets of la Condesa were slick with rainwater. A dog ate scraps of food and lapped water from the gutter. Despite the hour, Manuel wasn't tired. He was energized and inspired by his experience, and more than a little aroused. The woman with the braids had been enchanting, and over the course of the evening it had occurred to him that he would like to make love to her. The ache of desire in his body was palpable. He walked on breathing in the cool wet air. He passed a row of brightly painted houses and a dimly lit cantina filled with loud men. As he was about to flag a taxi to the hotel, he glimpsed three women down an alley, each with long black hair that shone in the light of the rising day. He stopped. Two leaned into a doorway smoking cigarettes. The third, older, sat on a chair in front of a red painted door wearing a man's oversized shirt and a look of boredom in her eyes. The shirt was unbuttoned and her naked chest exposed. Manuel stared. A crest of desire rose within him. He wanted her as he'd wanted the woman at the café, but had no idea how to make it happen. He took her in with his eyes; her body was beautiful enough, although what she offered was a transaction void of subtlety, more to his brother's liking, he thought, arrogantly. Would paying render the experience less erotic because of the whiff of desperation that surrounded it? His mouth watered and he swallowed hard. Recognizing his need, the woman sat up and kicked the red door ajar with her bare foot. "Come on, man," she said. "What are you waiting for?"

LUNA WAS HUNCHED OVER in the hotel bathroom, with her feet spread. She folded the cumbersome rag Marisol had left for her, into a long rectangle, and pulled it through the small pocket sewn into the crotch of her underwear. *How embarrassing*, she thought. *How humiliating!* She didn't want the men to know, and yet a flimsy ribbon on the open side of the pocket wasn't going to hold much in place when she was practising. She fiddled with the rag, awkwardly adjusting it while she fought back tears. Her body had betrayed her with cramps in her lower back and bleeding. And she'd bloomed. As if by some cruel destiny, she'd grown breasts — further reminders of her dubious place in the ring. She'd have to adjust her movements during a performance to accommodate her changing body. Already that first traje corto from the young novillero who'd died in the mud was too tight. She watched as red spots of blood fell onto the rag between her legs. The only time a man saw blood spilling out of his body was when he was injured. Was she injured? As a bullfighter, the idea offended her. She'd fought like a man, approached the penetration of the bull with her sword as men did, ritualistically, symbolically almost as though they were penetrating a woman, but she had become a woman. She tightened the ribbon and unhappily pulled up her underwear.

ARMANDO RECEIVED AN OFFER of a contract for the new plaza Santa-maría in Bogotá, Colombia, under the condition he fight Morillo, one of the largest fighting bulls of the day. The previous season, Morillo had killed an experienced bullfighter by goring him in the neck, and so the killer's mother had been slaughtered to ensure that no future tragedies were born. If Armando agreed to the fight, his international reputation would be secured. He'd receive top billing and twenty thousand pesos, a good sum of money.

"But what about the curse?" Luna said, as they walked out from under the covered training ring into the dying sun. "A torero who fights a bull that has killed is sure to be killed by a bull himself."

Armando waved her off. He wasn't prone to superstition. Despite a convent childhood, his lonely path had led him to shun belief in luck or fate or God, anything intangible that promised a home. Unlike most toreros, he believed solely in himself.

"I've trained diligently," he said. "I know the breed's temperament and I've heard about Morillo's quirks. He's not that imposing."

"Size comes from the father," Luna said. "But the danger is from his heart, and that's from the mother. There will be other contracts, Armando. Safer offers."

His face turned placid, as though shocked into submission. He disappeared behind his own eyes. "You don't believe in me?" He was more hurt than angry, and more ambitious than she knew. "You doubt me," he said.

"No, I don't."

She'd wanted to say, he shouldn't do it because if he were stolen by death she would be alone again. *Don't do it* she wanted to say, because she wasn't ready for such a challenge and if he was they could no longer remain in the same place. She still had much to learn from him; he was the lone person who understood, first-hand, what it was to wonder whether there was a lesser God for people like them. Instead, a long silence passed as they continued towards the house under a rusted sky. A perfume of sweet rind and fading sunshine wrapped around them and Armando looped his arm through hers.

"Luna, if I don't accept, Don Ramón will have no choice but to let me go. His reputation, the school's reputation. How would I survive? This is all I have. They've asked, but it's not a question."

"You could return to Spain with me next season," she said, disentangling from him. "We could perform there together. Don't you want to be confirmed in Madrid?"

His empty eyes were fixed straight ahead. His face, a grave. When he spoke again it was with the soullessness of one who was already gone. "All the skill you're acquiring," he spat. "Our talks of being successful, of becoming great matadors, and you would be willing to throw it all away as soon as a little fear sets in. You disgust me!"

"I'm not willing to throw you away."

"You should be."

Her heart beat against her chest as if to remind her she was still there. "Armando," she called after him. "Armando!"

Was it the practice of love she'd been fighting, in the ring at Don Ramón's? Not the bulls' inborn aggression or the blank horror of her own mortality, but the vulnerability that loving brings. Was she destined to fight for love and lose? Armando believed he was finished without taking a risk with Morillo and he was right.


STEPPING OFF THE AIRPLANE and onto the tarmac in Bogotá, Luna was met with a light rain and the overpowering scent of jasmine. An early evening fog dispersed like smoke, and through it, the Andes came into view. She felt the high altitude sitting inside her chest where air fell through her lungs, weightless, as though she wasn't breathing at all. Armando and his team had arrived two days earlier. Had his body had enough time to adjust?

Don Ramón lifted his fingers to his lips, whistled sharply. "Taxi!"

A black car pulled up with a small Colombian flag in its window, and the driver, a big man with the word, "Jesus," tattooed in black down the side of his neck jumped out and held a door open. "This city is a new Spain," Don Ramón said, climbing in beside her. "The Spain of the colonies. It is full of possibility." As they sped downtown, a feeling of dread began to swirl around inside of Luna's body. She hadn't wanted to travel with Don Ramón as her chaperone, but Manuel had been making great progress with his poetry collection and refused to break from the rhythm of his writing day. Pedro had made no offer to come. She looked out the taxi window and told herself not to be so anxious.

The buildings they passed were a mix of old and new, and sat next to one another as stubbornly as tombstones in a cemetery. The colour of the sky was gunmetal grey, and each face of a beggar child in the streets had its own cloud hanging over it. Luna couldn't tell whether the knot in her stomach was dread that Don Ramón would make a pass at her, or whether she sensed something more menacing on its way.

At the hotel restaurant the waitress wouldn't stop staring at her pants and the unwanted attention was annoying. Luna sat in silence while Don Ramón ordered for both of them, and when the meal arrived she drank her tinto and maracuya juice and ate bread with caldo. She tried to enjoy the clear soup with large chunks of potato and meat, and the mild flavour of cilantro teasing her tongue, but Don Ramón was gazing at her across the small table with a moony look in his eyes that made her squirm in her chair. "I didn't think Manuel was going to permit you to come," he said. "But he understands this is also an opportunity for you."

"Thank you for bringing me."

Don Ramón dunked a piece of bread into his soup, chewed slowly, sneaking a peek down her shirt. Luna resisted the urge to do up the top two buttons. Was this what Marisol had meant by thinking like a woman? "After the fight tomorrow I'll introduce you around," he said. "Perhaps, in the future, you will be invited to perform here."

Luna straightened, caught sight of Armando looking for them, and was relieved. "Mira, there he is now. Armando, over here!"

Armando strode towards them wearing his short suit and a broad smile. Restaurant patrons craned their necks to catch a glimpse of him. Having been notified of his arrival by the maître-d', the Colombian President stepped out of a private dining room, with security guards at his sides. Luna watched as he offered his hand to Armando. They shook, and exchanged a few words, and then the President returned to his meal. The maître-d' followed Armando to Don Ramón's table with a bouquet of calla lilies, and if Luna had any lingering doubts about the wisdom of Armando's choice to accept the contract, they vanished. "Hola," Armando said, embracing Don Ramón and taking the seat beside her.

"You look ready," she said, ignoring the superstition that prohibits discussion of a bullfight beforehand.

"We toured Santamaría today," he nodded. "It holds almost fifteen thousand people and still smells new. I am blessed to be among the first to perform there."

THE FOLLOWING AFTERNOON LUNA took her seat on a steel bench beside Don Ramón. The impressive Moorish entrance to the plaza de toros, which looked as if it had been transplanted directly from Andalucia, was deceptive and could not make up for the sterile space inside. The plaza was barely half full and that worried her. Part of a successful performance was the ability of the torero to feed off of the crowd's energy and connect with spectators. She wondered if Armando was thinking the same. "How did he look this morning?" she asked.

"Focused," said Don Ramón. He paid a vendor in the aisle for a stick of roasted corn-on-the-cob and a fresh pomegranate, passed her the fruit, already sliced in half.

She picked out the juicy red seeds, one after the other, and crushed them between her teeth. "Have you seen the bull? Is he as large as people claim?"

"You ask a lot of irrelevant questions," said Don Ramón. "If I didn't know better I'd think you were concerned about Armando."

"Aren't you?"

Don Ramón bit into his corn and shook his head. "As you know, my toreros are expertly trained and generously supported. The rest is up to them."

"Yes, Patrón," Luna said. But the sun had clearly hidden itself behind the clouds, and the modernity of the plaza erased the comforting history toreo was built upon. She couldn't so easily shake off the feeling that something bad was about to happen.

When Armando stepped onto the sand she watched his face for clues as to how he was feeling. There were none. His eyes sparked with the keen vision of a predator, his lips were parted; a sign he was generally relaxed and breathing well. As he swept his cape across the sand, she began to relax, although an ominous dark cloud moved in and shrouded the arena. It was time.

The chute flew open and out charged Morillo — a black thunderbolt with powerful legs and the thickest shoulders ever seen on a caste bull. Armando appeared to be unfazed, until a moment later when the earth shuddered and shifted with the tremulous beginnings of an earthquake, spooking Morillo. Luna didn't know if she'd imagined it, or if vertigo was looming, but hailstones as large as hens' eggs began to fall. Morillo bucked and kicked at the air, and in a disoriented panic charged indiscriminately — the burladero, the shadow of the Colombian flag on the sand, waving from the eastern edge of the arena, and at Armando, regardless of what he asked with his cape.

Luna prayed under her breath, and the vendor threw himself into a vacant seat nearby. "I have corn!" he cried. "Come and get your corn!" Hailstones landed and melted on the sand, creating wet spots, better traction for Morillo, and once he set his spirit to chasing Armando and Armando ran, Luna was on her feet with Don Ramón and the rest of the crowd.

"Regain control!" she shouted. Armando had dropped his cape and tripped and Morillo was charging straight for him, with the sharp tips of his curved cuernos aimed low. "Get him out of there!" someone hollered, and when other spectators turned around and stared, Luna realized it was her voice calling out the orders.

The vendor stood up. "Who wants water? Corn and pomegranate!"

At full speed, Morillo slammed into Armando, impaling him through the ribcage with both horns, and flinging him, like a ragdoll, high into the air.

Spectators gasped.

Luna reached for her crucifix with one hand and looked up to the sky, but God, if he existed, was in hiding; there was no hint of light anywhere.

Armando landed on his back with a horrifying thud.

Luna scrambled clumsily over the seats in front of her, rushing to the edge of the burladero. Frantically, she waved for the toreros on the sidelines. "Get in there, hurry! Before he charges again!" But it was too dangerous for anyone to enter the ring, and within seconds Morillo had charged for a second time. "No!" Luna screamed, as Armando flew towards the sky again, covered in his own blood.

The vendor and the crowd fell silent; all earthly creatures seemed to hold their breath and Luna heard the dreaded click in her mind that started the spinning. Armando landed on the sand, this time twisted and broken, and Don Ramón cried out, "Someone get the priest!" Spectators shrieked and turned their faces, but Luna didn't take her eyes off centre ring. Armando's neck was broken and his rib cage crushed, and yet he was still scrambling to get up, one dying eye fixed on the clouds, blinking ...

THEY BURIED HIM IN Mexico on his twentieth birthday, in a sarcophagus in the cemetery behind the Catedral of Nuestra Señora de la Asunción. Many people came to pay their respects. The nuns of the Santa Mónica convent, Don Ramón, some of his powerful friends, Armando's fellow students including the other Mexican torero from the school who'd been slated to share the bill with him that fateful afternoon, and had dutifully escorted his body home. Aficionados who'd been following Armando's career and two famous bullfight reporters also attended. His real family. His only family. With Pedro and Manuel on either side of her, stone pillars, and her cuadrilla an army behind, Luna stood at Armando's graveside trembling and dizzy as they placed a Colombian ruana and his best muleta across his casket, and though her heart tolled inside her chest, an iron bell, no one heard it.

After the funeral, Don Ramón was standing on the patio of his house looking out at the school, in a white suit and tan shirt. "Fate is a fickle whore," he said. He lit an expensive Cuban cigar and tossed the match into the flowerbed. The tiny leaves and stems of the gardenia shook and swayed, as though stifling sobs. Their scent became, for Luna, the scent of grief.

"No entiendo," she said. "I don't understand."

"One torero's misfortune is another's good luck, my dear." Don Ramón turned to her. "The school now has an opening for a star pupil."

"Armando is barely gone," Luna whispered. "We shouldn't speak of such things." Yet despite grief her heart pounded ambitiously; it was a rotten pulse, and that time it meant betrayal. "I'll be returning home in a few months," she added. "You have ten good Mexicanos. All with more experience than me, and all in need of sponsorship."

"But none as lovely," Ramón said, taking her hand in his.

She stared at their fingers entwined — Ramón's thick with grey veins, and hers, so much smaller. Her stomach clenched. An impulse to protect herself rippled under her skin. She scanned the room for Manuel and found him engaged in conversation with Javier González, one of the picadors.

Don Ramón blew large puffs of smoke up to the clouds and gave Luna's hand a squeeze. His gaze was polished with false sympathy. "Do not decide now," he said. "You have other things to pray on. But think of it soon." He sounded almost sincere, reassuring, although the gravelly bottom of his voice suggested otherwise. "Pedro tells me that by next season you could be ready to fight on foot," he pressed. "You will need contracts. I have the money and the friends. It would please me to take care of you."

"Manuel takes care of —"

"Give me your answer tomorrow," he interrupted.

She tried to steady her hands; it was as if the places on her body that could not hide or contain grief were the very places she needed to hold her reins, and her sword, and where she'd last held onto Armando. "Of course, Patrón," she said.

Don Ramón released her hand as spontaneously as he'd taken it up and she watched him make eye contact with Pedro, across the patio, while Pedro stuffed an empanada into his mouth. Whatever her new benefactor was proposing had already been agreed upon.

LUNA SPLASHED HER FACE with water from a wooden bowl in the guesthouse washroom and peered into the small mirror that sat atop the commode. In reflection, with the room spinning around her, she looked surprisingly out of place, surreal. She held on to the sides of the commode for balance. A moment later, she crept to her bedroom leaning against the wall for support, and fell into bed. Nauseous, she called out to Marisol who was in the kitchen preparing molotes and spiced coffee. "What's wrong?" Marisol asked when she stepped into the doorway. "Why do you cover your eyes with that pillow?"

"The light," Luna said. "I need an herbalist."

"I could ask Don Ramón?"

Luna shook her head, feeling worse. Who would be helpful without asking questions? "Talk to Chucho," she said. "But don't tell him it's for me."

Two days later, a slight man named Raul Nunez arrived at the rear door of the guesthouse smelling of garlic and echinacea. He had straight black hair and a long face, and skin the colour of burnt sugar. He wore bright white cotton pants and a shirt, and snake-skin boots. There were strands of turquoise, red, and black beads around his neck. The strap of a brown leather bag was slung across the front of his body as an aristocrat might wear a sash. Marisol ushered him through the kitchen, down the hallway and into the bedroom where Luna was still in bed.

Luna poked her head out from beneath the pillow. "I can't get up. I'm dizzy."

The man slipped the leather bag from around his neck and hung it on the spool-head of Luna's bed. He sat beside her. "How long have you been ill?" he asked.

Luna regarded him with curiosity. He had no hair on his face. There was a large gap between his two front teeth. Though the muscles in his arms were defined, he had a catlike build and his voice was a pitch too high for a man's. "A friend was killed last week," she said, quietly.

The herbalist reached over and placed his soft palm on her forehead, his two delicate fingers on the side of her neck to check her pulse. "Have you had the feeling before?"

"It usually lasts a few minutes. Sometimes an hour. What if it doesn't stop this time?"

"Any numbness in your face?"

"No."

"Ringing in your ears?"

Luna noted the herbalist's gentle, deliberate gestures. His legs were crossed at the knee. "None," she said.

"Try and sit up," he said. "Stick out your tongue."

Luna did as she was asked. The herbalist leaned in to take a closer look. "You're dehydrated," he said. Turning to Marisol he added, "She needs water."

"Do you know who I am?" Luna asked as soon as Marisol left the room. The herbalist nodded. "Then you understand you mustn't tell anyone about this; they won't let me perform."

"You need rest," he said. "And to stay out of the sun. I've seen it before." The herbalist tapped his forefinger on the side of his head as if discerning the connection between her mind and her body. "Your eyes are filled with grief," he added. "And fear. What are you afraid of?"

"Aren't you listening?" said Luna. "I will pay whatever you ask, but I need a remedy."

The herbalist lifted the flap on his leather bag, reached inside for a small bottle of oil, which he opened and rubbed all over his hands. The smell of eucalyptus, menthol, and clove was instantly calming. "This is for the treatment," he said. "Sit over there." He pointed to the chair Marisol occasionally sat in to mend clothes with her needle and thread. "Can you walk by yourself?"

Luna hesitated. She didn't want to move for fear of making the spinning worse. "What will you do?" she asked.

"I know about herbs, but I'm also a sobrador."

"Massage," she said. Paqui had occasionally massaged the

workers at Sangre Mio to help alleviate their aches and pains. She was willing to try anything.

Marisol returned with a glass of water as the herbalist was helping Luna into the chair. "Here," Marisol said, handing Luna the glass.

The herbalist stepped behind the chair. He rubbed his hands together vigorously to warm the oil and placed them upon Luna's head, with his thumbs pressing on the centre of her scalp. Gently, he massaged downwards and outwards, down and out. "We'll know more in an hour," he said. Once again Marisol left the room.

After a few minutes, Luna felt the tension in her neck and shoulders begin to pull away. She breathed in deeply, took in the gentle but firm fingertips that seemed to unwind her. Her hair and skin absorbed the oil, and before long the room smelled of eucalyptus and clove. The eucalyptus tingled on her skin, waking her senses. *Am I afraid?* she thought.

The herbalist placed his fingers behind her ears, and massaged there, in a circular motion. Luna closed her eyes and sank into the chair. If she hadn't seen him for herself, if she'd merely heard his high voice, she would've assumed it was a woman behind her, and when he pressed his thumbs into the back of her neck muscle, by her hairline, she forgot who she was too, and thought, *Am I afraid of death? Or, being permanently immobilized by vertigo? Maybe of being alone.* Her stomach turned and she opened her eyes. She was afraid of herself. She was afraid of feeling love, outside the ring, where she couldn't control it. "Stop," she told the herbalist. "That's enough."

The herbalist helped her into bed. He lifted the flap of his brown leather bag and revealed two small bottles, one labelled *bee venom*, and the other, *snake oil*, a string of garlic bulbs, and a half-full bottle of tequila. He pulled out a small cloth sac filled with dried leaves, from among a pile of sacs. "Mix one spoonful of this into boiling water with honey and drink it each hour for three days," he said. "It'll reduce your anxiety. Take no salt. No coffee and absolutely no sun."

A FEW DAYS LATER, when she was well enough to sit up without being sick to her stomach, Luna asked Marisol to bring a pen and some notepaper to her bed. Propped up on two pillows, she wrote to Paqui, relaying news of Armando's death, and explaining that she would be taking his place at the school. That meant staying away a little longer, she said, hoping Paqui would understand. She doodled a simple line drawing of herself in the centre of an arena, facing a bull on foot. *I miss you*, she wrote. *All the way to the stars and back.*

SUNDAY, ONE MONTH AFTER the funeral, at a table in a hotel suite in Zacatecas, Marisol slipped gaily between Pedro and Luna, handing each their coffee. Marisol floated and fluttered about like a woman in love. Her newfound levity offended Luna.

"You're in a good mood," she said, bitterly.

Outside, below the open window, cars sped through the main avenue and a throng of voices confirmed that anticipation for the fiesta was growing. In an hour the cuadrilla will gather to discuss strategy for Luna's fight, which capote passes would be best, the personality of the crowd. Her mozo de estoques will be in charge, giving orders to the others.

Too tense about performing to feel hunger, Luna was picking at a chilaquiles that Marisol had fetched from the restaurant downstairs. Would she be able to focus on Fortuna, and visualize the moment when the bull entered the ring, or would she lose her balance and become the school's next casualty? It had been a mere two days without dizziness, and she hadn't slept more than a few hours at a time since the funeral. If she fought today she could very well be killed. Was that the answer to the guilt she felt for being the one who survived?

"If you're tossed," said Pedro, to provoke laughter and break the tension of the morning, "remember to smile and wave at the ring promoter as you fly before him in the stands."

"Pedro!" Marisol swatted him. "Don't say such things. No one will be tossed."

He nudged Luna. "I hear the bulls are ferocious."

"Mexican bulls are the most docile," she said, flatly. "Manuel says so all the time, don't you?"

Manuel lifted his eyes from the latest edition of *Frente a Frente* that he was reading. "You look ashen," he said. "Did you not sleep?"

Luna took a sip of coffee, and her nervous hands spilled some on the table. "Some," she said. "It was hot."

Manuel had also been awake for most of the night, absorbed in a poem, metaphors and similes sparking out of him. For once he hadn't worried about the quality of the material, and tried to keep his pen moving. This morning he could see the dark circles beneath Luna's eyes, and an uncharacteristic self-doubt within them. "You're not Armando," he said softly. "You don't share his fate."

Luna nodded, unconvinced.

"I slept very well," Pedro said, grabbing Marisol around the waist and pulling her down onto his lap. He gave her a proprietary squeeze. "Tell them," he said.

Marisol looped her arm around his neck and kissed him on the forehead. She lifted her hand and waved her ring finger for Manuel and Luna to see. "Vamos a casarnos," she announced.

Manuel was on his feet in a flash, embracing them. "Felicitaciones! What good news." He kissed Marisol on both cheeks and winked at Luna. "Now I'll have two sisters."

"Yes, congratulations," Luna said, sounding less than enthusiastic. It was the first time Manuel had spoken of her as his sister without it having to do with her career, and she was forced to share the title. "Does Chucho know?"

"Don't preoccupy yourself with contracts," said Pedro. "A wedding can wait until next season, when we've secured our reputations. My parents will want to sail for a wedding." Marisol's expression shifted slightly; the decision had not been hers.

Manuel reached for his mug and lifted it to make a toast. "Luna, raise your cup," he said. "When did your heart grow so hard?"

She did as he asked, though her heart was no longer an organ made of muscle, but a grey stone in her chest. "May your future together be long and happy," she said.

"And filled with babies," interrupted Marisol.

Pedro lifted the coffee to his lips and grinned. "To making babies."

Marisol blushed, though she was looking beyond her gold ring at Luna, and her eyes were victorious. She thought marriage would make Pedro hers and hers alone, but she was mistaken; not even a contract with God could guarantee that; love belongs to no one, Luna knew, and Pedro was capable only of being faithful to himself.

LUNA WAS KNEELING INSIDE the crude chapel of the bullring, before a single burning candle, praying to the Virgen de la Tlaxcala Macarena for protection.

"There you are," Chucho said, entering. "It's almost time for the paseo."

"I can't," she whispered. "No puedo," she repeated, sounding as certain as she'd ever been of anything.

Chucho towered over her, unmoved by her protest. "Get up," he said. "You've drawn Dolor."

She lifted her head and the chapel tilted, slightly. This is it, she thought, *I'm to be killed by a bull named for his sorrowful stance.* Her hands began to tremble. "Where's the priest?" she asked. "Look?" She held them out for him to see. "Soon it'll be the same and worse inside."

Chucho grabbed her by one arm and yanked her onto her feet. "I told you to stand!"

"Don't touch me!"

They both knew there was no shame in fear, though much in admitting to it. "Gather yourself," he told her. "You can't enter the ring in this state."

"You heard what happened to Armando!" she shouted. "Doesn't anyone care! Morillo ripped him apart. A front-page photograph in El Tiempo and a minute of silence is all he got for his life."

Chucho squinted through his impatience, to understand her better. "Armando is not the last one you'll see killed, Luna. You are a student of death. Learn from it. It chases us all. Armando faced death with honour."

"I know about death," she said. "Tell them I'm ill. Make something up. Maybe people are right what they say," she tried weakly. "Because I'm a girl."

"Stupid bitch!" Chucho's bird-claw hand stung her cheek. "How dare you," he said. "We've all worked hard. Do you mean to make fools of us? Have we wasted our time and risked our reputations for nothing?"

"No," she said, stunned by his words and the force of his blow.

"It's not up to us who lives and who dies," said Chucho. "Armando knew that. He received the Colombian president before he was gored; the hotel lobby where he was staying was full of flowers. Can I say that about myself if I die today? Can you?" He took Luna sharply by one arm and led her out of the chapel, past the enfermería where the médicos had arranged their instruments and removed their white gowns as a gesture of solidarity and confidence in the bullfighters. They passed animated reporters on their way to the stands, photographers from the papers adjusting their cameras, toreros helping each other to drape their embroidered parade capes over their shoulders and tuck them under their arms. When they heard the announcement of the arrival of the bullfight association president, Chucho released her in the patio of

the cuadrillas. "You're El Corazón," he said. "And there's a contract to fight this afternoon. You know what to do." He stepped
behind her mozo de espada and Fortuna. "Now, do it!"

For a moment she wanted to run, leave her horse and cuadrilla,
and her pride, and flee to some safe place, but where was that place?
The crowd in the plaza applauded and chanted for the fiesta to
begin. She heard the picador's spurs clinking on his stirrup and she
turned around cautiously, as though Armando was behind her, his
breath pressed to her neck. He'd been a brief, beautiful accident
she'd fallen upon, but his love wasn't hers to hold; the threat of
vertigo reminded her of that. She was a bullfighter, her job was to
take the pain of loss and turn it into something hard and glittering.
*Out there*, she thought, looking into the arena. *That's where I am
meant to be loved.* She reached into her pocket and pulled out a
slice of fresh ginger, placed it on her tongue as a priest places the
host at communion. The familiar sun hit her, warming her features.
She forced herself to turn inward, visualize a large, round clock and
herself, stepping into time. "San Juan de Ávila," she whispered as
the trembling in her hands stopped. "Patron Saint of Andalucía.
Today, I need protection." Amidst the others in their colourful suits
and the singing of the national anthem, she crossed herself. At precisely four o'clock, when the bugle blew and the band began to play
a pasodoble, the doves were released from the stands and she felt
she was being propelled upward, onto Fortuna by instinct. She took
her place and proceeded to make the paseo with the others.

Dolor was a wild, fiery, calcetero, dark grey with white feet, and
an unusually long, ratty-looking tail. His horns were widely separated, and their tips the colour of molten lead. When he charged
into the ring Luna saw the Laguna brand, the mark of the premier
ganaderia in Mexico, burned into his hide. *He would rather die
fighting*, she thought, *than relent*. She kicked Fortuna hard, asking
her to gallop around the ring. Dolor chased them.

After two circles of the bullring, Dolor slowed. He stopped on the
sunny side to catch his breath and Luna passed by the president's

palco. She tipped her hat and saw that behind the palco, beyond the bullring, sat the city's ancient limestone viaduct. She turned, gave a quick kick, and moved Fortuna to the chalk line.

Gripping the reins in her left hand and the red and white pole in her right, Luna again kicked Fortuna. They galloped straight for Dolor and then, from two feet away, turned at a sharp angle. Dolor skidded, and raced to catch up. Seconds later, his head was so close to Fortuna's hindquarters that her tail swiped him in the face. Twisting around in her saddle, Luna kept her eyes on his horns. "You won't scratch this horse," she muttered under her breath. She lifted the rejón high and brought her arm down fast, placing it on his back. Dolor slowed, surprised by the stabbing pain, and stopped in centre ring.

Luna galloped past the burladero and showed Chucho two fingers, indicating two rejones. When she came around again, he held them out, and she grabbed both in one hand. She wound the reins around the horn of her saddle. A moment later she and Fortuna moved to the shady side, and taunted Dolor.

He charged at top speed.

Luna held one rejón in each hand, clung onto Fortuna with her knees. When she had a clear view of Dolor's withers, she lifted herself out of her saddle, leaned forward, and simultaneously placed both rejones on his back.

"Bravo!" she heard someone cheer. She craned her neck to see who it was and found Don Ramón standing ringside between a reporter and a photographer.

Luna was pleased. She easily placed three rejones, and the rejón de muerte, the killing lance. When Dolor finally fell onto his knees, she leapt off Fortuna's back and ran to him. She stood before him, moving her hands in front of his face as if to dare him to rally. Only when he collapsed at her feet, disoriented, did she see the sorrow in his eyes that had earned him his name. She lifted her arms in victory, and the crowd cheered. The lens of the photographer's camera was aimed at her, and she turned to pose for a picture.

WHEN LUNA WAS NINE years old, she'd followed Manuel up the mountain behind the ranch house, without him knowing. The wind was strong and warm, and their steep path cut with heather. They passed a denuded cork forest where hundreds of bright sienna trees stood with their trunks exposed and vulnerable, the unharvested tops as steely grey and wrinkled as the skin of an elephant. Luna heard the far away clanging of tin bells as a herd of sheep grazed in a pasture. The higher she climbed the cloudier it got, and the air thinned. Manuel stopped at the mouth of a cave where an old farmer stood picking at moss growing on the rock face. Luna hid behind a giant boulder.

"What do you want?" the man barked in an odd voice that came more from his chest than his throat. Luna peeked and saw that he looked weary as he walked over to Manuel. "There's nothing in there except broken tools," he said.

"I've heard otherwise," said Manuel.

"If bat shit is a treasure, I suppose you heard right."

"People say there are paintings."

"Oh that." The farmer nodded and stretched his arms out at his sides to show the scale.

"Charge me entry," Manuel said. "I'll pay to see them."

The old man's mouth fixed into a grimace. "From time to time your father buys goats from me," he said. "Why does he send his son to insult me? You tell Don Carlos this is my sanctuary. There's no hidden treasure here, and no more goats either."

Luna popped out from behind the boulder. "Don Carlos needs nothing from you," she said.

"Luna, you shouldn't have followed me!" said Manuel.

"But I was afraid you wouldn't return."

The farmer pointed at her. "You're the orphan of Sangre Mío?"

"The one," she said, fanning the heat with her hands.

Manuel pulled her to stand properly before the man. "I present, Luna García Caballero," he said, lending her his family name, and she noticed that one of the farmer's eyes was brown and the other milky white, including the pupil, as though a small cloud sat over top of it. She made an obligatory curtsey.

"I'm Francisco Pintado," he said, almost deferentially. "I've heard about you. You were born on the greatest day of the year. Maybe you bring luck to my crops?"

"Maybe," she shrugged.

Francisco observed her with his one good eye as though he might find evidence of magic or a miracle on her face, though what he saw was the dark skin and tired eyes of an indentured servant not unlike himself. He bent down with breath smelling of rotten goat meat, and peered closely. Behind his cloud eye there was an outline of another eye peeking through. "To her, I will give a tour of the cave."

"If she goes in so do I," said Manuel.

The cave was blacker than black, and slippery. They squinted to see by Francisco's oil lamp and Luna held onto Manuel as they descended the crude staircase through an odourless fog. She ran her hand along the damp wall but withdrew it instantly, as though she were touching a living thing. Trampling her fear, she reached out for it again.

"Are you sure he isn't crazy?" she whispered.

"Sí, está bien."

Francisco held the lamp high over his shoulders and the flame blazed in his milky eyeball. "Look, he said, illuminating a veil of bats as they swooped out of the lamp's glare. Luna ducked, but clumsy wings grazed her forehead and she squealed. Francisco's deep, raspy laugh echoed throughout the chamber and Luna looked up again. The cave was partially aglow and their shadows loomed like giants on one wall. "It's one hundred feet high," Francisco said. "Sixty wide. I've measured the best I can. I believe this is where they slept. There are other rooms," he said, "but what you want to see is over there." He swung his lamp and on another wall, in faded red dye, Luna found the unmistakeable outline of a bull.

She stepped closer. The length of the bull's horns was exaggerated, as were his genitals, and his legs had been drawn in such a way that he appeared to be charging. She examined his dark eye, set at an angle that evoked sorrow as much as the instinct to fight. A strong, hot draft blew through the cave and she leaned into it, as though allowing her body to be passed back and forth between God's capable hands while He decided what to do with her next.

Beside her stood an enormous stalagmite with a companion stalactite above it, stretching down. She watched as a single drop of water prepared to fall from the tip of one pillar onto the tip of the other. It looked, to her, as though the cave was crying.

"They've been trying to come together like that for centuries," said Francisco. "At this rate it'll take another thousand years before they succeed."

Luna reached up, caught the fallen tear in her palm. It was warm. All at once, she felt lightheaded. The air was thick and she struggled to breathe.

"Get me out of here," she said.

Francisco led them out along a slippery incline made of quartz, and through a narrow passage where minerals and stone had formed a wall of curtains. He banged his fist against each hard fold, sending vibrations along the curtain that made alluring organ music. A moan, a tang, again an echo. Outside, Luna and Manuel said their goodbyes and walked the long walk down and around the mountain to the ranch house in silence.

DRIVING BACK TO DON RAMÓN'S after the fight in Zacatecas, Manuel handed Luna a telegram written by his mother and dictated by Paqui. *Sometimes at night when I look at your empty bed I am very sad*, Paqui had said. *Then you send news of your success and I am happy again. I know the world is your arena now, but I belong to Sangre Mio. Luna, come home to me.* Luna fiddled with the telegram, felt a sharp-edged tweak of remorse. She read the words a second time before folding the telegram, and quietly slipping it into her pocket.

MARISOL WORE THE MOST brilliant, candle-white wedding gown, and Doña García's antique lace mantilla. At the family's request, Paqui had made the gown from two bolts of satin and packed it in a trunk to cross the ocean. It had taken an entire month to embroider the bodice using silver thread, and another month to sew on each crystal bead. As Marisol glided down the aisle on Chucho's arm, with the cathedral train flowing out behind her, she shimmered, light itself.

There were easily three hundred guests at the reception — Mexicans, a few Spaniards and Colombians, one famous Argentine promoter, friends who'd been invited by the cuadrilla, or by Don Ramón. It was an uncomfortable turn of events for Luna to find herself in the background of activity, not to be the focus of all eyes. Most awkward was the role reversal between her and Marisol, for it had become Luna's job as Dama de Honor to tend to Marisol's needs. "Are you thirsty," she'd ask, wearing the pale yellow dress Marisol had begged her to wear. Is your corset too tight?" Marisol accepted the attention gladly, sometimes making demands simply to see Luna struggle. Perhaps to punish Luna for all the things she'd had to do for her.

It was Marisol's day after all, the day she'd been waiting for since they'd met, and probably longer, but Luna was resentful. Being cast in the role of maid of honour reminded her of being a servant and all she wanted to do was escape. "Look what I've accomplished," she complained to Manuel. "I risk my life each Sunday and all Marisol does is marry. Why should she have a party?"

Marisol was oblivious to Luna's resentment, exalted, delirious, and if she had any doubts or fears about marrying Pedro they didn't show.

They were standing outside, on the lawn at Don Ramón's school, waiting for the photographer to focus his camera — Manuel, Chucho, and Pedro on one side of Marisol, Doña García and Don Carlos and Luna on the other.

"What is it?" Luna asked, adjusting Marisol's train.

"Mi madre," Marisol said, her voice breaking.

Luna peered up at the blue sky, directly into the sun, to conjure Paqui's face. She needed a mother herself today and, until recently, hadn't thought it possible for an orphan to miss anyone as much as she missed Paqui. She had been mistaken. A sluice of light pulsed through the dense branches of the overhanging fir tree, brightening the place where she stood; connecting her to the past she'd left behind through its pale charge. "You're not alone," she said, as the photographer lifted his camera.

AFTER THE MEAL, MANUEL stood with his parents under a large white tent where a mariachi band played. Seven men in silver studded charro suits, with wide-brimmed hats, played songs of desire with a quality of longing that could break the hardest of hearts.

"Qué buenos, no?" Don Ramón came up behind them with a lit pipe hanging from between his lips. "What do you think?"

"It was good of you to find them," said Carlos. "The one on vihuela is most impressive."

"Yes, but he's no Salamancan," said Manuel.

"Aiy," scolded Doña García. "Not politics tonight, por favor."

"What politics?" Manuel said. "The charros come first from Spain, tú sabes."

"No Spaniard ever made a serenade as good," said Don Ramón. "We're too proud for it. Look how they play to the women."

The two on violin and the two on trumpet walked towards Marisol, and the others followed to surround her. The one on guitarron bent his knee and played at her feet while she laughed and danced for him. Pedro feigned jealousy.

"I would've made them a proper wedding at home," said Carlos.

"They're young," said Don Ramón. "Waiting is an eternity for the young."

"This is true," Carlos laughed. "When did we become old men?

"I think it was yesterday," said Don Ramón, pointing at his white hair.

Doña García swatted him. "You have made a good life here. Be proud of this school."

Don Ramón sucked on his pipe, puckered his lips, as though savouring the compliment. He fidgeted with his wristband, admiring his gold watch. "This country has rewarded me generously," he said. He turned to Manuel. "What about you? How will you make your name?"

"He's a poet," said Carlos, flatly. "A brilliant poet." He met his son's dark eyes, caught the shadow of injustice hovering there and once again knew he'd been harsh. He couldn't stop himself. Maybe because Manuel was the firstborn, or because he was the one who challenged authority? But no, it wasn't any of that, nor was it that Manuel hadn't become a bullfighter. It was about Luna. Because he couldn't openly love her, he'd held all of his children at a distance.

Don Ramón tried to conceal embarrassment for his old friend. "Yes," he said. "I knew that. Remind me, what have you published?"

Manuel's face flashed red. The one thing worse than struggling to create art was defending it. "I hope to have a collection finished by next year," he said.

"Marvellous." Don Ramón glanced at his wristwatch again, noted the hour. "My staff tell me you receive many letters and telegrams," he added. "Maybe there's a girl back home?"

Manuel shook his head. "Good friends who keep me informed."

"In that case," said Don Ramón. "I will introduce you to the daughter of a colleague. She's got a dog's face but she's smart enough, and her hips will bear you children."

Manuel's heart compressed. He resisted the urge to rail against the unspoken assumption that he was a pathetic waste of skin. "You make a tempting offer," he said. "Perhaps you should keep her for yourself."

"Manuel!" his mother whacked him with her fan. "Apologize."

"For what should I apologize?"

"Por ser bocón, hombre! For you being a big mouth."

"That's all right, Helena," said Don Ramón. A minute later he jostled Carlos. "Good that you've got one with talent, hmm?"

Carlos stiffened. It was one thing for him to disparage his son and another thing altogether for someone else to do it. He flicked at the fingernails of one hand with his thumb as though discarding stanzas in a poem, along with his manners. "A man wants to find his own way," he said. "It's natural."

Manuel lifted his eyes; grateful and surprised that his father had bothered to defend him. "I want to write other things too," he said, emboldened. "Essays about the class struggle."

"Struggle?" his mother scoffed, indignantly. "You sound like a communist."

"A socialist, Mama."

Until recently, Manuel hadn't truly understood what his family's privilege meant, or how it shaped his view of the world. Intellectually he knew. He'd read books by scholars on the plight of peasants. He'd combed over articles on the role of the Army and Church in maintaining social order. He'd debated with educated

friends. But watching Luna train as a bullfighter, seeing her development in the ring, her skill and courage, and her dedication changed
that, and turned over any lasting notions he held onto about life
being a meritocracy. It wasn't. Luna worked hard for what she
wanted, harder than he had or would ever need to, and for her there
was no guarantee of success. Being born with nothing, controlling
nothing, seemed to be her greatest motivator and he believed others
of her class would also succeed, given the chance to realize their
dreams.

"You want to shame me, is that it?" said his father.

"I welcome reform."

"The Republic had its chance! They destroyed the economy
and inflamed tensions. I've made major concessions to my men."
He turned to Don Ramón. "There is a serious workers movement
gathering strength in the south. Some of my men go to meetings. I
want no violence at Sangre Mío."

"Will it come to that?" asked Doña García. "Surely it can't."

"Take caution, Carlos. You are highly regarded. You have no need
to align yourself with trouble. Remind them of who is in charge
or the ranch could suffer. Business hinges on our reputations; you
know that."

"This is what I tell him," said Doña García. "He won't listen."

Don Ramón's posture stiffened, his face wrinkled with disapproval. "I see where Manuel gets his sympathies."

"I'm no Republican," said Carlos. "I'm a Christian, but with
some complaints. I try to be fair."

"Spaniards sent a clear message in the last election," said Don
Ramón.

"We were swindled out of those seats," said Manuel. "A hungry
man can't vote honestly with his landlord's armed thugs hanging
around the voting urns."

Doña García snapped her fan shut, tapped it against her hip, in
time with the music. The tenor of the conversation was growing
tedious, and she'd been three hours without slaking her thirst.

"I would like to dance at my son's wedding," she said. "Which one of you politicians will escort me?"

In Ramón's arms Helena felt young again, free, which was foolish, since she was an unhappily married woman. She couldn't remember the last time her husband had held her — a long, long time ago perhaps. She wasn't sure. Don Ramón spun her around twice, and she saw Carlos standing beside Manuel, both of them looking as though they'd rather be somewhere else. A feeling of profound emptiness came over her, a terrible calm that follows a tragedy. It was the feeling she normally drank down. She fixed on Don Ramón's pockmarked face; it wasn't nearly as handsome as her husband's but it was, she assumed, an honest representation of the man who wore it. "Luna is not my daughter," she said, as the band brought the high-pitched serenade to an end. "You should know."

DON RAMÓN SIDLED UP to Luna with a calculated look in his eyes. "From here, Spain feels like another world."

"Sometimes," she said. "I miss it." She admired the expensive weave of his grey-striped suit, his crisp shirt and suspenders, the shiny gold cufflinks. She stopped herself from picking lint off his shoulder. "You're dressed like home tonight," she said.

"Soon it'll be your turn," he said, gesturing with his chin to Marisol. "Or are you to be married to your bulls?"

Luna looked away, beyond the dance floor, across the lawn, to the covered training ring. It would be prudent to pay him further compliments, and yet, she couldn't think of one. "Have you secured any fights for me on foot?" she asked instead.

"You know, seeing you dressed as you are, it's hard to remember you're the same girl who faces the bulls." He ran the back of his hand along the sleeve of her dress and she stiffened. He took her chin in his hand and raised it so she met his eyes directly, and all at once she wasn't El Corazón anymore, or a servant girl, but a nervous and inexperienced young woman, without parents or brothers to protect her. His meaning was undeniable and it frightened her that he would make such a gesture in public. She wanted to run but that would've drawn attention, or been an admission of fear, so she faced him head-on.

"Someone might see," she said. Then, she allowed him to lead her out from under the tent, inside the foyer of the house, and through the servants' kitchen where five girls her age and younger were busy clearing empty plates and washing and drying glasses and cutlery. She averted her gaze the way visitors to Sangre Mio once averted theirs. She couldn't acknowledge them, couldn't show them they were visible to her, because that would've meant acknowledging her past. Besides, she knew her recognition made no difference to their daily existence and might've been interpreted as condescending.

At the end of a corridor Don Ramón found his office with the Tlaxcala coat of arms, and the splintered cuernos of an enormous Rancho Seco bull mounted above the door. Inside, in the dark, he pressed her backwards, stumbling around his large wooden desk, until a wall closed in behind her. "I think of you often," he confessed. "During the day. In my sleep." His breath was wet and heavy with the smell of pipe tobacco.

Cautious, she permitted him to press his chest to hers, stroke her face and hair. Would this be enough to secure her next season? He slipped one arm around her waist and held her tightly, and before she knew what he was doing Don Ramón had unzipped his pants and was urgently guiding her hand inside his trousers. She met the silkiness of his skin. He was instantly vulnerable to her in a way she did not desire. She tried to pull her hand away but he held it there.

"Please?" he begged. "I can't wait any longer."

"We should go," she said, all the while giving him a firm squeeze.

He groaned and moved to kiss her, but she refused him her lips; his sex in her hand was a rejón or a muleta she could control but his mouth on hers would've been too much of a threat. The power she had in that situation, maybe the only power a woman has over a man, lay precisely in not giving all that was wanted. She held and stroked him until her eyes adjusted to the dark and his face turned warm against her own and his breath came hard, hard and he said, "I must have you." He grew more aroused and absent and pressed his fat lips to the side of her neck. "I must tame you," he whispered, and in one great jerk forward, he slumped against her body.

*Tame her!*

She eased him off, and slipped out from under his formidable weight. Her hand was wet and she rubbed the viscous film between her fingers and raised them to her nose. The smell was as skunky as the bleach she'd once used for washing clothes.

"There's no need to worry what the others will think," he said, fixing his trousers. "I want for us to marry."

"No," she blurted, before she could stop herself.

She was sickened by his graceless show of weakness and the evidence of such weakness that he'd left in her hand: he assumed he could have her for his woman as easily as he'd assumed she'd accept his offer of sponsorship after Armando's goring. She felt a shudder of shame, for her complicity, and knew this time she couldn't give him what he wanted, and if she could he'd remain unsatisfied; any man ruled by acquisition grows hungrier and hungrier the more he acquires. She was the same; the more skill she gained on foot the wetter her appetite for it had grown.

"Our families have been friends a long time," he said, pressing her.

"No," she repeated.

"Think carefully before you cause regrets." He reached for her, stroked her hair. "I will build the biggest house in Mexico," he said. "You'll have servants and all the dresses you desire. I am your servant, Luna García."

"I don't want a house," she said. "I don't need a dress."

"You would be the envy of other wives."

She pushed his hand aside. "Ramón," she whispered. "Please stop."

"Not until you agree," he said.

"But I don't love you!"

His eyes flashed with anger, he stepped away from her. "I know who you are," he said. "I know all about your scheme. Very clever. I thought it was odd that I'd not heard of Carlos having a daughter. What frauds! And you, you are a two-faced nothing, passing for a García, with all that their privileges allow."

"I don't know what you're talking about," she said, panicking, and fighting an old expectation that she buckle under a crippling sense of inferiority; she'd worked too hard and come too far for that. If she gave into it now she might as well have stayed in Spain.

"Don't play innocent with me," he said, spitefully. "Surely, a dirty little rag like you wouldn't expect a better offer? I could ruin you in a day."

Luna's stomach turned, she wondered who'd told him and how much he knew. "It's true that without your sponsorship I wouldn't be fighting on foot," she said, trying to control the tremor in her voice. "I am grateful. But each time I place myself in front of a charging bull I repay the debt. I owe you nothing more." She lifted her gaze defiantly. "Go ahead and tell," she said. "Stain your reputation." She turned and hurried out of his office.

Down the corridor, she stopped outside the servants' kitchen to lean against the wall. Should she find Manuel and tell him what had happened? Would there be consequences for refusing Don Ramón? At Sangre Mio whenever she'd dared to argue with Doña García or had refused to be intimidated by her, some form of punishment would inevitably follow — a week of cold, alienating silence, unreasonable demands that kept her scrubbing floors or pots for hours until her hands and fingers were raw. *"No" is the most dangerous word*, she thought, *for it's only once you've said no to someone that you truly discover what they're capable of.* She heard Don Ramón's office door slam and his leather heels fast approaching. She swung open the kitchen door and stepped inside.

Five girls looked up from their workstations: two drying glassware and bowls and setting them upside down on the shelf to dry. Another two were washing plates at a double sink. The youngest was polishing silverware at the table and setting the utensils into a felt-lined box.

"I need to wash," Luna said, lifting her hands to show what she meant.

The girls at the sink stepped away, made a place for her.

She turned on the hot water tap, lifted a thick bar of soap. She could feel their eyes watching, as if they knew the stain she was trying to remove. *Had they, too, been led into Don Ramón's office?* Luna looked down at the water scalding her hands and the idea enraged her. Don Ramón profited from them, as he did from her. They were all here to serve his needs. She turned off the tap. Compared with these girls she had been lucky, but all her success in the bullring hadn't changed the way even one man saw her.

"Here," said the youngest girl, holding out a dishtowel.

Luna turned, accepted the towel and dried her hands. "Thank you," she said. She set the towel on the counter beside the sink and slipped out of the kitchen, and down the corridor, while outside, the mariachi band still played.

CARLOS HAD STEPPED AWAY from the music and the celebration, where the night air warmed him and helped him to relax. At first, the visit to Mexico had been exciting, but he was beginning to feel he should be tending things at home. He looked out across Ramón's property and by moonlight saw the rough outline of the Huamantla Sierra in the distance. This place, like Sangre Mio, sat safely in a valley, and being surrounded by mountains had often been a comfort to Carlos, as though the natural world helped wall in his heart. Here he was feeling landlocked and vulnerable, too far from an ocean.

Ramón's suggestion that he was weak with his workers had angered him, and yet he knew he was. Over the years, he would see the field girls hauling water at Sangre Mio, or catch sight of a peasant skirt blowing in the wind, and he'd remember Elisenda. Her beauty and boldness, her ability to bear happiness. Loving someone who wasn't his equal had made him more human. He could lie about Luna, but he couldn't deny the humanity of her class.

Such were the thoughts he was having when Don Ramón fell into the chair beside him, with two glasses of spiked pulque.

Carlos accepted the fermented cactus juice and lifted it to his lips. Ramón guzzled his. "Why did you lie to me about the girl?" he asked.

Carlos's neck and face flashed red. His heart lodged in his throat. "Helena told you?" he said, fiddling with the glass in his hand. When Ramón didn't respond he said, "No importa. I've been thinking of how to tell you myself. How to apologize. I shouldn't have agreed to this scheme in the first place; vanity made me do it."

"But a housemaid, Carlos? Jesus! How could she bring you any honour?"

Carlos felt his throat constrict. His wife hadn't told the whole story; she'd merely forced his hand. Setting his drink on the ground, he dragged his chair closer to Ramón's. "There's more you don't know," he said. "Luna doesn't know." Ramón waited for him to continue. "She is mine."

Ramón stared, as the meaning of these words shuffled through his brain. All at once, he burst out laughing. "Qué Cabrón! You bastard!"

Carlos lowered his voice, leaned in closer. "Have you never done something because you were compelled? I didn't set out to deceive you; she had the talent my boys didn't have. She was my one chance for glory."

Ramón removed his suit jacket; lay it across his lap deliberately, calculating what strategy, in this turn of events, would serve him best. "If you thought I wouldn't agree to a maidservant attending my school, you were right, but she's here and she's earning more than the other toreros." He cleared his throat. "From now on, this will be business. I'll want a percentage of her earnings."

Carlos was taken aback. He wanted to refuse, but any lie, including a self-serving one leaves us in its debt. "Pedro will ask questions," he said.

Ramón nodded. "There's no need to involve him. Pay me directly."

ONE SUNDAY MORNING IN February, with no fight scheduled, Luna was tucked into the window of the guesthouse living room, legs bent at the knee and her arms hugging them. Don Ramón had been acting as though nothing had changed between them and she'd been maintaining the charade and with it, his honour, although recently she'd decided that if the truth about her past did spread, so what? She was a professional bullfighter, a fact that couldn't be ignored; her public wouldn't care about the rest. But she was still plagued by a superstitious feeling that in rejecting a proposal of marriage by the man who'd sponsored her career, she might've condemned herself to a future without love, any sort of love at all.

Marisol had gone to church and Manuel had taken Chucho along to some gathering of Leftists in the capital. Pedro was sitting at a table in the guesthouse, drinking his way through a bottle of tequila although it was eleven o'clock in the morning. "You look like a thundercloud," he said.

Luna ignored his drunken ill humour. Outside, a young couple kissed fervently. The man was a student from the school but she'd not seen the woman before. "Pedro," she said. "Why do men love?"

He looked up at her with blood-shot eyes, surprised — no, amazed — by the question. Not once had she sought his opinion on anything unrelated to bullfighting.

"Aren't you asking the wrong brother?"

"You're the one who is married," she said.

Pedro laughed, his face flushed with drink. "Marriage has nothing to do with love."

"I should've known better than to ask," said Luna.

He peered overtop of his bottle, circled the top of the neck with his thumb. "A man has needs," he said. "He can try and ignore them, deny them, abuse them, but he's drawn to fulfill them like a bull is drawn to the cape."

Luna rubbed the curtain between her fingers, tugged it all the way aside, to let in the sun. "Is that why you visit the brothels?"

Pedro coughed and choked on a mouthful of tequila. He looked around to make sure Marisol was still at mass. "Mira, that's none of your business," he said. "I respect Marisol. In her arms I am happy, she knows me. She accepts me."

"Then why ask for more?"

Pedro tapped one finger on the side of his drinking glass, set it on the table. "Even my brother won't deny he sometimes wants the passion without the poetry."

"Manuel wouldn't!"

"You think he's some kind of saint?" Pedro took another swig, swiped his mouth with the back of his hand. "We all want a good fuck, Luna."

Luna scrunched her face, regretted having started the conversation. She changed the subject to something else that had been on her mind. "I want to manage my own money," she said. "I can count as well as you."

Pedro fiddled with a package of cigarettes on the table, tapped one out. "The money is my job. You knew from the beginning. You are earning a fortune. That's all you need to know."

"Pay me weekly," she said. "As you pay the others. And I want my own bank account. I don't like feeling indebted to you or Don Ramón."

Pedro lifted a cigarette to his lips and struck a match. "There was a time when you knew no other way," he said. "It seems freedom has spoilt you."

"No it hasn't," she said.

It was true she slept in the best hotels and wasn't at the ranch wondering what the rest of the world looked like. Because of bullfighting she was experiencing things she otherwise couldn't have, and yet in some ways she still felt like a servant — of tradition, confined to the diameter of the barrera, where each move was scripted and rehearsed and carried out under the crowds' cold scrutiny, or to the locked suites of strange hotels. Being loved for what she did, hadn't freed her.

"When are we going home?" she asked.

Pedro laughed again, but this time it was a hard sound, treacherous, like a crooked staircase. "Would you risk your fortune?" he said. "Alone in Madrid or Sevilla, in Ronda where the García name is known, what cuadrilla do you think will support you? Without a promoter and a team what empresa would gamble on a servant girl?"

"You gambled," she spat. "Surely you're not the only greedy brother in Spain."

Pedro's jaw stiffened. He regarded her with fury, as though she'd attacked him at his most vulnerable place. "Ask Don Ramón," he said. "Ask your precious Manuel. It's illegal for a girl to fight on foot in Spain. Remember?"

Luna pulled her shirt away from her chest, self-consciously. "You mean you've arranged for me to fight here on foot?"

Pedro pressed his cigarette into his empty glass. "Listen, the horses are unpredictable. They can be injured on the road, or catch pneumonia. If we travel by boat they could become seasick or die. Better if we didn't have to rely on them. You're ready, and Mexicans are open to it, they still talk of that girl from Perú. What was her name?" He rubbed his hands together as if to warm them, or prepare them to receive a gift. "Yes, it's time we test this openness with an espontáneo."

Espontáneo: an illegal sabotage. A thief's chance to prove herself.

"At one of the village events," he added. "Now that the formal season has ended."

"It's risky," she said.

An espontáneo usually involved an overeager spectator at a country fiesta who would, to his great peril, interrupt the real program by jumping onto the sand to confront the bull, not a serious bullfighter building a reputation. Yet she had heard of rare successes where a single, foolish performance had elevated a novillero's reputation and earned important bookings during the main season. "This was your plan all along," she said. "You don't intend for us to return."

Pedro shrugged, with a devilish expression on his face. "If you make a good impression it'll be worth gold in seasons to come. Contracts here, but also all over the colonies, maybe in Colombia and Argentina." He looked at her. "If you think you can handle a sword."

"I handle one already," she said.

"But professionally. In front of a crowd. For money."

Luna sat up higher to stretch out her legs. She looked to the lovers outside but they were gone. Was Pedro right and an espontáneo was what she needed to do? After all, each spring at Sangre Mío he'd brought out his slingshot and devised clever ways to hunt little birds — raiding their nests, smearing grease on a stick and sprinkling it with seeds, or pouring whiskey or Cognac into the grain and, once they were drunk, trapping them. If there was one thing he knew it was how to play and win at killing. "What does Manuel think?" she asked.

Pedro took a deep drag off his cigarette, exhaled while he spoke. "He sits on his ass all day. Why would I ask him?"

"And if I'm killed during the espontáneo?" she said. "Have you thought about that? I'm the one who lines your pockets. You say I could buy five houses tomorrow and still have plenty of money left over. Without me, how would you eat?"

Pedro pushed the glass across the table. "That's not the question I asked. Do you want to go back to be a maid, or will you reach for respect?"

She hesitated before answering him.

"Loudly," he demanded.

"I'll do it!" she shouted. "But I will have my own bank account."

He faced her, his smugness gone. "You're smarter than you look," he said.

Luna turned away from him, hated him in that moment, more than she ever would again. Pedro knew a good venture when he saw one — he hadn't changed. Neither had she; she was still driven by a bottomless need to prove her worth that would swallow all other needs. She should've known that first day when she placed the rejón on Payasín's withers; somehow, in some way, she would always be moving in the direction of death. "And get me a new suit of lights," she said. "Like the men wear. Blue and gold, with red cabos."

IN MAY, THE CUADRILLA drove southeast, to a dusty town with an off-season bullring, where a large crowd of aficionados gathered in the countryside the last two Sundays of the month. Don Ramón and Doña García enjoyed a meal together in the hotel restaurant, while upstairs, Carlos read a Mexican bullfight magazine and waited with his sons. Marisol helped Luna dress for her surprise debut on foot. As requested, Pedro had ordered her a suit of lights traditionally worn by a matador or a matador-in-training, not the short jacket she'd worn on horseback. The suit had been measured and cut by an expert tailor in the city, and weighed twenty-five pounds. It offered no protection against goring, its layers and tightness would restrict her movements, further testing her agility and grace in the ring.

Marisol was tugging the new pantaloons over Luna's calves when a loud knock came at the hotel door. "Ignore it," said Luna. It was bad luck for anyone other than intimates to witness a bullfighter dressing.

Again, a knock.

"Not now!" Pedro barked.

Luna drew a sharp breath and tugged her pants up over her rib-cage, so Marisol could button them. She squeezed into one sleeve of her chaquetilla. It was powder blue and gold encrusted, with white piping along the cuffs and seam, and silver tassels sewn along the shoulder pads. Her cabos were blood red. The silk socks were fuchsia, and her slippers black. She needed to pin no coleta as the others did, because her hair was long enough to make a tail at the nape of her neck.

"Señorita García," the voice on the other side of the wall said. "El Corazón? I come with an important message."

"Might be an offer," said Carlos, so he got up from his chair and cracked the door open. There stood the concierge from the lobby, holding out a telegram from El Mayoral. "My sympathies," he said. "Let us know if we can be of assistance."

Luna leaned backwards, straining to see and hear. "Is there a problem?"

Carlos accepted the telegram thinking there had been unrest at the ranch, and instead read of Paqui's sudden death. He shut the door slowly and turned around. Marisol was kneeling to tie the machos on the knee strings of Luna's suit and they were all waiting to learn his news. He shoved the paper into his pants pocket. "Business at home," he said. "It can wait."

A moment later, he presented Luna with a gift. "This for you," he said, displaying a small turquoise and red sac across his out-stretched, callused hand. Marisol stopped buttoning Luna's jacket long enough for her to accept the gift.

"Muchísimas gracias, Don Carlos," she said, as she hurriedly untied the ribbon and dropped the small enamel pendant of Mary and the baby Jesus into her palm. Mary's bone-white face stared. Her eyes were pained though confident.

"She'll need a miracle today," said Pedro, putting his arm around his father. "You should see the size of the La Vina."

"Stop it," said Manuel. "Do you want to shake her confidence?"

Luna turned to see her reflection in the standing mirror. The suit flattened her chest, and concealed her hips and thighs. It fit her properly, a heavy, second skin. "A bullfighter can't have too many miracles," she said, transferring the pendant from one hand to the other, noting its weight.

"Do you like it?" Carlos asked.

Luna kissed the pendant, and for the second time in her life, she kissed Don Carlos. "One more thing," he said, and from behind the closet door he pulled a leather sword case with a bull's head embroidered in gold, silver, and white thread. She caught her breath reading her name tooled in the leather. "A torero must have acero like this one," he said, helping her to open the case and lift out the steel.

"I will use it with honour," she said. "One day I'll take my alternativa with it."

He couldn't help but smile. "Today is your first fight on foot and already you dream of becoming more."

Pedro whistled sharply when he saw her holding the sword out as she would to kill. "Look at you," he said. Then, turning to his father, "Can you believe what we've made of our little Luna?"

She snapped her fingers three times in rapid succession. "Eh. Eh. Eh. Who made whom?" She was her own elegant creation, a glittering blue bird.

Carlos laughed, rubbed his nose, and paid the highest of compliments: "You smell like a matador," he said.


RED WAS EVERYWHERE IN the Tlaxcala countryside — crimson on the bright paper decorations of the picadors' lances, which flashed like sirens when pitched at the bulls, excitement in the faces of the bankers and diplomats and local tradesmen in the makeshift stands as they scrambled for shade. The sand on the ground in the ring made a ruddy beach as Luna prepared to jump over the barrera and take control. Manuel had smuggled in her muleta beneath his long coat so no one would suspect what she was about to do. She appeared confident, but was a web of nerves. *It's about preparation and luck, she told herself, this clock of death, this dance with death.* The doors swung open and the bull charged into the ring.

When the La Vina stood at eight and the torero who intended to fight him stood at twelve, Chucho nudged her and she clambered over top of the five-foot high barrera, landing on the other side, not far from the arrastre. Manuel passed her the capote and muleta and in a flash, mere seconds before the officials could interfere, it had happened: she was standing in the ring in her suit of lights calling the bull.

"Toro!"

How different it felt without her horse. Terrifying. Exhilarating. She'd practised it more than a thousand times during training, but until now she couldn't have known that Fortuna, sharing her performances, diluted some of the fear and honour that went along with them.

"Toro!" she repeated.

The crowd whistled and stomped, at first annoyed with her for interrupting the fiesta, but almost as soon, when the officials charged to remove her, they rallied by applauding and tossing carnations into the ring. Some threw orange and pink streamers, which ribboned through the air. A woman seated near Carlos fainted on realizing a girl was in the ring, and was taken to the enfermería to be given smelling salts.

The bull was confused to find he faced two opponents. His tail swept from side to side angrily, and he swung his heavy head from one to the other of them.

"Eh, Toro!" Luna called again to show that she was the bigger menace. She waved her heavy capote.

"Get out of my way stupid girl!" hollered the other torero. "Someone remove her!" Then, when he saw she'd stepped into the proper position for a Farol de Muleta, a difficult cape pass, he relented. "It's your death!" he shouted, and he slipped out to safety through the nearest burladero.

She wouldn't be frightened into withdrawing. The corrida was the flash and flicker of life, of her adopted family, of all she believed human — the pain and the red pleasure, and her need to be more than that. It was not a fight between man and bull, as she'd assumed up until that moment when she stood on her own two feet facing a two thousand pound beast, but a kind of civil war, where the more universal need we each experience to conquer our own fear is at stake. Sweat trickled down her sides as she passed her right arm, and with it the muleta, high over her head.

The bull charged.

Thundering across the sand, he passed so close to her body that she saw his long flat eyelashes. When he stopped and turned to face her again she sized him up, watched him lick his nose. Then, she lifted her muleta and let him feel his raw power and the force of his rage. She permitted him to think he could crush her with those white cuernos. Once she'd tired him the second time, he was like a pear in syrup, and she had only to site down length of her sword, to the spot between his cuernos, and wave him into the perfect choreography. As she injured she loved, as she killed she was reborn, and when she wanted him to, he fell to his knees and clumsily rolled onto one side. She reached her bloodied hand under her collar and pulled out her mother's gold crucifix and the pendant that hung beside it.

"Co-ra-zón! Co-ra-zón!" She heard Carlos shouting — driving the crowd into a frenzy. "El Corazón!" He was cheering proudly, hollering for her, as if she was his real daughter, calling her name up and sending it into the forgiving sky.

Manuel was cheering too and for an instant he and his father looked at one another, and Manuel saw the love in Carlos's eyes. Tears were rolling down his face. Such warmth — or was it gratitude? — hadn't been sent Manuel's way since he was a small child. At first he thought they'd found a way to share the corrida again, that which was most important in his father's life, but when Carlos's loving gaze fell to Luna in the ring Manuel knew it was something else. His father was cheering as though he'd sired a winner. The hair on the back of Manuel's neck stood. Was that possible?! Luna's connection to the family was random and coincidental; the dark, mysterious curl of her widow's peak, or her appreciation of the bulls. Wasn't it?

Luna easily defeated the La Vina on foot and at the crowd's insistence, they awarded her the tail. Her first tail!

RETURNING TO A HOTEL in Mexico City through a bank of fog, Carlos took a seat beside Luna and Manuel in the rear of the bus. "You gave a marvellous performance," he said. "I've seen few better."

"The next time I will try a more difficult cape pass," she said.

Carlos chewed on the tip of his cigar, looking anxious, and Manuel noticed how grey his temples had turned over time. Silver whiskers salted his dark moustache. The flaws that made him who he was grew more apparent to Manuel with each passing second, and his suspicion grew. Was his father hiding an illegitimate child? "I wanted to wait until after the fight to tell you something," Carlos said. "The telegram that came earlier. It brought sad news from Sangre Mio."

"What did it say?"

He searched for words to ease the impact, but there were none. "It's about Paqui's heart," he said. "El Mayoral found her out by the chickens. She was dead."

"Dead?" Luna mouthed the word inaudibly, as if a sensation of weightlessness, of slipping outside her skin, had moved through her body and she no longer had a voice. Her physical self remained, of course, but it was as if her spirit had fled, was soaring high above them, higher, too high, and as fast it was falling and spinning and slamming into her body, where the fleshy clock inside her own chest wanted to stop ticking. "Paquita!" she screamed.

"Lo siento, Luna. I'm sorry."

"It's not true," she said, frantically. "I don't believe you!" She couldn't bear to think of Paqui gone, of her dying alone, and of not having had the chance to say goodbye. But shock gave way to heartache, and the pain was instantaneous. Before either Carlos or Manuel could stop her, she'd reached behind the seat and found her sword. Bereft, she flailed it through the air, sending both men scrambling to the front of the bus, along with the cuadrilla.

"Stop!" they hollered. "Drop your sword!"

She staggered, flashed her wild dark eyes around looking for something to destroy. She held her sword out with both hands and hacked at a seat over and over, scarring the wooden back, tearing into the leather cover as if destroying grief.

Chucho, at the wheel of the bus, swerved sharply, to knock her off her feet. This sent her spinning up the aisle with the long blade in hand. As the bus skidded to a stop, Marisol cowered next to Pedro and his mother, and the doors swung open. Pedro was the first one out, followed by the others. Chucho tried to pull Manuel outside, but he wouldn't go. He remained in the doorway, one foot on the step of the bus and the other hanging off, ready to leap. After a few minutes, Luna exhausted herself and he approached her slowly. "Luna?"

Heaving and sweating and too dizzy to stand, she dropped her sword and collapsed onto the seat. "Who's that you were calling?" she said, wiping her runny nose on the sleeve of her shirt. "Without Paqui to remind me, I don't know her anymore."

Manuel kicked the sword up the aisle, and slid in next to her. "I know you," he whispered. "You're the girl who names all the animals, and hides in the sunflowers, and steals small treasures to comfort the dead. I still know you."

She nodded wordlessly and stared out the window, unconvinced. Everything outside was spinning in darkness, and this time she was sure the vertigo wouldn't stop. Paqui's death marked the end of her childhood, and any lingering innocence. She wasn't the same person anymore and hadn't been since she began fighting bulls;

as a professional she learned each animal's weight and height and temperament but not his name, and the lone comfort she offered was the promise of swift death in the ring. Sitting at the side of that desolate road she felt alone again and pining for love, real love, enduring love. She'd worked hard and been lucky and she'd won the momentary kind, love from spectators on Sunday afternoons. Would it be enough now? When Manuel tried to put his arm around her shoulders she shook him off. She didn't want consolation. There was no consolation: she'd come all the way around the world to prove she was worth something, that she was worthy of love, but in so doing she'd left behind the first and only person who'd ever loved her. There was no distance wide enough, no ambition profound enough, to muffle the deafening peal of that loss. She glanced up at the cloudy Mexican sky. No stars, no moon, nothing left worth believing in.

WHITE LIGHT, WHITE VEINS, empty of blood and pulse, she carried on. She carried on for the cuadrilla, and she carried on for her art. She leaned on it, and turned cold colourless earth and flesh into afternoon upon afternoon of fine spectacle. Driven by compulsion, she moved through her days fulfilling contracts, as though still bathed in immortality, and through her nights with low, heavy eyelids, two small flags hung at half-mast.

At the end of June, Don Carlos and Doña García returned to Spain, and the team began a gruelling travel schedule. They stopped in dozens of cities and towns; but, for Luna, each crashed into the next: Torreón, Queretaro, León, Toluca. The bulls were indistinguishable to her. There was little fresh energy to her passes, a mime's performance of life. As if to honour Paqui, and all the lives that had been lost, she wrapped herself in death's red elegance, concentrated on the choreography of sword and blood. Tasted revenge. When she made the tiro de gracia, it was punishment of the God she now hated. She killed to kill what was left of herself too, because she had again been spared. Once more, she'd been charged with surviving, left behind, an empty blue shell that glittered and shined, but had been cast off by the sea. Manuel watched in horror as she ran at the bulls in a style of killing called Volapié, forsaken and filled with wild daring. Charge me, she dared. Charge me, impale me. Take me from this endless bright light.

She deliberately stood too close to the bulls, using passes she'd barely practised, and she no longer allowed Chucho to blunt the bulls' cuernos. "Either I fight clean," she told him. "Or I don't fight."

"The others saw off the tips," he said. "We used to do it regularly."

"Not me. Not anymore."

"So you are trying to kill yourself!"

Then, in September of 1935 a letter arrived from Jorge Vidal, informing Manuel that their artist's circle was planning to meet and tour, performing in a number of Spanish cities, including at a week-long arts festival in Madrid. Jorge had bought a hotel there, he said, and would be hosting.

"I need to see my friends," said Manuel.

"Don't leave me," Luna begged. "I couldn't bear to lose you, too."

"Soon," he said. "When my collection is finished."

IT WAS DURING THIS period that Luna and Marisol grew closer. Marisol kept up a strict daily regimen of feeding and bathing Luna, and did so without resentment. She seemed to know that structure and routine were required to hold a fractured spirit in place. Marisol confided in Luna, that she'd been longing to feel life growing inside her, to hold a newborn in her arms, and yet each passing month without a pregnancy left her more desperate and fearful that it might not happen. She laid alongside Luna before they fell asleep, a child-less mother next to a motherless child, singing softly of Andalucía, and her sweet voice held both of their nightmares at bay. "Close your eyes," she sang. "Close your eyes and find the ocean and the mountains and the sea. Close your eyes and you will be there, with your true love and with me." Often, Marisol was still there when Luna woke, curled around her, holding on tightly, and it was unclear which one of them was saving the other from despair.

The following spring, Manuel received another letter from Jorge Vidal, this one informing him that Eugenia had moved to Paris and that he was working with the local branch of the UGT — the general union of workers, to negotiate contracts for his hotel staff. The political mood of the country felt unstable, Jorge wrote. There were rumours of two rogue generals hoping to make their names.

Meanwhile, aficionados and bullfight reviewers regularly noted Luna, but mistook her sorrow for bravery and declared her to be an astonishing success. *She's among the most courageous bullfighters of our day*, wrote one reviewer. Era Gran Amazón. Another wrote that in the faena her stance was one of pure accomplishment, and to reassure his readers he wasn't reporting second-hand gossip he added: *I saw her kill with my own eyes and I like her for her bravery and style. She has no fear of death. First place: El Corazón.* What appeared to be courage to the aficionados wasn't any kind of courage to Luna, it was a lonely orphan's posture. And luck.

One afternoon at the Plaza de Toros in Mexico City, the largest bullring in the world, fifty thousand spectators, Luna faced a blond La Punta, number 356. As the bull charged, she spun out a second too late and his round-pointed cuerno ripped, fast as light, into her flesh. The pain was a deep, fiery brand. She was tossed into the air, a wounded bird unable to fly. It's what she'd wanted to feel, something other than the tight twist of anguish. Her sword and muletta fell onto the sand, and she landed, by instinct, face down. She covered her head with her hands, and waited for the end. Sand and sawdust filled her mouth, and she coughed, struggling for air. She heard the low growl of the audience's broncas, and her own belabored breathing. Chucho was ordering the cuadrilla to get her out of the ring and there came a flurry of feet and hooves and capotes, and someone, Manuel, shouting at the bull. Luna lifted her head, opened one eye. The bull was charging straight for her. Panicking, she tried to drag herself to the burladero but was too weak to move. Her red muletta was lying twisted in the sand just out of reach. She strained for it with her right hand, strained with all her will, and grasping it, flung it as far from her body as she could. With mere seconds to spare, the bull diverted his path. Luna dropped her arm. The bullring spun in dizzying circles around her. Her leg was a current of lightning. As shock set in, blood poured through her pantaloons, and pooled like an open heart in the sand.

*Death*, she imagined, *her gateway to everlasting immortality. A reunion. A real possibility.* But ... she lifted her head higher, worsening the vertigo. The sun was blinding and she closed her eyes. Black day, drawn curtain. Darkness calling her. It was a surprise to her as much as it was to anyone: She was gored and yet she wasn't ready to die.

"Manuel!" she whispered. "Ayúdame! Help me!"

THE WAN LIGHT OF an overcast afternoon filtered through the hospital window painting Luna's face with a pallid yellow sheen. Dizziness had subsided, and she inhaled the sweet smell of fresh cut roses and carnations. Vases lined the windowsill, stood on the bedside table, crowded together in one corner of the floor. Marisol sat next to the bed, worrying a rosary, while Pedro smoked furiously in a corner. Manuel paced.

"Chucho saved your leg," he explained. "When they wheeled you from the plaza he ran through traffic alongside the stretcher. He tied the straps of his suspenders to keep up pressure."

"Thank God for that," said Marisol.

Manuel stopped at the foot of the bed, chewed his thumbnail. "God had nothing to do with it. It was pure luck she wasn't killed."

Luna threw off the sheets with one hand to reveal the thick pink and white braid that ran from the top of her inner left thigh down to her knee. "The wound is already healing," she said. "As long as there's no infection I'll walk in a week or two."

Pedro nodded, stubbed his cigarette on the window ledge, and tossed the butt out the window. "A real torero doesn't quit," he said. "He longs for the next afternoon to redeem himself."

"She is a real torero," Marisol said, patting Luna's hand. It was the kindest thing Marisol had ever said about her, and without having to prove herself Luna hoped it was true.

"Did you not hear the doctor?" said Manuel. "She could have permanent nerve damage! If she doesn't heal properly she'll lose range of movement." He turned to Luna. "How long do you expect to go on? Two more years, five? Ten?"

"What are you trying to do?" said Pedro. "She has everything she needs. Ramón will cover our lodging and training again next season, and I've lined up twenty-three contracts. Would you have me unsign them?"

"I don't care about Don Ramón," Luna said, rather bluntly. "He's not the main concern."

"You're avoiding him," Manuel said. "Why?"

Marisol set her rosary beads on the end table. "Stop it," she said. "Both of you. There's no need to speak of this now." She tugged the sheets up over Luna's body. "I was going to wait and tell you," she said. "At last, I am pregnant."

"De verdad?!" Luna opened her arms. "Come, let me congratulate you properly." She hugged Marisol tightly and kissed her on both cheeks. "Cuánto me allegro por ti. I'm happy for you. This is the kind of hopeful news I need to hear. You'll be a wonderful mother," Luna said, squeezing her hand.

"I used to cry for Sevilla," Marisol said. "Now, my home is with Pedro. Wherever he is I am home. But what about your future, Luna? Each day your mood grows heavier. I see that. Since Paqui's death, toreo has become a second mother, like the good nuns who run this hospital. Like me," she smiled. "I fear the longer you go on fighting, the more you'll grow to resent it, and possibly yourself."

Marisol had rarely made reference to her old life in Sevilla. She'd behaved as though time began anew each morning and ended again at sunset, as if there was no history or continuity to her life. Indeed,

Luna had done the same. She sank backwards onto her pillow, fiddled anxiously with the frayed edge of her hospital sheet. To what family did she belong? She'd watched over two hundred corridas and performed in as many, killing one hundred and eighty bulls. She'd cut one hundred and thirty-four ears, sixty-five tails, and five hoofs, and yet she didn't carry the title of matador de toros. She remained a novillero, a professional bullfighter who hadn't taken her alternativa and been formally recognized by the senior matadors.

She turned her head, peered out the window. Surviving the bull had changed her. It had reaffirmed her will to live and strengthened her motivation. She wouldn't fight primarily for the money now, or for the adoration of the crowd. With Paqui gone, she needed a new home for her heart and there remained one way to be legitimate: She must take her alternativa in Spain, facing a bull on foot. A rare ambivalence shuddered through her. No woman had done it.

"Leave us," she said. "I want to speak with Manuel alone."


"SPAIN IS HOME TO the corrida," she said, before he could open his mouth. "If I can't succeed there I am nothing. Ultimately, it doesn't matter what I've accomplished here, or anywhere else."

"I don't believe that," he said. "You have a remarkable career. Does Ramón have something to do with this?"

"No," she said. Her face was almost angelic as she spoke, eyes deep and endless, skin as flawless as it was smooth. He had no reason to think she would lie to him.

"You do everything a matador does. Carrying the official title doesn't matter."

"It matters to me!" she snapped. "When I was face down on the sand all I could think was I didn't want to die ungraduated."

"What about the law?"

"We can get around it."

"If we can't, you'd be stuck on top of a horse. The others won't go, I can tell you. Here they live like kings."

"Chucho and Javier?"

"Javier has a wife and son now. And Pedro won't be convinced."

"That's the easy part," she laughed. "Tell him it will please your father. I'll pay him whatever he wants. People have been saying I would fail at every turn and I've succeeded." She pushed her shoulders back as if to challenge anything that dared to get in her way. "I'll be the exception at home too."

Manuel smiled sympathetically. "I've been watching all your life," he said. "The world itself could not fill the emptiness inside of you. What makes you sure that taking the alternativa at home will satisfy your ambition?"

"Respectfully, Manuel, for you there's been enough food and wine, and the assumption of more. If I need a bigger audience, who are you to challenge it?"

"I can't help my advantage," he said. "I haven't held it against you."

"No, you haven't." She avoided his eyes, rubbed the edge of the hospital sheet between her fingers. "I've been ashamed," she said. "Of who I am. I thought I could prove I was as good as you and your family, but without a title I've proved nothing. Not to myself."

"Of course you have."

"How would you feel writing but not completing your manuscript, never publishing it? Could you live with that?"

Manuel raised his hand, palm out, fingers spread, and she lifted her right one to his. "We're more alike than not," he said. "But if art doesn't cure our loneliness, or if we don't succeed, we'll both have to find something else."

"This is all I can do now," she said.

"I should show you Jorge's last telegram. Power in Spain has shifted dangerously to the right. The future is uncertain."

"You sound like you want to be there."

Manuel nodded, felt that old affinity with her again. He tangled his fingers tightly around hers. They'd been co-conspirators — against his parents, against the roles that tradition forced them both to play. Perhaps they could conspire to return. "When we left Sangre Mio I was looking for my inspiration," he said. "For my paradise, and to some extent I've found it. I write here, better than before, but wherever we go I find things from home — the rosemary, the way bread is made, an item of clothing. Even the corrupt class system here was inherited from Spain. We encounter people every day who want to visit there. I've asked myself why, and I think I know: we have the Mediterranean and the sun; the inspiration I was looking for, the paradise other people seek, is already mine. I want to go home to write about it."

Luna strained to shift position on her pillow. "Madrid could be my masterpiece," she said. "If there's a chance I must try."

"Look at our hands," he said, growing braver. "Look at my face. Do you ever see yourself in it?"

"It is remarkable."

He leaned closer. "Listen, if you had a real family, would you consider retiring?"

She blinked and blinked again, and he thought she might've understood what he was hinting at but she pulled her hand away. Perhaps a heart can stretch so much before it bends and breaks and hers would go on beating as long as nothing more was asked of it. "It is a risk," she said. "But the ring is mine. You gave it to me and I belong there. All I'm asking is that it be formally recognized. When I'm buried it should be at home with my sword and cape, in a marked grave."

He was pensive for a long moment, searching his heart for a soft cadence, perhaps wisdom. There was a good chance she would destroy her career by leaving Mexico, or be arrested for attempting to fight on foot at home. Returning, she might lose all she had gained but she wasn't afraid of taking the risk. His chest tightened and he locked onto her: pale and gaunt, with arms that lay at her sides limply, broken wings, and yet in her eyes there still shone an impressive bid at hope for the future. "You inspire me," he said.

ONCE LUNA WAS HEALED and business taken care of, they crossed the ocean in a luxury liner, along with Chucho, Pedro, and Marisol. In the mornings, they met on deck to enjoy the sun and drink coffee. Luna exercised. In the evenings, after the meal, they gathered in the first class smoking room. It was there, one night, seated around a card table, that the ship's captain appeared looking haggard and anxious. His bearded face was illuminated by the overhead light emanating from a crystal chandelier. He removed his white hat and held it to his chest. "There has been unrest at home," he said.

A series of telegraphs had been sent from other ships and from land, informing him that a group of right-wing generals, including General Francisco Franco, had made a declaration of opposition to the Republican government. Franco's Army of Africa had invaded Andalucía. They were moving northward, according to the telegraphs, slaughtering peasants and taking land. "And at Sangre Mio?" Manuel asked, fearful of the answer. He and Luna exchanged worried glances. Marisol squeezed Pedro's hand. "I will relay the news as soon as I hear it," said the captain.

Three weeks later, days before they reached land, a telegraph arrived confirming that the García family was alive and unharmed. Don Carlos had not fled to safety as had many landlords, nor had he brutally come down on his workers to keep them in line. He'd avoided a revolt by conceding some land to his men. No one knew how much he'd paid the Fascists to spare Sangre Mio.

# Act 3

*Sangre Mio & Madrid*
*1936–1937*

THE SUN BRANDED LUNA'S face as she and Manuel approached the main entrance leading into Sangre Mío. Pedro, Chucho, and Marisol followed. Clouds moved overhead sending everything they passed into alternating patterns of shadow and light — the iron gate, the pileta storing water, the chicken coop where Paqui had been found dead. It was eerily silent, and Luna took Manuel's hand as they moved through the arches and into the first courtyard, where the old mulberry tree offered momentary relief from the sun. When they reached the oak doors a girl younger than Luna stood waiting in Paqui's old apron. "Bienvenidos," she said with gigantic coppery eyes that seemed to leap from their sockets as though there was something wild behind them trying to escape. Her voice and demeanour were as restrained as they ought to have been, given her position.

Luna stood motionless as though, until that moment, she'd somehow been expecting to find things as they'd been before the invasion, with Paqui still there. It's hard to believe in death from a distance, but the sight of this young replacement confirmed it; Paqui was gone and everything at home had changed. A flood of tears pressed up behind Luna's eyes. "Who are you?" she asked, rudely.

"My name is Elvira," said the girl. "Come, step in from the sun."

LIGHT-HEADED, LUNA SAT on the edge of what was once Paqui's bed. She swung her legs up overtop of the covers, pressed her face into the feather pillow and breathed deeply. Not a trace of Paqui. We assume that when the people we love die, we'll forever retain the look of them, the sound of them, the smell of them, but we don't. Time steals the essence of a person as surely as it claims their last breath. For a while, after Armando was killed, Luna had still felt him standing beside her when she practised. His skilful posture, his hands manoeuvring his cape, and the feeling of those hands moving over her body as though in search of deliverance. Yet, within months of his death she could barely hold on to the memory of his kiss.

She rolled onto her back, stared at the painting of the dancing girl hanging on the wall. It had faded a little. As she studied it, she thought, *we're all shadows, shapes cut out of light or light imposed on darkness, not fully seen or heard or known.* Her mood broke, and she laughed at herself for sounding so maudlin. Paqui would've scolded her for it, and reminded her that she hadn't dulled one bit with time. If anything, time had sharpened her into a more self-aware version of herself. She flipped onto her side, and was caught off guard when she noticed Doña García hovering in the doorway, watching her. Doña García appeared reluctant to enter, respectful, perhaps offering a truce. "Elvira told me you'd arrived," she said.

Luna sat up. In the sunlight Doña García's long face bore deep grooves and wrinkles, which, on another woman her age, might've looked distinguished but on her were ugly battle scars. "I saved her things," she said, pointing at Paqui's wardrobe. "I thought you would want them." There was a newfound humility in her voice, and yet Luna knew better than to trust her. Her gaze was frantic, fearful, the kind of fear that masks itself as indifference and says, Don't come too close, you have no need of me now and it frightens me not to control you.

Luna stood wordlessly and walked over to the wardrobe, opened the door. Inside were three identical black housedresses, widow's wear, or maid's attire, each on its own wooden hanger. Folded over the left shoulders were pale blue aprons. A pair of worn, rope-soled sandals sat neatly on the floor. "I trust she was properly buried?" Luna said.

Doña García nodded. "Full rights. Father Serratosa came immediately. Would you like to see the stone?"

"Yes."

Luna followed out behind the house to the small plateau where she was shown the engraved lettering of Paqui's full name. Pasquella Maria Martínez Ortiz. In childhood she'd often sat there, where a few crooked headstones bore the García family name, wishing that one of the plots cradled her mother's dead body. It struck her that for all her pining and searching, Paqui had been the mother she'd needed all along.

"I have the new girl cut fresh flowers in the mornings," said Doña García, pointing with her silk fan to the vase propped up against the headstone. "Don't you think this is a lovely spot, closest to the kitchen?"

Luna glanced at the kitchen window out through which she and Paqui had gazed daily. There was no radio crackling, no songs from far and wide offering another life. "Why not a view of the hill?" she asked. "You couldn't give her the sunflowers or the cows she milked for you each morning?" She turned to face Doña García. "Why would she want to spend eternity next door to that stinking kitchen where she stood until her heart gave out?"

Doña García stopped fanning herself. "How ungrateful, Luna!"

"Call me El Corazón," she said. She reached out for the headstone. "You know nothing about what Paqui would want, what any of us want."

Doña García folded the fan with one snap of her wrist. "I've been trying to make this easier for you."

"There was a time when I would've appreciated that, Señora. But I'm not so sentimental now. I know you've wished I wasn't here."

Doña García sharpened her gaze, chose her words more carefully. "It's true," she said. "I won't bother to deny it. Did you not also wish I would disappear? You hated me because I was in charge. What do you want from me, an apology?"

"Tell me where my mother is buried."

Doña García clasped her hands together to hide the tremor. She'd been fighting the urge to drink since returning from Mexico, but the war had made it impossible. "I would if I knew," she said. "Speak with my husband." She took a step towards Luna trying to pay her a compliment. "Elvira does what I ask well enough," she said. "But she lacks your nerve."

"I pity her then."

Doña García stiffened. There would be no reconciliation after all. She pursed her lips. "Lunch will be served at two o'clock," she said. "I'll let the others know." She turned and walked away.

"HOLA?" LUNA KNOCKED ON the office door, knowing Don Carlos typically took his coffee and read the newspapers before lunch. The radio inside blasted a commentary about Franco's troops fanning northward into Extremadura. Mass killings had been reported at Badajoz. She pressed the door open to be heard. "Don Carlos?"

He looked up from behind his desk where he sat in an oxblood leather chair. "Come in," he said, snapping off the radio. "I didn't expect to see you until later."

Luna stepped into the room. It looked exactly as it had before — two large, wood-framed oil paintings of Manuel's great, great grandparents on one wall, curtainless windows on another, a small cabinet with a glass door, guarding a cigar collection and another similar cabinet holding expensive bottles of sherry and cognac. It had once been her job to remove each bottle, dust it, and return it to the shelf. Doña García had occasionally snuck sips, she knew, or dipped her fingers into the necks to taste that way, but she hadn't. The cast-iron sculpture of Plateadito was also there, on the desk, Don Carlos's famous prize-winning bull, and the first to compete in the ring. The sculpture had been buffed to a shine, no doubt by Elvira's oil cloth, and it reflected the unusual silver sheen in Plateadito's coat. "I was hoping to speak with you alone," she said.

Carlos unbuttoned his grey vest, pushed a bowl of pistachio nuts across the desk. "Would you like?" She shook her head. Although no longer his servant, it still felt wrong to eat from the same bowl as he did. "How does it feel to be home?" he asked.

"Too quiet." Luna fingered the statue of Plateadito, decided it was best to be direct. "Tomorrow Pedro will leave for Madrid," she said. "To put my affairs in order. I've returned to take my alternativa."

"So I read in Manuel's letter." Carlos's thin lips were chapped and his breath gave off the stench of too many cigars.

"You don't approve?"

"It's not a matter of approval." Carlos picked through the nut bowl, cracking shells between his teeth, and scooping out the meat with his tongue. "We have Franco to contend with now." He brushed the shells from his chest, glanced out the window and across the field where, a month earlier, he'd seen the Army of Africa marching onto his property. He'd paid them off, but how long would it be before they returned? He looked beyond the field, to where his training ring sat, and his heart compressed at the bittersweet memory of Luna proving herself there years ago. It was unlikely, now, that she would fulfill her dream — or his. He opened his mouth, as if to finally spill the secret that sat upon his lips like an unclaimed prize. Instead all he said was: "If war doesn't prevent you fighting in Madrid, the law will try. You know this."

"I do," she nodded. "And I want you to know I dream of the Real Maestranza. Being celebrated in Ronda where your bulls are so prized would be the greatest honour. But Las Ventas is where I must be confirmed."

"You're here to ask for my endorsement?"

"No." She made herself as tall as she could be. "I'm here to ask about my mother."

He was surprised by the intensity of her words, and the demand in her eyes. His pulse quickened and for an instant he panicked, then a wave of relief washed over him; the opportunity to unburden himself had come. He angled his chair a little towards the window. "Her name was Elisenda," he said.

"Elisenda," Luna repeated. "That's very pretty. What do you remember of her?"

"She had flecks of gold in her eyes," he said. "In the sunlight." He twisted the ends of his moustache nervously. "She came here to work with two older brothers when she was your age. Later, her brothers went north and she stayed on."

Carlos ran his palm along the silver statue that represented his wealth and success, and all at once those things meant less to him. He fished in the top drawer of his desk for a small key, fumbled with it, and used it to unlock the bottom drawer. He produced a wrinkled and faded black and white photograph and handed it to her. "Take it," he said.

Luna accepted the photograph. On it there was a young woman waving from the edge of a cliff. Her face was overexposed, her features grainy and impossible to distinguish. But she was obviously pregnant. "Is this her?" Luna asked.

"Turn it over," he said.

Zahara, summer 1919.

It was his handwriting.

"I paid a fortune to a Swedish military man for the camera," he said. "That's the one picture I still have from those days. It's yours now."

Luna stared at the image trying to find herself in it, but couldn't: The woman had a solid, curvy body, ample chest, and long straight hair. She brought the image closer to her eyes and then, there it was, faded with time and reflecting the sun: the same gold crucifix she wore around her neck. Breath caught in her throat and she reached up and touched the chain.

"Paqui thought I should've told you," Carlos said. "I'll tell it to you now. I loved your mother."

"Loved her?" Luna peered into his dark eyes, noted the familiar angle of his jaw, the way he held his head slightly to one side when he was speaking, as she did, as Manuel did, and all at once time folded backwards, a house of cards. "You?" she said, looking from him to the photograph and at him again. "You're my father?!" She shook her head. "No, Paqui would've told me."

"And humiliate my wife? It wasn't her place."

. Luna's face flashed red. Her arms and legs weakened and the room began to spin. All the years she'd felt like the dirt that blew whichever way the wind blew, praying for a family of her own, to belong to someone, waiting for her father to return and claim her, and he'd been there all along! Rage spilled into confusion and back to rage. "How dare you!" she shouted. "How dare you deny me!" Her knees buckled slightly, and the floor seemed to give way. She slammed her hands down on the desktop in front of her for balance. At one time, she would've traded anything for a legitimate name and a place at her father's table, but not any longer. "I should hate you," she hissed, and by the tormented expression on his face she knew he'd had the same thought many times. She hoped he'd anguished over it.

"I won't blame you if you do," he said.

"Don't try and sound noble." For the first time Luna understood Doña García, or pitied her; she too had lived with a ghost hovering in the shadows, unable to capture it, unable to bury it. Worse, she'd been a consolation prize.

"I loved your mother," Carlos repeated.

Luna's voice quavered. "Then why couldn't you love me?"

Carlos felt his body tense. He wrung his dry, cracked hands. He'd relinquished his rights as a father almost eighteen years ago and he wasn't so arrogant as to claim them now. Only her success was any comfort. "If I had raised you as my daughter," he said. "With your needs attended to, would you have wanted to become a bullfighter?"

She stared at him, dumbstruck. "I'll never know," she said.

"You would've married well. Filled a house with babies. That would've been the limit of your ambition. I've known some of the greatest matadors in the world and it's pain that drives them into the ring."

"It did nothing to motivate me," said a voice from out in the hallway.

"Manuel!" Luna spun around, feeling instantly nauseous. "Did you know?"

Manuel stormed up to his father. "That's why you agreed to let her train in the first place, wasn't it?!"

Carlos's face blanched. His eyes flickered with old wounds, and he wanted to say something that would release them from the silent war they'd been fighting through the years, but he stared at his son with a mixture of defiance and regret. "Life is not like the ink you set down on paper. It is not so black and white."

"I suspected in Mexico," Manuel said. "When I saw your reaction to her fight."

Luna clenched her jaw to hold back the tears, tried to suppress vertigo. "It's too late for a confession," she said. "You should've taken it to your grave." She lost her balance, grabbed onto Manuel for support. Hot tears streamed down her face and she wiped them away to make room for new ones to fall. "Show me a thousand photographs to prove we are related," she said. "But it's only by blood." She looked up through wet, blurry vision. "I am not your daughter. I would never turn my back on love."

Manuel pulled her closer. "Does Pedro know?"

Carlos shook his head. "I doubt he'd want to, but I suppose that's up to Luna now." He watched her clutch the photograph of her mother to her chest. "I buried her under the cypress tree," he said. "At the north end of the property."

WITH THE TASTE OF bitter herbs on her tongue, Luna sat against the tree. She held the featureless photograph of her mother in one hand. A pile of stolen items from her hiding spot in her lap. Glancing down at the gifts she'd long ago hidden — pieces of her younger self, and of others, taken to mark what had previously had no marker, she felt a new disorientation. Until Don Carlos's confession, she'd believed that God had taken her mother's life as payment for her own, left no father, not a coin to trade up on, because she didn't deserve one. She didn't know what to believe anymore. The cows on the hill were lowing, and the wind, up from the Straits of Gibralter, caressed her skin as gently as a dog licks its wound. One by one, she carefully set each item at the tree's base.

Manuel remained a few feet away, tentatively observing. He looked solemn, doleful. "It's love you've needed," he said. "Not more grief. I regret my father delivering more." He chewed his fingernail, tore at the cuticle with his teeth until it bled. "I should've told you my suspicions," he said.

Luna rubbed the thin paper of the photograph between her

thumb and forefinger. Don Carlos's confession had called every-thing into question, including Manuel's loyalty. She craned her neck. "Recite a poem about me," she said.

"What?"

"Can you not find one little poem inside yourself for me?"

"I started one a long time ago," he said. This was a test and he hesitated. Unlike him, Luna was a natural artist, with an elegance and grace about her when she performed that couldn't be achieved through practice alone. It wasn't so for him with his writing. Each word he set down on paper was wrung out of him as though he was squeezing the last drops of water from a cloth.

"Go ahead," she said, waiting.

He approached, crouched down in front of her. It took a moment to free his mind of insecurities, find his metered self. He delivered the lines out loud:

*When the sky is black and stars pulse air*
*a pale seam glows on the horizon*
*higher, higher, the white eye opens*
*staring down, an incandescent lover,*
*betraying the sun.*

*Look how the moon defies us!*
*making a silhouette of the trees*
*turning darkness into a new dawn*
*behold, behold this Cyclops of the night*
*rightful custodian of the sky.*

"It's beautiful," Luna said. She looked up, to the very top branches of the cypress tree where the hot sun streamed down on her face, drying her tears. The sun was still there, burning up the sky. The sky, decorated with birds, the birds still believing in flight. Maybe not everything had changed with Don Carlos's confession. Yet one important thing had. She looked to the ground, to the unofficial grave she'd been waiting to discover all her life and felt guilty admitting it: loving a dead mother was a feat only a child could sustain, and she'd outgrown the burden. She took a deep breath and the dry air filled her lungs with relief.

THE FOLLOWING AFTERNOON, LUNA and Manuel watched as Pedro, Marisol, and Chucho tore off down the driveway in one of Don Carlos's trucks, headed for Madrid. "See you in a week!" Marisol called out the window. Pedro honked the horn.

An hour later, Luna found herself sitting under the cypress tree again, with Manuel at her side, writing in his notebook. She was trying to think about Las Ventas, to visualize herself standing on the sand there, sword raised opposite a bull, but thoughts of Don Carlos interfered. *How could he have lied to her all these years, without her knowing? Did he regret it now?* A dust cloud formed up the road, far in the distance. Luna heard pounding on the ground but couldn't see any horses or riders through the haze. She and Manuel stood and started toward the house. By the time they neared the stone wall they saw a scruffy band of Rightist soldiers made up of civil guards, men from the Army of Africa, and local Falange who'd been rounded up and sent by regional landlords. The soldiers rolled in like thunder — thrump, thrump — marching in five columns of six men each. Along the dirt road they came, with their leader carrying a framed picture of Christ. They stopped by the palm tree in the outer courtyard. Luna and Manuel ducked behind the wall.

Elvira was the first outside, followed swiftly by Doña García and the two daughters of the field hand, the one with the overbite carrying a live chicken by its legs. El Mayoral and Don Carlos emerged from the barn with Carlos bearing a branding iron. "Get off my property, Luis Mendez!"

The local boy with God on his side stepped forward. "You are under suspicion of being a Republican sympathizer," he said. "Will you surrender?"

Carlos laughed. "Your grandfather has been treating my blood pressure for more than twenty years. What does he think of that ugly uniform you wear?"

Luis' face reddened, he glanced self-consciously over his shoulder at the boys and men awaiting his response. "My grandfather is a wise man," he said, setting the picture of Christ against the palm. "Like your neighbours, he knows how to protect himself."

"I don't need protection," said Carlos. Again he lifted the hot poker.

The soldiers raised their guns in unison, and aimed them, but Luis Mendez raised his hand to stop them firing. "Wait!" He advanced a few steps, lowered his voice. "Don Carlos, surrender your land and your family will not be harmed."

"And the others?"

Doña García sipped nervously from a silver flask. "Don't antagonize them, Carlos!"

He looked at her, and beyond, as though searching out someone else, a soul who might perhaps understand him better. "Sangre Mio is mine," he said. "I am in charge here, and a dictator's greedy followers won't change that now." He turned and whistled sharply, and that whistle was followed by another, and another, each one a reply from a different worker stationed somewhere farther out on the property. Within seconds men began to walk in from the fields, a half dozen inching over the hill, six from behind the house, most of them hardline communists from Montejaque.

"Don't be a fool," said Luis Mendez. "They would as soon slit your neck."

El Mayoral moved in behind him. "No. Don Carlos is an honourable landlord," he said. "Not all men who wear ties are unjust bourgeoisie."

Luis sneered. "He does little to convince us of your innocence, Don Carlos."

Doña García tugged at her husband's sleeve. "I'm begging you. Give them what they want." Carlos shook her off. "We are women and children here," she said, appealing to Luis directly. "God will not forgive you harming us."

"Silence!" Luis shouted.

Doña García pulled Elvira to stand in front of her. "We've prepared the afternoon meal," she tried, in a less threatening tone. "Come inside and eat. Drink some good sherry."

"I said, silence!" Luis was pacing, agitated. The upside-down chicken flapped and squawked and became hard for the girl with the overbite to handle. All at once, Luis lifted his pistol and shot the bird, ending the noise that disturbed his conscience.

The girl screamed and dropped the bird at her feet, frantically wiping its blood from her clothes.

Luna tried to stand, almost as a reflex, but Manuel grabbed her arm. The hunting dogs were barking loudly and one of them raced over to sniff at the chicken. Manuel feared it would sniff them out next, until Luis raised his gun for a second time and pulled the trigger. The dog fell.

"Oye, cañijo!" Carlos shouted. "Hey runt! You're the mutt that should be silenced!"

Luis turned, pointed his gun at Carlos and then, losing courage, turned it on El Mayoral.

Carlos gripped his branding iron. "Your complaint is with me," he said.

"All of them together are not worth your life, Don Carlos."

Carlos thought of Luna, one of his own, of Elisenda, and the years of loving her that had taught him otherwise. He lifted his iron, lunged and swung.

Luis ducked and rolled to avoid decapitation, and Carlos accidentally smashed through the picture of Christ leaning against the tree. At that, Luis lifted his arm and signalled to his troops who opened fire, hitting Carlos in the chest with a dozen lead bullets, sending him bent forward over the wall. Luna shuddered. Manuel let go his grip on her. From the other side of the wall, Manuel crawled to his father on hands and knees. Luna followed.

Blood spilled from Carlos's mouth. His lungs no longer held air. But for a few seconds his eyes still saw, and he knew he was dead because the anger and judgment he'd last seen on Manuel's face had been replaced with grief. Luna reached up, touched Carlos's lips with her fingertips. It was too late to mouth any final words: Luis Mendez grabbed Carlos by the ankles, and dragged him over the wall, smashing his face into it. "Enemy of Spain!" Luis cried.

Manuel and Luna flattened against the hot earth and held their breath, expecting to be the next to die. They lay stiff, terrified. Gunshots blasted and echoed throughout the valley. Bodies slammed together, knives were drawn. They smelled gunpowder and blood and tasted the salt of their own fear. When most of the workers had been slaughtered, Luis ordered those remaining to stand against the white stone wall beside the women. Manuel clamped his hand over Luna's mouth and one by one shots rang out as bodies fell:

El Mayoral.

Elvira.

The girl with the overbite.

Doña García protested. "Don't shoot! Please. I've done nothing wro—" Her warm blood splattered over the wall, raining down on Manuel and Luna. Manuel gagged, swallowed a mouthful of bile. It burned down his oesophagus like venom.

He wanted to kill. Not a bull, but a man. He wanted to ram a gun down Luis Mendez's throat until every Godless bullet had been swallowed, take Luis's life and make him suffer while he did it. Death leaves scaring scars, turning the living into machines for destruction, and he was not immune. He tried to rise and couldn't. Boots reverberated on the ground as Luis's men on the other side of the wall darted from one wounded or dead body to another, scavenging in warm pockets. "Plant our flag over there," Luis commanded. "We'll return for the animals."

Hours later, hours after the sun and soldiers had retreated, and the cries of the half-dead had stopped, Manuel slipped over the blood-soaked wall. They were all there, in incomplete poses, midway through some attempt at escape or attack: His mother in the dirt, face beside the chicken, with Elvira a few feet away. The girl with the overbite and her sister, El Mayoral, the other workers who'd come to protect his father; all shot in the head. Carlos was the one Manuel couldn't find, but as he began to pick up speed towards the house, with Luna chasing him, he tripped on a body, stumbled and fell beside it.

Carlos's face was smashed and his chest blown open. The branding iron lay on the ground nearby. Manuel moaned, and the best of him turned black as a crow, spread its ugly feathers and disappeared into that unholy night. "San Juan de la Cruz," he muttered, in a final, feeble attept to believe in anything at all. "In the darkness of your worst moment you found Him. Help me to have faith now." Still, he felt nothing but nothing. Where was God when those guns were being pointed? Where was God when his mother had begged for her life? Wearily, he pushed up onto his feet, backed away, and ran, slamming his fists into the sides of his head. "There is no God!" he cried.

Luna caught up to him, reached for one of his hands and wrapped her trembling fingers around his. "We can hide in the cave," she said.

They searched the barn for a hunting rifle and some ammunition, and the house for candles and match sticks. They packed two bags each, one for clothes and one for bread and cured ham, and filled wineskins with water. Then, they headed up the mountain.

Once there, they sat awake in the cave all night, holding onto each other tightly, disoriented, numb, with bats swooping and diving overtop of their heads, and the primitive painting of the red bull looming. Death was not always orchestrated with the beauty or majesty found in the ring. Death was a random, hideous promise, and without redemption.

Early the next morning, Francisco Pintado, the old farmer, found them and brought them to his wife who served garlic soup. Luna paid him, and when night fell, he hid her and Manuel in the back of his rickety truck, within cloth sacks usually reserved for bat and goat manure. He piled some of those around them in case he was stopped and his cargo inspected, and drove to the train.

LUNA AND MANUEL SAT next to one another on the train, staring out the dirty window. Luna's hands were still trembling. The farther she travelled from Sangre Mio, the closer to safety and Madrid they came, the more her body absorbed what she had witnessed. She was exhausted from mental anguish. Her thoughts were incoherent, and yet she couldn't stop thinking, nor could she sleep. Afraid to close her eyes and see the violence again, she didn't know how she would carry on. She'd barely had time to absorb the news that Don Carlos was her father when he was taken from her. How could she grieve him? Would she tell Pedro that he'd been her father too? The rhythmic clacking of the train on its rails was soothing. She rested her head on Manuel's shoulder.

"Again, we start over," he said.

"Yes." Luna nodded, but she was no romantic; some things cannot begin again and home was one of them. From now on her home would be nothing but a round house, with a carpet of sand. Her family, the muleta and sword. These things were not made of flesh and bone, they wouldn't deceive her or abandon her for death.

An hour later, the train stopped to refuel and a man boarded with a canvas bag slung across his back. He walked through each car, selling newspapers. As he approached, Manuel sat up. "Over here," Manuel said, waving a coin.

The vendor held out the newspaper, and reading the front page headline, Manuel gasped. *Lorca Dead!* it declared. Manuel scanned the article. Anti-Republican rebels near Granada had arrested and shot his favourite poet, the great Federico. All at once, the melancholy that had lived in Lorca's poems fell like tears upon him. He began to sob. With each Fascist victory from then on, he would struggle to hold onto poetry as if it was a fickle lover who couldn't commit.

LUNA AND MANUEL STOOD in the centre of Madrid's Puerta del Sol beside a faded flower stall with droopy, dehydrated geraniums. The streets looked to be in ill repair. Garbage tumbled in the gutters. Few trucks or motorcars passed and some storefronts hadn't yet opened, their windows drawn with steel shutters. A crier peddled newspapers on one corner, his music competing with the song of men selling Republican ballads for a few centimes on the opposite side of the street. When the bell on top of the clock tower on the Casa Correos sounded the hour Luna looked up and found a faded Catalan recruitment poster for the Popular Army pasted to the front of it. The illustration was of a woman in red overalls waving a rifle and it read: *Les milicies us necessiten! The militias need you!* A gang of militiamen passed them in the street wearing dusty blue overalls, zipper jackets, and peaked caps. They moved with authority, like the boys and men who'd marched into Sangre Mio, though their gait was buoyed by Republican optimism. She glanced at Manuel, whose face had aged ten years in a matter of days.

"How do we tell the others?" she said.

He kicked at a loose stone on the ground. Guns and blood and grief were blasting through his brain, and every minute of the day, Luis Mendez's face sat grinning behind his eyes, burning him with mocking laughter and red-hot tears shed of his mother's blood. "We start with the truth," he said.

Luna slipped her arm through his and together they walked, arm-in-arm to join Pedro and Marisol in the apartment at the hotel, in the Plaza Santa Ana, two renegade links in a longer chain that had already been broken.

LATER THAT NIGHT AT the hotel, after the horrors of the massacre had been shared, Marisol found spots of blood on her skirt. She hoped it was the result of shock and exhaustion, nothing more, but soon cramps began in her lower back and much stronger ones in her abdomen. Luna accompanied her to the hospital where she lost the baby gradually, over many painful hours. When she returned to the hotel a few days later, Marisol was frail and withdrawn and the womanly confidence that had made her so attractive to Pedro was replaced with shame and insecurity. For the next few weeks, the long, empty wail of her despair filled the hotel suite, as if it was the cry of the future, warning them all of what was to come: unmistakeable sorrow, sorrow, with its ugly endless echo.

IN SEPTEMBER, FRANCO'S TROOPS took Talavera, while the Soviet Union agreed to send arms to aid the Spanish Republic. Manuel followed the news closely, reconnected with old friends. The massacre at Sangre Mio had turned him into more of himself, more defiant, determined to join the resistance. Socialism made the most sense to him intellectually, Communism was a close second, but when he thought of home, his heart was an anarchist.

Meanwhile Luna waited for Pedro to find alternates and secure her a bullfight in Las Ventas, but day-by-day, the muscle in her left arm weakened, along with her spirit. There were fewer bullfights now, especially in Republican-controlled Madrid, and Pedro could find no colleagues willing to share time with her in the ring. She couldn't train and she couldn't fight, and soon, she knew, the capote would be too heavy for her.

"I've been crawling on my knees," Pedro said, one afternoon as they sat around. "I beg the impresarios and they laugh in my face."

"Try harder," she said.

He'd been dining in private homes with a group of aficionados, all Nationalists. He claimed he was using these meetings to stir support for her career, though Luna suspected the meetings were about more than that. Still, she wanted to believe her people would eventually accept her on foot, give her their respect as they gave it completely to the other toreros, and yet, as the war was proving, change comes not because it is politely requested, but because it is demanded. Why should her career as a matador be any different? "No more back room dealing," she said. "Tomorrow we visit to the Association office."

At first President Leal refused to see them but Luna wouldn't leave the marble foyer. She stood beside Pedro for two hours, with the suspicious eyes of the security guard upon her until her patience ran dry. Without a word, she slipped past the guard and vaulted up the staircase, pushing open the doors to the president's office. Pedro rushed to catch up.

Rafael Leal leapt behind his desk. "How dare you storm in here without an invitation?!" He was close to seven feet tall, and pole thin. On the wall behind him, a pink and gold capote was spread like the wings of a dead butterfly.

"I'm Luna García Caballero," she said, extending her hand. "And this is my brother, Pedro. We ask that you give me what I've already earned."

"Oh that," he said, dismissively. "I thought I'd settled that nonesense."

"Surely," said Pedro. "Such a cultured man doesn't mean to suggest that Spain's national pride is trivial?"

"I have an indisputable record of success abroad," Luna added. "Grant me permission to fight on foot in Las Ventas."

President Leal folded his arms across his scrawny chest, looked through her when he spoke. "There's no accounting for the Mexican authorities, but clearly here we must protect you from yourself."

"I've killed bulls ten times your body weight!"

Leal moved to his wooden filing cabinet, withdrew the top drawer, shuffled through a folder and pulled out a sheet of paper. "Here is a list of bullfighters your brother has been bothering," he said. "They've all declared their refusal to fight on any bill that includes your name." He handed her the paper and she read over two-dozen names, some of them friends and colleagues with whom she'd shared the ring in Mexico. "They won't waste bulls on a woman," he said, with smug satisfaction. "Now, are we finished?"

Luna tossed the list across his desk. "Not until you grant me permission."

Leal walked over to the door where the security guard was hovering, held it open. "Señorita García, some men might find your aggressive nature to be admirable. I am not one of them."

"There was Fransisca García," she tried. "I've studied her. She petitioned Pamplona for permission."

"She was the wife of a bullfighter. It was long ago."

"Teresa Alonso, La Fragosa. What about Las Noyas?"

"Novelty acts."

"All sold-out performances," said Pedro. "All on horseback."

"And all in dresses," said Leal.

"Martina García retired at sixty-six!"

Pedro took Luna by the arm, pulled her aside. "Keep your mouth shut! The virility of Spain is in question. A woman in the ring is more of a threat in times of war."

"A threat?" She looked as if she wanted to laugh, but feared she'd dissolve into tears instead. Her career had been an exercise in proving that, despite her sex, she was a formidable opponent, and now she was too threatening! "Which is it?" she asked, bitterly. "Am I too weak or too strong?"

Pedro noticed a monarchist newsletter lying open on President Leal's desk. It featured an article about the right-wing group, Renovación Española, advocating for the restoration of King Alfonso XIII to power. He turned to Leal. "We do not wish to jeopardize the law," he said. "Your laws are not in question." He took a step forward, sounded deferential when he lowered his voice. "Now, more than ever, we must all maintain tradition. But I think you can agree no woman has performed on foot so elegantly and with as much success as El Corazón?"

"I suppose," said Leal.

"Therefore she cannot be a real woman," said Pedro. "You see? It's a matter of category." He smiled and patted his pockets to show how simple and profitable the adjustment would be. "Grant her the status of a man and there will be no confusion."

"But I'm a woman," said Luna.

"No," Pedro shot her a silencing glare. "You are varonil."

"Varonil," repeated President Leal, weighing the outrageous proposal against Luna's appearance. Varonil was a manly term of praise, Luna knew, applied to girls who showed qualities valued in boys and men, but it suggested something unnatural about her. She slipped her hands self-consciously into her pants pockets.

Leal took in her height, tilted his head in appraisal. He walked around her twice to study her profile, her bottom and her thighs. He stared at her chest. "She's tall, like a man, but ultimately, she's too beautiful," he concluded. "If she were flat-chested, maybe. Or ugly. Her appearance, it works against your argument."

"On horseback then?" Pedro pressed.

"Absolutely not!" said Luna. "I refuse to —"

"For free, the first time," interrupted Pedro. "Or, to raise funds for a a local charity. We could donate the ticket price," he said. "What about to Renovación Española? There's a good cause. If she promises not to bother you again will you agree to that?"

"Fine," said Leal, exasperated. "To be rid of you. But she stays on top of her horse, and it'll be at an insignificant novillada after the main season ends."

"No!" said Luna.

"And her name will be listed last when the day's bills are printed and hung."

"Of course," Pedro nodded. "Thank you."

AT A YOUNG AGE, Pedro had learned that negotiating with those in power necessitated persistance and ingratiating yourself, often at the expense of others. His father had returned home from a long trip bearing perfume made of gardenia, a thick index about birds of the region, and a trim little slingshot. Pedro had wanted the slingshot as soon as he'd seen it, but it wasn't intended for him.

"There's a photograph of a Booted Eagle on page 56," Carlos had said, tossing him the index. "Like the one that circles around here in the fall."

"Oh," Pedro flipped the pages, dispassionately. He set the book down.

"What's the problem?"

"I'd rather have the slingshot," he said.

Manuel tentatively lifted the band of the slingshot, stretching it between his hands to see how far it would pull. "We can trade," he shrugged. "I don't mind."

"I do," said Carlos. "You're older and I gave it to you."

"Why should he get everything?" said Pedro, stomping his boot.

Perhaps if Pedro hadn't already believed some people were more deserving than others, he would've adjusted his attitude and appreciated what he'd been given. Perhaps if he'd understood that a sense of entitlement, his own included, was an approach to life that would deprive him of knowing genuine gratitude, he would've halted the meanness knitting under his skin. But he didn't know those things, so he determined to do whatever was required to advance his own cause.

"He doesn't like it," he said, of his brother. "You can tell."

"Yes, I do," Manuel lied.

"He'll be afraid to use it. You know he's spineless in the ring!"

Manuel chewed his thumbnail, avoided eye contact with his father.

"Give it to your brother," Carlos sighed.

"What? No, but I —"

"Give it to him!" Carlos grabbed the slingshot and placed it in

Pedro's hands. "It'll be good for birds and small creatures," he said, turning away from them both. "Don't ever let me see you aim it at a person."

AFTER LEAVING THE BULLFIGHT Association office, Luna and Pedro walked in silence for a few blocks, until Pedro stopped into a tobacconist to buy a cigar. Luna waited outside, feeling offended and deflated by the deal he'd struck. Under such conditions, how could she hope to graduate to the status of matador? It took a stranger's voice to bring her back to herself.

"Perdóneme?"

She turned cautiously to find two people — a girl a few years younger than herself wearing glasses and a navy zipper jacket, and a clean-shaven young man. "You're the bullfighter, yes?" he said.

"We've heard much of your last season in Mexico," said the girl. "You were in *El Toreo.*"

Luna smiled. "Probably for the blond bull," she said, humbly. "I remember him well." She touched her thigh as though a residual memory of her goring was permanently cut into the muscle along with the scar. She flexed her leg, straightened her shoulders, and assumed the posture of an experienced matador. It was reassuring to come upon these fans today. "Are you carrying a pen?" she asked, expecting to sign an autograph.

Without warning the girl spit on Luna's shoes. "You should be ashamed!" she said. "The bulls you've killed would feed hundreds and the land they were raised on would feed thousands more!"

Luna was shocked by these words and disgusted by the clear gob of saliva dripping from the toe of her right shoe. "Look what you did!"

The young man pulled a placard from behind his back, lifted it and waved it in Luna's face. One side of the sign bore the colours of the Republican cause and the other the words, *Occupy the land! End the corrida!*

Luna swatted the sign away, knocked it out of his hand. "Get that thing away from me!"

"I grew up working on an estate," said the man. "The landlord reserved his best soil for fighting bulls, and he rubbed it in my face every day that I would never eat that prize-winning meat. The first time I did was after the rise of the Republic, and it was the sweetest thing I'd ever tasted."

Pedro stepped out onto the street, holding a lit match to the end of a cigar as he inhaled. "What's going on?"

"They're anti-taurinos," Luna said, and before she could say more, both protestors had darted across the street and were running in the opposite direction.

"Hijos de puta!" Pedro waved his fist in the air and shouted obscenities. "I shit on the mother who bore you!" He hated these activists who called for an end to the corrida. Like all Republicans, they were morally weak, he thought. Sympathetic to foreign ideals. Though it had been Fascists who'd taken his home and his parents, Pedro blamed Republicans for having incited the war by going too far with their reforms. "Run, cowards!" he shouted.

Luna bent down and examined the placard. She had heard of such people, but this was the first time she'd encountered them in person. They were angry, hostile, and yet she couldn't dismiss them as easily as Pedro had. Bullfighting was the ultimate aristocratic conceit, it represented the class tradition that starved so many, and had once impoverished her. She felt her face burn. What had once been a radical, progressive ambition now made her feel like a traitor to her class.

"What do they want from me?" she asked.

"Your contrition," said Pedro. "Forget them."

THE EVENING LUNA ACCOMPANIED Manuel to a café in a run-down neighbourhood near the university it was raining lightly. A tough-looking youth of sixteen leaned up against the window of the café, partially blocking a sign informing them that tipping was forbidden. Manuel greeted him with the word *progreso,* which was used to identify militiamen to one another.

Inside, resistance posters hung on the walls. Red and blue notices declared that barbers had collectivized and bootblacks were no longer slaves. There was an image of a peasant woman who resembled Paqui, standing in a field of barley with her bare foot pinning her landlord's face to the dirt. Through the haze of thick tobacco smoke, at the rear, on a door leading somewhere private, there was a call to prostitutes to give up their trade. Luna was surprised to see Chucho sitting at a table strumming his guitar; she was about to ask Manuel about it when they were both distracted by a conversation in broken Spanish.

"Is that her, Karl?"

"Yes, I think so. Must be."

They turned and found two international volunteers. The first was a blond man with a square jaw and broad shoulders. The woman at his side looked to be about twenty-five. She had long red hair tied up in a practical way, but one thin strand snaked across her forehead, one cheek, and down her slender neck. She was tall for a woman, though she had more than a swell of hips, and her canvas mono was the very smoky blue of her eyes. She wore a hammer and sickle sewn onto the front of the overalls, over her heart, and beneath it, a Yiddish folk saying: "*If all men pulled in one direction, the world would topple over.*"

Manuel studied the foreign alphabet, unable to decipher it, until the man saw him staring and extended his hand. "I'm Kalle Kiiski nen," he said, in a jagged, unfamiliar accent. "Of the 15th Brigade. People call me Karl."

"Con mucho gusto. I'm Manuel García Caballero. This is my sister, Luna."

"El Corazón," she corrected.

"Of course, we know you by reputation," Karl said. "You're the one who wants to fight in Las Ventas. I saw your photograph in the papers. What an honour, truly an honour to meet the best lady bullfighter in all of Spain."

Luna smiled. "You are far too kind, Señor. Some people claim I'm no lady at all."

Karl laughed, and then, feeling indiscrete, looked at his boots.

"And may we know your lovely wife's name?" Manuel asked.

The redhead raised her cutting eyes. "I am Grace."

Manuel shifted in his clothes, feeling warm. Grace's skin was smooth alabaster, cheeks dusted with fine freckles, and her lips were full and red. Hers was a carnivorous beauty that suggested hunger. "Your husband is something of an aficionado," Manuel said. "Do you also enjoy the corrida?"

"I think it's cruel," Grace said, flatly. "It should be outlawed."

Luna winced at the prospect of another confrontation with an anti-taurino. "Is that so?" she said.

"Yes, and Karl is not my husband."

"We met on a train full of miners and lumberjacks," Karl explained. "She boarded in Toronto. The only woman. I offered my seat but she refused all the way to New York."

"He told the border guards he was visiting family in Finland," said Grace. "I said I was going to Paris to see the World Fair. It was easier than we thought it would be."

Luna folded her arms across her chest. "So you've come to Spain to defend the bulls?"

"I drive a mobile transfusion truck," Grace said, gesturing with one arm extended as though to clarify. "Blood transfusions," she said, proudly. "If we reach the men at the front they have a chance."

Two drummers and a Flamenco dancer took to the plank stage and a man tapped Karl on the shoulder. "Pardon me," said Karl, I hope you won't think me rude," and he turned from Luna and Manuel before they could protest.

The dancer's hair was pulled back off her long face and pinned at the base of her neck, with red flowers that matched her lips and the dress. Dark fringes spun out from her shoulders and from her waist, like feathers, and her black crinoline held the shape of her skirt. More impressive than her costume was the way she wore it: with confidence, with arrogance. She was a woman who knew what it meant to be a woman.

"You're American then?" Manuel asked.

"Canadiense." Grace spoke in a colourless Spanish accent. "My parents emigrated from Russia to escape the pogroms. I'm here with the help of the Canadian Committee in Support of Spain. Her lips moved to deliver the information though her eyes held the meaning. She played with the ends of her hair, eyes set on Luna, watching her closely, so closely Manuel began to feel invisible. "Tell me, El Corazón," Grace said. "Are you ever frightened by what you do?"

"Nunca. Jamás," Luna said. "Never." Of course she'd lived each day with fear, though not of the bulls. "Have you seen a bullfight?" she asked, defensively.

Grace shook her head. "Too much of death cannot be avoided. I've no need to search out more."

Luna's brow furrowed. She didn't know whether to be insulted by Grace's arrogance or dismiss her out of hand. "Then allow me to convince you what I do has meaning," she tried.

"I don't think that's possible," said Grace.

The dancer stomped her black heels, demanding their attention and flashed a bold smile that was as much a tease, as much a dare as Luna's expressions in the ring were a dare to her bulls. The dancer was sensuous and profound, and watching her, it didn't matter that she was beautiful, because her statement of survival was more beautiful. She waved her shawl at Luna to mimic a capote in the ring; she too danced with the shadow of death beneath her feet.

"Are you always so sure of yourself?" Luna asked. She searched Grace's blue eyes, waiting for a retraction or an apology. None came. Grace's face betrayed the faintest hint of humility and a carefully guarded heart. "Perhaps we're not so different," Luna said. "After all, it seems we're both in the business of blood."

Grace laughed, breaking the tension between them.

"You sound like a diplomat," came a familiar voice from behind. "Not a bullfighter."

Luna swivelled around and found Jorge Vidal, after more than five years, with a snifter of cognac in his hand. He was squat and balding but wearing a bow tie. He'd lost much weight and had a flat, ferocious face seen up close; one that made her certain time had treated him with the bluntness of a hammer. "Maravilloso!" she said, embracing him. "I was wondering when you'd turn up. How wonderful to see you again." She glanced around the café. "Is Eugenia also here?"

"In Paris," said Jorge. "Still painting and infuriating the masses."

"Jorge has pledged his considerable resources to the resistance," said Manuel. "It's through him that I originally secured our hotel suite."

"Few men possess a greater sense of honour," Luna said. "It doesn't surprise me."

"I've followed your career," said Jorge. "How far you've come from that grimy little girl who thought a glass of water was a treat."

"Apparently not very far," Luna said, aiming her words at Grace.

Karl returned to Grace's side. "I was talking with our Cuban friend over there." He pointed to a wiry young man with high cheekbones who was wearing a black beret. "He says Germany and Italy have recognized Franco. This will help him choke off Madrid."

"Impossible," said Luna. "Madrid will never fall."

An uneasy stillness settled across their part of the café. The crowd of socialists, Brigade members and trade unionists, stood around pretending not to hear. Franco had issued a decree forbidding political and union activity and his spies could be anywhere.

"Franco's already traded your souls for greater power," Grace said. "He'll stop at nothing. Where are these planes from that fly overhead? Where do you think he finds weapons? Germany and Italy and Spain are lovers now, like it or not. They share a passion for power that cannot be satisfied. We need to mobilize before it's too late."

"Lovers," was all Luna heard. "Lovers, like it or not."

"More of us should document what's happening," said Manuel. "Outside the country they hear only lies. I've been trying to send news to friends in Mexico."

Jorge sipped his cognac and held his snifter out for a passing waiter to refill. "The papers here lie too," he said.

"I don't trust what's happening on the Left," said Karl. Infighting had divided Leftists when he'd fought against the Whites in the Finnish war.

Manuel nodded. "We play into their hands and they'll crush us." He turned to Jorge. "What do you think of Largo Caballero's position within the party?"

"That Marxist bastard!" Jorge slapped Manuel on the back,

waved to acknowledge Chucho in the corner. "We must win the
war first. Later we can talk about revolution."

"This is what moderates always say," pressed Manuel. "But later
never comes. The social democratic position is self-serving. We
cannot please peasants and the middle classes, not if workers are to
have real control over the land."

"I agree," said Grace. "I'm in Spain to fight against a dictator —
not to fight for democracy. It's a big difference."

Manuel felt a surge of excitement well up inside of him at the
thought that he and Grace were political allies. He had an impulse
to find a pad of paper and scribble down some notes for a poem to
be composed later, but he resisted. It was harder than ever to see
the importance of any individual dream, including his own. "Since
Britain and France refuse to intervene perhaps we should work with
the Russians," he said. "The Marxist wing of PSOE is ready."

"Don't be naïve," said Jorge. "We should distance ourselves from
radical members. Don't you agree, Luna?"

Luna felt all eyes upon her, though none so penetrating as
Grace's. Her palms were sweating. She should side with Manuel,
she knew. No one had come upon her under the night moon, as
he had, looking a fighting bull in the eyes, nor would anyone else
see, as he did, that when she threw a perfect lance she was proving
more than her worth as a bullfighter. But Leftists opposed the
corrida and she was still set on getting to Las Ventas. She glanced
around the room, scanned the faces and clothes, the posturing, and
guessed that only she had been a servant. "I don't want to think
about it," she said.

Manuel pushed his bangs off his forehead. *We've been fighting
for your rights,* he thought. *The Republic would take hundreds of
thousands of girls like you and give them real jobs.* "But you have
an opinion?" he pressed.

"I don't know."

Manuel stepped closer, so close Luna could smell the sharpness
of his breath. "Here, before us all," he said. "I want to know what

the Great El Corazón — famous bullfighter of the people — will stand up for?"

"Let's return to the hotel," she said, advancing to show that she wouldn't be physically intimidated.

"No." He raised his voice childishly; this was the one arena in which she couldn't outperform him. "Whose side are you on, Luna?"

"I'm here tonight as your guest. That's all." It almost sounded like an honourable answer, but the truth was far less flattering and Grace, for one, recognized this.

"There's a clear line in this conflict," she said. "You must choose sides. If not, the choice will be made for you."

"I'm only interested in circles," Luna said. "Not in lines."

Grace scoffed, appalled by such blatant self-interest. She stared for a moment too long, to discern whether Luna could be as selfish as she sounded. Working in the unions at home, Grace had met but one person as confounding; the boss's daughter in the factory where she and her mother sewed clothes, the one with a knack for Yiddish storytelling and furtive kisses, the one who'd ultimately broken her heart. Grace was aware of Luna's body, lean and muscular from years of physical exercise, her face weathered beyond its nineteen years. "We may have as many opinions as you've had corridas," she said. "But at least we care." She looked at Manuel. He was wise to the difference between bravery and courage. He would sacrifice his life for the cause. She smiled at him, passing a current of appreciation his way.

Manuel was electrified. A wave of desire rippled through his body. Grace was beautiful and she was brave, and it seemed impossible not to want her. But was she Karl's woman? Manuel reached for his beer, took a sip and tried to shake off the disquieting idea, along with his nerves.

A FEW DAYS LATER, the evening before Luna's performance on horseback, without any warning, Eugenia called from downstairs in the hotel lobby. She'd made a trip in from Paris, she said, to consult with an epilepsy specialist, and she wanted to see Manuel. So, after changing into a clean white shirt, he headed down to the lobby to meet her.

They sat opposite one another, in gold velvet chairs. An immense floral arrangement stood between them. Eugenia was wearing a short black dress, black stockings and heels, and a long purple scarf wrapped twice around her neck. Her face showed the strain of time, or perhaps too many seizures.

"I heard the terrible news about your parents," she said. "I'm so sorry, Manuel."

"Thank you." He felt guarded, untrusting.

"My brother enjoyed receiving your letters while you were out of the country. He told me of your news whenever I asked."

"And did you ask often?"

Eugenia flashed her kohl-painted eyes. She smiled, but not indulgently. "You haven't forgiven me," she said.

"There was nothing to forgive."

She shifted awkwardly in her chair, crossed and uncrossed her legs. She'd made a mistake rejecting him all those years ago and questioned it now. She'd come to see about a second chance. "I wouldn't have guessed you'd look so good in a beard," she said. "But it suits you."

Manuel rubbed his face, self-consciously. "How is your health?"

She shrugged. "I can still hold a paintbrush."

"Yes, Jorge brags about his famous sister."

Eugenia fiddled with the fringes of her scarf. "Maybe you'll come to Paris to see me," she said. "I promise you'd be inspired."

He met her gaze and saw the flicker of temptation in her eyes; the possibility of what he had once desired so badly returning to him. For an instant he was excited, but nearly five years had passed. He wasn't the same man anymore.

"I don't write much poetry these days," he offered, gently.

"I see," Eugenia said. "I understand." She pushed up onto her feet. "I hope you've found your happiness. That is what's important."

He stood too. "Love, you mean. You hope I've found love."

Eugenia tossed the end of her scarf over one shoulder. "It's wonderful to see you," she said, kissing him on both cheeks. "Let's not take so long between visits again."

THE SUN WAS ALREADY setting as Luna prepared to enter the ring on horseback, when a thin, serpentine alguacil half-slithered, half-marched up to her. He was dressed in black velvet and a plumed hat, and the contrast between his uniform and the bloodless skin on his hands and face was stark, almost deathly. His eyes were of such a pale blue that they resembled a snake's. He spoke with a pronounced lisp.

"You shouldn't be wearing that suit for a novillada."

"Nothing else fit," she lied.

"It's too late to change, but you are not to dismount in the arena," he hissed. "Remember, you're under penalty of a fine and barring if you do."

It was infuriating to be forced back on top of a horse as though she was a child being punished for bad behaviour. She was less than a child, reduced to God's first idea of her — something worthless and ill formed. "Tell the president and your associates that El Corazón is their well-behaved prisoner," she said.

Determined to win over the crowd and compel the officials

to invite her back to fight on foot, Luna charged into the arena on an intelligent roan that Pedro and Chucho had bought at the police auction for the price of meat. She was immediately met with heckles from those who were offended by the sight of a woman in the ring, piercing whistles and insults so vulgar they would've pricked most women and children with their filthy, jagged syllables. "Mamarracho!" they called out — grotesque — and "marimacho! Butch!" — to ridicule what maleness in another torero, or in another place, would've received praise. Her skills hadn't changed since her injury in Mexico and yet here the tradition she had embraced was being used against her.

The stands were packed, a sea of rippling flags, including those the Governor and his wife waved — la tricolor — red-yellow-purple. Far off, at the top, were the glorious stone archways, one hundred unblinking eyes peering down as though in judgment. Luna saw that anti-taurinos had bought prominent seats and were waving their hand-painted signs. Sitting near Pedro, Marisol, and Chucho, tendido bajo, she recognized the two who'd accosted her in the street. She also recognized a few faces from the evening at the café, though there was no sign of Grace. With so many detractors, she began to fear that all the skill and confidence she'd accumulated over the years would evacuate her bones; she was nervous in a new way, perhaps in the way the bull is nervous, for she was the day's target. *Is there not more than one master of death?* she thought. *The matador, yes. But what about politicians and protestors who kill reputations?*

Before she could respond, someone in the stands shouted, "Girl, take off that suit!" and an anti-taurino called out for an end to bloodshed. Soon spectators were making the Fascist salute or arguing about the war, their anger bleeding into an invisible wave that threatened to drown her. Luna squeezed the roan's thick chest with her thighs, gripped the reins tightly with one hand, and with the other, steadied herself against his saddle. She tried to shut out the hostility surrounding her, to remind herself she had a right to be there. The larger crowd of aficionados, mostly pro-Fascist, turned on the anti-taurinos and she saw Pedro and Chucho leap over their seats to defend her honour, or to stain it, their tan hats with black ribbons popping into the air. Manuel shouted, "Fascistas, maricones!" and shook his fists, defending both Luna and Republicanism, and in his fury Luna heard something akin to the bull's seductive lament. *Try me, catch me, kill me if you're able. Slay me with grace but you won't conquer me.* Was the Left that beast, backed into a corner, or was she? She gave her horse a kick and turned towards the bull, galloping straight for him, a stupid, black-horned novillo named Angel Maker with curly hair on the crown of his head. She swore he cried real tears with each dart she threw. Her blue suit had faded with the sun, its brilliance dulled, and yet, somehow she made each precise target. As soon as she was done tiring the bull, the trumpets sounded and it was time for her to abandon her rival and remove herself from the ring.

"Your time is up!" shouted an alguacil.

"I can finish it," she said. "He's mine."

"Don't make me ban you!"

With the tightness of her satin jacket holding her high, Luna forced her legs to give a kick, asking her horse to lead her out of the ring. She wanted nothing more than to swing her sword — at the bull who should've been hers, at the young novillero — to make a descabello of him, or turn the blade upright on its handle, and plunge her neck down onto it and relieve the pain. Instead, she trotted past the picador's dying nag, towards the barrera, leaving any speck of glory behind, and the bull, to be finished by another, less skilled torero. Something shifted within her then, changing the route her blood made travelling the circuitry of her body, altering the perception her eyes held of the world. Justice was injustice, left was right, and no amount of supposed luck could help save her career.

Passing through the exit, she glanced over her shoulder to take a final look at the ring. For so long she'd believed justice could be relied upon inside that circle — the brave measuring their lives against the eternal clock of death. She'd learned from Manuel and Armando, from so many, that what mattered most was the emotion between torero and aficionado, her artistry and skill, but these were lies, as ugly as any others, and jealousy was a yellow boil spontaneously exploding inside her chest. She had trouble catching her breath. Rage, rage, the putrid pulse was spreading to her throat as though she was being strangled. It didn't matter how talented she was, or what pedigree she carried, in Spain she was no blue bird, wouldn't be anything but an illegitimate worm crawling in the dirt.

From centre ring, the novillero was making ridiculous clowning gestures. He ran at the bull and somersaulted over his broad back to show dominance. He placed a pair of banderillas de fuego, poder a poder, which exploded on the bull's back. Luna cast her eyes to the sand, embarrassed by her colleague. Though some found it distasteful to kill bulls in public view, she found it unforgivable to humiliate them. When she looked up again, her eyes flashed on something red; a long auburn mane that flickered fire under the sun. Grace was sitting in the contrabarreras, second row, behind the breeder and a line of impresarios. She wasn't cheering or arguing with anyone. She was watching the young novillero finish what Luna had begun, with a pained expression on her face. Her cheek was wet and Luna was touched, touched by the sweetness of the sentiment. Grace had been moved by her predicament and drawn into the spectacle, and for a moment Luna felt vindicated. But then, a second later, when the novillero killed the bull, she saw Grace cover her eyes with her hands, and knew she'd been wrong — Grace's tears weren't meant for her; they were meant for a more deserving animal.

Luna dismounted quickly, found her sword case where she'd left it with her cape coat by the chapel, and tore off past the peurto de caballos, and the area behind where the bulls had been drawn and quartered. She didn't stop to answer questions from reporters there, or permit rogue aficionados to dig the dagger in deeper. It felt as though her career was over. Barely holding back tears, she threw the cape coat around her shoulders and ran until she'd gone all the way around the corridor and burst out the side doors by the parking lot.

Catching her breath, she ambled along the side of Las Ventas, slowly moving closer to the main entrance where again she heard chanting. "Feed the poor! End the corrida!" They were waiting for her outside. She felt her stomach clench and peered around the front of the plaza. Two peasant women were tearing the cartel from beside the ticket window. They waved strips of it in the air, and cursed the bullfighters, accusing them, and the ring promoter, of murder. Soon, the whole crowd joined in, violently shaking sections of the torn paper.

"No more blood! No more hunger!"

Luna ducked, tried to hide behind the collar of her cape coat, but it was too late. "Look! Over there!" shouted one protestor. "It's El Corazón!"

The mob approached fast and Luna struck a defensive posture, on instinct, ready to fight. Her mouth filled with a salty paste. She gripped the handle of her sword case tightly in one hand.

"An end to brutality!" they chanted.

Brutality? It was the random cruelty of birth. A child without entitlement. Brutality was a dictator's dream, not hers. She looked around to see if Manuel had perhaps followed her outside, and was startled to find Grace peering down from the second floor balcony. In her overalls and white shirt she stood out against the brick background, reminding Luna of a bird she'd once seen high up in a tree. Luna raised her hand but Grace ducked out of sight.

The protestors advanced, and Luna stood her ground, prepared to defend her art with chivalrous determination, as if she was a man defending a woman's honour. "I hold the bulls in the upper-most esteem," she said. "A torero, more than anyone."

The demonstrators laughed and waved their signs. "Lay down your sword!"

"Mira, a bravura is a fierce competitor," she explained. "He'll kill without hesitation, if given the chance. It's my duty to honour him as an equal in the ring. Surely you understand that."

"Assassin!" They chanted.

"But I love the animals!"

"Mur-der-er!"

All at once, she was dizzy, as disoriented as she'd been after Armando's death, and after Paqui's. Rage mixed in with a shame that originated at birth but hadn't truly left; her own innate wrongness, the curse she carried like a secret in the bloody pocket of her heart. Did they see it? "Lay down your sword, El Corazón!" they shouted.

Instead, she lifted it higher.

If relinquishing her passion was the price required to show loyalty to a cause or a country that didn't want her, she'd be loyal to nothing and no one but herself.

Undeterred by her threatening posture, the protestors closed in on her. Trapped, Luna again did the wise but cowardly thing. She charged through an opening in the wall of people, and tore off down Alcalá Street. From the balcony above, Grace watched her flee.

ON LUNA'S TENTH BIRTHDAY, Manuel had offered to take her bird watching. She'd thought it sounded like the most boring activity, but had agreed to go because it would get her out of the house. Who wanted to squat in the tall grass all afternoon, sweltering under the sun, waiting for the possibility of something beautiful to appear? If they were lucky enough to see the dazzling bright yellow of a golden oriole or the tricoloured bee-eater it would be for a few seconds, at most. *I hate my birthday*, she thought. *He knows that.* Her heart squeezed a little too tightly. Birthdays reminded her of the parents she didn't know and the ambition she couldn't hope to fulfill.

Manuel looked at her as if to say, *be patient, see what comes.* He was proud he could identify birds by their calls. Or their silhouettes at dusk and dawn. Some of them he recognized from the flash of their bright wings on air. To Manuel they weren't merely birds in flight; each one was writing a secret message to the sky. Luna rolled her eyes. *Let's get this over with*, she thought.

They found a good spot from which to watch, partially shaded, and it didn't take long before they heard a tapping noise. They followed the hollow sound to the side of a dead tree where a great spotted woodpecker was hammering away, searching for food. Its quick, busy noise was impressive and Luna reached for Manuel's binoculars to have a closer look.

Magnified, it was easy to see the bird's black and white patterned wings, the crimson patch on the bottom of its belly, its stiff tail feathers helping it to balance on the side of the tree. It looked as if it should fall. Luna adjusted the focus on the small round lenses. Was it a female? The woodpecker stopped tapping. She gave a loud call. Without forethought, Luna mimicked the call and, to her amazement, the bird answered.

LUNA STAGGERED INTO AN alley, vibrating with panic. Vertigo had taken over and she couldn't go on until the spinning slowed. She removed her cape coat and slumped onto the ground beside it, where she remained for over an hour. Finally able to walk without feeling as though she would fall, she grabbed up her cape coat, stepped out onto the main street again, and flagged a taxi. She sped towards the hotel, past a boarded up pharmacy and a block of tapas bars, until the driver turned her sharply down a cramped street that lead to the Plaza Mayor, where another storm of people, this one singing Republican ballads, waved their fists in the air chanting, "No Pasaran!" and "Viva la Republica!" Luna peered up at the salmon-coloured Baroque facades of the plaza, to the balconies, a green blind rolled down in each window. In previous centuries people had flocked to this place for celebrations, including public bullfights. Now they gathered for a different kind of spectacle.

At the hotel, she dragged herself up four flights to their suite, number 409, and stepped inside, hanging her cape coat on a hook. Marisol was stretched across the sofa, with her feet in Pedro's lap. She had missed her period for the second month in a row and was secretly hoping she might be pregnant again. To guard against disappointment, she busied herself with mending a shirt while Pedro rubbed her feet. The room smelled of cigar smoke and the radio told news of Mussolini sending more arms and troops to aid Franco. A goatskin lay across the back of the chair where Manuel sat at an open window gazing out at the small Plaza Santa Angel, trying to write. He was jolted from his thoughts the instant Luna stepped through the doorway.

"Where have you been!?"

Luna fastened the lock on the door and fell onto the second sofa. Her damp and dusty suit was stretched and hung inelegantly off her bones.

"I looked everywhere," said Manuel, setting down his pencil. "You know better than to roam about alone."

She removed her slippers, untied the machos on her knees.

Manuel's back went rigid. "Quién?" he asked, with false calm. She was practically a full matador and she'd earned wages that supported them all, the equivalent of nearly thirty thousand pesetas a fight in Mexico, but she was still his responsibility and he wouldn't tolerate strange suitors. "I asked you a question, Luna. Who have you been with?"

"The anti-taurinos came after me!" she snapped.

Marisol looked up from her sewing. "Did they hurt you?"

"No." Luna shook her head.

Pedro lifted Marisol's legs, slipped out from under them. He'd had it up to here with activists. They buzz, he thought. Maybe they pinch. But they were easily squashed. The next time he saw them he would call in military force. "Those malditos idiotas should go back to Barcelona where they will find sympathy," he said. "Six grown bulls offer four thousand pounds of beef. A good sum for the local meat market."

Manuel fiddled with the strings of the goatskin on his chair. "The poor don't eat meat and you know it." It was his brother's bourgeois friends who profited from the corrida.

Pedro sucked his teeth. He caught sight of something on the table beside him, a copy of El Pueblo, the socialist workers' newsletter. The cover page featured an article Manuel had written. He picked it up and flung it at his brother. "Keep writing for that rag," he said. But remember what happened to that big mouth, faggot, Lorca. They shot him twice up the ass."

Manuel clenched his jaw. His lips tightened across his face, two pulled stitches. Was his brother threatening him? "Your Fascist brain has been twisted so tightly you can't think for yourself," he said. "You'd turn a swan into an armadillo if money could be made."

Pedro lit a fresh cigar, took a deep drag. "I suppose you think writing pretty poems is real work?"

"Vete a la mierda!" shouted Manuel. "Who broke union regulations with the old cuadrilla? Who short-changed them by making them sign receipts for full payment?"

Luna's eyes widened. "Pedro, you didn't!"

"Tell her," said Manuel.

"Fuck you!"

Marisol rested her needle and thread and draped her mending over the arm of the sofa. Though she wouldn't risk jinxing herself by telling the others she might be pregnant, she was already feeling cautious and protective, and wanted nothing to compromise her health. She looked at Pedro as if to say, *Please, let's have peace tonight.*

Luna stood and marched into her bedroom where she peeled out of her chaquetilla and pulled off her fuchsia socks, angrily. Was Pedro the reason no one wanted to work with her anymore? Then another terrible thought occurred to her. Had Manuel seen her as one of his causes? The thought of his pity, or condescension, enraged her.

Pedro began pacing in front of the glass doors that faced the Plaza Santa Ana. He stopped for a moment, and rapped his fingers against the pane of glass. His brother had a way of needling under his skin and making him look bad. Manuel had to see himself as a saviour, didn't he? Maybe there is no good dictator, he thought. But there are worse. He looked at this brother with contempt. "You'd rather see Russia in charge," he said. "You can have your Godless volunteers. No foreigner is giving me orders."

Seething with anger, Manuel turned to face the open city outside the window. The waxy yellow sun lit his dark face, as would a lantern and he reached for his pencil. He made a few hasty scribbles but nothing good came. *Was poetry another enemy? Not a ruthless dictator or a brother who resented him, but traitorous language, which wouldn't permit him to express what he needed to say.* He scraped his pencil across the page again, and found one compelling word left inside of him: *war.*

LATER, WHEN THE OTHERS were in bed, Manuel passed through the living room on his way out to a meeting and found his satchel and notebook missing from his writing chair. He noticed a light coming from under the bathroom door.

"Luna?"

She ignored him, rustled through his bag, expecting to find an editorial or a political treatise — something to explain what he'd been up to.

"Open this door!" he fumed.

She lifted out a ten peseta note and a crumpled handbill from the CNT, Confederación Nacional de Trabajadores, which she quickly tossed aside.

"Open this goddamned door!"

She wrapped her fingers around a small handgun, pulled it out of the bag slowly, assuming it was loaded, and stared at it a moment before setting it aside on the edge of the marble vanity. Next, she retrieved a tight wad of paper, unfolded it and shuffled the pages. To her surprise, it was a poem dedicated to Grace, laid down in practiced flowing script. She read the first stanza:

*The things that can't be said*
*reach beyond the world of war, into my nights*
*where I hush this shrill desire*
*renounce it, rededicate to our commitments.*
*And yet, I am adulterer;*
*as we spin resistance I grow two impossible hearts*
*for the good fight and for you.*

Manuel beat on the other side of the door while Luna slouched against it. "I swear I'll break it down!" he shouted.

She scanned the next page where he'd copied out Lorca's "Sonnet of the Sweet Complaint" and likened himself to a dog and Grace to its master. He'd devoted stanzas in admiration of Grace's face and the flash of her hair. Several passages found exquisite ways to describe the sound of her voice, to imagine the touch of her fingertips on his skin. *My body burns to be close to you*, he'd written, and each poem was signed, *Manuel Carlos Elonzo García Caballero, yours in struggle*. It was obvious to Luna that he'd fallen in love again. He needed Grace in the same passionate way she needed permission to fight on foot. There was no mistaking the desperation he felt to prove himself.

*She's not that beautiful*, Luna thought. *He exaggerates.*

Manuel crashed his boot through the door and for the first time in her life Luna was afraid of him. When he kicked at it again it flew open. He raised an arm to strike her but she prepared for the blow and he stopped himself. He turned and stomped past Marisol and Pedro who were standing in their nightclothes, staring.

Luna chased him out of the hotel apartment and into the stairwell, with his poems in hand. She shouldn't have snooped, but had wanted to understand him again. He'd been so far away. *Was it about the foreigner, Grace? He loved her more than he'd loved Eugenia?* She hurried to keep up, descending two steps at a time.

Manuel flew down the stairs and burst outside through the rear exit of the hotel to find half a dozen International Brigade members nailing posters on storefronts. "*No Pasaran!*" The posters declared. "*They shall not pass!*" He looked around for Grace but she wasn't among them.

Luna tried to tug him inside once again but he jerked his arm away. Her suit of lights was a kind of uniform that identified her with the enemy.

"Franco must be stopped," she said. "But it's the Republicans who would send me back to the kitchen and I won't go!"

"Shame on you!" he said. This struggle was about the very system that had once been responsible for negating her life and creating much of the pain that drove her ambition, and had taken her into the ring in the first place. He looked at her with dark eyes that were much older, older than his twenty-eight years. He was weary and accusation slackened and fell back against his bones like wilted branches.

"You're turning on me," she said. "But I know you still care about your writing."

Manuel sighed. Of course he cared, but there was no art in an artless age. *How could he write with a gun in his mouth?* He took both her hands in his, as he'd done so long before when he agreed to train her as a bullfighter. His palms were damp and she felt a fast pulse in their centre. "I'm on the side of those who have nothing," he said. "Whatever happens, remember that."

ON THE DAY REPUBLICAN forces beat back the rebel offensive at the Battle of Jarama, a soldier in a Nationalist army uniform arrived to help Pedro move belongings to a private location in the wealthy Salamanca district, where Nationalists were said to reside. Marisol, three and a half months pregnant, had just learned she was to relocate. She stood in the doorway of the hotel apartment with her hands spread protectively over her abdomen, blocking his entrance. "There's no need for us to leave, Pedro," she said. "Be reasonable."

"Get out of the way," Pedro said, shoving her aside.

"Luna, try and convince him."

"She's right," said Luna. "We should stay together."

The soldier walked towards the mantle, lifted the radio and turned to carry it out. "You'll be safer where you're going," he said.

Luna stepped in front of him. "Why? Because Nationalists won't bomb their own kind?" The soldier was young, perhaps fourteen. "You smell like a butcher as well as a thief," she said.

He laughed, sniffed the air between them. "So do you, lady bullfighter."

"Ignore her," said Pedro. "The radio belongs to me. I paid for it."

"With my money, you paid!"

"Luna, come if you want," said Pedro. "It's up to you."

"I'm not going with that assassin!" she shouted. "And I wouldn't leave without Manuel."

Pedro looked at her bitterly. "He doesn't share your sense of loyalty."

"Qué quieres decir?"

"He's chosen them; that's what I mean. Check his room. His clothes are gone."

Luna braced herself. She looked at Marisol for confirmation. "I'm sure he'll return soon," Marisol said.

Pedro moved about the room with the soldier, pointing out belongings with sharp, impatient gestures, the grasping abrasiveness Luna had abhorred in him as a child. She and Marisol had become liabilities to him and it occurred to Luna that if Marisol hadn't been carrying his child, Pedro might've also been willing to abandon her. She watched him lift a brown envelope, already opened, from his breast pocket and hold it out. "It was hand-delivered this morning," he lied.

"My permission!" Luna grabbed it from him and ripped into it. She scanned the words typed onto the page and her heart sank. *El Corazón is to be admired for talents unusual to her sex*, it said. *However, tradition prevails. We decline her request for an alternativa on foot, and we consider this matter closed.* It was signed by a high-ranking General in the National army, a colleague of President Leal's and a new friend of Pedro's.

"Tradition!" Luna spat. "Unusual to my sex!" She crumpled the letter into a ball and threw it at the soldier.

"Señorita," he said too calmly. "You are not being gracious."

Pedro waved him over to wait by the dining room table. "Mira, Luna, there are no more favours to call in. It's time to quit."

"I can't quit myself," she said. If ever there was a moment to tell him they were siblings it was then. But she didn't want his love if it could be traded as easily as a name. "Now you earn your living as a Fascist, is that it?" she said. "You intend to purify the nation? Cleanse it of people like me? Well, you need me. You've needed us all, and more. Admit it; without us who would you blame for your own inadequacies?" She shoved him towards the soldier. "Get out! Go with your new friends! See how long it is before they turn on you."

"Vamos," said the soldier. "Let's go."

Marisol began to sob. "You're out all night, Pedro. Here I have Luna for company. Please, I am begging. Let us stay together."

"Don't beg, mujer. It's weak. Soon you'll have my son for company."

Marisol crossed herself and Pedro laughed, mockingly. "Yes," he said. "Father, Son, and Holy Ghost, the one team left around here."

Luna clutched Marisol's hand. "We'll still see each other as often as we like. I'll meet you at the Rastro. We'll go to mass."

Marisol couldn't stop crying long enough to speak. The thought of bringing a child into this madness was unbearable. If Luna were there too, she reasoned, she might manage. Strange how two people who, at first, had avoided each other could've become so close. She and Luna were family now, in the truest sense. Being the only women in a house of men a bond had been forced, one the rest of them couldn't see. Marisol hadn't seen it fully either, until they were about to be separated. "You'll come for the birth?" she said, as though she and Luna would need an excuse to be together.

"Claro que sí," said Luna. "Of course. I'll help you name him."

Marisol gave a weak smile. Like Pedro, Luna assumed it would be a boy. I hope it's a girl, Marisol thought, so we'll outnumber them. She wiped her eyes and permitted Luna to pull her close, inhale the lemon and oleander in her hair. It might be a long time before they would see each other again, and, if they did, things would've once more changed. Pedro bellowed for her from the stairwell.

"I'll light a candle for you," Marisol said.

"I won't need your prayers anymore."

Marisol stroked her abdomen with a trembling hand.

"Then light one for me."

LUNA RAN ALL THE way to the café to find the place empty, except for two wrinkled aficionados standing at the bar, and a table of painted whores. The acrid smell of cigarette smoke lingered, but she noticed that the resistance posters were gone, and in place of one there hung a sign that said, *Se prohibe cantar. Singing is forbidden.* She waved to the bartender and he set down his towel and came out from around the counter.

"You're the sister of Manuel," he said. "The bullfighter."

"Do you know where he is today?"

"No sé y no quiero saber. Don't know, don't care to know."

"You don't mean that," she said, preparing for another argument.

"Each night your brother and his friends pass as I am closing," the bartender explained. "'If you're a Fascist you will lock that door,' they tell me. 'Only a Fascist would refuse us to meet here.' What can I do? I have a wife and three children upstairs. I see their guns. But this morning two Falange soldiers passed. 'If you're one of us you'll lock that door,' they said. 'This is no refuge for traitors, right?'" The bartender was nervous to speak with her, his face a grey moon with dark clouds for eyes, and in them the turbulent look of Spain itself. "So I am whatever I need to be," he said. "I can't have trouble here. Tell him. Tell the other one too."

"Cuál otro?"

"The one with the claw," he said, fixing his hand as if he were an eagle. He gestured with his chin. "Back there."

She reached across a small table, lifted a newspaper and tore off one corner. "I need something to write with," she said. The bartender moved over to the counter and returned with a pencil. She scribbled in the margin of the newspaper, folded it, and handed it to him. "If you see the Canadian woman, give her this, from me. Tell her it's important that she come." She pulled two ten peseta notes from her pocket, and slipped them across the table. "For your troubles," she said.

She turned the cool brass doorknob at the back of the café expecting to find a secret meeting of Republicans, but it was quiet and dark on the other side, and she barely saw her own shadow. As she stepped further along a slim hallway she heard whispering and the shuffling of clothing. The sound stopped, then, when she neared a red curtain, it resumed. Chucho's unmistakeable voice was on the other side, full and heavy with urgency, and there was something desperate in it that made her uncomfortable. It was warm, without fresh air, and the odour of spilled Cognac and Absinthe closed her in. She slipped the curtain, barely an inch, to one side — enough to catch the shock of Chucho's dark head and broad, naked back glistening with sweat. His powerful arms were spread, raptor's wings, each one reaching around in front of Jorge, steadying them both as Jorge bent forward, eyes squeezed tightly. She read the strained, almost pained, expression on Jorge's face. Chucho's claw was stuffed into Jorge's open mouth to stifle his pleasure. Then, Jorge turned and they kissed.

Luna dropped behind the curtain, covered her own mouth. She crossed herself. "Santiago," she prayed, "what guidance can you offer?" Should she run and pretend she'd not been there, or, throw the curtain aside and confront them, men sick with the fever of sin? Frozen in place, she listened to the frantic flutter of Chucho and Jorge claiming each other.

Their passion was a dark delight, unstoppable, oblivious. Carnal. It terrified her. Her stomach twisted, and lower down, and yet, she envied them their liberation. She'd embraced passion on Sundays at five in the afternoon, the stall of day, but there were parameters to those interactions and she was in charge. What passed between Chucho and Jorge defied rules, disregarded institutions. Before she could be discovered, Luna ripped herself away, crept out along the dark hall, and burst into the bar where the bartender looked confused by her shocked expression. She returned to the empty apartment and threw herself onto her bed, breathless. Conflicted, she couldn't help but touch herself. It had been a long time since she'd been kissed, and longer still since the girl with the overbite, but that's what she thought of: another girl's lips upon her own. She'd been denying the need for human touch, and now her hand between her legs denied nothing. She shuddered, and when she brought her wet fingers to her lips she found she tasted salty, more like the sea than the sky, and Grace's name was slipping off her tongue.

LUNA WAITED OUTSIDE THE bullring, beneath the ancient midnight moon. A scattering of derelict men scampered about Alcalá Street in search of dropped coins and wine. An old woman dressed entirely in black and red sniffed her out, and grinned the greeting of the mad. She was missing her front teeth.

Luna stepped from under the darkened main gate when Grace appeared, her face wrapped in a blue scarf, and startlingly white beneath the lamppost.

"I'm not sure I want to be here," said Grace.

"Surely someone who drives on the front lines cannot be afraid of me?"

"You kill," Grace said, without irony. "I'm fighting against you."

Hurt, Luna motioned for her to follow through the main gate. It had been left unlocked by a security guard who'd been all too happy to accept her bribe. They walked the length of the round corridor with moonlight as their guide, fanning in through the semi-circular iron grills, and casting intricate patterns at their feet. Each step echoed on the red stone floor. Grace crept closely because at two feet apart, they became invisible to one another. When Luna found the door they slipped through it, and through the arrastre, where she smelled the stale blood of dead bulls who'd been dragged out. They stepped onto the dry sand of the bullring and fell off into silence. Grace moved gingerly, as though afraid to step on something live, or dead, or perhaps to stain her shoes.

"Here," Luna said, reaching out to offer a hand. She was surprised to find Grace's palm dry and chafed like her own; Grace had worker's hands that seem a poor match for her kind of beauty. They moved out into the centre of the ring, where Luna knew, from memory that they were standing at the exact spot where she'd last sat atop a horse. They might've been the only two people to have stood under an open sky, inside that empty Plaza de Toros in the middle of the night, and what she learned was this: without aficionados to fill the stands and bear witness, there were souls within that stone and dirt circle, ghosts of other matadors, ghosts of the brave bulls they'd fought, and she could feel them all there with her. Once they stopped, Grace immediately let go of her.

Luna turned to face her, though her mind was empty. She'd asked Grace there for reasons she didn't fully understand. "Manuel hasn't come home," she managed, grinding her feet into the sand. "I think he's in trouble."

Grace hesitated before revealing anything. "We're preparing for another battle," she said cautiously. "At Guadalajara, on the northeast front. With men like your brother leading the charge, there is hope for Madrid."

The slow, even rasp of breath. The distant thrum of traffic in the streets.

"My petition to fight on foot has been refused," Luna blurted. Saying it out loud felt like a condemnation and right away she thought she should explain. "They find one excuse after another to exclude me. They claim I make a parody of the corrida and it's not true. When I'm here, when I stand in the centre of a ring and face the bull, I too am staring down death."

"No," interrupted Grace, "you're preparing to kill."

"Yes," she said, flustered and on the defensive.

Grace scoffed and Luna felt her judgment. Others gave their lives for freedom while she merely satisfied her own ambition. She knew Grace believed what she did was not fighting, but barbarism. There was silence and Grace had turned from her, although in the dark there was no need to do so; the moon was obscured by a cloudy sky and Luna couldn't make out the coarse details of Grace's expression. Did she always have such fierce convictions and absolute confidence in them? Perhaps other Canadians were the same, innocent in the way the young are innocent, not having been corrupted by too much history. "The corrida is Spain," Luna said. "Sweet, sweet Andalucía, where the country's soul has long struggled against itself — the coast's hot summer against mountain cold, the dry tabernas desert in Almería against the rainy Sierra de Grazalema in Cádiz. We are the sun, more than any place in Europe, and though our history has long been a battle, few argue about whether a fighting bull deserves the ring."

"Then let me go and we won't argue."

All at once, Luna needed to convince Grace that she was a good person, and that her life was of value. She told herself it was because Grace was the closest she could get to Manuel, but it was something else.

"You don't know anything about me," Luna pressed. "Or what I do. Spain is thousands of years old, and your country too young to be civilized yet." Luna kicked at the sand with the toe of her shoe. "I've devoted myself to bullfighting, it's my family and before it I had none. When I stand in front of a charging bull I remember that, and I don't move because I would rather die than feel so lonely again. Is it wrong to hold onto that in the middle of the war?"

"Boys as young as twelve die every day," Grace said, impatiently. "A grenade fails to unpin, a forty year old Mauser jams. They die from hunger, lack of sleep and the night wind. Lice drives some of them mad. Occasionally, a Fascist machine-gunner makes his target."

"But you save them?"

"No, I merely drive." Quietly, more quietly than had there been light, Grace was crying.

"Oh, don't," Luna said. "Don't do that."

Grace wiped her tears, her unpredictable emotions. "I'm sorry," she said.

"Maybe it's because you come from far," said Luna, "and foreigners look with borrowed eyes. I don't know, but if you would try and understand; beauty does exist inside of this great spectacle." She spread her arms into the blank slate of night. "Beauty and valour and the true art of performance." She faced Grace, stepped closer so Grace would hear the honesty in her voice. "Wherever there is beauty there must also be a little tragedy, no?"

"Life is not a three-part act," Grace said. And more softly, "Your suertes. To watch the horses suffer. How can you?"

Luna took a deep breath, and tasted the faint flavour of old blood on her tongue. "There's pain everywhere," she said. "For the animals, for toreros. Here," She wanted to raise her hand and sweep Grace's hair to one side but didn't. "Right now, I see pain behind your eyes."

Grace stiffened. "I should go."

"Wait," Luna reached for Grace's hand. "This circle is a clock to me," she said, pointing to their enclosure. "The measure of my life, of any life, I suppose."

"That's a beautiful image," Grace said. "If only what it represented wasn't so hideous."

"Maybe you should go!" Luna snapped, then felt mean for speaking so harshly. She sensed Grace needed something to believe in, even if it wasn't her. "Look up," she said, arching her neck to face the stars.

Grace caught her breath. The sky was unusually clear and whole constellations flickered brightly against the obsidian night. Luna remembered the orange grove on Don Ramón's property where she and Armando had strolled, the bullring where she was gored, Sangre Mio. Nothing of beauty existed without a dark side.

"I came tonight because of Manuel," Grace said. "He seems to love you as he loves no other."

"Who do you love?" Luna asked, and quickly, she dropped her eyes. "Perdóneme, I'm sorry, we're strangers. I make you uncomfortable."

"Have you ever seen a falling star?" Grace asked. "It's good luck."

Luna shook her head. She needed no more luck. She'd been luck's prisoner, and luck had forsaken her.

"If we see one tonight we can each make a wish," said Grace.

Luna waited next to Grace and felt the heat of her body, wondering for the first time what it would be like to kiss someone so different — and yet so much the same. *Had Manuel and Grace already kissed?* When no star fell Luna said, "No matter. Somewhere a star is falling. We can wish on it from here."

Grace smiled, one thin crack that said hope was her salvation.

"Where's Manuel?" Luna whispered.

"I'll take you," said Grace.

Then, standing in the centre of the bullring where she'd been refused her rights, Luna caught Grace looking at her in an unguarded way, as though what she did for a living had been forgiven. She smiled and when Grace blushed she felt the unmistakable rush of blood that warned of danger. She'd known something similar once before, with Armando. She'd tried to win his favour too. Was love chasing her again, as death chased? She gave up counting the stars above them. Paqui had been right; there were a million illuminations to be found, gifts of light from out of nowhere, and standing under them Luna knew Grace was the one. Grace held the power to break her heart.

INSIDE THE TRANSFUSION HEADQUARTERS the sterile residue of hyperbaric oxygen, citrate and blood lingered. They passed a dozen volunteer donors sitting on chairs against one wall, waiting their turns. Above them hung a photograph of a balding médico in a mono similar to Grace's, with the word *Canada* stitched on his shoulders. The volunteers' clothing was threadbare and tattered. One man wore no sandals or boots; his toes were bloated and purple and stank of rotting flesh. They sang and cursed Franco, pledging revenge against the high number of casualties that had been suffered by the Left.

Luna pointed to the photo. She wanted to know about the Canadian man. His name was Bethune, Grace explained. Spaniards called him Médico de Sangre. Doctor Blood, because the mobile unit was his idea. Grace turned a corner into a windowless room. There were three beds on one wall and a stack of medical supplies propped along another.

The gangly médico from the photograph leaned over the foot of a grey iron bed feeding blood into a patient's ankle through a thick rubber tube. Around his neck he wore a stethoscope. A fat nurse in a white apron monitored the patient's heart rate and tucked a stiff sheet and two blankets under his chin.

Without looking up, Bethune fogged the lenses of his glasses with his breath and wiped them using the edge of the bed-sheet. He replaced his glasses, peered up at Luna. She had come to help soldiers. At such a time of low morale this was a great show of solidarity. He nodded in appreciation and Luna felt like an impostor.

Grace led Luna to an empty cot in the corner where Luna sat and rolled up her sleeve. Grace produced a Jube syringe from a metal tray on the table next to them and held up a 500 cc glass bottle. She would collect in this, and after the doctor would check Luna's blood group and the bottle would be sealed and refrigerated. In a week or two someone would drive it to the front. Could be her. "You could save a man's life, Luna. Have you ever saved a life?"

"Only my own," she said.

Grace wrapped her long fingers around Luna's wrist. "Squeeze your hand into a fist," she said. "Good." She inspected Luna's arm, ran her pointer across the crease on the inner side of Luna's elbow a couple of times and pressed down firmly. "I feel a vein," she said, smiling up at Luna and for an instant Luna forgot to breathe and thought they might stay in that position with Grace holding the arm she used to swing her capote, and that being close to Grace might be a kind of victory. Anyone would've felt the same next to Grace — instinctive, restless, a little too willing to do whatever she asked.

"Manuel's not far," Grace said. "But you promised; this first." She flicked a vein hard with her index finger and rubbed alcohol over the spot with a piece of cotton. The smell was as cold and sharp as a blade. Then, Grace carefully inserted the point of the needle into Luna's arm. "Didn't get it," Grace said. "Your veins are deep." She dug the needle around beneath the skin, pushing her face closer. "Do you feel that?"

Warm breath.

Temptation.

Luna shook her head. "Like a mosquito bite," she said.

"That?" Grace was frustrated.

"No."

"There?"

"Aiy, sí!"

Grace sat up straight. "Good. Now, open your hand."

A slow red liquid flooded the syringe, down along the rubber tube, and into the glass jar. Luna thought of Christ, she didn't know why. And the stigmata. She felt a sacrifice — passion required it. She watched Grace's lips, noticed the tendons in her neck. Her pulse. The memory of the goring in Mexico returned to her, her blood pooling out onto the sand. It was an odd sensation to know she was capable of being emptied. Her arm began to tingle.

"You're pale," said Grace. "Maybe you should lie down." Grace gathered a pillow under Luna's head and neck, and helped her to lean backward onto it without tugging at the tube. That was when Luna felt it without question — desire, coursing through her veins, her body burning towards betrayal. She shuddered as the weight of Grace's breasts swung into her smelling of warm, yeasty bread.

THE TRUCK GRACE DROVE was a long black Renault with the words *Servicio Canadiense de Transfusión de Sangre al Frente* printed on the side. She steered purposefully away from the headquarters and up a small incline; she'd made the journey many times. The roads circled and circled as though they were trapped inside a game of darts and Madrid was the bulls-eye. With one foot on the clutch and the other on the gas, Grace clamped her right hand around the gearshift. Karl, who'd met them at the truck, was slouched against the passenger-side door in khaki pants and a dark green shirt. He shifted to make room for Luna in the middle.

"Is it true you're forbidden to fight in Spain?" he asked.

"On foot," she said. "But one day I will perform in las Ventas. It's my dream."

"Such a small dream," murmured Grace.

Luna's body tensed and Karl noticed. He rolled down the window and his blond hair blew into his eyes. "Manuel says you're a poet in the ring."

"Killers are rarely poets," Luna said, no longer willing to tolerate anyone's judgment or disapproval. She'd been born for the ring and for the tight suit of lights she wore to honour it. Her palm had been chiselled perfectly by the better hand of God, to hold a sword. Grace didn't think so but it was true. Light from the sun eclipsed Grace's face, momentarily erasing her from vision, it retreated and once again Luna found the tangle of red hair, freckles scattered across Grace's face like tiny stars. Despite her anger, a sensation of pleasure rang through her body. She straightened in place and tried to ignore it. "I'm a matador," she added. And because one truth bleeds into the next she added, "maybe we're not all born to be heroes." She reached for a goatskin on the dash, squirted a stream of water into her dry mouth without touching her lips to the bag.

Grace turned a fast corner and sped them over a bridge. Her truck lurched and jolted, and she accidentally grazed Luna's hand. She steadied herself against the dashboard, folded her right hand in her lap so it wouldn't happen again. "Tell us about Manuel," she said.

Luna closed her eyes, conjured him writing in his notebook — in hotel lobbies, in the back of a bus, in the pasture at Sangre Mio with the whitewashed ranch house in the distance, clean and pure against the dusty earth. Manuel had always been there, somewhere in the background of her life. "He's patient with me," she said. "He understands me before I understand myself."

"I believe that."

Luna stared. How could Grace think she knew Manuel if she couldn't understand the corrida? Much of Manuel's life had been defined by it. Because of bullfighting, he was tethered to her as the bull is tethered to his caste. She'd already tried, in the arena, to explain: Love is an imperfect circle, from the forgotten curve of her mother's womb to the open mouth of her first kiss, to that sandy enclosure that had secured her freedom, it was a knotted promise that must be kept. "Manuel will return to the hotel with me," she said.

Light fell on Grace once more, a gauzy veil, shrouding her expression. She blinked in a flutter to the blinding light. "I don't think so," she said.

The tires of the mobile unit scratched and turned over in the dirt, and wind picked up, blowing dust in through the open window. Luna coughed. "What of Finland?" she asked Karl, but he kept his eyes fixed out the window.

"Spain would fit inside of Canada thirty times," Grace offered. "Maybe more."

"Are there mountains, like here? Workers fighting for their rights?"

"Committed socialists," nodded Grace. "My mother organized the Amalgamated Clothing Workers Union. She sews in a sports-wear shop. My father made deliveries for the warehouses."

"What did you do?"

Grace smiled. "You can't imagine me without the war, can you?"

"I suppose not."

"When I was young I sometimes rode a carriage with my father," she said. "Later, they changed to trucks. His was much like this one but painted blue. Eventually I worked in the needle trades with my mother and the other women. We had half a day off on Saturdays when our family attended picnics and barbeques. When the Depression hit there were no jobs." Sadness seemed to wrap around Grace and squeeze tightly. "A few years ago we lost our house," she said. "My father left to look for work. We moved in with another family and my mother disappeared too, in her own way. We don't know my father's whereabouts; but from time to time he sends money."

"You miss him."

"Yes, of course. I stayed with my younger sister Rose, she's … how would they say it here, Karl?"

"Retrasada," he said.

"Yes, retrasada. She's twenty but her mind is that of a child."

"Ah sí," said Luna. "I've watched them begging for bread by the cathedral."

"Rose does not need to beg!" Grace was adamant. "She is loved. I cared for her."

"So who's caring for her now?"

Grace cast her blue eyes to the dashboard, fidgeted with her hands around the steering wheel. Her fingers were slender and white but their tips callused, red and sore looking. "I joined the Resistance," she said.

Luna nodded knowingly. She faced the distance where the heavy hills sloped and arched, leaning into one another like soon-to-be lovers. "You didn't rush to Spain to save us from anything," she said, sounding a little disappointed. "You ran away to save yourself."

A BLAZE OF ORANGE swept across the sleepy sky as Grace approached Ciudad Universitaria, where a nurse was standing next to a militia-man on a gurney, one of his legs cut off at the knee, exposing a stump of rotten flesh. He was covered in dried blood, and his clothes and face were caked with mud.

"Gangrene," Karl reported. The nurses had stopped it before it had spread throughout his bloodstream. He'd had a transfusion but there was no room for him at the hospital. The legless man was conscious, but not lucid. His head rolled on his neck as though loosely hinged, and his eyes roamed — the sky above, the mobile unit as they slowed. Karl gave him the anti-fascist salute and the wounded man tried to return it.

Minutes later, the sun slipped below the horizon, bringing a chill, and night came thick around them. "So we're even?" Grace

asked. "You gave me your blood and I'm bringing you to Manuel."
A low flutter opened up in the distance, the sound of metal cutting
air high above them. The noise grew louder, sharper, more mechan-
ical. An airplane descended, and looked, for a second or two, to
be suspended over top of them, its sinister grey body like that of an
enormous shark.

"A Gustav," said Karl. He'd seen gold on the wings.

Grace switched off the headlights. Should she pull over and wait
until it passed?

"They already see us," said Luna. She preferred to be a moving
target.

The aircraft flashed past and turned back again, flying so low the
trees shook, and their bones rattled, and a swirl of wind sent dirt
flying. Karl and Grace rolled up their windows and Luna covered
her ears to block the grinding noise. There were two figures in the
cockpit and they tracked Grace's truck for less than half a minute
until she parked in front of a large brick building, and they were
gone.


THE SECOND FLOOR OF the old philosophy department was crammed
with bodies, International volunteers propped up on their weapons,
trying to sleep, others straining to make the night watch at the
windows. It stank of neglect, filthy clothes and the putrid tang of
human waste. Great thinkers and writers had studied on this campus
and now it was occupied by Manuel's charges, mainly volunteer
soldiers. As soon as they entered, Karl joined a group of men, one of
them Chucho, and Manuel appeared.

"Luna, my moon," he said, embracing her.

She ran her fingers across the dark stitches on his brow. He'd left
without saying goodbye. She'd thought she wouldn't forgive him
but she already had. His clothes were damp, made of useless cotton
that couldn't hold much heat. His teeth were chattering. Luna rubbed his arms for warmth and found crumpled, yellowed pages poking

out of his collar and the cuffs of his sleeves. His jacket was also stuffed with soggy paper. She tugged a page from around his neck.

"Literature makes for good insulation," he said, turning to a mound of charred books, the once hoped-for legacies — pages torn from their spines, littering the department floor, miniature paper tombstones. Behind the mound was the library. "There are no more blankets," he added. He'd given what was left to his men.

Grace pulled a package from beneath her coat and handed it to him. "These came from our Irish friends," she said. "There's more bread and wine in my truck, but no cheese."

"A feast," he said, devouring her with his eyes. He kissed her on both cheeks and turned the package over to the five men kneeling on the hard stone floor nearby. They were passing a panikin between them and heating its contents over a single candle. "Mi hermana," he said, explaining Luna's presence. "I think she's come to take me to the city."

The men laughed, and so did Grace, but Luna didn't. The dark, damp cold made her impatient. She pulled him aside. "Return with me to the hotel," she demanded. "We'll leave now."

Manuel glanced over at Grace, emboldened by her beauty. "This isn't some far away noise you hear about on the radio," he said. "Look at them. They're half starved, injured." His eyes were large and melancholy. "Some will die tonight."

"I don't need to look," she said. When she closed her eyes she saw the others lined up against the stone wall. She couldn't escape the pitching and sounding of guns blasting in her head, and she didn't need him to die to know what all of it meant. She panned over the reading room where anti-tank guns slept on tables next to students, thinkers, perhaps former poets like him. "I'm responsible for my mother's death," she whispered. "I couldn't help Paqui or Armando, or our father."

"I don't want to be saved."

She removed her cape coat and swung it around his shoulders. He was the one who'd saved her time and again — with kindness and friendship. He was the one who'd called her 'sister' for the first time, before they knew it was true. "Don't be so proud," she said.

"I expect you to understand. You, of all people." He raised his bayonet as if it was a muleta. "This is my pen now." Rain flew through the shattered glass of a large window, spitting on their faces. "Join us," he added, straightening. "This is your fight too."

"My fight is in the sun," she said.

Manuel glared at her, as though she was his enemy, and all at once she might've been. "Where is your heart!" he shouted.

"Still in the ring," she said, defiantly. "Where you placed it."

The candle the men had been using to heat their food flickered and died and with it went any lingering hope Manuel had that she would join the Resistance. "If I made you what you are today, I'm sorry for it now," he said, and he might as well have unnamed her. "There's been a barricade," he added coldly. "Travel tonight is impossible; the roads may be bombed." He turned, started walking towards Chucho and the other men, then called over his shoulder. "Stay in the truck. I'll find you in the morning."

LUNA AND GRACE HUDDLED, shivering, under one blanket in the truck, desperate for warmth. They were curled, seahorses, shaping into each other. It was awkward for Luna to be so physically close, but the cold made it necessary. They were surrounded by the echo of a lone sniper and the keen scent of blood — blood that had poured from open wounds and dried. Blood, that had been rejected by bodies, spilled from loose tubes, splattered onto the machines and motors above them. Luna opened and closed her right hand, intuitively grasping for her muleta, and felt a pinch in her arm from where Grace had drawn her blood. A clock on the dashboard announced each second, each minute, and she could not erase the Godless irony that if Manuel's life was spared it would be by the grace of Spanish literature, some thick copy of a renaissance book stopping a Fascist bullet.

"Manuel may not forgive me," Luna confessed.

"For speaking to him as you did?"

"For meaning it." She rubbed her hands together under the blanket to bring warmth. Her teeth were chattering.

Grace pressed closer. "I felt trapped at home," she said. "With the depression on, I was one more mouth to feed. My sister wasn't the only reason I left." She gave a small laugh. "You'll think this sounds foolish, and it does: I hoped it would be better here."

Luna thought of her own demand to leave Mexico to fight on foot in Spain. "Staying would've been a kind of death," she said.

"People die in small ways."

Luna tried not to touch Grace more than was necessary. She couldn't speak anymore of death without also speaking about the bulls. "I know that," she said.

"The corrida," Grace said, caustically.

"You know, if I doubted myself as much as you do, my blade wouldn't go in and I would lose my life, and with it the one love I can call my own. There have been moments since my return to Spain when I've questioned it," she admitted. "But not for long. If my art is ugly, as a painting can be ugly or one of Manuel's poems a failure, that doesn't mean there's no value in what I do."

"Manuel writes poetry?" Grace asked. "He hasn't told me that." She shifted slightly. "When I see the two of you together I miss my sister."

Luna was pleased Grace didn't know Manuel as she did. "He was meant for softer things," she said.

"You can't believe that," said Grace. "He's a strong man."

But she did believe it. Manuel was all heart, her heart, dancing outside her body. Her life had depended on him from the start. He was strong, to be sure, though his kind of strength was governed by the need to act on behalf of others, and that left her, left all of them, vulnerable. Luna shivered uncontrollably. The possibility of losing him too, shattered everything she knew about herself.

"Sshsh," Grace reached around, pressed a cool palm to Luna's lips like a sacrament. She rubbed Luna's arms for warmth. "You two are so alike," she said, tracing Luna's jaw and brushing hair from her eyes. Grace's lips grazed the back of her neck and warm electricity swam under Luna's skin. *Did Grace mean to do it or was it an accident?* Perhaps they could find comfort in one another knowing it might be their last chance for any kind of comfort. The scent of old blood coiled and clung to her lungs with a raw desperation she'd not found in any ring. Blood that Grace had used to save lives.

"Do you want to see a picture?" Luna asked, rolling over and pulling out the photograph Don Carlos had given her.

"All right." Grace accepted the tattered image and strained to see it in the dark. "You have the same posture," she said. "Who is she? Your mother?"

They locked eyes, and for a moment Luna felt Grace could see her, recognized in her the longing and loneliness she'd carried inside. Desire flooded her body and though she knew it was wrong to feel that way about another woman, especially the one Manuel loved, all that mattered was that she did.

"Luna? Who is it?"

"You could persuade Manuel to leave with us tomorrow," she said, grabbing the photograph and tucking it away. "He would listen to you."

"I wouldn't try," Grace said firmly.

Luna untangled her feet and rolled onto her back. Her mother's death had saddled her with a thin, empty shadow she still caught glimpses of in certain light — a soul wandering without a body, a hollowness waiting, in vain, to be filled. Losing Armando and Paqui, witnessing the massacre at Sangre Mio had added more. She recognized them when they appeared. Another was looming over Manuel. If they lived through the night she was afraid she might once more survive someone she loved, only to be haunted by him. "Despite my reputation for chasing death," she said. "It seems death is chasing me."

Grace bristled. "Manuel is as determined to win as you are," she said.

Luna bit the flesh of her bottom lip. "We're alike but we're different too," she said, thinking he was not the lucky one.

"AMBUSH! WAKE UP, LUNA!"

She flipped over as Grace was bolting from the truck. The doors swung wide and she was hit with a blast of cool, dry air. Two Condor biplanes flew over a nearby administration building. A boy not much older than her crawled along the ground toward the truck, one eye hanging from its socket, the other imploring her to help. She scurried out of the truck, her stomach twisting into knots, and stepped over him pretending he wasn't there, and over a viejo who was dragging his useless limbs. She cowered with Grace behind the ground-level barricade. Together they watched in disbelief as a German tank rolled over the hill and shot a parade of grenades through the windows of the philosophy department.

"Manuel!" Luna screamed, running toward the building. A machine gunner flew low, but before he could take aim again, she'd disappeared into dust and smoke.

"Come back!" Grace shouted.

A body exploded in the air in front of Luna, scattering a great puzzle. Bits of flesh rained down. An arm, completely intact, hit

the dirt at her feet with an angry thud. She gagged as she entered
the building, and flew up the stairs, choking on embers and smoke.
She covered her eyes to break the sting, and was forced down again
by a wave of heat.

"Luna! Where are you?!" Grace had followed.

"It's too hot," Luna said, frantically. "Is there another way up?"

Grace traced the wall with her hands, found the door handle
she knew led to a second stairwell. It was cool. "This way," she
said, pulling the door open.

They entered the library from the other side where the remaining
stacks of books along the far wall were ablaze. A grey and black
cloud filled the room and the inky air was dense with the odour of
paper, each page within its careful binding a fold of skin, peeling
and curling and burning. Manuel was fifty feet from a shattered
window, uninjured. His bayonet was leaning against the wall, and
a rifle slung across his shoulder.

"Vamos!" Luna said, pulling on him. "Let's go!"

He shook her off, reloaded his gun. "I'm not leaving my post."
He reached into his pocket, pulled out a wad of folded notepaper,
which he pressed into Grace's palm. "These belong to you, as I do,"
he said.

"There's no time, Manuel."

"Take them," he insisted.

Grace accepted the poems, roped both arms around his neck and
Luna felt the hair on the back of her own neck bristle. Manuel held
Grace — a hand there, and there, and he kissed her — a passionate
act, filled with the urgency of the moment, and Grace let him do
it. Luna's mouth turned desert. Jealousy crackled inside her chest.
Had she and Grace kissed the night before, once their words had
all been spent? Had she pressed her weight down on top of Grace,
warmed herself against the fear of never and nothing. No, of course
not. She'd laid there, hour after hour, imagining it. But she had
thought that perhaps Grace was imagining it too. She spun away
stiffly, and triggered vertigo.

Grace noticed something was wrong. "Luna, what is it? Are you injured?"

"No." She wasn't injured, she was once more off balance, unstable, like the country whirling into chaos around her, and she ached all over for love; ached most in the places she'd not been touched. She parted her lips to speak, but uttered no sound. After years of cloaking herself in nothing but the art of red, she felt exposed and raw, almost bleeding from want of something more.

Manuel unwrapped himself from the cape coat she'd given him the night before, and held it out to her. "The road is still intact," he said. "Grace can drive out, if you leave now."

"I'm not leaving you," said Luna.

The heavy material, covered in soot and smelling of cigarettes, swung heavily between them. "If you're not going to help," he said. "Then get out of our way." Somewhere, far off, Nationalist soldiers took a Republican stronghold, and bells cascaded with the tears of the saints. Manuel looked from Luna's dark eyes to Grace's overpowering blue ones. "She'll be safest at the hotel."

Grace hesitated. With the supplies in her truck she could dress five hundred wounds. She could probably administer a transfusion by herself, if she had to. She should stay. But what about Luna? "I'll drive her and come back," she said.

Manuel nodded, threw his arms around them both and held on tightly. He let go when another grenade exploded outside, and war again gripped them as a rabid dog grips. Grace and Luna broke away from him, fled together down the rear stairwell and outside to the truck, with the cape coat covering their heads.

TWO WEEKS LATER, GRACE was still sitting at Marisol's old sewing machine pulling fabric from one of Luna's useless muletas over its rusty teeth to pass the time. Her foot on the pedal made a rickety purr, which was a welcome comfort for Luna. She stood in front of the large glass doors of the balcony. A pastel sun washed over the plaza Santa Ana, more diffuse than the pointed vermilion dazzle of an Andalucian sun, it set the old city in relief against a bleak military backdrop. Madrid had been surrounded, and they'd heard no news since University City. They couldn't bring themselves to speak of Manuel.

"Anything out there?" Grace asked, without looking up.

"No one," said Luna. Two gutter dogs scrounged for something to eat in front of the Teatro Español. An old lamppost with its broken globe stood like a jagged blade. "To me, this city once represented possibility and freedom," she said. "Now look at it. It's our chiquero."

"It has to end soon," said Grace.

Luna bit her lip. What if Manuel had been injured. Her skin

turned as cold as a hooked fish. If he wasn't dead, his dream of being an artist was. So was hers. She turned around, uncertain what to wish for now.

A part of her was grateful to be locked in with Grace, where no one else could see what she shouldn't be feeling. Day after day she'd watched Grace discretely, lifting what was left of their food to her lips, or moving gingerly from one room to the next, soothed by the swift caress of Grace's shirt-sleeve. She stayed awake nights, as though wakefulness was the drug, and sleep akin to death. She wanted to press open Grace's bedroom door, beg like a dog to sleep at the foot of her bed, to be near her, and sometimes she convinced herself that this was what Grace wanted too.

If she'd been a man and Manuel, a stranger, she would've crept into Grace's room. Her longing would've been over. She'd have played Zeus to Grace's Europa, turned herself all the way bull and ravaged Grace. She'd dreamt it, though Grace had offered no consent; but, in those moments of swollen desire, Luna could've taken her and been satisfied.

She paced in front of the glass doors, looking out at the plaza. After a few minutes she unlatched the doors and stepped onto the balcony where a spray of rain cooled her face. Somewhere far off an oboe cried, its music oddly disturbing, and before long she couldn't stand being stuck inside the hotel a minute more.

"Take a walk with me?" she said.

"I don't know, Luna."

"You're not going to sleep anyway. Come out."

"But the curfew. I hear sniper fire," Grace said. "We shouldn't."

"Just to Retiro Park." She grabbed Grace's coat from the hook, and her own. "The rain is stopping and I know a shortcut."

Quietly, they slipped downstairs and out through the vacant hotel lobby and the deserted plaza, passing a few men, though no military police. The air was clean and the streets slick with rainwater. The sun had almost completely disappeared. They hurried down Calle del Prado to the small Plaza de la Cortes where the monument to Cervantes stood, and farther down to the Plaza de Canovas de Castillo and Neptune's overflowing fountain.

"I feel eyes on me," said Grace.

"It's not far now."

Inside the park, iron lampposts illuminated their path and their shoes crunched on sand and gravel. Maples and cedars and palms watched over them and Luna wasn't afraid of being arrested for breaking curfew, as much as she dreaded turning back. They didn't speak. What was there to say? From the inside of war their own voices sounded superficial.

The scent of wet jasmine was inescapable and once Grace saw that they weren't being followed she began to relax. "It is good to breathe fresh air," she said, walking through a thicket of trees. The lamplight softened her features and made blue moons of her eyes.

"There it is," said Luna. "That's what I wanted you to see."

The Crystal Palace stood out from the night, cut glass on velvet.

Grace rushed towards it pressing her face up to one of its large plate glass windows. "Luna, come and look with me."

She did and found it empty inside. They walked around to the front entrance where she spread her coat on the white marble steps and they sat facing the pond. A large sequoia loomed to their left, its heavy dark branches stripped of green needles. "Mothers bring their children here to feed the swans," she said.

Grace peered across the pond. "I see nothing."

The sound of a small waterfall came fast and hard, and the ruffling of heavy wet feathers. "They're black," she said. "It's hard to see them in the dark."

They stepped up to the edge of the pond where three slow-moving shapes, vague shadows, floated across the water. They paddled closer, closer, until their thin red beaks were visible. One was bathing and stretching his long neck to swallow a drink of water. The second made an unexpectedly high-pitched squawk. The third swan paddled up to the lip of the pond ambitiously, hoping to be fed, and moved off alone, to swim in the centre of that watery circle. Luna's shoes pressed down on a pile of soggy sunflower seeds and she thought she heard the whistle of a train pulling out of the Atocha station across the city.

"I want to be a mother," Grace said.

"You do! Why?"

"To know a love that lasts. To come first in someone's eyes." Grace lifted a piece of paper from out of her pants pocket and unfolded it. "It won't happen," she said. She fiddled with the page, holding it close to her face so she might make out the words. "One of Manuel's poems," she said.

Grace knew he loved her. Did she know that Luna did too? Luna bent down, grabbed a handful of sand and sunflower seeds and tossed the wet shells at the surface of water. She'd not thought of motherhood as anything but pain and loss. Now she thought of Marisol, who would be almost six months pregnant.

"Would you read it to me?" Grace asked.

"I don't know."

"I think I understand it," she said. "I've translated it as best I can. But I'd like to hear it in Spanish, as you would say it."

Luna hesitated. What she wanted to do was draw Grace nearer, whisper a dare. Love me, she wanted to say. Love me and I'll make it last. Instead she turned, a fog of breath on her lips, and whatever she was going to say or do evaporated and she stared.

Grace held out the page and, helpless, she read it:

*At the café I leaned into your words*
*found the softness of your skin with my eyes*
*What if I had reached for you, taken you*
*into the night, under the rain*
*tasted each moment of exile laid onto your skin*
*without asking first.*
*If I had murmured something crude*
*would you have blushed?*

Luna returned the poem without comment and Grace folded the paper, was slipping it away when they heard a car door slam, and the footsteps of a man racing through the park behind them.

"Help!" he cried. "Someone help me!"

They spun around, and behind the crystal palace, four Nationalist soldiers streaked by in pursuit. She and Grace ducked, and heard the sharp fire of a bullet, and another blasting and echoing inside their bones, and then nothing. Death rang under darkness and Luna reached for Grace's hand as instinctively as Grace reached for hers, and they fled in the opposite direction, along the wide boulevard lined by statues, through the sculpted garden, and out onto the maze of cobblestone streets. Breathless and damp, they didn't stop running until they reached the hotel.

AFTER THEY'D CHANGED INTO dry clothes, Grace resumed her sewing and Luna again stood in front of the glass doors of the balcony looking out at the plaza, though she no longer had any desire to escape. Madrid had become two cities; the mythic celestial one above, where brass and copper statues of Gods on rooftops drove iron chariots, or danced on the balls of their feet, and the gritty, dangerous one they'd tried to explore on foot. By day, the sky was lined with gold and silver, but after sundown, in the darkness of civil war, it was as if heaven had collided with earth and left behind ash. Luna thought of the three black swans, oblivious to war, and her mother and Paqui, somewhere up in a corner of that sky, beyond the stars. Would she ever see Manuel or Marisol again? Marisol had become one of the losses of her life and, when she thought of her, it was as though Marisol too was among the dead.

Outside, a supply truck with smashed windows was an empty steel carcass parked crookedly at the side of the road.

"You drove a truck," Luna said.

"Pardon?"

"You drove a truck in Canada."

"No," Grace said. "My father did."

Luna turned. "For a clothing warehouse?"

"Yes." Grace looked up from the sewing machine. "He liked to brag that his bumpers were made from chrome and his tires had white hubcaps. I know he felt sharp sitting at the wheel. He'd say, if you can drive, you can go anywhere."

They were both silent for a moment, the thought of freedom now a cruel joke.

"I miss my horse," Luna said. "I don't know what Pedro did with her."

Grace rethreaded the needle, carefully squinting to find the tiny opening, and pulled the fine string through with her thumb and forefinger. "I had a favourite horse once," she said. "Before the company changed to trucks, when my father made his deliveries by carriage. Her name was Mae."

"Mae," Luna repeated, throwing herself onto the sofa, and dangling her legs over one end.

"She was sixteen hands high and part Clydesdale. Her coat was tan, but the quarter horse in her, gave her a dark mane and tail."

"Why was Mae your favourite?" Luna asked.

"She was in love."

To Luna love still sounded decadent, and dangerous, even for a horse.

Grace tied off the thread and resumed sewing sections of the capote to the fabric she'd cut from one of her shirts. "If Mae and the other horse weren't placed in side-by-side stalls for the night, Mae whinnied and kicked at the doors, and kept the barn awake. She'd injure herself if need be."

"Foolish," Luna said.

"Hmm." Grace ran one hand, the one without the needle, through her thick red hair, and scratched her head. "When Mae pulled the carriage, I sat on my father's lap wearing his navy wool cap with the black patent visor. I would sing to reassure her, and she'd peak one ear forward for the road while the other was turned a little back to hear. The customers knew her by name. Some would offer a carrot or a lump of sugar."

"Sing for me," Luna said, growing more interested.

Grace blushed and shook her head.

"Por qué no?"

"I have a terrible voice, like a saw. It's embarrassing."

Luna propped herself up on her elbows. "Please," she whined. "I'm so bored being stuck inside. Let me hear what you sang to the pretty horse."

"Oh, all right." Grace stopped what she was doing, and turned in her chair. "But I can't look at you while I do it." She closed her eyes and took a deep breath and it was easy for Luna to imagine her atop a carriage with the breeze fanning through her coppery hair: "When night falls, and the moon sleeps," Grace sang, "I will be waiting, I will be waiting." She opened one eye to see that Luna was still listening and continued. "When day breaks and your heart does too, think of me. Then I would do this," she said, taking a big gulp of air. "Whineee!" Her cheeks and neck were bright pink. "Whineee!"

Bursting out laughing, Luna gestured with her hands as if to say, not bad.

"It rhymes," Grace smiled. "Mae and my father appreciated it." She joined Luna on the sofa, forcing her to sit up and make a place. "Your turn," she said.

"I do not embarrass myself."

Grace rolled her eyes and slapped Luna gently on one arm. "Fine, think of something else."

Luna shrugged. "There's nothing silly about my life."

"That's so sad," said Grace.

"Is it?"

Grace examined her closely, as though there must be something revealing she was keeping to herself. "As a child didn't you tell riddles or play practical jokes?"

Luna thought for a moment and said, "When I was small, maybe four or five, Manuel would come up beside me like this." She reached her hands around Grace's ribcage, "and he would do this." She tickled Grace mercilessly.

"Don't," Grace said. "Stop!" She was soon crying and out of breath and squirming to get away, but the sound of unbridled joy after days and weeks of gloom was unimaginable. Grace's eyes were laughing as freely as the rest of her, and it made Luna feel like a girl again, the girl she might've been, before the bulls, before the war, before she lost so much. Not even Armando had cut through to the place inside her where anything felt possible, and for an instant there was no one but Grace and nothing else to want — the lonely nights of imposed curfews were gone — the dreaded darkness after sunset, and their empty days of vigilance and mistrust — it felt as if bad luck could return to good, so she kissed Grace.

"I, I'm sorry." She stood immediately. "I mean no disrespect."

Grace reached out, "Luna, it's ok. We were playing."

"No, I must go," she said. She turned away, although there was only their suite for an escape so she marched into her bedroom and closed the door.

LUNA STOOD IN THE centre of the room dressed in her blue suit of lights. The epaulets broadened her shoulders, the gold sequined panels on the sides of her pants narrowed her hips. There was something reassuring about being in the costume that most resembled her self-image and she admired herself in the standing mirror, from the front and twisting around to see behind, but reassurance was fleeting. She hardly knew who she was anymore. *The kiss was a sin,* she thought, all the while feeling it wasn't. Sin was a country divided, brothers divided, permissions ungranted, and a government that censored her art.

She ran her hand across the decorated breast of her suit as she had so many times before, felt the scale of sequins graze her palm.

Strange, with the lingering press of soft lips upon her own, the one thing she thought she'd always need, the corrida, held less measure against the insatiable sanguine need she had to be with Grace. She unbuttoned her collar. Reluctantly, she stepped out of her slippers, a traitor, and a deserter.

She dropped to the floor, tearing her pink stockings, and there, on her knees, by the blue note light of the moon, with the faces of dead poets carved into the façade of the Teatro Español for an audience, she tried to pray for the hardness of a stone, but underground passion had already grabbed hold and she couldn't deny it anymore. You can't deny love; the best you can do is to endure it privately. She'd worked hard to be recognized. Not as a servant, or a sister, or as a daughter, but as a matador, punto. *Be brave*, she'd told herself since she began to train. *Show courage, find grace.* And instead what had happened? "Grace," she whispered. "You have made a cave of my heart."

Feeling a presence behind her, she leapt to her feet and spun around. "Who's there?" Grace's figure stepped out from the shadow of the doorway in a dress the colour of antique rubies, and Luna felt her bones fold. "You shouldn't be here," she said.

"I want to show you what I've been sewing all these days." Grace fanned the skirt of her dress. "I've finished. Do you like it?" The dress hung below her knees. It was cinched tightly at the waist with a wide panel and a skirt that flared. The neckline exposed her elegant throat and the ivory skin of her breasts.

Luna nodded. Her mouth was dry and shame coloured the moment. She couldn't give shape or sound to her feelings.

"Say it," said Grace. "Say what you want."

"No, I —"

"Say it." Grace wasn't leaving until she made the confession.

"I need you," Luna whispered.

"Yes."

"I crave you."

Grace moved towards her.

"And?"

All at once Luna found herself laughing again, as they had in the living room, though it was an absurd thing to do. "What I want doesn't matter," she said. "Loving what I cannot have is a mistake I was born to make." She touched her chest with open hands. "This ragged armour is meaningless," she said, and she began to unhook her vest.

"Men envy and respect you," said Grace.

"You don't."

Grace faced her, their mouths inches apart, and Luna tried to slip from her jacket. "Leave it on," said Grace. "I want to touch it." She ran her strong and slender hand along the shoulder, played with the gold tassels. She pressed the lapel with her fingers as if gauging the quality of the material or the figure wearing it, and she flicked a single gold sequin with her nail. "You are magnificent in your suit of lights."

"Don't mock me," said Luna. "You hate it." She wanted so badly to reach for Grace again, close her mouth overtop of Grace's, and silence her, along with all the bullets. But Grace was meant to be Manuel's woman and the kisses belonged to him. "There's no glory inside of betrayal," she said.

Grace slowly traced the button of Luna's shirt with one finger, from neck to sash. "You would rather betray yourself?"

"Leave me alone," Luna said, but she didn't mean it.

"I've seen you swagger, in and out of the ring. Your arrogant manner and unselfconscious charm. Your kind has your way with the world and blames it on the stars. You're too stubborn to admit it." Grace's breath came fast. "But you are all bull." She tugged gently on the bottom of the jacket. "Your suit feels as I suspected it would."

"Cómo?"

She leaned in and her lips brushed Luna's ear. "Rough," she whispered.

"Rough."

"Yes, and the smell." Grace inhaled deeply. "You smell of —"
she sniffed Luna's neck and cheek and ran her tongue along Luna's
bottom lip. She pressed her body closer, the skirt of the dress
bunching between their legs. Luna's knees buckled. Grace drew
back and gathered her skirt in both hands, lifting it so her bare
thighs showed. "You're brave in the ring, El Corazón, but where's
your courage here, outside of it? You seduce ten thousand spectators at once and know nothing of seduction." Slowly, melodically,
Grace began to sway, side to side, all the while holding her skirt
away from her body, and with the flick of her wrist, waving it, mes-
merizing, taunting, daring Luna to uncover what lay behind that
red material. Grace was the cape. Grace made the pass.

"Forgive me, Manuel," Luna said, as she charged.

CONQUERED AND SLAIN, LUNA sat in the white light of dawn propped up against the headboard of her bed with Grace reclining on her naked chest. The pulse of what they'd done still beat beneath the surface of her skin. She was embarrassed by the force of her desire, what she was capable of feeling. She wondered if Grace was embarrassed by it too.

"You were going to tell me why you cried at my performance," Luna said, curling a strand of red hair around her thumb.

"It wasn't because of you," Grace teased. She ran the fingers of one hand casually along Luna's scar. The dress was a puddle on the floor beside them.

"No?" Luna felt Grace's lungs inflate as if they were her own.

"I was thinking of it from the bull's perspective," Grace said. She rolled over and pushed up on her knees so they were facing one another. "He wakes and is driven somewhere foreign in a small container. He's kept in a stall with several of his own kind. On death row," she added, dramatically. "He grows nervous that something unusual is going to happen and wants to escape. When he is released out to meet you in the ring he thinks he's found that escape, but instead finds a screaming mob that wants to see him defeated."

"Yes," Luna said. "And this is when he's either brave or he gives up."

"He can't be brave. You tire him until his front legs give out. If he's aggressive you kill him, and if he resists he's led out of the ring and slaughtered. Don't you see? Like the proletariat; he's doomed no matter what he does."

Luna was silent. For once, she didn't want to think about bull-fighting, she wanted to understand how to feel about what they'd done. It was the very notion of being doomed to a caste she'd fought against for most of her life, and Grace's words returned her to the bastard servant she was born. "Am I supposed to feel guilty," she asked, "so you can feel superior?" Her tongue curled around the question, but she was surprised not to be delivering it with stronger conviction. Love had softened her defences. Did that mean how she felt about the corrida would also soften? "My picadors and banderilleros bring us to the same point," she said firmly. "When I face the bull for the faena we are as equals."

"Equals! That would be you alone with the bull when he charges. No, not then," said Grace. "To be fair the bull must have the right to live. Where is the mystery or the art if it's a foregone conclusion he'll die?"

Luna stiffened. "We all know we die," she said. "Does that make our lives less elegant or mysterious?"

"Death," said Grace, shaking her head. "It's about death and power."

"That's all you saw? A powerless animal and my cruelty. How can you lie with me here if all I am is a murderer in your eyes?"

"That's not all," Grace said, cupping Luna's face in her palms. "Despite myself, I admired you in your suit that day. It was as if I was there, on the sand with you, and had been handed your light. You do that. You make us feel immortal and we love you for it." Grace was quiet for a moment and in a bashful voice she added,

"Watching the bulls suffer and die was horrible, I can't lie, but watching you, I knew I'd never been truly loved. Passionately, foolishly, recklessly loved."

"Is that why you followed me on the balcony?"

"Yes."

Luna blushed, wrapped her arms around Grace once more. There was a little light inside of her, she knew, but there was also a crowd of shadow. The heart Grace imagined to be so pure, the righteous, generous pump Grace dreamt of, beat inside of Manuel's chest, not hers. She pulled Grace to her, inhaled skin and breath and hair. There would've been one other time she was this close to a woman's body; when she was placed at her mother's breast. She clung to Grace; for as long as she could remember she'd struggled to hold onto a sense of entitlement — to believe she deserved more than her class allowed, more than her sex allowed, and after all this time and struggle she would have something more. "Is this foolish?" she asked. "Is this reckless?" She kissed Grace ardently and felt long hair tickling her shoulders.

"Make love to me," said Grace.

Embarrassed again, Luna tried not to sound nervous. "How?" she asked.

"As I did to you."

"I haven't done anything like that before."

Grace smiled tenderly. "I knew another woman once," she said. "She wasn't my match. It's true I don't understand how you love what you do, Luna, but I can't help whom I love either."

Luna nodded, thinking of Chucho and Jorge together in the café, remembering how she'd kissed the girl with the overbite. But the thought of Grace with anyone else made her feel jealous and inconsequential. After all, whom had she loved? Armando, yes, desperately, for his beauty and accomplishment and for the power he'd gathered around himself despite his humble beginnings. She'd wanted him with the reverential passion of a student for a mentor. Wanting Grace had nothing to do with ambition or the corrida and yet loving her felt like a tempest in the blood. Grace had opened her to a passionate resurrection; each time they touched, Luna came more alive. "What are we doing?" she asked.

Grace ran one finger along Luna's collarbone. "According to some people, a woman fighting bulls is wrong but that hasn't stopped you. Perhaps the life worth leading is the one we aren't supposed to lead."

"I was once a servant to the García family," Luna confessed. "You saw the photograph of my real mother. Manuel trained me to the bulls, without him I would still be penniless, and scrubbing pots."

"He told me," said Grace.

"Did he also explain how I am his real sister after all? You do see the resemblance?"

Grace rolled onto one side, pulling Luna along. "I would like to see more," she said, gently biting Luna's neck. "I would like to see and smell and taste every inch of you."

Luna froze. Her eyes began to water. She'd surrendered to desire and was without defense or protection.

"Should I stop?" Grace asked.

Luna shook her head. She wanted the newness of Grace, to be unburdened from the weight of tradition. "No," she said. She was inexperienced and frightened but this moment was inevitable.

Grace ran one hand down Luna's naked back and said, "Tell me what you feel."

"Fear," she admitted. "I don't know what you want from me."

"Everything," Grace said, pushing Luna's head lower down on the bed, between her legs. "Forget talking. Without words your tongue can still be a most persuasive muscle."

Trembling, Luna once more gave herself up to the curves and folds of Grace's body, and its will to be satisfied. She pretended she was Grace, touched and tasted by instinct, as Grace had done with her in the night, and before long she'd forgotten to pretend. Her confidence grew; she was no stranger to desire after all, and any body was merely a cage of flesh and bone. She was gentle and greedy, by turns, but when Grace moaned encouragement she became as fierce as the fiercest bull in the Sangre caste.

After, Luna said nothing more about Manuel or the corrida or anything else, though she was thinking that from the moment we're born we are dying. Perhaps it's a contradiction only a matador can reconcile, and yet the most miraculous thing is that we love anyway. We love love. More than we fear ourselves. It's absurd and it's reckless, and Luna knew it once she knew Grace; our taste for living, especially when surrounded by death, is at its most undeniable. For the first time in her life she wanted to live forever.

"SALTAR LA COMBA," SHE said, resting her head on Grace's stomach.

"Pardon?"

"I remember another game from when I was young. Saltar la comba. Jump rope. The workers' daughters played it at Sangre Mío."

"I did that too," said Grace. "In Canada. Do you remember any of the songs?"

Luna sifted through her memories, grabbed hold of a clear one. "This was popular," she said as a street sweeper began to work his broom below the window. "One girl on each end, turning the rope, and two jumping in and out."

"Go on."

She sang it with a bouncing melody, as she'd heard it when she was a child.

*"Al cementerio subí
con sangre escribí un letrero
arriba puse María
abajo te quiero
ay qué Montaña tan alta
ay qué balcón tan dorado
ay qué dolor de está niña
qué el novio la ha abandonado."*

"Something about mountains and a gold balcony," Grace said.

Luna hadn't considered the words before, but there was nothing innocent in them. "It's very serious," she said. "Let me see if I can explain. It says, I went to the cemetery."

"To the cemetery."

"Yes. I went to the cemetery, and with blood I wrote."

"Blood!"

"Shshsh, let me finish or I'll forget it."

"I went to the cemetery
with blood I wrote
a sign in the upper part said, Maria
the lower part said, I love you.
how tall is the mountain.
how golden is the balcony
how much pain is this girl suffering
because her fiancé has abandoned her?"

Grace was silent. She took up Luna's hand, raised Luna's fingers to her lips and inhaled the lingering scent of desire. "You're thinking of Manuel," she said. "That he's abandoned you."

"No," said Luna, as though delivering a eulogy. "I've abandoned him."

IN THE MORNING, LUNA shot upright and pulled the cotton sheet around her body. "Do you hear that? There. I hear something."

"It's nothing," Grace said, nuzzling in closer. "A pigeon on the ledge sunning himself."

"No, Listen." There was a faint knock at the front door, almost a scratch.

Luna leapt from the mattress and scurried to pull on a pair of pants. She grabbed a shirt and tucked it in on her way to the door. Grace followed, slipping into the red dress.

"Quién es?" Luna barked. "Who is it? What do you want?"

"Luna, it's me."

"Manuel!" She swung the door open to find him with Chucho slumped against his bare chest, a bird with a broken wing. Manuel's face was swollen and his beard matted. He had two black eyes. Both men's clothes were covered in dried blood. They stank.

"Hurry," Grace said, helping them to the sofa.

Manuel met her bright eyes. He was tired, so very tired, and yet each stinging muscle in his body that had, until now, wanted sleep, roused for her. "You're both here," he said, sounding relieved.

When they'd left him at University City he'd felt a crack in his soul, as if any poetry that remained unwritten inside of him had disappeared with them. He'd been angry with Luna and thought the worst when Grace hadn't returned to the Front, but the long, cold days and nights of fighting hadn't put a stop to love, and seeing his sister and Grace again was like coming home twice. He decided that when the war was over he would ask Grace to marry him.

Luna propped Chucho's head under a pillow, loosened his collar. His right arm was wrapped in Manuel's torn jacket. "We were on our way for water," said Chucho. "The well exploded."

Luna stared at his ragged wound as though the last of an endangered species had been rendered extinct. "That's your sword hand," she said.

"They might as well have cut off my balls. I'll never work again." He struggled to sit up but the pain in his arm was searing. "Aiy!"

"Don't move," Grace said. She pulled off his shoes, one after the other.

"I tried to carry his weight for a mile or two," explained Manuel. "Then the Cuban — Grace you remember him from the café meetings? The one with the cheekbones? He drove by in a truck. We sat on stacks of dynamite and I thought we'd explode before Chucho bled to death, but the Cuban had been making the route, in and out of the city, for weeks. I had him drop us a block from here. You can't be sure who to trust now." Manuel tilted a wineskin to Chucho's swollen lips, noticed the old muletas Grace wore as a dress. "I see you've become a fan of the corrida," he said.

Grace and Luna exchanged a furtive glance and Manuel wondered why. A shudder of ambivalence about Grace's feelings for him rippled under his skin, the self-doubt he'd once carried in Eugenia's presence. He'd thought it was gone, beaten back to pulp by the passage of time, though he found he carried it with him still, as one carries love for the dead after they too are dust. Maybe he'd been wrong to assume Grace felt anything more than friendship for him. "Why didn't you return?" he asked.

Grace looked uncomfortable and sank beneath the weight of her own thoughts. "I couldn't leave Luna," she mumbled.

Grace was thinner than she'd been at the front, her hair longer and unruly, but it was her oddly aloof disposition that suggested something had changed. "What's going on?" Manuel asked.

"Nothing!" Luna said defensively. She tossed him an old cloth bag containing sections of leathery orange and crusty bread, and tried to slow her racing heart. *I must not want this anymore*, she thought. *I cannot want this.* And yet she needed Grace, needed her as a shadow needs the sun, to be shaped by its angle and light, to be carved into colour. She'd been half-dead before Grace. Without her she'd be half-dead again.

Manuel took a bite of the bread and fed the rest to Chucho. "Luna, we parted angrily," he said. "I've regretted that."

"We're together now," she said, avoiding his eyes. She moved across the room, remembered having seen something hanging on the hotel door when she'd opened it. Sure enough, out in the hall nailed to the wood frame, there was a small cream-coloured fold of paper. She tugged it off the nail and broke the wax of the military seal: *Meet me on Sunday*, she read. *If you're still a matador.* Her pulse quickened. *This is your last chance at Las Ventas*, the note said. *I will be there with a Serrano.* It was signed, *Private Pedro García Caballero, Spanish National Army.*

Quickly, she folded the note and pressed it under the heel of one shoe. Grace couldn't know about the possibility of a bullfight. She would try to stop her, and Luna already knew she didn't want that. Love, as wonderful as it felt, hadn't changed who she was. If anything, loving Grace had renewed her confidence, a truer confidence, not the bravado she'd used to mask a sense of inferiority. She stepped into the suite and found Grace picking through Marisol's old sewing basket looking for a clean needle with which to stitch Chucho's wound.

"What were you doing out there?" Grace asked. But before Luna could respond, Grace disappeared into the bathroom and returned with a pan of water, which she placed on the floor, next to Chucho. "I'll try to be fast," she told him, beginning to clean his wound.

"Just do it right," he said.

Luna looked away because Chucho was a strong man, and his vulnerability pained her. "What of Marisol?" she asked to distract him.

"When I saw her last she wouldn't eat," he said. "Not a grain of rice. She sang to her belly." Chucho clenched his teeth as Grace pulled the needle through his shredded skin, shutting out infection. The smell was of uncooked meat. "Hijo de puta!" he said.

"And Pedro knows about this?"

"He's rarely home," said Chucho. "When he is, he brings other women and they drink."

Luna took up the wineskin and drank greedily. She wanted to ask about Jorge, what she'd seen behind the curtain in the café. But they couldn't speak of such things. "What happened to the other one?" she asked instead, of his claw hand.

"Born that way," he said.

A few minutes later Grace tied off a knot of thread. "There, I'm done," she said. It was a clean stump with a good seam.

Manuel hoisted Chucho onto his feet, and swung one of Chucho's heavy arms around his shoulder. "I'll put you in my old room," he said.

As soon as they were gone, Luna followed Grace into the bathroom and watched anxiously as Grace scrubbed her hands with the last of the soap.

"I haven't seen you drink before," said Grace.

"It's my business what I do."

Grace dried her hands on the skirt of her dress and, turning said, "Should we tell him together or do you want to do it?"

"Tell him? What are you talking about, we can't tell anyone."

Grace reached out to stroke Luna's cheek. "Don't be afraid," she said. Her palm was warm, reassuring. Luna pushed it away.

"He's my brother."

Grace stepped closer. "Claim me," she dared. "If you love me you would."

They were standing near enough to each other that Luna could taste Grace's breath, feel her heat, all it would've taken to hold onto her was courage. In love, as in the bullring, Luna was given rare, fleeting moments to save herself and if she hesitated, if she failed to feign and dodge and lunge with bravado, the moment would simply be gone, and so would she. She leaned forward, and pressed her lips to Grace's mouth. "You know I want to," she whispered.

Grace wrapped her fingers around the back of Luna's neck sending desire twisting down her spine, dampening her with it. This is the love she'd longed for, the kind she could call home. But Grace spoke again.

"We're lucky to have found each other."

Luna flinched, loosened her embrace. She'd grown to mistrust the notion of luck. Luck was a lonely, bloody ambition, the sharp shiny lie she'd told about herself, to make sense of pain and fear, to open another day. Luck was a Fascist's promise of hope, and believing had made her its slave. "If I could return to the ring," she said. "Would you still want me then?"

"You can't," said Grace. "That doesn't matter anymore."

Luna wanted to weep. Grace still didn't see her, not all of her, and she wanted to punish her for it, and for the deception loving her had caused, but that was also an excuse. Pushing Grace away was easier than waiting for her to leave. "You're not my match," she said, tilting the wineskin and willing the remainder of its contents to spill onto her tongue.

Grace dropped her hand, stepped away. "That's cruel, and you know it. You're afraid of what you feel. Don't you think I am too?"

"Tomorrow I perform on foot," Luna said.

"What?! You could be shot!" Grace ripped the wineskin from Luna's hand and tossed it across the floor. "A relationship or the ring," she hissed, as the last drops of wine dribbled onto the grey marble like beads of blood. "You'll always feel torn between the two, won't you?"

"You wouldn't have noticed me, if not for bullfighting," Luna said. "Admit it. And yet you'd have me give it up." Must love come to this ironic death, she thought, killing the thing that originally sparked it? "I will fight," she repeated, angrily. "You have no right to ask me to do otherwise."

"Did last night not give me any rights?"

"No!" For an instant Luna hated Grace for the way Grace made her feel about herself — vulnerable, disloyal, and powerless to stop it, and she hated herself. "Try and understand," she said. "I must do this."

Grace tried to brush past her. Luna grabbed her by the wrist. "One last time," she said, hoping to barter for both passions.

Grace tore away from her clutch. "No wonder you kill so well," she said. "You're heartless. And a coward. You'll never be happy, Luna. You choose the wrong things to love." Grace turned and flung the door wide open.


MANUEL WAS STANDING THERE, stunned. For a moment it felt as though time had surely stopped and the world no longer rotated for anyone, but Luna advanced and everything again shifted into motion. "Let me explain," she said. "We didn't mean to —"

"How could you do this to me?" He pointed at her. "Qué decepción! What a disappointment you are."

"Manuel don't."

He turned to Grace. "What is it?" he said. "I'm not enough of a fighter for you? You need someone who kills with her bare hands."

"Leave her alone!" shouted Luna.

"But I want to know," he pressed. "Is it about the tits or the sword!"

With that, Luna shoved him hard and he fell backwards into the doorframe. "Stop it!" she fumed. Her anger was palpable, fed her courage. "I ... I ..." She wanted to say she loved Grace and didn't care who knew it. Grace was waiting for her to say it. But the word, 'love' was wedged someplace deep and dangerous inside of her where artists were killers and lovers died. She shook with the effort. "I ... I ..."

Grace began to sob, her red hair matted and clinging to her wet cheeks. She pushed past both of them and ran into Pedro and Marisol's old room where she slammed the door.

A FORMER REPUBLICAN-CONTROLLED tank groaned outside Luna's bedroom window, casting an immense, ugly shadow across the ceiling. She closed her eyes to it, and to regret, but there it was, waiting for her with the other disasters she'd sidestepped, or caused. Pedro's note was still pressed inside one of her shoes, under the bed. She'd hung her suit of lights on a proper wooden hanger on the doorknob, to permit it to fall out, and in the darkness it twinkled a galaxy, though duller than it once had been. Her Montera was balanced on the doorknob. She lay on her back straining to hear, and not to hear, as Manuel pressed open the door to Grace's room.

Grace switched on a bedside lamp, creaking the bed as she sat up. "Have you come to deliver more punishment?" she asked coolly.

Manuel crossed the floor, sat beside her on the bed. He wanted to tell her that yesterday some of the volunteers had evacuated. Karl among them. Jorge had left for France. "I've drawn the escape route across the Pyrenees on this map," he said. "You should memorize it. There's a house near Marennes where you'll be safe until you fly home. But you must leave with Chucho in the morning." He took a deep breath, remembered the softness of her lips at the university. He still felt entitled to her. For a moment he told himself Grace had loved him all along, that the war had made her doubt it. Sometimes a lie can be enough. "I'm returning to the front," he said. "I could die tomorrow, or next month." He paused. "But, tonight I live."

By the creaking of the bed Luna knew he'd been moved to kiss Grace again and the fury of a seed bull overtook her. She threw her head into the mattress, twisted in the sheets that still held Grace's scent. She pressed her face into the pillow to block their noise and conceal her own, and soon madness enveloped her, where night was day and day was death and she knew what she'd instinctively known — love — not any brave bull, was to be the ruin of her.

Grace pulled back, shuffled away from Manuel. "I don't want to hurt you," she said. "I know bullfighting is all your sister needs. She'll never want anything more than it. But I only want her."

Luna felt her heart squeeze inside her chest painfully. Grace was loyal to her, was choosing her, and she was choosing something else. She lifted her fingers to her mouth, bit hard, and found the taste of her own blood. Tears funnelled down her cheeks and into the crook of her neck. Was she like her father, turning away from the chance to be loved? Gazing out her window at the mercury sky, she tried to imagine waking the next morning alongside Grace and not entering Las Ventas. But she could already feel the passion of the bull pounding across the sand, thundering toward her, climbing up her, through the soles of her feet.

When she heard Manuel step across the floor of Grace's room to let himself out, she stopped crying. She felt light-headed, but resolved to do what she did best; fight her most impressive fight in a familiar circle. If, taking her alternativa, she lost Grace, if she was killed in the bullring by a red-coated Serrano or with a police bullet, she'd fail brilliantly, with the lights of Andalucía upon her breast and the afternoon sun in her eyes. If she didn't fight, her failure would be a dull and dreadful certainty. *Don't come to me for kisses*, she thought, as she willed herself to sleep. *Come for the kill.*

The next morning when she woke, the others were gone. The map was on the table, beside the sewing machine. Grace had left the red dress.

CARRIAGES AND MOTORCARS JAMMED Alcalá Street threatening pedestrians who tried to pass along the main thoroughfare leading to the plaza de toros. Not before, not in Spain or in Mexico, had Luna heard such a rumble about the corrida rolling through the street. The people were starved for a few hours relief from the cinches and shackles that had taken them prisoner. The corrida hadn't meant more to any aficionado — including a Republican — than it did on that day. It hadn't meant more to her.

Men in shabby clothes were drunk before the ticket kiosk opened, and loud arguments spontaneously erupted between those who could afford the shade and those who had no choice but to burn. Still a bit hung-over from the night before, Luna watched them forming a parade of sorts, a gruesome procession fuelled by a gaiety that was absurd, given that with each passing day the hands of a dictator were clamping more firmly around their necks. This is the wonder of the fiesta brava, that it cannot and will not be stopped by any force, it swells in the face of attempts at suppression. She stood outside the plaza feeling a mixture of pride, anticipation and dread.

That the matador kills is not in question, but what is it that she kills, exactly? Is it time, which has been ticking down her days since the moment she first gulped air? Is it something in herself she fears; the animal urge to inflict pain so evident in small children and in times of war? Or is it simply loss, sewn unavoidably into human skin? Death is the ultimate loss. Is that what the powerful bull allows us to conquer?

At half past three, along with the others, Luna collected her ticket and filed inside. She went unrecognized in her cape coat, her slippers and bright pink stockings concealed under common shoes and clothes. She'd left her embroidered sword case in the hotel and was balancing the sword's handle in one of her palms, the long, thin body of its sheaf flat against the length of her. Her suit of lights and white shirt were rolled tightly around her Montera and pressed into a heavy leather carry case, which she held in her other hand.

Men on the sunny side of the plaza wore blue and grey overalls. Their skin burned and blistered under that beaming yellow disc, and they wiped their faces with rags. On the shady side, wealthier patrons rested comfortably. The war hadn't changed that. Women were scattered throughout. In large white hats they bloomed against the clear blue backdrop, frantically fanning the heat. Some held children on their laps. The music was deafening and thousands of spectators shouted and laughed, despite the grey future they'd been assigned. The brass band bellowed a pasodoble and men lit matches for cigarettes and snuck sips from hidden flasks. "Helado, helado!" called out the vendors. "Who wants ices? Panales y agua, quiere agua? Do you want a snack, do you want water?" Coppers flew. Pages from *Arriba* and *El País* shuffled along the ground with photographs of toreros on the bill, score sheets, and used programs. The corrida is a menacing, showy event, and the crowd is what makes it so.

Luna found her seat in the contrabarrera where she wouldn't risk sitting behind impresarios or a bull breeder who might turn and recognize her. She settled onto the hard stone without a cushion and watched the crowd to judge their mood. Did they hunger for a certain kind of pass or were they merely looking out for blood?

A violent clash erupted at one of the entrances to the plaza where a couple of Nationalists attacked a Republican, the Cuban, Luna thought it was, who was announcing that socialist, Juan Negrín, had been named the new Prime Minister. One Nationalist threw a heavy stone, and it hit the Cuban in the side of the head. He stumbled and fell to his knees, grasping his ear where blood spurted into his hand. "Fascist pig!" he shouted. A line of six guards appeared. They dragged the Cuban and the other men through a side exit.

Luna surveyed the crowd for the ring promoter, the president, and what she might see of Pedro through the toreros' entrance, but it wasn't yet the stroke of the hour and the entrance was sealed. Did Pedro intend for her to fight today? Maybe this was a trap. She squinted on the toril at twelve o'clock, at the burladero at eight, and searched around the callejón. It was the same; if Pedro was in the plaza she couldn't know. Sweltering in her coat and extra clothes, she wondered how she would make her way into the ring without being recognized and arrested? What if there were anti-taurinos in the stands preparing to stir trouble? Where would she change into her suit or find a capote or a muleta?

The sudden call of the clarion excited the crowd, and settled her into a finer peace. This time Las Ventas would be hers. It belonged to her, after all, as it belonged to Belmonte or Frascuello — and was a loop from the ganadería at Sangre Mío, through her, to all Spaniards. It was her inheritance.

When the trumpet sounded a second time she knew the cuadrillas were ordering themselves behind the shelters although, from her seat, she could see nothing but their winged monteras. She gripped her sword handle and the warm metal sent a charge up her spine; she sat higher. The red plank fence was calling to her. Would the first bull out charge it, send spectators clambering to higher seats? She was impatient to be down there, in the middle of the ring, with the keenness of the sand lining her nostrils. She stood, and made her way along the aisle.

Before she knew it, a cushion boy of about ten had come up behind and taken her by the cuff of her sleeve, as though she was his mother. "Sshshs," he said, lifting his finger to pretty pink lips. She permitted him to guide her through the dense crowd, as she struggled to follow with her case and sword. He parted a path, like a small burrowing creature, until he came to the closed door of the plaza enfermería. He knocked three times, paused and knocked twice more, looking up with the face of an angel, round innocent eyes the colour of coffee. The door opened, and the boy jutted out his hand. Pedro, wearing a khaki army uniform and a red cap, dropped a coin in it, pulled Luna inside, and bolted the door.

"You look thin," he said, appraising her with a pungent smelling cigar between his teeth. He was robust by comparison, with plump cheeks and colour to his ruddy skin, and yet he'd aged. He felt the muscle in her left arm. "Can you still work a cape?"

"I don't have one," she said, removing her coat and laying her sword across the table. "I don't have my muleta either. I was counting on fate."

"I have what you need," he said. "But the wind is high; we must wet it."

She regarded him suspiciously, sniffed brandy on his breath. Why was he helping her? Had he somehow learned she was his real sister or did he want to use her talent to impress some of his new, ignoble friends? "Who did you bribe this time?" she asked.

"Do you care?"

Luna opened her case and lifted out the heavy suit, giving it a strong shake. Silver sequins fell and scattered across the floor like abandoned stars. She draped the suit over the back of a chair while she slipped out of her common clothes. "Marisol?" she asked. "Is she here? I could use help with dressing." Pedro didn't answer so she stopped what she was doing, and looked at him. "Pedro?"

"The child was born dead," he said, stubbing his cigar on the wall. "Marisol delivered too early. She blames God," he added. "And me."

"Aiy, no!" Luna steadied herself against the chair. "I'm so sorry." Her heart wrung for him and for Marisol.

"I held the baby," he said, sounding almost boastful. "She was tiny and cold and her skin as white as the top of the Sierra Nevada. I dug her a grave myself, deep, so the dogs won't find her. When it was done I thought, why does everything to do with me turn out only halfway good? At home I was the second son. Here, a husband with an unhappy wife." His shoulders drooped. "I was almost a father," he said. "Then, I remembered you, Luna. If I finally arranged it so you fought on foot here, I would indisputably be the single greatest bullfight promoter in Spain."

Luna swallowed hard, felt a lump in her dry throat. "I'll go to Marisol as soon as we're done here," she said. "She will need me now. I've missed her terribly."

Pedro reached behind himself to grab a blood red muleta and passed it to her unceremoniously. His hand was shaking when he said, "She took herself to heaven with the baby last week, Luna."

AS SOON AS THE picadors and horses had done their job and the first bull charged the first torero, Luna made her way to the edge of the arena, far from the managers who could've seen her and alerted the authorities. She stayed close to Pedro, who was on guard, and did her best to blend in with the crowd. Fully dressed, with her sword at her side, she was prepared to step in for the faena, but couldn't stop thinking of Marisol and her dead baby, the randomness of death. Toreo was a hard business, but it hadn't hardened her to that. She held her mother's crucifix between her teeth, touched her chest where the photograph was pressed up against her bare skin. Soon she might be joining them, she thought, and a part of her wanted to fold into the earth below, but she wouldn't allow grief, her oldest companion, to rob her of this moment.

The torero in the ring stood behind his magenta capote, holding out a large square, sighting the Serrano they called Diablo, for a Delantal pass. He pivoted correctly with the bull's charge, side-stepping those caramel-coloured cuernos, and the capote billowed, though the crowd was unimpressed. The torero appeared nervous, his gestures stiff. *Sinverguenza*, Luna thought. *What a fake.*

The bull stopped at the barrera closest to her, turned; this was when she looked at Pedro and lingered on him. It could be the last she'd see of a blood relation. She opened her mouth, to tell him she was his real sister, but he spoke first: "It was me," he said. "Not Manuel, who got you here."

He handed her the dampened muleta and she flew over the barrera.

At last she was there, on her feet, in the sand at Las Ventas, and for that supreme moment she knew she would've traded her soul. Perhaps she already had. The sun pounded her face and her suit of lights, and she took one graceful step forward.

"Espontánco!" Somcone ycllcd, and thc crowd gaspcd and shouted for her to leave. "Ándate! Get out of there, let him fight!"

The torero marched up angrily, waving his arms, "Vete fuera!" He swatted at the air as if she could be gotten rid of as easily as a barn fly.

"Con permiso," she told him, making a bow. "With your permission, Padrino, I will take my alternativa, and kill this bull."

"You will not!"

Diablo snorted, standing securely with his back to his querencia. He lowered and raised his heavy head, grunted loudly, and thick white froth on his chunky lips ran to the ground in a single stream.

"El Corazón!" Pedro shouted, to rile the crowd to her defence. "Mira? Look; it's the great El Corazón!"

The crowd swelled and roared around her, but they were loudest when they saw the Bullfight Association President, Raphael Leal, and the guards, funnelling up to remove her from the ring. It was as though in defiance they were one and if she succeeded, stole this bull and made the descabello, Madrid would be united again and they would all be free of the oppressive feeling of their own mortality, if only for an instant.

The guards, afraid to join her on the inside of the ring with the angry bull, organized themselves around the barrera. The torero she'd dethroned faced the ring promoter in his palco. "This woman castrates the nation!" he shouted.

A few whistles came from the stands, but Luna ignored them and spat at her colleague's slippers. She placed her sword over the wooden barrera and bent it to test its quality. At this, the majority again cheered.

"I've been denied my sword!" she called out. "But not today!" She made a show of testing the point of the blade with her fingers, pricking herself once, twice, to prove she was satisfied that it was indeed sharp enough. She raised her bloody fingers to the spectators. Once more they cheered and stomped and the other torero had no choice but to leave the ring to her.

She made no acknowledgement of the officials, instead she advanced past the tercios, stopped and held her hat, first to the crowd on the sunny side, and next she turned all the way around to el sombre. "I dedicate this bull to you!" she shouted. "For your love."

"Olé!" came the first cry of approval.

She moved to stand on the shaded side of the ring with feet together, arms high, the red muleta in her left hand, and the sword in her right. Her Montera was snug on her head. She tucked her chin in close to her body, resting her gaze firmly on Diablo. His eyes were two oily pearls, his red and black coat lit by the hot sun. The sand beneath her slippers was hot and dry, and the long, fuchsia stockings she wore under her heavy silk pantaloons itched, but she wouldn't move. Unless she brought him out of his chosen refuge, she would surely be gored. The ring smelled of manure, fresh blood, and the oranges tossed down by wealthy spectators. She could practically taste the sweet meat and rolled her tongue around in her dusty mouth as though she were rolling an orange seed. The crowd grew impatient. "Ándate!" shouted one man on the bench behind her. "Qué traigan el próximo!" called another. They expected entertainment. Bloody poetry. Luna hesitated; whose face was it there, in front of her? Manuel's, not a bull's? Or, was it hers? The bull no longer appeared dangerous to her, but desperate, trapped. He was anyone who'd ever tried, against the odds, to rise above circumstance. He had sad, wizened eyes. Could she kill again, under his gaze? Spectators tossed a cushion, hurled fruit, a wine-skin, a woman's shoe. Someone threw a dead cat and missed the bull by three feet.

Luna adjusted her focus.

Two banderillas were hanging, bloodied, from the thickest part of his neck. He was tired and irritated by the delay. The dying horse was moaning a few feet away where she lay on the ground, her entrails tangled in her own hooves. Diablo had gored her in the second act, when the picador had done his job. Now his tail twitched and his right ear matched it and Luna knew he favoured his left side. He'd come at her that way if given the chance.

She moved her left wrist, and with it the muleta, for the first in a series of Verónicas. The crowd grew still, seeing her promise to deliver the oldest and most beautiful of passes. Diablo stood with his forelegs far apart and she beckoned, directing his attention towards the muleta — her body the hour hand of a clock, resting at one. Leaning, to make space between her body and his cuernos, for the charge, she extended the muleta, its bright fabric taunting. The remainder of the material was gathered in her right hand or hanging to the ground. She repeated these movements twice but Diablo was stubborn and resisted. She stood taller and with honour, dropped one hand, and slanted her body forward, relaxed and unmoving, tempting him again, making him believe there was a solid figure on the other side of that material.

He charged.

She pressed her heels into the golden sand and stretched her neck, until tendons pulled and vertebrae cracked. She let him get close, within an inch of her thighs, with his sharp curving daggers.

"Olé!" Aficionados shook their fists in the air. She'd shown no fear. She'd demonstrated her talent and stood perilously close to the beast. Any detractors she had were silent.

Diablo turned and faced her, realizing he'd been duped. She saw anger in his square jaw, and his nostrils flared with hot breath, though it didn't matter. He was tiring to the point where she needed him. Again she positioned herself — left arm out at the side so the red material teased. Again Diablo charged, head down, and in a split second, when he was almost at her side, close enough to her body that she would feel the heat of his muscles, she decided on a Farol instead.

She faced him dead-on, her legs spread, shoulders down, holding the muleta, and she dropped onto her knees at an angle, without dropping her eyes from his. She swung the muleta around and over her head as though she was going to wear it in her coffin, and Diablo, presented with the inside of it, burst through that cloud of colour like an army of resisters. He appeared furious, his instinct for self defence snapping and boiling under his coat. He turned without a thought to charge again, and she summoned with the muleta in her right hand.

This time, when Diablo's head passed, Luna spun clockwise and he caught her pantaloons with the razor-sharp tip of his cuerno and ripped off a patch of gold sequins. Spectators in the front bleachers gasped and stood, but she aimed, plunged down with her sword, the thrust an exclamation mark putting an end to the years she'd struggled to get there, slicing into him gracefully, in the exact position she wanted, missing his spinal column and ribcage, and allowing his own great weight to draw the steel further between his shoulder blades.

In an instant, they were one.

It was holier than communion.

Her sword was in to the pommel, hasta la bola, and she felt the bristles of his withers tickle her fingers. She stopped him in his tracks and her feet remained solid in the sand, though the force of the impact of their bodies caused her montera to come loose from her head and sent it flying to the ground. She felt the pulsing sting of a shallow wound on her left thigh and they both knew, though it could not yet be discerned by any first-time spectator, she was barely injured and he was already dead. Still breathing, still standing, but dead.

She'd cut his spinal cord clean.

"Torero!" Spectators shouted. "Torero!"

Diablo's front knees buckled and he crashed down on them.

Thousands waved handkerchiefs, small white flags to signal his surrender, and a thrilling sense of victory rushed up inside her, for though she'd stolen the opportunity to take her alternativa, she was no longer a novillero. She was a full matador! She stepped back so she and Diablo could stare at one another for this last moment of truth.

His black eyes were wide and glassy. In them she saw her own reflection: Tall and thin, a crescent of a moon.

Co-ra-zón! Co-ra-zón!

She knelt at Diablo's head while some in the crowd groaned and shouted, "no, no!" and she leaned into him, to show him her tears. She bent to kiss him between his great cuernos, and then, as fast, scooped up her Montera and turned to permit the crowd to see the bright sash of fresh bull's blood that crossed her body.

The crowd leapt to its feet, stomping, hooting. Boots and shoes reverberated in the stands. Luna saw the surprised face of her fellow torero near the ring, and behind the barrera, the ring promoter and President Leal, waving their arms in the air, demanding her immediate arrest.

She took a full bow.

Anyone can kill, but few seduce a beast towards its own demise.

Before she could complete her triumphant vuelta around the ring, catching the bota, kissing handkerchiefs and tossing them up into the stands, the guards scrambled onto the sand to arrest her, and somewhere a siren was sounded. Many in the crowd jumped over the barrera and onto the sand to confront the guards. They ran past Diablo to her, and a group of them lifted her high onto their shoulders, as though she were a rare blue bird who'd forgotten how to fly, and with the sun burning into each gold and silver sequin on her suit of lights, they rewarded her with a salida en hombres, carrying her out of the arena and the plaza, into the streets of Madrid. Dogs trailed. Crumpled handbills and newspaper littered the entrance. Paper was caught by the wind, and sailed, in airy pulses, this way and that. Empty bottles clinked and rolled in the gutter. This was the music of her final ovation, this, and the roar of the people celebrating her.

She wept.

From high on her perch Luna searched the streets for Manuel and Grace. She wished they were there, knowing they weren't; Manuel was on his way to the front where Condor Legion biplanes would come fast and low in waves, nine across, wingtip to wingtip, and Grace was on her way out of the country with Chucho. Luna searched for Pedro, but he was being arrested for complicity in her illegal act by the Fascist friends who'd taken his bribe. She lifted her eyes and both arms to the cerulean ocean above as the crowd chanted — "Corazón! El Corazón!"

Was there ever a heart so ambitious?

A dry wind blew. The air tasted of sand and steel. She looked up at the Spanish sun.

*Was it worth the fight?*

Then, the horizon tilted. Everything began to spin.

As her admirers found an opening in the crowded street, and brought her awkwardly down to her feet, Luna heard the sky rumble. Disoriented, she craned her neck to see four huge bombers. The crowd scattered and fled along Alcalá Street, taking cover. She didn't move. There was nowhere to go. Trapped, dizzy, she closed her eyes and conjured Grace's face, listened hard for Grace's voice, but all she heard was the hiss of falling bombs and the peal of her own lonely heart echoing inside her chest.

# Note to Readers

In writing this novel, I didn't question whether bullfighting ought
to be permitted. There are others whose books, articles, and essays
address that controversial subject and are readily available. However,
information about the unique position of women inside the corrida
is not as easy to locate. Therefore, here I offer a partial background:

Julia Escamilla (a.k.a. Pajuelerra) is said to be the first woman
to have dedicated herself to bullfighting. There is a painting of
her on horseback in Goya's Tauromaquia. Escamilla was born in
Valdemoro, and appeared in the Madrid plaza in 1776. However,
according to my research there are only two Spanish women to
have achieved the status of becoming matador de toros: First,
Juanita Cruz, who began fighting bulls as a novillero at the age of
fifteen. After years of struggling against the hostile attitudes of her
fellow bullfighters and various governments, including making a
constitutional appeal based on gender, Juanita Cruz was eventually
outlawed from the bullring altogether by Franco's regime.

More recently, through the 1990's, Christina Sánchez built a
highly respected reputation as a matador, though this daughter

of a banderillero retired early, reputedly citing on-going sexual harassment as the reason. Mexico's, Juanita Aparicio was born in 1936 and was one of the first female bullfighters to be taken seriously. She appeared on the same program with men though did not compete against them. Instead of drawing, smaller bulls were assigned to her.

Arguably, the most successful female matador de toros in history is the Chilean born, Peruvian trained, Conchita Cintron, who enjoyed a fabulous international career during the 1940's and 50's. She drew for bulls, competed against men, and was generally accepted as skilful among her peers. Conchita Cintron, success aside, was never permitted to perform on foot in Spain. She died of natural causes, in February of 2009, as I was writing this novel.

*Matadora* is a work if literary fiction, wholly imagined by me, its author. While respecting political and historical fact, particularly Spanish Civil War chronology, I occasionally bent the facts of history in an effort to reach for a greater poetic or literary truth. Historians may note, for example, that the Battle of Ciudad Universitaria de Madrid took place between 15 and 23 November, 1936, not, sixteen months later, as I have it occurring in the novel. (I simply could not resist having Manuel, a poet, battle among the books in the university library.) Similarly, the fact that women were not legally permitted to fight on foot in Spain did not deter me from imagining otherwise. Such alterations are in no way meant to detract from the horrors of the Spanish Civil War.

Finally, it may interest you to know that after Madrid fell, and during the Franco dictatorship, the poetry and plays of Federico Garcia Lorca were censored. Today, Spaniards openly revere Garcia Lorca, his work is widely known and studied, and a statue of him stands proudly in the plaza Santa Ana, in Madrid.

# Sources

The following were most inspiring during the writing of this novel:

The poetry of Federico García Lorca.
*Out of the Shadow, Into the Sun* (film), a documentary by Kathryn Klassen.
*Memoirs of a Bullfighter* by Conchita Cintron.
*Toreros Del Romanticismo* by Natalio Rivas, Prologue by Juan Belmonte.
*On Bullfighting* by A.L. Kennedy.
*The Spanish Civil War* by Helen Graham.
*Death and Money in the Afternoon* by Adrian Shubert.
*Reflexiones Sobre José Tomas*
*The Spanish Civil War: Reaction, Revolution, and Revenge* by Paul Preston.
*Homage to Catalonia* by George Orwell.
*Death in the Afternoon* by Ernest Hemingway.
*Renegades: Canadians in the Spanish Civil War* by Michael Petrou.

*Note to Readers*

*Sweatshop Strife* by Ruth A. Frager. (The Yiddish folk saying Grace
   wears on her dress appears in English on page 35 of this book)
*Anatomy of a Bullfight* by Arthur Greenfield. Longmans, Green
   and Co Ltd. New York, 1961.

# Glossary of Bullfighting
# Terms Used in This Novel

*Acero*: steel, sword.

*Adorno*: an action that shows control over the bull.

*Afeitar*: the practice of shaving or shortening the bull's horns.

*Aficionado*: a dedicated, knowledgeable fan of bullfighting.

*Alguacil*: a mounted constable, who open the ceremony by riding ahead of the bullfighters as they parade into the ring. They also relay orders of the president.

*Alternativa*: ceremony in which a novillero becomes a matador de Toros. A more senior matador concedes his first bull the novillero. The alternativa may be taken in any plaza but must be confirmed later in Madrid.

*Anillos*: marks or rings on the bull's horns, which denote the animal's age. The first appears at the age of three.

*Antitaurino*: someone who is opposed to bullfighting.

*Arena*: the sand that covers the floor of the bullring.

*Arrastre*: the gate through which the dead bull is dragged, the act of removing the dead bull.

*Arroba*: A measure of approximately twenty-five pounds. Bulls are often weighed in arrobas — thirty being the classic, desired weight. Now they are often weighed in kilos.

*Aspero*: a bull's coat is described as aspero, which means rough.

*Astiblanco*: bull horns that are mostly white.

*Astillado*: type of bull's horns known as splintered.

*Banderilla*: twenty-eight-inch-long, steel-barbed, wooden shaft decorated with paper.

*Banderillas de fuego*: banderillas with firecrackers attached to them.

*Banderillero*: one who places the banderillas in the bull, also the name of the three men on foot who assist the matador.

*Barrera*: the wooden fence around the bullring.

*Barreras*: the first row of seats in the bullring.

*Becerro*: a bull calf of one or two years of age.

*Bota*: a wineskin tossed down to the bullfighter.

*Broncas*: an argument or protest by the crowd against a bad fight.

*Burladero*: a narrow opening into the bullring with a wooden shield set in front through which people enter and leave.

*Cabos*: the sash and necktie worn by toreros.

*Callejón*: passageway between the barrera and the stands.

*Capa*: cape. The proper name for a bullfighter's cape is capa de brega. It is usually called capote.

*Capote*: fighting cape. Traditionally pink and gold.

*Capriole*: when the rejoneadoro's horse jumps directly up into the air, all four legs tucked up to its body, off the ground. The rider appears to be flying on a horse.

*Carniceria*: part of the bullring where the dead bulls are dressed into beef. It takes only ten to twelve minutes for the butchers to draw and quarter the bull.

*Cartel*: long colourful poster announcing the fight.

*Chaquetilla*: the gold or silver encrusted jacket that forms part of the suit of lights.

*Chiqueros*: stalls in which the bulls are kept prior to release into the bullring.

*Cite*: from citar, to direct attention to the bull toward the cape or muleta.

*Coleta*: pigtail.

*Contrabarreras*: second row seats.

*Cornada*: horn wound.

*Corrida*: bullfight.

*Cuadrilla*: the matador's banderilleros and picadors. His team.

*Cuerno*: bull's horn.

*Delantal*: cape pass begun like a veronica but with the cape billowing out in front.

*Descabellar*: killing the bull by severing the medulla, placing the sword between the cervical vertebrae.

*Descabello*: The straight sword used in descabellar.

*Desplante*: an arrogant gesture, synonymous with an adorno.

*Emoción*: emotion.

*Técnica*: technique.

*Empresa*: the company producing the bullfight.

*Empresario*: bullfight impresario.

*Enfermería*: the infirmary.

*Escobillado*: broom-shaped type of bull's horns.

*Espontáneo*: one who illegally enters the ring and performs passes with the bull.

*Estocada*: full sword thrust.

*Estoconazo*: a full sword thrust that kills the bull.

*Estribo*: the low wooden rail around the side of the bull ring about one foot above ground level.

*Faena*: the third and final part of a bullfight in which the matador uses the muleta.

*Farol*: a pass in which the cape or muleta is passed over the head.

*Festival*: an informal bullfight.

*Ganadería*: a bull ranch.

*Ganadero*: a bull rancher.

*Garrocha*: the long pole used by a rejoneador.

*Hasta la bola*: refers to a perfect sword thrust.

*Indulto*: a pardon or sparing the life of a particularly noble bull.

*Machos*: los machos specifically, refers to all the tassels on the knees strings of the suit of lights.

*Malettila*: bad learner, refers to a bullfighters who trains informally or illegally.

*Manso*: a tame bull who will not charge or who demonstrates cowardice. Manso is the opposite of brave, in this context, and it connotes an undesirable intelligence. An intelligent bull is not a brave bull.

*Mamarracho*: grotesque figure, inept, insult of Spanish audiences.

*Matador de toros*: a killer of bulls who has taken the alternativa.

*Mayoral (el Mayoral)*: a lead cowboy or foreman on a bull ranch.

*Media verónica*: a veronica in which both hands stop at the hip. This is a remate.

*Médico*: a doctor.

*Medios*: inner third of the bullring.

*Monosabios*: the costumed men who primarily assist the picador.

*Montera*: the hat commonly worn by bullfighters, introduced in 1835.

*Morillo*: the hump of erectile muscle at the base of the bull's neck in front of his shoulders. I have used it here as a nickname of a bull.

*Mozo de estoques*: sword handler.

*Muleta*: heart-shaped red flannel cape most often lined with a wooden stick and used in the latter part of a bullfight.

*Muleteros*: mule drivers.

*Natural*: a basic cape pass in which the bull follows the palm of the hand.

*Navarra*: a cape pass based on the veronica.

*Novillada*: a bullfight with bulls under four years of age.

*Novillero*: a professional bullfighter who has not taken the alternativa.

*Novillo*: a fighting bull of less than four years of age.

*Ojalao*: means "buttonhole" and refers to a bull with a circle around his eyes.

*Olé!*: shout of approval, like "bravo!" for a bullfighter when the bull's horn passes a few inches from his or her body.

*Padrino*: godfather, or sponsor of a novillero when he takes the alternativa.

*Palcos*: box seats.

*Palillo*: the notched wooden stick supporting the muleta.

*Pase*: a pass with cape or muleta.

*Paseo*: the opening procession of participants in a bullfight.

*Pases de castigo*: passes of punishment, short, chopping, low passes designed to tire the bull and make him stand for the kill.

*Pasodoble*: type of music associated with bullfights, played before and during.

*Pata*: hoof.

*Peon de confianza*: chief banderillero.

*Pera de dulce*: a pear in syrup, a term for an easy bull.

*Perfilar*: to stand in profile to the bull, preparing for the kill.

*Peto*: mattress-like pads used to protect the picadors' horses.

*Picador*: traditionally a man on horseback armed with a lance, the point of which he places in the bull's back.

*Pinchazo*: sword prick.

*Poder a poder*: a method of placing banderillas.

*Presidente*: the authority and presiding judge who directs the bullfight.

*Puntilla*: a short, spoon-bladed knife used by the puntillero.

*Puntillero*: traditionally the man who administers the coup de grace to the fallen bull.

*Querencia*: the bull may take a special liking to a certain spot in the arena where he feels safest. This is his refuge.

*Quite*: the act of luring the bull away from a picador or a fallen man.

*Rebolera*: a remate in which the cape is swung out like a flaring skirt.

*Recibiendo*: a method of killing in which the matador receives the bull's charge without moving forward himself.

*Glossary of Bullfighting*

*Rejón*: the lance used in bullfighting on horseback.
*Rejón de muerte*: the killing lance used in bullfighting on horseback.
*Rejoneador*: the Portuguese style of fighting bulls on horseback.
*Rejoneo*: bullfighting on horseback.
*Remate*: a pass used to finish a series.
*Salida en hombros*: refers to the high honour of a matador being carried out of the ring on the shoulders of the crowd.
*Sandunga*: arrogance and elegance shown in the haughty way a bullfighter walks in the ring.
*Sorteo*: the drawing of lots to determine which pair of bills will be fought by which matador on a given day.
*Suerte*: luck, or any action or series of actions that take place during the bullfight. For example, a pass, the kill, placing of banderillas.
*Temple*: the appearance of slowness, rhythm in making a pass.
*Temporada*: the bullfight season, or a series of bullfights.
*Tendido*: section of seats in the plaza, right behind the barrera.
*Tienta*: testing of the young bulls and heifers.
*Torero*: the matador or the members of his cuadrilla.
*Torera*: a female torero.
*Toril*: the gate through which the bull is let into the ring.
*Toro bravo*: a wild fighting bull.
*Traje corto*: informal bullfighting suit.
*Traje de luces*: suit of lights, or formal bullfighting form of dress.
*Vara*: the picador's lance, and each time the picador lances the bull the act is referred to as a vara.
*Veleta*: a type of bull's horn where the wide apart sharp tips are both pointed directly upwards.
*Verónica*: the basic two-handed cape pass.
*Volapié*: a style of killing in which the matador runs toward the bull.
*Vuelta*: the promenade around the ring made by a successful matador.
*Zajones*: leather chaps worn on ranches in Andalucia.

I wish to acknowledge Barnaby Conrad's *Encyclopedia of Bullfighting* for many of the definitions provided above.

# Civil War Acronyms
# Used in This Novel

CNT: Confederación Nacional de Trabajadores (National
   Confederation of Workers).
POUM: The Workers' Party of Marxist Unification
CEDA: Confederación Española de Derechas Autónomas (Spanish
   Confederation of the Autonomous Right).
PSOE: Partido Socialista Obrero Español (Spanish Socialist
   Workers' Party).

# Acknowledgements

I am eternally grateful to: Elisenda Vidal and Pablo Serratosa for sharing their home and history with me at Cortijo Las Piletas, in Parque Natural, Sierra de Grazalema, Andalucia, Spain. Thanks to Raphael Puerto for his detailed tour of a working ganaderia, Álvaro Peralta at Hotel Miau in Madrid, and the countless other Spaniards who answered my questions. Not the least, I am indebted to the brave bulls of Madrid and Ronda who died in the ring while I researched.

For their generous support enabling me to develop and complete this work, I humbly acknowledge the Canada Council for the Arts, the Ontario Arts Council, the Toronto Arts Council, and The Woodcock Fund, administered by the Writers' Trust of Canada. The Banff Centre for the Arts provided time and space to begin. For conversations about writing, I thank Edna Alford, Greg Hollingshead, Anne Simpson, Anita Rau Badami, and Helen Humphreys.

For his brave impulse in acquiring this book, I thank my intrepid editor and publisher, Marc Côté, of Cormorant Books. My thanks also to the whole Cormorant team who've worked hard on my behalf.

*Acknowledgements*

To my agent, Hilary McMahon of Westwood Creative Artists: it remains a pleasure to have you and your colleagues in my corner. Thanks to Lisa B. Rundle who offered thoughtful feedback on an early draft. Thanks also to John Miller and Sally Cooper, whose invaluable insight and commitment to our little writing circle, Big Canvas, has sustained me through the years. Thanks to Farzana Doctor, the newest member of Big Canvas. With the brutal honesty that only an old friend can provide, Margarita Miniovich reminded me to ignore all voices but my own.

I thank Erin Rielly Clarke, Joanne Vannicola, and Evalyn Parry for donating their time and talent to create my book trailer. Thanks to historian David Goutor for his consultations on the Spanish Civil War, and for reading recommendations. Thanks to Ron Hawkins for loaning me books on the subject, Suzanne M. Steele for sharing her thoughts on Flamenco, Virginia Santos Nerlich, and Diana Rodriguez Quevedo for helping with my rusty Spanish. Thank you Kathleen Olmstead for the videos and much more.

For offering to provide childcare so I could write, I thank Lori Ross, Shannon Neufeldt, Cheryl Champagne, and Dana Rudiak. Thanks also to Andrea Németh, Steve Nugent, Howard Kaplan, and the late Frenchman, André Flon de Neré, who was my first writing mentor.

Throughout the long nights, when most of this book was written, one song kept me going: Perla Batalla and Julie Christensen's interpretation of "Anthem" by Leonard Cohen. Thank you, all three. As always, thanks go out to my mother, Linda Dawn Pettigrew, for ongoing support and guidance. Finally, and especially, I am grateful to Shannon Olliffe for love and patience, and for photographing numerous bullfights. This book would not have made it through the years without you.